Templar Tales, Book 1:

St. Louis' Knight

by

Helena P. Schrader

ISBN-13: 978-0-989-1597-3-9
ISBN-10: 0989 1597 36

More information under
www.HelenaPSchrader.com
www.Tales-of-Chivalry.com

Introduction

This is the first of three interrelated novels set in the mid-thirteenth to the early fourteenth century. The inspiration for this particular novel came during my first trip to Cyprus almost twenty years ago and resulted in a short novel, *The Cypriot Knight*, published in 1995.

That was a mistake. My enthusiasm had outrun both my research and my skills as a novelist. Influenced by advice on "what would sell," I warped the story and lost the thread. The product was half-baked — and it rightfully did not sell very well.

This past year, while looking for a new project after finishing my Leonidas trilogy, I looked again at this, the first novel I ever published. Even as I cringed at the product as it stood, I recognized that it had great potential. I decided it deserved a second chance.

The new novel incorporates some scenes from the old, but it is essentially a new work, hence the new title. It has greatly benefited from much more research on the Albigensian Crusade, the Seventh Crusade, and the crusader kingdoms generally. I hope it has also benefited from greater skill on my part as a novelist. It has certainly benefited from the skilled editing of Christina Dickson and the cover art by Charles Whall.

Helena P. Schrader
Addis Ababa
January 2014

Chapter 1

Captive!

The Kingdom of Cyprus
April, Anno Domini 1250

"The French King and all his nobles have been captured by the Saracens," the herald intoned. His deep voice, more commonly used to proclaim the ancestry and deeds of knights at tournaments, was muted with respect and shock. His bright livery was shrouded in a dark cloak as if he were in mourning for a lost cause, and his boots and hose were splattered with mud, betraying his haste to bring the news to the Dowager Queen of Cyprus.

His words provoked an eruption of shocked and frightened exclamations from the little audience. The Dowager Queen was on her deathbed, and had been for months. She lived in almost complete seclusion, served only by a household of Cypriot servants and four ladies, three of whom were almost as old as she was herself.

One of these ladies began crossing herself repeatedly and reciting the Rosary in a tone of almost hysterical desperation. Another clapped her hands over her mouth and stared at the herald as if she expected Saracens to come storming through the door behind him. A third protested, "But that can't be! King Louis had the greatest army anyone had ever seen! He had *scores* of barons and nearly *three thousand* knights. They can't *all* have been captured! Not all those brave knights! And the King's brothers! And what of the French Queen and the ladies of the court?"

"When the messenger left Egypt, the French Queen and her ladies were still in Damietta with the handful of knights and men-at-arms left there for their protection, but I doubt that is still the case. With the King captive and his army destroyed, the Sultan of Egypt will undoubtedly try to recapture Damietta. The knights with Queen Marguerite are urging her to remove herself to safety immediately. If she chooses Cyprus over Acre, she could be here any moment." The herald glanced toward the large double-light window that looked south, towards Egypt, as if expecting to see the sails of a Genoese round ship straining to bring the French Queen to safety. But the window offered only a view of the walled garden of this isolated manor.

The Dowager Queen clicked her tongue and drew the herald's attention back to the interior of the room. "What did you expect?" the old woman asked rhetorically. "All these foreign kings and princes think crusading is a lark! They think we hang onto only the fragments of the Holy Land because we, the nobility of Outremer, have become weak, cowardly, and luxury-loving. They all come out here thinking that *they*, so splendid and so brave, will chase the Saracens back into the desert. Ha!"

The herald did not contradict her. There was some truth to what the old Queen said. Although King Louis himself had seemed a sober and far from lighthearted crusader, his younger brothers and many of his knights had been as arrogant and ignorant as the Queen suggested. Besides, the Queen was a woman who knew more about politics in the Holy Land than almost anyone else alive. Alice of Champagne had been widowed when her son, King Henry I, was only eight months old and had acted as his regent until he came of age — by which time she had weathered a civil war on Cyprus and a crusade led by the Holy Roman Emperor. As if that hadn't been enough, as the granddaughter of the Queen of Jerusalem, she had been Regent of Jerusalem for the underaged King Conrad IV as well. While it was fair to say that Queen Alice's politics had not been crowned by particular success, no one could deny that she *understood* the complexity of surviving in the crusader kingdoms.

"So," the old woman scoffed, "the Sultan of Egypt has humiliated the most powerful monarch in Christendom. The Holy Roman Emperor must be dancing for joy to see the Pope's favorite humiliated like this."

"Madame! How can you think in such terms when a Christian monarch and all his knights and nobles are at the mercy of the godless Saracens?" one of Alice's ladies admonished her — inducing her praying colleague to raise her voice even more shrilly to the Mother of God.

The old Queen silenced both ladies. "Enough of your howling, Catherine! You have the brain of a hen, Eschiva! Godless or not, the Sultan loves gold. He'll let them all go when enough ransom has been paid, and if France is beggared, then the Holy Roman Empire will be stronger." The Dowager Queen had always sided with the Holy Roman Empire against the barons of Outremer, and now she smiled to herself. Then she cleared her throat and announced, "Thank you, Sir Herald. Blanche, give the herald ten *livres* for his trouble! Eleanor, see him to the kitchens and tell the cook to give him a hearty meal. I weary."

The interview was over. The Queen signaled for assistance to rise, and two of her ladies sprang to help her from her armed chair, while the third retrieved her mistress' purse and doled out the promised reward. The herald found himself following the fourth of the Queen's ladies, Eleanor de Najac, down the spiral stairs from the Queen's tower chamber toward the kitchen on the ground floor.

Eleanor was the only one of the Queen's women who was less than sixty years of age. The herald guessed she was no more than twenty or twenty-one. All the herald knew about her was that she was a ward of the Comte de Poitiers, the French King's younger brother, and had had the misfortune to shipwreck on the coast of Cyprus on her way to join the Comtesse de Poitiers' household.

The storm that struck in March of the previous year had been one of the worst in living memory, and it had scattered half the French King's fleet then assembling for the invasion to Egypt. In the confusion following the gale, hardly anyone took note of a small French vessel that went ashore on the west coast with the loss of all hands — especially since the only corpses found were those of common sailors and tonsured men, presumably clerics bound for the Holy Land.

Weeks later, however, a second ship from France brought letters making reference to the passage of the heiress of Najac aboard a previous vessel. The Comte de Poitiers, who was by then in Egypt with his brother, asked the King of Cyprus to find out what had happened to his ward.

A search for her corpse was instituted along the coast, and to the wonder and amazement of those sent to find her body,

Eleanor was found alive — albeit severely injured — in a fishing village. Since Eleanor spoke no Greek and the fishermen no French, Eleanor's rescuers had not realized she was a highborn lady and heiress; they had not thought to notify the authorities.

The herald was familiar with the cramped, stinking cottages of the local fishermen. He was certain that for a French noblewoman the weeks in the Cypriot fishing village had been a hell — especially since one of her legs had been crushed in the wreck and she was in pain and feverish.

Even now, more than a year after the wreck, she walked with a limp as she led him across the inner courtyard to the kitchen tract. The experience had also left its mark on her face and soul, the herald surmised, for her face was too guarded and sober for a gentle maiden still in the bloom of youth.

Furthermore, although the herald knew professionally that the sires of Najac were ancient and wealthy lords, Eleanor neither looked nor acted like a haughty heiress. The simplicity of her dress, a soft linen gown with a pale-blue surcoat, would not have been out of place on the wife of a country squire or town merchant. Her auburn hair was neatly braided down her back and her head covered with a flat, modestly embroidered hat, held in place by simple white veils. The effect was neat and attractive — but not suited to an heiress. The Cypriot court was filled with young women who adorned themselves much more lavishly and brightly, although they claimed hardly more than a thimbleful of noble blood rather than a barony! They compared to Eleanor of Najac like butterflies to a moth.

Not that Eleanor was plain. The herald considered her with the eyes of a connoisseur of women as Eleanor gestured for him to sit at a table in the passageway before the kitchen. She was pretty in a soft, understated way, he decided. She had wide-set hazel eyes, dark straight eyebrows, and an elegant long nose in an oval face. Her skin was flawless and very pale. Her only bad features were her nearly colorless, narrow lips — but even this defect would have been forgotten, if only she smiled.

"Wait here, Sir Herald, while I inform the cook of your needs," she told him simply, before lurching down the stone steps leading to the kitchen.

Waiting for her, the herald wished he had some means to make her smile. If only he had brought good news instead of word of this catastrophe! It was only too natural that Eleanor was deeply troubled. Her guardian was in grave danger, a prisoner of the Saracens, and even if the Sultan was unlikely to harm a prince of France, she must worry that the ransom he imposed would impoverish her, since the income from her inheritance flowed into the Count's coffers as long as she was unwed.

While the herald was still lost in these thoughts, Eleanor returned with a bronze aquarelle in the form of a lion and a linen towel.

"My Lady, it is unseemly that you wait on me. Send for a servant, and sit with me instead," the herald urged, indicating the bench on the other side of the table from him.

She seemed flustered by his remark, hastily putting the aquarelle down and stepping back as if she had done something wrong.

He smiled to reassure her and gestured to the bench opposite him again, urging, "Sit with me a moment, My Lady. Perhaps I can be of service with some information? My travels take me all over the island." The herald had long since learned to use his natural access to information to satisfy the interest of others in gossip.

Eleanor nodded, but not with eager curiosity as he had expected. Instead she sat very stiffly on the bench opposite, and there was so much tension in her that the herald felt compelled to reassure her. "You must not distress yourself too much. I'm sure the Comte de Poitiers is in no great danger." In the herald's experience, maidens of Eleanor's age were rarely interested in the fate of their fathers or guardians. It was far more likely that Eleanor was worried about some young knight who had courted her or otherwise caught her fancy. But no modest maiden would confess such an interest to a strange man, so the herald knew he had to pretend to talk about her guardian.

Eleanor drew a deep breath. "Would you — would you mind telling me more of what has happened in Egypt? I have been very isolated here," she hastened to excuse herself.

"I would be delighted, My Lady," the herald answered enthusiastically, as a serving woman brought a loaf of bread on a cutting board and wine in a jug, along with cheese and sausage. Cutting himself a thick slice of bread, he began his tale. "Where should I start, My Lady? With the Battle of Mansourah?"

Eleanor nodded shortly, a slight frown creasing her brow, and the herald had the impression she didn't really know what this was, so he expanded his narration slightly. "Well, you know that after defeating a Saracen army that tried to block the landing of his fleet, the French King found the great city of Damietta abandoned. Then a council of war was held, and the barons of Outremer urged an assault on Alexandria in order to secure a great port through which supplies could be shipped to the crusaders. But the King's impetuous young brother, the Comte d'Artois, insisted that "a snake must be killed by crushing the head," and urged an assault on Cairo. So the crusading army started up the Nile until it came to the great walled city of Mansourah, which guards the route to Cairo.

"The Saracens were determined to defend Mansourah, and had collected a large army with many powerful war machines. Initially, because of the river between them, the armies could not get to grips with one another. Yet then, just as the King was in despair, a Bedouin came and offered to show the King a ford across the river."

"Are there traitors even among the Saracens?" Eleanor asked, evidently astonished.

The herald, a native of Cyprus, laughed at so much naiveté. "Have you not heard, My Lady? Why, the crusader kingdoms would long since have been destroyed, if the Saracens did not spend more time fighting among themselves than fighting us. Indeed, the very Sultan that King Louis set out to destroy a year ago was poisoned by the Sultan of Homs in the midst of this crusade!

"But to return to my tale: The traitorous Bedouin showed the crusaders a ford, but the ford was narrow, deep, and difficult. Only a few mounted men could cross at a time, and as a result, the army could only cross very slowly.

"Robert d'Artois was one of the first to cross, and he did not want to wait until the bulk of the army had forded the river before attacking the enemy. The Grand Master of the Knights Templar, who commanded some three hundred knights of his Order, tried to dissuade the Comte d'Artois. He pointed out that even with the whole crusader army, the Christians were significantly outnumbered. But the Comte d'Artois would not listen to reason. Scoffing that if the Templars were afraid to fight the Saracens, he would attack alone, he spurred his horse forward, his own knights in his wake.

"Master de Sonnac, although a wise man, is also a man from the Languedoc." Eleanor abruptly sat up straighter, but by now the herald was too swept up in his own story to notice her reaction. He continued, "Like all men from that sunny province, he is hot-blooded and hot-tempered. He was outraged by the stupidity and pigheadedness of the King's brother, but he would not suffer to have it said that the Templars had been afraid to go where a Prince of France led. So the Templars couched their lances and charged at the Saracen with their battle cry on their lips.

"The sight of three hundred Templars on their great destriers, spurring forward in a solid block of shields and spears, broke the courage of even the bravest Saracen. The Saracen army fled in all directions before their lances, and those few men who tried to stand were cut down and trampled. But the Comte d'Artois did not stop when he had scattered the foe. He kept riding through the open gates into the city of Mansourah itself!

"No doubt —" the herald paused to reflect — "no doubt he believed that Mansourah, like Damietta, had been abandoned and would be vacant. But it was not. Within moments, the knights were lost and separated from one another in narrow alleys and dark side streets. The momentum of their charge was broken by the cobbles, the winding streets, and the shop stalls. Before they could extricate themselves, the inhabitants swarmed around them, cutting them off from one another, overwhelming them by their numbers. From overhead the women flung furniture and poured boiling water from the balconies and rooftops, and children darted out from the doors to stab the frightened horses in their bellies.

"Meanwhile, the Saracen army that had scattered before their initial charge closed again behind them, like water rushing around a stone as the tide pours in. The Comte d'Artois and the Templars were cut off within the city — while outside, the French King and the rest of his army faced the undiminished force drawn up against them.

"What followed was a bitter battle in which many knights and nobles were killed. The Christians fought bravely, but so did the Saracens. By nightfall the French King was in control of the Saracen camp before the gates of Mansourah, but his brother's body was hanging from the ramparts, and inside the city the Saracens lit bonfires and beat their drums, shouting in triumph, 'Allah is Great!'"

The herald paused dramatically and looked at his audience. He had captured Eleanor's attention at last. She was gazing at him with large, intelligent eyes, leaning slightly forward in her seat, and she kept licking her lips nervously.

The herald pushed aside his plate, with its crumbs of bread and rinds of sausage, so he could lean toward Eleanor across the table. "It was only now, after the apparent victory before the walls of Mansourah, that the King noticed that supplies of food and war equipment were long overdue. He sent scouts north to see what the problem was, and they returned to report that Saracen galleys had taken control of the river downstream from the Christian camp. Every Christian galley that tried to come up the river to supply the crusaders was seized. The scouts reported that the Christian dead were piled high on either side of the river, and that black, buzzing clouds of flies were visible long before the heaps of unburied, headless bodies could be smelled, much less seen."

"Headless?" the gentle maiden asked in horror, making the herald regret that he had been quite so vivid in his images.

He now explained, "The Sultan has promised a reward for every killed Christian, and the heads of the Christian martyrs are sent to the Sultan as a means of collecting payment. Only those who convert to Islam are spared."

"Are there many such men?" Eleanor asked.

The herald tilted his head in uncertainty. "It is hard to know how many accept Islam, My Lady, since they become slaves, and are no more likely to return than are the dead."

"Oh!" Eleanor was horrified by this news.

The herald, pleased that she was thawing enough to show emotion, pressed ahead with his story. "Now, when King Louis learned what was happening to his supplies, he realized that he could not remain where he was. His army was slowly starving, and a terrible sickness had seized many of his men as well. Their skin was covered with horrible scabs, and their gums started to rot so that their teeth fell out. On top of all that, dysentery was spreading, felling the King himself. King Louis had no choice but to order his army to withdraw down the Nile, back to Damietta.

"But it was too late. The King's army was now so weak it could not defend itself. The Saracens overran the Christian camp and took King Louis, and all his remaining knights and noblemen, captive."

"Including the Comte de Poitiers?" Eleanor asked.

It seemed a stupid question in light of the situation the herald had just described, but the herald answered patiently, "Yes, My Lady.

Including both the King's surviving brothers, the Comtes de Poitiers and d'Anjou."

"But they will not be forced to convert to Islam or be enslaved, will they?" Eleanor asked, frowning slightly.

"No, My Lady. The Saracens respect other monarchs and their nobles. The Sultan will negotiate a ransom. Only those who have no means to pay a ransom need fear for their lives."

For a moment they were both silent, contemplating the magnitude of this catastrophe and its human cost. But finally Eleanor asked, "So when, Sir Herald, do you think the French King and his brothers might return?"

The use of the term "the French King" on the lips of one of his vassals jarred the herald. Shouldn't this maiden, a ward of the King's brother, refer to him as "King Louis" or "the King"? But the herald responded to Eleanor's question. "I think the negotiations could drag out a long time, My Lady. The Saracens will first try to retake Damietta to ensure King Louis cannot use it as a bargaining chip. The Queen of France, as you may know, is in her eighth month of pregnancy and very vulnerable. She will undoubtedly take refuge here or in Acre. Negotiations will have to be conducted with the King's mother in France, since she controls the French treasury in his absence. Communications with France will take months. I believe, My Lady, we will be lucky if the King and his brothers are home for Christmas."

Eleanor nodded slowly. "And there is no chance the King of France or his brothers could come to harm in the meantime?"

"We are all in God's hands, My Lady!" the herald protested. "The messengers said King Louis was so ill with dysentery at the time of his capture that many did not believe he could survive the night. He was taken to a peasant hut, and when the Saracens entered the mud hut they found the French King, wet with the sweat of fever, lying in the arms of a French slave woman. It was God's will that she had set out on pilgrimage from Paris to Jerusalem half a century ago, only to be captured and enslaved. We know now that she had endured that humiliation and misery so, in the moment of his greatest need, she could give comfort to a King of France. She held him in her arms when the Saracen troops took him prisoner." The herald stopped and held his breath. He did not know exactly what he was expecting, but some exclamation of horror or prayer to God.

Instead, Eleanor nodded and then drew back from the table. Her composure, so briefly relaxed, was restored. "Thank you, Sir Herald," she said in a soft and formal voice.

How controlled she was, the herald thought, as if she thought carefully about each and every word she spoke — so unlike most maidens her age. "It was my pleasure," he told her as he reached for the jug and upended it over his goblet. The jug was empty.

"Should I fetch more wine for you, Sir Herald?" Eleanor asked, already getting to her feet.

The herald glanced out the window and noticed how low the sun was. He had stayed far longer than planned, and now he would have a hard time reaching Limassol before dark. Reluctantly he shook his head and got to his feet. "I regret, My Lady, I must be on my way. Thank you for your kindness and hospitality."

"And it is *I* who thank you for telling me in such detail what has transpired in the past months."

"I regret, My Lady, that I had such a sad and dismal tale to tell. I wish I could have told you a story to lift up your spirits rather than burden your heart."

"It is quite all right, Sir Herald," she assured him with great poise as she held out her hand, suddenly the highborn lady after all.

The herald took her hand and bowed low over it, a courtly bow intended to flatter the young woman. Consciously impudent, he glanced up as he bowed, and was stunned to catch Eleanor de Najac smiling broadly.

Chapter 2

The Lame Lady

Waves were pounding on the beach at the foot of the steep cliff to Eleanor's left, while threatening clouds obscured the rugged limestone hills to her right. As the wind hissed in the pine trees, Eleanor felt fear welling up, uncontrollably, spreading from the pit of her stomach to her throat. What was she doing out here? In the middle of nowhere? What madness had induced her to leave the safety of the Dowager Queen's manor?

Eleanor knew the answer: she had wanted to get away from the Cypriot ladies, who day and night lamented the fate of the French King and bickered over favors from the dying Cypriot Queen. She had wanted to get away from their ugly Norman French, their petty intrigues and sniping comments. She had wanted to escape ....

Ever since the herald had brought the news that King Louis — the great crusading King, who had destroyed everything she loved — was now himself a prisoner, she had felt an irrepressible joy. For the first time in a decade, the threat that emanated from the French King was banished. Her heart sang an almost forgotten Easter melody, to which she composed her own lyrics:

King Louis is a prisoner! Rejoice!

His army is obliterated! Rejoice!

His greedy, grasping nobles are humiliated! Rejoice! Rejoice!

Eleanor had felt like jumping for joy, while the music of her happy childhood flooded back to her. The melodies in her head were the songs the peasants sang as they danced the night away around the summer bonfires on the Feast of St. John's, the songs sung in the barns at harvest time and in the Great Hall at Christmas. They were melodies to set feet dancing, and Eleanor, for the first time in a decade, had *wanted* to dance.

But around her had been only gloom: the dying Cypriot Queen, the bad news from the crusade, the uncertainty and worry for the health and safety of the French ladies trapped in Damietta .... Eleanor felt she couldn't stand it a day longer, but it was more than a week before she had the idea of requesting permission to go on a pilgrimage "to pray for the safe return" of her guardian.

The Dowager Queen had blessed her venture at once — in principle — but it had taken another week before everyone had agreed on where she ought to go and how she was to get there. In the end, the Queen agreed to provide an escort in the form of one of her Genoese archers and a Cypriot serving woman. She also provided Eleanor with one of her mares and ten livres to cover expenses.

So a fortnight after the arrival of the herald, Eleanor and her two companions set out just after Prime. No sooner was she through the gates than Eleanor felt transformed. The world outside the obscure manor seemed made of lush green fields of sugar cane. The sun was bright and warming, despite the chill in the early morning air, and the sky a vivid blue. Farther up the slopes, above the sugar cane, the olive trees waved at them cheerfully, and larks frolicked to greet the rising sun.

Eleanor was so intoxicated by the beauty and her freedom that she wanted to gallop, but she dared not. The archer was a dour, elderly man with a drooping mustache, a graying beard, and a sour frown, apparently anything but pleased about being sent on this mission. The Cypriot woman was a widow in black widow's weeds reeking of garlic sweat. Furthermore, the woman rode only a little donkey, the archer a sturdy but plodding cob, and even Eleanor's once-fine palfrey was as old in horse years as the Dowager Queen in human ones. She had long, yellow teeth, a gray muzzle, and numerous scars and spavins on her legs. The fastest pace the little party managed was a shuffling trot.

Eleanor soon discovered she could not keep up even this pace for long. It had been too long since she had ridden. She had been brought to the Queen's manor in a litter, hardly able to sit up after the wreck. And to join the ship in Marseilles, she had traveled in a wagon with a half-dozen nuns. The last time she had ridden, she calculated backwards, had been when the Inquisition — but she didn't want to think about that! She turned her attention back to her surroundings.

The Cypriot countryside was very different from the landscape around Najac. In the north a massive hump of mountains glowered, purple in the haze, but to the south a chain of steep, scruffy hills cut off the view to the sea. Between these heights lay a rich, fertile valley, first filled with sugar cane plantations and later, to Eleanor's delight, lemon and orange orchards. Oranges were outrageously expensive at home, and she had never seen an entire orchard of them before.

Eleanor could still remember the first time her father brought the family a dozen oranges for Christmas. She had been very little, and had leaned in so close to watch her father peel her first orange that she had been squirted on the nose with orange juice, making everyone laugh.

When Eleanor realized she was riding past a whole orchard of oranges, she had begged the Cypriot woman to pick up one of the fallen ones. But the old woman refused, saying they were rotten, and they rode on.

Eleanor surrendered to her memories, sinking into them so completely that she no longer took note of the countryside around her. As the youngest child and only surviving daughter, she had been spoiled shamelessly by her father, she reflected. No matter how she tried, she could conjure up no negative images of him. He was always smiling through his long white beard. He held her on his lap as he shared the orange. He carried her up to bed in her tower chamber and tucked her in with a fur-lined blanket against the cold. "Tell me a story, Papa! Tell me story!"

"Shall I tell you about how the Duc d'Aquitaine, the famous Coeur de Lion, once came to Najac?" his soft voice asked with a chuckle. "Or would you rather hear about his sister, the Fair Joanna, and how her brother rescued her from her prison on Sicily?"

And she had drifted off to sleep with images of the ever-laughing, golden-haired troubadour-duke in her dreams.

But her father died when she was still very young. She could remember sitting in the front pew of the chapel below the castle, still so small her feet dangled, and she had stared and stared at the long black box that held her father's familiar and yet frighteningly alien body. They had hammered the coffin shut, and she had winced at each unremitting crack.

Her brothers had come home for the funeral. She hardly knew Henri then; he had seemed a stranger, and she had resented it when he sat down in her father's place at the High Table. "That's *Papa's* chair!" she told him angrily. "*You* can't sit there!"

Her mother had hushed her. "Hush, Nel! You brother is now the Lord of Najac. He has taken your father's place."

Eleanor could remember thinking loyally, if silently, "No one can take Papa's place."

But Henri had, in his way. He had come home to live with them after his father's death, and he had taken up his father's duties conscientiously. He had been good to his little sister, too, bringing her a puppy on her eighth birthday and giving her a fat cream-colored pony on her ninth. He'd always had a smile for her, even when she interrupted him in his study when he was doing the accounts — maybe especially when he was looking over the accounts, Eleanor thought in retrospect.

Her other brother, Roger, had also spent more time at home after his father's death. Roger was not as serious as Henri. He could play the lute and sing wonderful songs, just like a troubadour. In fact, Eleanor had thought he *was* a troubadour at first, but he had laughed at that, and told her he "played the sword" even better than the lute. Eleanor sensed, as children do, a tension between her brothers, and now and then she heard heated words exchanged behind closed doors. More than once she had found her mother in tears.

As the years passed and she started to grow up, her mother started to change. By the time she was ten, Eleanor was aware that her mother went out more and more — not as a great lady, but dressed in a simple black gown, with a white wimple and black veil. She looked so much like a nun that Eleanor asked her mother if she had taken holy orders. At first her mother had looked astonished, even angry, but then her expression softened and she answered, "In a way, yes. Now run along, or you'll be late for your Latin lesson."

Gradually the people who came to Najac changed, too. In her father's day, the Lord of Najac had hosted many rich merchants traveling the road from Albi to Cahors with spices, scents, and silk from the Orient or furs, amber, and copper from the north. Traveling friars had been welcome, too, and occasionally knights of the militant orders with dispatches and money, passing to and from the rich commanderies of the region and the Mediterranean ports that were the lifeline to the Holy Land.

But in the years after her father's death, fewer and fewer friars and military monks passed through Najac. Their place was taken by men and women who came in humble clothes and exuded an eerie kind of apartness. Her mother called them "good men" and "good women," and her mother sometimes spent hours, even days, with these visitors. In fact, she so neglected her other duties that Henri complained. His mother retorted that it was time he stopped grieving for his dead bride. She admonished him to bring home a new wife to take over the duties of chatelaine so that she could "attend to her soul."

More fascinating to Eleanor had been the knights that her brother Roger brought to the castle. They usually arrived in a whirlwind of fluttering horse trappers and surcoats, all bright with the colors of heraldry. They dazzled her with their snorting stallions, their gleaming chain mail, their helmets, and their longswords and axes. They clattered down the narrow street of Najac town, scattering the chickens and the children. They shouted for the gates to open as they galloped up the last hill. Eleanor used to run to watch from the upper floor of the gatehouse as they streamed in over the drawbridge. They were always in a hurry, it seemed, and the heavy planks had hardly fallen into place before they thundered in.

On two occasions there had been wounded among them, and once a man had been so sorely injured he had been left in her mother's care. Eleanor was not allowed near him, and she had not learned until days later that he had died and been buried, apparently in secrecy, during the night.

Abruptly Eleanor's mare stumbled. The off-hind fetlock slipped in a muddy puddle and the mare's hip buckled under her. She threw up her head, whinnying in surprise and pain. Eleanor was yanked out of her memories as she clung to the pommel to keep from falling off. The mare lurched forward for several strides, hobbling in obvious pain, and then stopped stubbornly in protest. Too late, Eleanor took in the changed surroundings. The road she was following had turned south, following a gorge that led to the sea. The road was steep and rocky and filled with potholes, while the slopes of the hills grew nothing but scrawny scrub brush on the white surface of the limestone.

The archer, cursing, turned his cob around and stopped beside Eleanor. He jumped down to take a closer look at the injured mare. After a cursory inspection, he declared, "It's no good, My Lady; she's twisted her fetlock and scraped her hock to the bone. She can't go far like that. We need to turn back."

Turn back? Back to the dismal manor of a dying woman and her bickering serving women? Back to be buried alive? Eleanor refused to consider it. For the first time in six years, she had felt alive. For six years she had known neither freedom nor the beauty of the world. She rationalized that the archer had not wanted to come on this journey from the start. He simply wanted to return to his comfortable life at the Queen's manor. She refused. "We will continue on to the next castle and ask for a remount there," she told the archer, in a tone of voice that reminded him she was a noblewoman and he a hired mercenary.

The archer frowned and protested, "Cyprus isn't like France. There aren't castles everywhere. We're at least twelve miles from Paphos, My Lady. At the pace that horse can hobble, it will take us twelve hours."

"Then we will stop at the next village, while you ride ahead to fetch a remount."

The archer made another face, and tried again. "Who'll look to your safety, ma'am, while I ride to Paphos and back? I can't take responsibility —"

"No one is asking you to," Eleanor cut him off. "I'm not returning! We will continue our journey, and that's the end of it."

Muttering under his breath in Italian, the archer remounted, and the journey continued. Behind him Eleanor sat stiffly on her mount, trying not to feel pity for the poor mare with each step as she limped forward in obvious pain.

At this agonizing pace, they at last emerged from the gorge to find themselves on the coastal road. To the left the shore reared up in steep white cliffs to form a headland several miles to the east, and straight ahead the rocks had broken off from the cliffs and spilled out into the little cove at the foot of the gorge. The sight was spectacularly beautiful, but the sound of the waves and the wind reminded Eleanor all too sharply of the wreck, and to make matters worse, clouds seemed to have come out of nowhere to scud across the sky, low and ominous. The sea was an iron gray, except for a tiny sliver of silver far out to sea and fast retreating. The sound of breakers hammering the beach was so reminiscent of the wreck that Eleanor had to stop herself from covering her ears.

Even without her hands on her ears, fear deafened her. The archer had to shout at her to move out of the way of riders approaching from behind at a fast pace. Only then did Eleanor look over her shoulder and register two men in armor with a packhorse on a lead, approaching at a purposeful canter. Their chain mail chinked in rhythm with the canter, and their kit banged against the flanks of their horses. The shod hooves pounded the hard-packed surface of the road.

She tried to guide her mare to the side of the road, but the lame horse balked, as if this were one demand too many. Eleanor kicked her heels into the mare's sides to no avail, humiliated by being reduced to such undignified methods. A lady shouldn't have to ride a horse as insensitive as this, she thought to herself, tears in her eyes.

A dark horse loomed beside her. The smell of horse sweat and leather was overpowering, and she glanced left, keeping her eyes down out of embarrassment and modesty. What she saw were black suede over-the-knee boots with golden spurs studded with blue enamel fleurs-de-lis.

The King of France!

But it couldn't be! He was a prisoner in Egypt. As were his brothers. But who else would dare wear spurs like these? She raised her eyes sharply and found herself staring at a young man with a neatly clipped brown beard and short hair — a style long since out of fashion in France. Next she took in his plain, shabby, unbleached linen surcoat. The surcoat was more suited to a common archer or a man-at-arms and completely out of place over the gold and enamel spurs. No knight in her experience ever dressed like this, but no one but a knight was entitled to golden spurs — much less ones with the lilies of France.

The knight seemed hardly less astonished by the sight of Eleanor than she was surprised by him. He drew up sharply, his massive and heavy-boned European stallion flattening his ears and flinging up his head in protest. "My Lady! What are you — May I be of service in some way?"

The question couldn't have been more chivalrous, but the man's tone was harsh and his expression forbidding. He certainly knew nothing of courtesy, Eleanor concluded, lumping him instantly with all the other brutes from France who had plundered her homeland and spoke the langue d'oil as he did.

"My horse stumbled and came up lame, but my man will ride for a remount as soon as we reach the next village," Eleanor told him haughtily.

This answer so astonished the knight that he was silenced for a moment. He turned and looked at the archer, who shrugged and whined, "I advised against it, sir. I told her we must turn back, but my lady wouldn't hear of it."

"And where are you bound?" the knight asked the archer rather than Eleanor.

"The Lady Eleanor de Najac is on pilgrimage to the Shrine of St. George to pray for the safe return of her guardian, the Comte de Poitiers."

"I see." The knight twisted in his saddle and ordered his squire to offload the packhorse and transfer Eleanor's saddle to it.

Only then did the knight turn back to Eleanor and announce, "We will bring you to Paphos, My Lady. We should be able to reach it before nightfall — if not before the rain breaks." He glanced grimly at the gathering clouds. "You are with the King's court in Nicosia?"

"No, I am temporarily in the household of the Dowager Queen. And just who are you, sir?"

"Sir Geoffrey de Preuthune, Mademoiselle," he answered absently, not even looking at her as he spoke. He was already turning to her archer, ordering: "Take the lame horse back to Her Grace the Queen. I will see your lady safe to Paphos, where I'm sure Lord Tancred will be able to provide her with a suitable remount and an escort to Agios Georgios." (He gave the shrine its Greek name, Eleanor noted.)

This solution clearly suited the Queen's archer, who nodded and agreed with alacrity, "Very good, sir."

Eleanor, however, felt like a child or a prisoner again. No one was even asking what she wanted, and that angered her. Besides, even if his name meant nothing to her, his spurs suggested he was closely associated with her enemy, the King of France. Certainly he spoke the French of her homeland's oppressors. She did not want his services! "I have not accepted your generous offer, Monsieur," she pointed out sharply, adding pointedly, "I do not travel with strange men."

The archer groaned out loud and rolled his eyes. The Cypriot woman crossed herself and started praying. The squire suppressed a laugh, and Sir Geoffrey stared at her, baffled. Then, after a moment, he reasoned with her. "My Lady, you cannot continue on that horse, and it looks like it could rain any moment. If you are new to Cyprus, perhaps you do not know how violent the storms here can be at this time of year. I beg you to reconsider and allow me to bring you under the shelter and protection of the Lord of Paphos as rapidly as possible."

His gesture toward the clouds and a renewed gust of wind made her look again at the dark, churning clouds gathering overhead. As she watched, a flash of lightning pierced them and she shuddered involuntarily. She could not stay here. She glanced toward the packhorse and noted with surprise that, stripped of its packs, it was a lovely fine-boned mare with a delicate face and large eyes. Indeed, it was beautiful, with the narrow legs of a racer and the arching neck of a proud palfrey.

Again Eleanor looked at the knight in confusion. The "packhorse" matched his spurs more than his plain surcoat. Something wasn't right about this knight, but the threat of the storm was tangible, too. Her whole body was in a state of alarm, and reason told her it made more sense to accept the offer of a good mount and a strong escort than to insist on remaining here on a lame horse with a sullen archer and a native woman she could barely talk to. If only he hadn't been wearing King Louis' lilies on his heels ...

Eleanor pulled herself together. "Your name means nothing to me, sir. Are you in the service of the King of France?"

"No, My Lady. I am Cypriot. My father was in the service of King Richard of England, and accompanied him on crusade, but remained here at the orders his liege lord."

"The Duc d'Aquitaine? Coeur de Leon?" The legendary Lionheart was so much a hero of her childhood that it was as if this strange knight had been transformed into a long-lost friend by his association with the late English King. As soon as Geoffrey answered her question with a somewhat baffled, "Yes, Mademoiselle," Eleanor nodded her consent and dismounted.

Within moments her saddle and the leather saddlebags with her modest belongings had been transferred to the knight's "packhorse," while Sir Geoffrey's luggage was distributed between his own and his squire's stallions. When all was ready for her, Sir Geoffrey swung himself down from his horse and went to hold the off stirrup, asking as he did so, "Do you ride well, My Lady?"

"I did as a girl," Eleanor answered unhelpfully as she approached the little bay mare, trying not to limp. She took hold of the pommel with her left hand, and facing back, turned the stirrup toward her with her right hand. Twice she pointed her toe in the stirrup, but it was no use. With a horrible sense of humiliation, she realized she did not have the strength in her right leg, the leg shattered in the wreck, to push herself up off the ground.

She withdrew her toe from the stirrup. "Sir, I have an injured leg; could we find something to use as a mounting block?"

"Forgive me, My Lady. I didn't know. Ian, give the lady a leg up!"

The young squire cheerfully jumped down from his horse again and came to help Eleanor. He locked his fingers together and held them for her to step into. She held onto the pommel with both hands, set her foot in the squire's hands, and he lifted her up until she could swing her right leg over the cantle of the saddle.

No sooner did her bottom settle onto the saddle than the mare started moving. The knight held her firmly just behind the bit, so she swung her haunches first in one direction and then the other. This mare was not like any "packhorse"

Eleanor had ever seen before. She could feel the nervous energy of the animal, and was instantly alarmed. It was too long since she had ridden a horse like this. Ashamed of her own fear, Eleanor reproached the knight. "This is a very nervous packhorse, sir!"

"She's not a packhorse, My Lady," he answered candidly. "She's an Arab warhorse. We killed her last master, but she refused to flee like the other horses. Should I take her on the lead?"

"No, of course not!" Eleanor answered without thinking. Only children — and prisoners — were led. "I can manage, sir." Eleanor thought the knight looked skeptical, but he did not insist. Instead he let go of the mare's reins to return to his own stallion. At once the mare broke into a trot. Eleanor reined her in sharply, so she danced in place uneasily.

"We'd best hurry, My Lady, and try to get as far as possible before the rain breaks," the knight told her.

"Of course," Eleanor answered despite her inner alarm.

At once the knight took up a trot, and Eleanor's mare followed without any urging, with the squire on her flank. Anna, crossing herself and lamenting in Greek, brought up the rear, while the archer set off in the opposite direction with the lame horse in tow, whistling happily.

Chapter 3

The Cypriot Knight

They were drenched to the bone by the time they reached Paphos and skirted the walled town by the coastal road to reach the castle on the shore. Eleanor had blisters on her hands from trying to prevent the mare from running away with her. Her thighs were so exhausted they were trembling, and if she had had any tears left she would have been crying.

Under these conditions, Eleanor found very little interest in the city of Paphos, which sulked behind its wall on the right. She thought she could make out the shape of what seemed to be a very large domed building, presumably a basilica, and a few other church spires, but it was very nearly dark. Only a narrow strip of gold on the horizon marked the setting sun and the end of the rain clouds.

Although the rain and wind had eased, breakers were still rushing in and smashing against the sea wall that enclosed the little harbor from the southeast, and even more dramatically against the mole that curved out from the northwest, footed by a round tower. The fishing boats and small trading vessels tied to the quays bounced up and down on the waves, and their ropes creaked as they were strained and halyards thwacked against masts.

Sir Geoffrey was clearly making for a substantial, if rather commonplace, castle squatting on a small promontory just beyond the harbor. Like so many of the crusader castles, it was low and concentric in shape, with a solid, square keep surrounded by a rectangular wall with round towers at each of the corners. The only unique feature was a canal that had been dug between the harbor and the sea on the north side of the castle, creating a salt-water moat on the landward side, while the rest of the castle was enclosed by water, the harbor in the east and the sea in the south and west. From the south side of the castle, a stairway led down to the western breakwater and so out to the round tower at the end.

Eleanor was cheered by the sight of two round-headed double-light windows on two floors of the keep, both faintly lit from the inside. But although the drawbridge was still down over the salt-water moat, when they reached the main gate they found it already locked and barred. Eleanor felt her strength give out and despair overwhelm her, thinking they had come all this way and were going to be left out in the cold and wet.

No sooner had this thought enveloped her than Sir Geoffrey raised his voice and forcefully demanded entry.

"Who goes?" a man answered gruffly.

"Sir Geoffrey de Preuthune, with the Lady Eleanor de Najac!"

"Who?" the man on the ramparts shouted back, as if hard of hearing or disbelieving.

"Geoffrey Thurn! With the Lady Eleanor de Najac — a ward of the Comte de Poitiers!" This announcement elicited only silence.

Just when Sir Geoffrey was getting impatient and had raised his mailed fist to pound at the gate again, it swung open to admit them. They rode into the outer ward, at once gaining shelter from the wind, if not the rain.

Sir Geoffrey jumped down from his stallion, turning it over to his squire, and went to hold Eleanor's mare for her to dismount. Eleanor tried to stand in her stirrups so she could swing her leg over the cantle, but pain stabbed up from her thighs so sharply it made her gasp. She sank back into the saddle. Before she could decide what to do, a commotion in the darkness to her right distracted her.

Accompanied by a pageboy carrying a torch, a broad man with a bushy white beard emerged from a door in the face of the keep. The door was a good twelve feet above the base of the keep. He called out: "Geoff? Geoff? Is it really you? We'd feared the worst when the news of Mansourah came! But then the most peculiar rumors —"

"Yes, My Lord, it's me."

"With a lady?" the older man asked in obvious amazement, clattering down the exterior wooden stairs that led to the ward.

"The Lady Eleanor de Najac, a ward of the Comte de Poitiers," Sir Geoffrey introduced her. "Her horse went lame and I offered to bring her here."

"Najac, did you say? Holy Mother of God!" the older man exclaimed as he reached the foot of the stairs and started toward the horses. "Not the same poor damsel who was shipwrecked and nearly killed? When was that — last year?" He reached Eleanor's off stirrup and peered up at her.

"Yes, My Lord," Geoffrey and Eleanor answered in unintended unison.

"You poor child! I mean, My Lady! Holy Mother of God, you're drenched to the skin! Isaac! Run as fast as you can and tell my lady we have a highborn lady guest! Tell her to get a chamber ready, and a hot bath! Run!"

The boy with the torch at once handed it over to his lord and then started back up the wooden steps. Meanwhile the old knight turned again to Eleanor, bowing deeply as he introduced himself: "Tancred, Lord of Paphos, at your service, My Lady."

He must be a forgotten remnant of the age of chivalry and troubadours, Eleanor thought. He clearly did not belong to this modern age of inquisitions and crusades against Christians.

"Please," he urged as he straightened from his bow with an outstretched hand, "let me take you in to the fire. We'll have a bath for you shortly, and wine and a hot meal as well."

Eleanor had built up barriers against hatred, contempt, cruelty, and scorn, but she had no barriers against kindness. The old man's well-meaning offer pierced clear through her emotional armor, and she felt tears running down her face, at a complete loss for words.

"My Lady!" Paphos stepped closer, his warm hand on her knee. "My Lady! What have I said to upset you? What is wrong?"

"It's just my injured leg, sir. I — I can't — I'm exhausted."

"Geoffrey! Don't just stand there!" Lord Paphos ordered, flustered and angry at once. "Help the lady down from her horse. Take her in your arms. You're strong enough to carry such a slim child!"

Eleanor sensed Sir Geoffrey's reluctance, but he stepped beside her saddle and reached out his arms to her. She had no choice but to reach down to him. He took hold of her under her arms, then stepped back, pulling her gently off the horse. The pain in her legs made her gasp again, and she would have fallen to her knees if Sir Geoffrey hadn't held her upright — at a respectful distance.

Geoffrey could feel that she was trembling, however, and realized her legs could hardly hold her. After only a second of indecision, he overcame his inhibitions, and in a single, fluid motion bent, caught her under her knees, and swept her into his arms. The Lord of Paphos was gesturing toward the wooden stairway leading up to the entrance of the keep overhead.

Eleanor closed her eyes and lowered her head on Sir Geoffrey's chest in instinctive trust. In that moment she was not conscious of him being a virtual stranger; she was aware only that he was helping her when she needed it.

"Put her down there, by the fire!" the Lord of Paphos ordered, and Eleanor opened her eyes to take in a comfortable solar lit by a gentle fire. There were carpets on the floor, wall hangings hiding the stone walls, and big, inviting cushions on the window seat. Two large hounds lying by the fire jumped to their feet, their ears pricked and their tails wagging, and trotted over curiously at the arrival of strangers. Eleanor thoughtlessly reached out a hand so they could sniff it, remembering her brother's hunting dogs, and her own ....

Sir Geoffrey set her down gently in a large armed chair with a leather back and seat, while Paphos grabbed cushions from the window seat and offered them to Eleanor, ordering her to "Make yourself comfortable for the moment, while I go see where my lady wife —"

"I'm right here, Tancred," a woman's voice answered, emerging from a narrow interior spiral staircase and striding into the room. Eleanor looked over and saw a short, plump woman with a round face framed by an old-fashioned wimple. Her eyes were clear and intelligent, while the wrinkles of her face had been formed by smiles, giving the woman a permanently benign expression. "May I present my lady wife, Rosalyn de Montolif," the Lord of Paphos intoned formally.

As Lady Rosalyn caught sight of the state Eleanor was in, her motherly instincts overpowered etiquette and she exclaimed, "My dear child! You're drenched. We must get you out of those wet clothes or you'll catch your death of cold!"

"The Lady Eleanor is exhausted, Ros; we had to carry her inside," her husband informed her.

"Well, then," Lady Rosalyn retorted, "you'll just have to carry her upstairs to the East Chamber. Eva and Fani are up there now getting the bed ready." Turning back to Eleanor, she assured her, "Don't worry about a thing. You'll be warm and dry before you know it."

Eleanor felt tears threatening again. When was the last time she had been treated with so much heartfelt kindness? Certainly not in the Queen of Cyprus' household, nor by the Dominican Sisters in Albi, not to mention the Inquisition … And before that, she had been a child …. "I can't thank you enough, Madame. I'm just so tired. I haven't ridden since before the wreck, and today it was more than twelve hours. I'm just exhausted …." Eleanor tried to explain her own helplessness.

"We'll get you out of those clothes, into a hot bath and a warm bed, and you'll feel much better in the morning," Lady Rosalyn promised, turning to look toward the men.

For the first time the Lady of Paphos noticed Sir Geoffrey, and her face lit up at once.

"Geoff! I mean, *Sir* Geoffrey! We were so pleased to hear you weren't killed!" She embraced the young knight and kissed him on both cheeks. Then she stepped back and looked him straight in the eye to ask in a tense tone, "And my Matthew? Have you any word for a mother from her son?"

"He lived yet, My Lady, when I left His Grace's camp. But that was almost two months ago. More I cannot say." Sir Geoffrey's voice was so somber that it implied his news was worse than it sounded. Eleanor was rapidly calculating that Sir Geoffrey had taken part in King Louis' crusade in Egypt, but for some reason he had not been taken captive with the rest of King Louis's army. He was also only newly knighted, which might explain his plain clothes — but hardly his spurs.

Meanwhile Lady Rosalyn sighed deeply, nodded, and patted Sir Geoffrey on the arm. "That is good enough for now, though we dread the ransom demands. We are not as rich as the King of France and his mighty nobles."

"We can talk of this later," Sir Geoffrey promised; "first let me see to the Lady Eleanor. Ian?" He turned to look over his shoulder and, as expected, his squire was waiting in the background with Anna in his shadow. He asked the squire about Eleanor's things, and the youth gestured to the saddlebags he was carrying over his shoulders.

Lady Rosalyn took one look at the Cypriot maid's drenched condition, and ordered her back down to the kitchens to dry off and get something hot to eat. Then she took the torch her husband was still holding and led the way up the spiral stairs to the floor above, where the tower was divided by wooden partitions into two chambers. Sir Geoffrey was told to set Eleanor on the large bed of the right-hand room. Ian left the saddlebags with her belongings on a chair. Then the two men retreated back to the floor below, leaving Eleanor in the competent hands of Lady Rosalyn and her serving maids.

In the solar, Paphos ordered his unexpected guests to strip out of their wet clothes, saying he'd loan them some of his own robes while their own things were washed and dried. His visitors did not need to be asked twice. Standing by the fire, they unbuckled their swords and propped these up against the wall, then helped one another out of their soggy surcoats and boots. Next they freed themselves of their cold, wet chain mail and peeled off their gambesons and undergarments, reaching for the towels provided by their host.

As they rubbed each other down with towels, Geoffrey's sword fell over with a clatter, and Paphos went around the young men to pick it up and lay it on a bench near the door. It was a splendid sword, he thought automatically — and then he froze, and his heart missed a beat. Splendid indeed! This was like no sword he had ever seen before: the hilt appeared to be of rock crystal, and enclosed inside were three small, slender bones, finger bones. This was a holy relic! Paphos looked sharply over at Sir Geoffrey and his squire.

They had just finished drying themselves off and stood naked, ready to pull the robes he'd provided over their heads. The sight of a welter of hideous scars across Geoffrey's right shoulder and back made the older man forget the sword. "Jesus, Joseph, and Mary! What happened to you, Geoff?" he cried out as he set the sword on the nearest chair and went to get a closer look at Geoffrey's scars.

Geoffrey shook his head to dismiss his concern. "It's all but healed now," he insisted, reaching for the robe, but Paphos stopped him and drew him closer to the light of the fire as he looked at the scars professionally. "Greek fire," he concluded.

"Yes, we were defending one of the King's siege engines," Geoffrey admitted. "It took a direct hit and some Greek fire splattered in my direction. I just barely managed to turn my back into it."

Paphos glanced up to look at Geoffrey's face. The Cypriot nobleman knew perfectly well what Greek fire was like and what it could do. Geoffrey was very lucky it had not splashed onto his face or neck. If it had, he would have been blinded and completely disfigured. Even here, on his back, the sticky, molten substance would have been excruciating. Paphos had seen Greek fire heat chain mail to a glowing red. Geoffrey's hauberk would have burned into him, and yet the flames on his surcoat and gambeson could only be extinguished by pressing them out — by pressing that hot metal into his flesh, leaving these distinctive wriggly scars.

Geoffrey kept his eyes averted, so Paphos glanced toward the squire to see if the youth might be more communicative. The young man was a stranger to him and spoke with heavily accented French, clearly no native. Paphos guessed he was an Englishman.

"Take the dirty things down to the kitchen," he ordered the youth, "and have one of the women see to cleaning them. Tell her to give the chain mail to my squire. He'll clean it for you, while you find a hot meal and a warm place to sleep."

"Yes, My Lord," the youth answered cheerfully, sweeping Geoffrey's and his own clothes, including chain mail and boots, into his arms. Paphos opened the door for him and gave him directions to the kitchens. Then he closed the door and turned to look back at Geoffrey.

The young knight had pulled Paphos' robe over his head, covering both his nakedness and his scars. He tied the robe firmly and modestly at his waist. Geoffrey had always been modest, Paphos remembered suddenly. Even as a little boy, when he'd been a page in the household, he'd been shy about his nakedness. He was the son of a second, late marriage. Geoffrey's elder brother — strong, healthy, and already a father by the time Geoff joined Paphos' household — was the heir apparent. Geoff had been destined for the Church from the day he was born, and he knew that.

Looking at him now, bearded, tanned and muscular, it was hard to remember that once he had been a frail, pale boy with a preference for reading over sports. While the other boys fussed, fought, and played silly games, Geoffrey had diligently learned his letters — in Latin and Greek. By the time he was twelve, he could read and write in three languages: French, Latin, and Greek. When the other pages took service as squires to other knights, Geoffrey had been sent to study at the school run by the Cistercian abbey in Nicosia, earning his keep as a copyist. Three years later, the Abbot of Bellapais had been impressed enough to agree to accept him as a novice. Then abruptly Geoffrey's father, old Sir John Thurn, decided he had to make a pilgrimage to Jerusalem, and took it into his head that Geoffrey ought to escort him.

More than one man, including Tancred's father and Sir John's liege lord, had tried to talk Sir John out of this trip to Jerusalem. The situation had been precarious for months. The risks were obvious and enormous. But the more people warned Sir John that Jerusalem could fall to the Saracens any day, the more insistent he became that that was the *very* reason why he had to go — now. Before leaving England, he reminded everyone, he had taken a vow to pray at the Church of the Holy Sepulcher — or die in the attempt. The fact that he had remained on Cyprus on the orders of King Richard was no excuse for breaking his word to God. He was seventy-five years old. The Saracens were threatening to seize the city again and cut off the pilgrim routes. If he didn't go, he would very likely die without having fulfilled his vow. Now was his last chance to save his soul.

So Geoffrey delayed joining the canons at Bellapais to accompany his father, acting as the old man's squire, body servant, and translator all in one. They traveled as pilgrims, unarmed and in company. But something had gone terribly wrong. Paphos never learned the details, but apparently the pilgrim convoy had been attacked by robbers and most of the pilgrims killed or captured. Sir John had been horribly wounded and left for dead. Geoffrey had somehow managed to hide himself, but then spent two days in the desert with his injured father and no water before a troop of Templars found and rescued him. The Templars buried Sir John in their graveyard in Jaffa and looked after Geoffrey until they could put him aboard a ship bound for Cyprus.

Geoffrey returned home eleven months after he departed — a totally different youth. He had completely lost his dreamy interest in theology, history, and learning. He was hardened, passionate — and obsessed with joining the Knights Templar. He flatly refused to join the canons at Bellapais, and when his brother tried to force him, he ran away and presented himself to the Templars at Limassol.

Most Templar recruits were men already knighted, or at least youths trained in the arts of war. Furthermore, the Templars did not have novices, although they allowed secular knights to serve with them for a period without taking vows, and hired secular squires. The problem was that Geoffrey was neither a knight nor a squire, and had none of the skills required for either.

Paphos could not imagine what Geoffrey had said to persuade the Templars to give him a chance. All he knew was that Geoffrey was indeed allowed to live, pray, and train with the Templars. The training could not have been pleasant for a youth with little physical strength or agility. Templar training was notoriously hard — even for men and youths already skilled in horsemanship and arms. It was therefore no surprise to Paphos that Geoffrey was still a squire five years later, when King Louis of France arrived to lead a new crusade. It made no sense to Paphos, however, that Geoffrey was now a knight, but not a Templar.

Paphos shook his head, pulled out a second chair before the fire, and gestured for Geoffrey to sit opposite him. Between them was a table laden with wine in a jug, bread on a cutting board, and a platter of cheeses. "Help yourself, Geoff."

Geoffrey looked at the food, but he did not take any. Instead he crossed himself, bowed his head, and prayed silently. When he finished, he admitted, "I have not heard Mass since morning."

"God will forgive you, boy. Eat up."

Geoffrey still hesitated. "I must confess ...."

"I'll make sure Father Benedict doesn't go to bed before he's heard your confession and given you the sacraments, but now you need food and wine to warm you up from the inside."

"Thank you, My Lord." Only then did Geoffrey reach for the bread knife and cut himself a slice of bread. He spread butter on it thickly and started eating with a healthy appetite — only to abruptly stop himself and put the things down. He swallowed.

"What's the matter, Geoff?"

"I — I was thinking of Matthew, My Lord."

That hurt. "Yes?" Paphos prompted. Geoff and Matthew were roughly the same age and had been pages together, but back then Matthew had been much stronger and more athletic than Geoffrey. They had not been close.

"It's true Matthew was still alive when I left the army," Geoffrey told the father.

Paphos nodded, his eyes boring into Geoffrey: "But?"

"He was ill, sir, when last I saw him; he was very ill."

"I see."

"The supplies were no longer getting through. Many secular knights had nothing fresh left to eat. Meat had spoiled. And the water was no longer safe to drink."

Paphos nodded, his stomach tying itself in knots as he thought of it. It was better not to think of it, he told himself, and changed the subject. "And you Geoff? We've heard the wildest rumors. They're saying you're a knight, but no longer with the Templars. And that sword," Paphos pointed to the magnificent weapon he'd left on the seat of a chair with its macabre crystal hilt gleaming. "That's no ordinary sword."

"No, sir," Geoffrey admitted, following his host's pointing finger.

"The bones in the hilt — they're some kind of relic, aren't they?"

"It's the finger of St. John the Baptist," Geoffrey answered. Paphos sprang to his feet, crossing himself in a mixture of alarm and awe. He felt his blood rushing in his veins to think he was so close to such an exceptional relic, that he had all but held it in his hand. He looked again in the direction of the sacred bones and was certain that they were glistening, almost luminous. "Geoffrey!" He turned and gaped at the young man who had been his page. "How, in the name of the Virgin Mary and all His Saints ...?"

"It was Master de Sonnac's sword," Geoffrey explained softly. "After Mansourah ..." He swallowed, and his eyes were fixed on the hilt of the sword no less than his host's were. "After Mansourah, the Master knew ... he knew the army was doomed, and that any Templars still with it would fall into Saracen hands and be killed." It was against the Rule of the Templars to pay ransom, so Templars taken captive were always executed. That was one reason they fought so well, Paphos supposed.

Geoffrey was continuing. "Master de Sonnac didn't want that sword, the sacred relic, to fall into the hands of heathens."

That made sense to Paphos, but there was a large unexplained gap between giving the sacred sword to a squire to get it out of Egypt and it lying on the chair of his solar here in Cyprus. Paphos turned his gaze to Geoffrey again. "But what are you doing with it here, now? And why aren't you wearing the coat and mantle of the Temple?"

"I have not taken the vows. Not yet." The answer did not make sense to Paphos. Geoffrey had shared the discipline and the hardships of the Templars for six years so that he could join the Temple the moment he qualified as a knight. That had always been the terms of his service; when he was skilled enough with sword, lance, and horse to take his place in a Templar charge, he would be allowed to take his vows.

"But you're a knight," Paphos countered, adding, "I've heard rumors that you were knighted by King Louis himself."

Geoffrey stared at the fire, unwilling to meet Paphos' eyes. He nodded.

"I don't understand. What happened?" Paphos demanded.

"We were at Mansourah. Surely you've heard what happened?"

"That that fool, the Comte d'Artois, insisted on attacking with just the vanguard, and your Grand Master — who damned well knew better! — threw away the lives of three hundred knights rather than stop him? Yes, I heard all that. What does it have to do with you?"

"I was with Master de Sonnac. I'd been acting as his squire ever since his own squire fell ill before we left Damietta. I rode with him into Mansourah ...." Geoffrey was staring at the fire. After a moment, he realized Paphos was waiting for him to continue, and he drew a deep breath. "We were cut off from one another. The Master was shot in the eye and lost consciousness. His horse was cut down under him. I only just managed to drag him across my saddle. I don't know how I got out. I don't know."

Paphos waited, letting Geoffrey sort out his memories, and then asked, "How many of you got out?"

"Seventeen. Four knights, eleven sergeants, the Master, and me."

"And then?"

Geoffrey shook his head sharply. "When Master de Sonnac came to again, and was told I had rescued him, he sent for me. He wanted to knight me and accept me into the Order. But I was angry. I said some stupid things." Geoffrey was staring at the fire.

"And?" Paphos prompted.

Geoffrey was seeing it again in his head. The confusion in a darkness lit only by the unsteady light of smoking torches. Wounded men and horses seemed to be staggering about everywhere, and the moans and cries of man and beast punctuated the night. Other men wandered about asking after one friend or another. Abandoned Saracen equipment, clothing, and weapons still littered the ground, tripping the unwary, while those with strength left in them were trying to erect tents. The stench of open latrines and foul water combined in Geoffrey's mind with the constant beating of the enemy drums as they shouted "Allah is Great!" from the ramparts of Mansourah. They must have lit huge bonfires, because the city appeared aglow from the inside; the men on the walls, shaking their swords and bows triumphantly, were silhouetted against that orange light.

Geoffrey had been dazed, unable to grasp what had happened in such a short space of time. All his brothers from Limassol — knights, squires, and sergeants — were dead. They had been one hundred strong when they sailed for Egypt, a significant contingent of the Templar force, and they were no more. Geoffrey had lost the one man who gave him a chance when all others spoke against accepting him into the Temple. He'd lost the men who'd taught him fighting and the ethos of the Temple. He'd lost his best friends — and there would not even be a Mass for their souls, because their bodies were all in the hands of the heathens shouting "Allah is Great!"

Suddenly someone was tugging at his sleeve and saying he must come to the surgeon's tent. The Grand Master had regained consciousness. He had followed numbly, without a will of his own. Sonnac, a bandage covering the gaping hole in the right side of his face where his eye had been, was struggling to sit up. "Geoff!" he called out in a rasping, ruined voice at the sight of the young man. "Geoff, come kneel and put your hands in mine, that I may take you into the Order at last."

Sonnac knew how much that meant to his squire. Sonnac knew that, unlike other squires, Geoffrey wanted to be a Templar. He understood that Geoffrey wanted to be knighted, not for itself, but because it was the prerequisite for joining the Order.

That night in the camp before Mansourah, Geoffrey knew that Master de Sonnac wanted to reward him with that which meant most to him, but he also knew that the vows involved saying the Lord's Prayer. He knew that the Knights Templar said the Lord's Prayer in place of Mass when circumstances made it impossible to hear Mass. The Lord's Prayer was central to their devotion. But what had, until that day, seemed self-evident, had abruptly been transformed into a demon standing between Geoffrey and what he wanted most in the world.

As Geoffrey stood in the tent staring at the wounded Grand Master, he became conscious of the blood drying on the links of his chain mail, his surcoat shredded and soiled, but between him and the Master crowded the ghastly ghosts of his dead brothers: some headless, some limbless, some gushing blood from wounds to their heads, others clutching their gutted stomachs or clinging to their disemboweled intestines.

Suddenly Geoffrey thought: If this is God's will, then I cannot say "Thy will be done!" I cannot say it!

Sonnac, seeing him hesitate, tried to smile encouragingly. "Come, Geoff. If this is the last thing I do, let me make you a Templar."

"No!" Geoffrey screamed back at him. "No! I don't want to be servant to a senseless God! If this is God's will, then he is a monster! And Christ — Christ died on a cross in Jerusalem, but he was not God's son, and was not our Savior!"

Still full of fury, Geoffrey had spun about and fled, leaving the astonished Grand Master struggling to rise. He heard the exclamation of horrified priests and surgeons, and he was shocked by his own words as much as anyone. But there was no place to go in the crusader camp. There was no escape except out into the desert to be killed by the Bedouins.

Geoffrey could not remember what he'd done next. He'd stumbled about in the dark until he'd found himself at the horse lines. There he sank down in misery beside the remnants of a once-great cavalry, and begged forgiveness from his stallion. The tall, dark gray had not only carried him and his armor all the way here, to the middle of nowhere; he had today taken the burden of two fully armored knights, and with the strength of an angel, he had jumped over a barricade to bring both Geoffrey and the wounded Grand Master to safety. But now he stood with hanging head and swollen fetlocks, covered in cuts and probably bruises, too. We can't even give you a decent meal, Geoffrey thought. What right have we, he asked himself, to take these gentle, loyal creatures into so much misery and almost certain death?

The herald had found him there. "You must report to King Louis at once," the man ordered.

King Louis? Geoffrey had never exchanged words with the French King. Like all the crusaders, he had seen him crowned and decked in gleaming armor at the head of his troops, and had seen him, too, when he went bareheaded to Mass. Once or twice he had glimpsed him as he moved among the tents surrounded by his advisors, his brothers, and his friends. What could King Louis want with a Templar squire who had just denied the divinity of Christ?

Geoffrey had quickly concluded that King Louis, who was admirably pious, must have heard about his blasphemy and wanted to repudiate and punish such a renegade. Maybe even execute him.

But didn't he deserve that?

The crusader camp was dark, lit almost exclusively by the lurid glow of the bonfires in Mansourah. All Christian voices were subdued by the distant chanting of "Allahu Akbar! Allahu Akbar!"

Geoffrey heard someone mutter that the body of the Comte d'Artois was hanging outside the city walls.

"Does the King know?" someone asked back in horror.

"He must," the first speaker replied.

"How can he stand the insult?"

"What can he do about it?"

Geoffrey felt himself being shoved into the royal tent. The fleurs-de-lis on the canvas walls still sparkled gold by torchlight, and there were carpets spread upon the floor, although these were covered by so much sand that their patterns were indecipherable. Geoffrey focused his attention on the carpets because Master de Sonnac, a bandage covering half his face, was standing beside the King, and Geoffrey was afraid to meet his remaining eye.

"Geoffrey de Thune?" the King inquired.

Geoffrey had not thought it appropriate to correct the King of France on the pronunciation of his name. What did his name matter? He had disgraced it with his stupid outburst to the Grand Master.

The King ordered Geoffrey to kneel and asked his constable for a sword. Geoffrey went down on his knees, expecting the constable to behead him then and there. It took him a little by surprise that justice could be so swift, but it did not strike him as unjust after what he had said. A crusader had no right to doubt the divinity of Christ. He bowed his head for the blade.

"At the request of our beloved friend, William de Sonnac, Grand Master of the Poor Knights of the Temple of Solomon in Jerusalem, it is our pleasure to knight you, Geoffrey." Instead of swooshing down to sever his head from his shoulders, the sword fell firmly but flat upon his left shoulder, and then on the right. "Rise, Sir Geoffrey de Preuthune."

Geoffrey stumbled to his feet, tears already starting to blind him. Master de Sonnac moved forward, and Geoffrey recoiled, but the Master caught him by the arm and then, with a sad smile, passed his own sword around Geoffrey's hips and buckled it deftly. King Louis, meanwhile, had knelt to buckle spurs on Geoffrey's heels. Bewildered, Geoffrey tried to step back. "Wait! Wait!" King Louis called. When the King stood again, he bestowed the kiss of peace on Geoffrey's cheeks. It was too much. Geoffrey started sobbing.

"This is no time for tears!" King Louis admonished gently. "We have lost so many good knights this day; let us rejoice at making a new one."

"And?" It was the voice of the Lord of Paphos, demanding an explanation of what had happened.

Geoffrey turned away from the fire and faced the aging Cypriot baron. "Master de Sonnac asked the French King to knight me because I — I refused to take the Templar vows."

Paphos raised his eyebrows. "You refused?"

"Yes, My Lord."

"And you're not going to tell me why?"

"It was a fit of temper, My Lord, and before I had time to repent, I was summoned to the King's tent."

Paphos considered the young knight sitting opposite him. There was clearly more to this than Geoffrey was willing to tell him, but he did not think it was his place to press for more information. Geoffrey was not his kinsman, after all, nor his vassal, since his elder brother held the fief. Geoffrey was a knight, but a landless one, and despite the honor that went with being knighted by a king, it would not put food on his table nor a roof over his head. "So what do you do now? Do you want to join the Canons at Bellapais after all?"

Geoffrey shook his head vigorously. "No. Master de Sonnac provided me with a letter that, he said, would assure me admittance to the Temple, whenever I was ready, but he first made me swear not to make use of it until — until I had fulfilled certain criteria," Geoffrey answered cautiously. Sonnac had charged him with nothing less than regaining his faith in God and his trust in Christ, but Geoffrey was ashamed to admit to the Lord of Paphos what his sins had been. He continued, "The Grand Master also gave me a sealed letter for the English Preceptor, Sir Thomas Bérard, who is due to put in at Limassol within the fortnight. I was on my way to visit my brother, before returning to Limassol to deliver the message, when I came upon the Lady Eleanor."

"Thank God for that, at least! What was she doing riding about alone?" Paphos demanded.

"She is on a pilgrimage to pray for the safe return of her guardian, the Comte de Poitiers. She had one of the Dowager Queen's archers and the

Greek serving woman you saw with her, but I sent the archer back with the lame horse, and your wife sent her woman below. Will you be able to see her safely to her destination?"

"First she needs to recover from today's misadventure. I'm surprised she could ride at all. At the time of the wreck it was said her leg was broken in multiple places, and by the time the Hospitallers found her, it was too late to reset everything. I thought she was a complete cripple."

Geoffrey said nothing. He had taken no note of Eleanor's wreck when it occurred, because wrecks were common on Cyprus, and seeing that he and his brothers had already embarked for the crusade, he had other things on his mind. Nor had his initial offer of assistance been more than sheer practicality: he would have offered his spare horse to any knight, merchant, or, indeed, practically anyone on the road in the same predicament as Eleanor of Najac.

It was not until he realized that she was in such terrible pain, and so weak she could not stand, that he had taken note of her as a person. Furthermore, when he'd taken her in his arms, he had realized that she was as fragile as a sparrow — all skin and bones. He'd felt as if he would have crushed her if he grasped her firmly. Only in that instant did he realize just how vulnerable she was. And no sooner had he thought that, than he realized with horror that it could so easily have been a different kind of man who had come upon her on that isolated stretch of road. What good would the Queen's aging archer have been then?

He had been right to offer assistance, but he should have been more mindful of how weak she was. After all, she'd had trouble mounting and had told him she was injured. Why had he ridden so hard? Why hadn't he at least been more solicitous of her condition? His failure to be more chivalrous shamed him, and Geoffrey got to his feet. "With your permission, My Lord, I would like to confess my sins and hear Mass before bed."

Paphos nodded absently. His conscience said he should go with his guest, but the chapel would be cold this time of night. He would take communion in the morning, he rationalized, gesturing to Geoffrey, "You know the way."

Chapter 4

The Shades of Montsègur

The maids were chattering as they stoked the fire under a large cauldron and filled it with bucket after bucket of water. Two of the kitchen boys had already set up a cork-lined tub, and Lady Rosalyn herself took linen towels from a large wooden cabinet and spread these around the base of the tub, laying others on a chair within reach.

All the while, Eleanor sat on the bed trying to collect the strength to move. Her feet were numb with cold, and her legs ached unbearably.

"Shall I help you undress, my dear?" the Lady of Paphos asked gently, startling Eleanor into nervous action. The offer of help was disorienting, especially since it came from an older woman, a noblewoman. At once Eleanor started to disentangle her scarves, which seemed glued together by the rain. As she pulled off her hat, water ran down her face, and Lady Rosalyn handed her a towel. Eleanor held it to her face and dabbed her hair with it to absorb the wetness.

"Eva!" Lady Rosalyn called to one of the serving girls. "Come help Lady Eleanor out of her wet shoes and stockings!"

The serving girl left the buckets to her companion and came over to the bed. As she bent to untie Eleanor's shoes, Eleanor raised her hands to untie the lacings of her surcoat.

Lady Rosalyn, finished with the towels, came to Eleanor's assistance. As she reached out to help, she noticed that Eleanor's hands were shaking, and then that the palms were bloody. "Good heavens, child!" she exclaimed. "What happened to your hands?"

Eleanor clenched her fists together in shame.

"Child! You're bleeding! Give me your hands!" the older woman insisted, holding out her own hands, but Eleanor shook her head and countered defensively, "They're just blisters. Sir Geoffrey's packhorse was so hot- blooded that she tried to run away the whole time."

"I'm going to give that young man a piece of my mind!" Lady Rosalyn concluded firmly.

"No, no!" Eleanor protested. "He meant well. Besides, he had no other horse."

"Then he could have taken you up on his own!" Rosalyn concluded practically. "His stallion, so I've been told, carried both him and the Grand Master of the Temple, fully armored, out of Mansourah. He could easily have carried a bird like you!" She paused and added more charitably, "But I suppose Geoffrey hasn't had much experience with women. Still, let me clean up your hands —"

"In the bath," Eleanor countered, increasing her efforts to free herself of her wet clothes. Rosalyn gave up trying to look at Eleanor's hands and instead helped her wriggle out of her clinging gowns. Meanwhile, the maids began to transfer the steaming water from the cauldron into the tub itself. As soon as the tub was half full, Eleanor — with a gasp of pain — got to her feet.

Rosalyn caught Eleanor under the arm and helped her hobble over to the tub. There she held the younger woman upright as Eleanor gingerly lifted her right leg over the edge. The maids gawked at the ugly scars on the lady's leg, then looked down quickly as they felt their mistress' disapproving frown. At last Eleanor sank into the water with an audible sigh of relief, and Rosalyn gestured for three more buckets of water, before retreating to her own chamber to get a vial of bath oil.

Meanwhile, without being asked, Eva shoved up her sleeves and knelt beside the tub to help soap down Lady Eleanor, while Fani started unbraiding her hair. Eleanor leaned her head back against the padded rim of the tub and closed her eyes, her hands clasped together between her breasts.

Returning, Rosalyn nodded her approval, then stepped beside the tub to pour just a thimbleful of the precious essence into the steaming water. A moment later the smell of lavender wafted up on the steam, and tears started streaming down Eleanor's face.

No one noticed. Lady Rosalyn had turned away to return her vial to her own chamber, and the maids were collecting the buckets to go fetch more water, leaving Eleanor alone in the now cozy chamber.

Eleanor put her hands over her face and held them there, trying to calm herself. She felt as if she had been tortured all day, and then this sudden vivid memory of home – the lavender fields in the sunshine. It was too much!

"Hush, child!" The voice came from the timber roof above her head and wafted down to settle upon her like petals shaken from a dying rose. "Relax, little one. There's nothing to be afraid of anymore."

Nothing? Eleanor wondered, opening her eyes. Nothing?

"You're with good people now," her mother assured her. "Good people, who mean you no harm."

Was that possible?

"And you, Mother?" Eleanor asked the voice, with all the pent-up fury of half a dozen years. "Did you mean me no harm when you abandoned me at fourteen? Preferring your sick religion to your own child!" Eleanor was so agitated that she sat upright, looking for her mother in the darkness of the rafters, sloshing water over the edge of the tub. She turned to look over her shoulder first in one direction, then the other.

"Child, child!" her mother protested in an anguished voice. "I never thought they'd harm a little girl, a child as innocent as you!"

"Never thought they'd harm a child?" Eleanor mocked back. "Never thought they'd harm a child?" she raged. "Hadn't they slaughtered children at Beziers? At Minerve and Lavour? What else did you expect, Mother? They put it in their very edicts — that the parents and children of heretics were to be persecuted and punished. You *must* have known what they would do to me!"

To Eleanor's distress, her mother did not protest. Instead, her voice fell to an almost inaudible murmur and pleaded, "You're right. I *should* have known. I — I deceived myself. Please forgive me, Nel."

Eleanor didn't want to forgive her. It was easier to rage than to forgive. She shook her head. For a moment it seemed as if this negative answer had banished her mother, but then her mother spoke from so near at hand that Eleanor thought she felt her breath on her cheek.

"At least try to understand. I was a known heretic. All I would have achieved by abjuring my faith would have been to be branded on the forehead and forced to live as beggar — a beggar that Christians were forbidden to support. Worse, I would have endangered the good people who followed Christ's commandments and showed me Christian charity. I would have died of hunger and cold eventually, but my soul would have been condemned to hell. And you — you would *still* have fallen into their hands."

Eleanor shook her head again and brought her hands out of the water to stare at the palms. On the left hand, beneath the broken blisters from today's ride, was a hideous, puckered scar. A single flame had caused it, and she had screamed loud enough to wake the dead. She had been unable to endure the flame for more than a second, but her mother had let them burn her alive ....

"You were never there when I needed you," Eleanor told her mother bitterly.

"How could I be?" her mother answered, already farther away. "They encircled you with their evil. I couldn't break through, not until today ...." Eleanor had to strain to hear her mother's voice. The sound of Lady Rosalyn's returning footsteps was obliterating her mother's voice. "You're with ..." thump, thump, "trust ..." thump, thump, "Sir Geoffrey ...."

"Are you feeling better now, My Lady?" the cheerful voice of Lady Rosalyn asked as she re-entered the chamber.

Eleanor lifted her head and smiled at her. "Thank you. I am feeling much better. I never knew — that riding could — be so exhausting. But then I'm so out of practice ...."

"Of course you are. I'm sure you haven't been on a horse since your accident." Lady Rosalyn settled herself in the armed chair on the other side of the fireplace. "And you mustn't think of continuing tomorrow. You need to rest and regain your strength. You can stay here as long as you please. I'd be glad of the company."

"That's very kind," Eleanor answered, overwhelmed by a sense of safety. She hadn't felt this safe in half a decade — except for that moment in Sir Geoffrey's arms ....

"Do you mind telling me where you were headed in such a storm?" Lady Rosalyn continued, curious more than reproachful.

"A pilgrimage," Eleanor answered defensively, knowing now how very foolish she had been and how easily her escapade could have ended in disaster. "My guardian, the Comte de Poitiers, was taken captive with his brother, King Louis of France. I wanted to pray for his safe return."

"Yes," Lady Rosalyn replied, crossing herself. "May God hear our prayers!" Rosalyn's cheerful face was instantly clouded with worry, and Eleanor realized she was thinking of her son. Eleanor felt a surge of sympathy for the older woman and reached out a hand to her, promising, "I will pray for your son, too, Madame." For him more than for the Comte de Poitiers, she added mentally.

Lady Rosalyn was too distressed to speak, but she took Eleanor's hand and clasped it, nodding in thanks, thinking that she would ask Geoffrey to pray for her son as well. Geoffrey was practically a monk, after all, and a crusader. God would surely hear his prayers ....

Eleanor awoke to sunlight pouring through the round-headed window of her chamber and tumbling down over the cushioned window seat to stretch across the checkered tile floor. A warm breeze followed the sunshine, carrying with it the caw of gulls. A knock at the door explained what had awoken her, and she called out 'Come in' as she tried to sit up. Every muscle in her body ached, so she gave up and sank back onto the soft bedding.

Lady Rosalyn entered with Eva behind her, carrying a tray. "We've brought you something to eat and drink," Lady Rosalyn announced, smiling, "but you mustn't think you have to get up."

Eleanor immediately made a new attempt to sit up. "Is it very late?" she asked.

"Almost noon, but that's no matter. As I said last night, you're welcome to stay as long as you like, and after exhausting yourself yesterday, it would be wise to rest a week or more."

Eleanor still could not fully believe her good fortune. She stammered, "You're so — so kind, My Lady!"

"No, I'm as selfish as they come," Lady Rosalyn retorted matter-of-factly. "I'm delighted to have a visitor. It's been a long winter, particularly since half our nobles are in Egypt and the King is awaiting his bride and so held no Christmas court this year. I'm quite starved for female companionship." As she spoke, she efficiently straightened Eleanor's bed-covers to make a place for the tray beside her. She helped Eva set the tray down, and then remarked, "By the way, we've had news that the Queen of France is refusing to leave Damietta! Can you imagine? She's practically defenseless there, surrounded by a sea of Saracens and Bedouins, with only a handful of Christian knights to defend her, but she flatly refuses to leave. Apparently she told the Marshal of the Temple, who urged her to flee, that Damietta was the most important bargaining chip she had in the negotiations for the release of her husband. She said she would rather die than risk prolonging King Louis' captivity." Admiration and amazement were mixed liberally in Lady Rosalyn's voice.

Eleanor smiled faintly. "Queen Marguerite is from the Provence, My Lady. We women of the Languedoc may smell of lavender, but we are made of steel." Eleanor sat up straighter as she spoke, proud both of the Queen she'd never met and of her own survival.

"You are from the Provence?" Lady Rosalyn asked, surprised, adding apologetically, "You must forgive my ignorance of French geography; I've lived my whole life on Cyprus. I had no idea where Najac was — beyond being in the West." As she spoke she pulled the armed chair away from the fire to place it beside the bed and settled herself in it. "Do help yourself to your breakfast, child. I'll just keep you company. You may go, thank you, Eva," she ordered the maid.

Eleanor only realized how hungry she was when she saw the feast prepared for her. There was fresh bread, butter, honey, olive paste, little boiled eggs, finger-sized sausages, fresh figs, and an orange. With delight, Eleanor seized the orange and started peeling it. "I'm sure your ignorance of the West is no greater than my ignorance of Outremer, My Lady. I hardly know where I am!" Eleanor was out of practice making jokes, and this one fell a little flat, but Rosalyn smiled encouragingly. "There will be plenty of time to show you around, once you're back on your feet again," she promised. "If nothing else, we must show you Aphrodite's birthplace, the ancient tombs, Bellapais, and the like. But first you need to recover from your terrible ride yesterday — and while you do, you can educate me about France.

Start by telling me more about Najac," Lady Rosalyn urged.

"Najac." Eleanor repeated the word wistfully, paused, and then admitted, "Najac isn't in the Provence, but it does lie in the Languedoc. It is on the border of the Aveyron and Quercy. My grandfather and his father were vassals of the Ducs d'Aquitaine. My father swore homage to Comte Richard, called Coeur de Leon, and came with him on crusade. When I was a little girl, my father used to tell me stories of landing on Cyprus and fighting at Acre with the Lionheart." Eleanor's eyes lit up at the memory, and Rosalyn smiled and nodded encouragement. Eleanor continued, "But our lands were part of the dowry King Richard settled on his sister Joanna when she married the Comte de Toulouse, so we became vassals of Raymond de Toulouse."

"Didn't the Comte de Toulouse rebel against the French King and get excommunicated, or am I mixing something up?" The Lady of Paphos was clearly more conversational than judgmental in her remark.

Nevertheless, Eleanor put a slice of orange in her mouth to give herself time to think before answering. Finally she said, "It is rather complicated. Raymond VI de Toulouse was a violent and self-willed man, but a fierce defender of the independence of the southern barons against the crown of France. The Pope excommunicated him twice, I think. Once for bigamy —"

"Good heavens! A French Count?"

"I'm not sure of the details. It happened before I was born, and people seemed to think I shouldn't hear of such things," Eleanor admitted.

Rosalyn laughed out loud. "The things that interest us *most* are always what men try to keep secret! All right, so your father's liege was bigamous and also a rebel?"

Eleanor didn't like the word "rebel." She squirmed uncomfortably before cautiously explaining, "He did not consider himself a rebel, as he did not recognize the suzerainty of the King of France. In any case, he was allegedly excommunicated for failing to suppress the Albigensian heresy in my homeland, but my brothers always claimed the real reason was that the French King wanted to seize control of his lands." Eleanor paused tensely, afraid she had said too much, afraid that Lady Rosalyn's kindness had lured her into the trap of letting down her guard.

Rosalyn unconsciously reassured her by remarking simply, "It's always the same, isn't it? Whether with the Capets and Plantagenets or the Holy Roman Emperor, the Pope allows himself to get dragged into these secular wars."

"Exactly," Eleanor exclaimed with relief. "So the Comte de Toulouse was excommunicated a second time, and this time his lands and titles were transferred to Simon de Montfort."

"Montfort? Surely not!" the Lady of Paphos protested, thinking of Montfort in the Kingdom of Jerusalem. "I'm sure Montfort never took an interest in affairs in France."

"Simon de Montfort was the Commander of the French crusaders," Eleanor explained.

"Crusaders?" Rosalyn asked, more confused than ever. "But the last crusade was led by the Holy Roman Emperor. I don't remember any French participation at all — or not in significant numbers."

"Not *that* crusade, My Lady," Eleanor corrected, shaking her head vigorously. "The crusade against the Albigensians."

Rosalyn frowned. "I've never heard of it!"

Eleanor was stunned. The conflict that had warped her childhood, decimated her family, and turned her youth into a living hell was utterly meaningless to her hostess. "It was a crusade against heretics, not Saracens," she tried to explain. "But the heretics lived among us, in the midst of our cities and towns and villages. It was impossible to eliminate them without destroying — everything."

Lady Rosalyn could see that Eleanor had become stiff and tense, and she guessed that she was remembering. Instinctively she reached out to her and stroked her arm. "Don't think about it, child; it is behind you. But could you explain how you came to be the ward of the French King's brother? I'm sure that's what Geoff said last night."

"Raymond VI de Toulouse was excommunicated and lost his titles, but his son, Raymond VII, regained most of them."

"He must have been a very exceptional young man to do that!" Lady Rosalyn surmised.

Eleanor smiled. "He was. He was the son of Joanna Plantagenet and so a nephew of Richard Coeur de Leon — and he too had a lion's heart! My brothers were both very loyal to him — and fond of him as well." Eleanor was proud of that, even though it had cost them both their lives. "But in the end he was not strong enough to fight the King of France. Eventually he capitulated and married his only child, Jeanne, to King Louis' brother, Alphonse de Poitiers. When Raymond VII died last year, his titles passed by right of his daughter to the Comte de Poitiers."

"And you were on the way to join the Comtesse de Poitiers when your ship wrecked?"

"Yes, exactly," Eleanor agreed.

"You may live to thank God for that wreck," the Lady of Paphos noted. "The Comtesse de Poitiers is now trapped in Damietta with the Queen of France, and God alone knows if they will not all fall into Saracen hands. There is nothing worse that can happen to a woman, I assure you! It is a fate far worse than death itself."

Eleanor nodded, thinking she was indeed happy not to be with the ladies of the French court — for more reasons than just their current precarious situation. To Rosalyn she remarked, "I am already thankful, Madame, not just to God, but to the fishermen who risked their lives and their livelihoods to rescue me on the day of that storm. They took me to safety at great risk to their lives and boats, and their wives and daughters nursed me as lovingly as my own mother and sisters would have done — although we could not speak a word of the same language. They were very good people, and I've never had a chance to thank them."

Eleanor felt her debt to the fishermen acutely. She had been raised to think gratitude was more important than charity. Giving alms, her mother told her, provided short-term material comfort, yet robbed the recipient of self-respect. Giving sincere thanks, on the other hand, dignified the recipient by underlining that they were the creditor rather than the debtor.

"I'm sure they were adequately rewarded," Rosalyn dismissed the topic offhandedly.

Eleanor shook her head solemnly. "I think not. I had the impression the Hospitallers were impatient, even rude, to them. They were contemptuous of the medical assistance these humble people had given me, and afraid that I might yet die. I don't think they were very generous." She paused and then asked timidly, "You don't suppose there is any way to find out which fishing village it was and go there to thank them, do you?"

"Oh, I am sure everyone hereabouts knows which village it was. The wreck caused quite a sensation — at least it did after the King sent word that a highborn French heiress had been aboard the ship. A reward was offered to anyone who could provide information," she frowned as she tried to remember. "Quite a few people came to us, claiming to have news of your whereabouts. The west coast is very treacherous, with many underwater ledges, and infamous for shattering ships. The wreckage of more than one vessel lies at the bottom of the sea near here, but I'm almost certain Tancred said your ship actually made it into Coral Bay before it foundered. I believe the wreck of your ship can still be seen to this day."

Eleanor's heart started racing. The memories of the storm always set off an echo of panic, but this was more than that. This wasn't just the memory of terror, it was a new fear. Brother Xavier had traveled with a strongbox in which he'd locked documents about her case and her mother. What if that strongbox had survived the wreck and was still there, waiting to condemn her?

"You mean," she asked cautiously, "it's in water shallow enough to see?"

"Oh, yes! I'm told the local boys swim out and scour for treasure. Half a dozen bodies were found trapped inside in the first few days after the wreck. Indeed, that was where the search for you began. The assumption was that you, too, had been below deck and trapped inside when the ship went down. Only after the bodies were removed and it was certain no women were among the dead on the ship did the search parties start scouring the shore for your body."

"Do you know …" Eleanor started, but then her voice failed her. She reached for some of the bread and dipped it in the honey instead.

"I think I'd better go down and see what's happening with the main meal," Rosalyn announced, getting to her feet. "Tancred will be hungry as a bear when he returns, but I'll check in on you in a couple of hours. We've dried out your clothes, but I'm afraid the dress you were wearing will never be the same." She paused, but then continued, "You didn't bring very many things with you. Shall we send to the Queen Mother for more of your things?"

"I don't have many things," Eleanor confessed without thinking. Then, seeing the astonishment on Lady Rosalyn's face, she hastened to add, "I lost everything in the wreck," which was true as far as it went. There was no need to tell Lady Rosalyn that she'd had almost nothing on the ship, either. The daughters of executed heretics were not treated to large wardrobes ….

"And the Queen Mother did not see fit to outfit you?" Lady Rosalyn asked with raised, reproachful eyebrows.

Eleanor shrugged. "She is not well, you know, and she lives in seclusion. None of her ladies have many things."

"Which befits them, since they are as old as Queen Alice herself! But you're a young maiden with your life ahead of you! Let me see what I can find," Rosalyn concluded. "I must have half a dozen gowns that I'll never be able to squeeze myself into again. There's no point in letting them rot in chests when they could be made to fit you!"

Eleanor thanked her and sank back into the pillows as her hostess closed the door behind her. She did not know if she should dare believe her good fortune or fear betrayal. If only she could start her life over again, as easily as she could have a new dress made. It would be wonderful to have new clothes, pretty clothes, bright-colored clothes, but part of her did not trust her good fortune. And what if the Inquisition records were to be found in the hold of the wreck? What if Lord and Lady Rosalyn learned the truth — or about Montségur?

Chapter 5

The Temple at Limassol

The Templar Commandery at Limassol was not an inviting building. It had been built after the violent revolt of the Cypriot population against the Templars in 1192, an austere fortress of white stone that frowned down on the surrounding streets through arrow slits rather than windows.

At the sight of it, Geoffrey drew up in the market square to collect his thoughts. He could remember as if it were yesterday the day he had come here to beg admittance to the Knights Templar. He'd been a scrawny fifteen-year- old boy, on the run from his brother and from previous presumptions about his destiny. By the time he'd reached Limassol he hadn't eaten in two days and his clothes were filthy from almost a week on the road, while his shoes were coming apart at the seams. He'd looked so much like a beggar that the Templar sentries had laughed at him for asking to speak with the Commander, telling him that alms were handed out at the back door by the Almoner.

Geoffrey had been forced to lurk in the shadows all day, until at last he spotted a troop of Templar knights returning from somewhere. He'd darted out and grabbed the stirrup of the leading knight, bringing the whole column to a halt as swords flashed in the dying sunlight. The men around the Commander assumed he was an assassin, and came very close to killing him — but he'd only realized that after the fact. At the time, he'd had his eyes fixed only on the man leading the column of troops. "Sir! Sir! Hear me out!" he pleaded, clinging to the man's leg and stirrup so firmly that he was dragged halfway off his feet by the forward momentum of the horse.

The men around the Commander were cursing colorfully, but the Commander just stared down at Geoffrey. "What is it, boy?" he'd asked at last.

"My father was Sir John Thurn, one of King Richard's knights, and I am his legitimate son, and I — I want to join the Knights Templar—"

They had burst out laughing, the other knights and sergeants, guffawing heartily, and even the Commander had smiled faintly — but he had nodded, too, not in agreement but in acknowledgment. "I have heard about you," he said, adding, "You look like you need a meal and a bath. Come inside and we will discuss your future in peace and private — not in the middle of a public street." He had gestured to the gawking shopkeepers and serving girls.

Geoffrey remembered the looks of astonishment on the faces of the sergeants who had turned him away earlier, and the sense of triumph, too. When the gates fell shut behind him with a resounding clang of metal and the thud of heavy wood, Geoffrey had felt a sense of jubilation that made him want to sing the Te Deum at the top of his voice.

Ruefully, Geoffrey wondered if they would let him in now. Commander Jules had died at Mansourah, along with the rest of the knights from Limassol. The only men who might remember him were sergeants, lay brothers, or priests. Geoffrey was not sure how they would feel about his return

— alone and without the mantle of the Temple. "Don't be surprised if we get turned away," he warned his squire, who had pulled up beside him.

"I saw a nice caravansary on the way into town," Ian replied hopefully, clearly put off by the grim exterior of the commandery.

Geoffrey nodded absently, envying the young man who served him. Ian had come to the Holy Land to get away from poverty at home. He'd come to make his fortune, and despite the disaster of the crusade, Ian remained an optimistic opportunist. He'd presented himself to Geoffrey as the latter prepared to leave the crusader camp, a newly made knight with dispatches from the Grand Master in his saddlebags, a head full of confusion, and a heart full of grief. "You need a squire, sir," Ian had announced, seeing a chance to escape illness, capture, and death on a crusade that was clearly headed for disaster. Geoffrey had been too numbed by the turn of events in the previous forty-eight hours to offer resistance. In fact, he wasn't sure he'd answered Ian at all. Ian simply took over the duties of his squire and followed him out of the camp.

At Damietta Geoffrey had reported to the Marshal of the Order, Renaud de Vichiers. King Louis had appointed Vichiers Commander of the knights left behind to defend the city and his Queen against possible Saracen attack, while he advanced up the Nile towards Cairo with the bulk of the crusaders. When Geoffrey reported the loss of three hundred Templars and the Grand Master's serious wound, de Vichiers had put Damietta on a state of alert, and sent Geoffrey on to Acre with his sealed dispatches for the Seneschal of the Order and the Commander of the Kingdom of Jerusalem.

These senior officials had received Geoffrey in Acre, read Sonnac's dispatches, consulted among themselves, and then asked Geoffrey if he wished to be received into the Order. Because he'd vowed not enter the Order until he could sincerely accept God's will — including the defeat at Mansourah — Geoffrey had declined. The senior officers accepted his decision without protest, too preoccupied with more important things to care, or so it seemed to Geoffrey. They had simply advised him that if he wished to deliver his last letter, addressed to the Preceptor of England, personally, he should be in Limassol by the middle of April; Thomas Bérard was bringing reinforcements from England and could be expected to put in at Limassol about that time.

So here he was, but Geoffrey's apprehension was growing the longer he sat here. Something, he sensed, was not right. Then again, maybe it was the dead who blocked his way — the dead and the sense of his whole life having been futile. First he'd rejected the path his father had laid out for him when he refused to enter the Premonstratensian Order at Bellapais. Then — after all but forcing his way into the Templars — he refused to join them as well. He was only twenty-one years old, but already he'd twice failed to fulfill a calling. That was surely displeasing to God, and made him a failure twice over.

"Do you want to go back to the caravansary?" Ian asked hopefully, evidently impatient with Geoffrey's indecision.

Geoffrey shook his head and urged his stallion forward. They rode up to the heavy arched portal of the commandery with the splayed cross of the Temple carved into the keystone. Geoffrey drew up in front of the sergeant on duty, and a thrill of recognition went through him. "Brother Bartholomew!" This sergeant had been the commandery's Marshal, or Master of Horses, as long as Geoffrey belonged to the community. He had taught the clumsy and inept Geoffrey to ride like a knight, a fundamental prerequisite of knighthood.

The grizzled sergeant squinted up against the sun. "Geoffrey?" he asked, frowning. "Then the rumors are true! You did survive — and did run away!"

There was so much reproach in those words that Geoffrey felt as if the sergeant had stabbed a sword deep into his guts. He jumped down from his stallion and went down on his knees in front of the astonished sergeant. "You are right to reproach me, brother. I have sinned deeply — but whether you believe me or not, I am following Master de Sonnac's orders."

The old sergeant looked at the knight kneeling before him, then up at the strange squire, who shrugged and smiled in embarrassment. The sergeant cleared his throat and tapped Geoffrey on the shoulder. "Who am I to question the ways of knights?" he concluded gruffly. "Why are you here?"

Geoffrey got to his feet. "I have a letter from Master de Sonnac for the Preceptor of England, Sir Thomas Bérard. He is —"

"What is going on there, Sergeant? What does the man want?" The voice was sharp and authoritative.

The sergeant and Geoffrey turned to look at a priest coming down the external steps from the keep. This keep rose up three stories to the west of the Byzantine basilica that the Templars had converted into their church. Geoffrey remembered this man, too — with far less affection than Brother Bartholomew. "Father

Alphonso," he acknowledged the priest with a bow of his head.

"Geoffrey Thurn — or should I say *Sir* Geoffrey." The priest looked pointedly at Geoffrey's heels as if he did not believe the rumors — only to start at the sight of gleaming gold studded with blue enamel fleurs-de-lis. He looked more sharply at Geoffrey. "Then the rumors are true? You were knighted by the French King himself?"

"Yes."

"And what brings you here?"

"I have a letter from Master de Sonnac for —"

"*Late* Master de Sonnac. Surely you heard that Sonnac was dead?"

Geoffrey tried to draw a deep breath, but his lungs didn't seem to be working properly. Perhaps it was only in that instant that he realized just how much he had loved the Grand Master.

"William de Sonnac died of his wounds after leading yet another futile attack against the Saracen that cost him his second eye," Father Alphonso continued, sounding almost self-righteous. "He was dead before King Louis was taken captive by the Saracen."

It is better that way, Geoffrey told himself, since the Saracens would have killed him anyway. It was better that they did not have the chance to gloat over capturing — and then killing — a Grand Master of the Temple. "Any letters you have from him should be surrendered to the proper authorities," Father Alphonso added, holding out his hand as if he incorporated that authority.

Geoffrey shook his head. Father Alphonso was a very powerful man — within the confines of the commandery of Limassol. He was the chief celebrant of the Mass, and he routinely heard the confessions of the brothers. Because of his education he was one of the chief advisors to the Commander, and Geoffrey had once been frightened of him, but Geoffrey was no longer the awed and humbled squire he had been a year ago.

"If you will not entrust the letter to me," Father Alphonso responded to his inaction, "then you will have to give it to the Commander."

"Sir Jules is dead," Geoffrey countered, astonished that Father Alphonso knew about Master de Sonnac's death but not that of his own Commander.

"I know. I was speaking of his successor, Sir Arnaud."

What an efficient organization we are, Geoffrey registered. It might take months to elect a new Grand Master, but mere Commanders were appointed with ruthless efficiency. No doubt the very same day he reported the casualties to the Marshal in Damietta, the orders had gone out ....

"I have a letter for the Preceptor of England —"

"Talk to Sir Arnaud about it," the priest insisted. "He's in Gastria at the moment, but we expect him back tonight."

Geoffrey looked back at Ian. The squire pleaded, "The caravansary looked *really* nice, sir."

But Geoffrey caught a look from Brother Bartholomew beyond Ian. He owed the men here a report on the last days of their brothers and friends. "You can go, Ian, and take the horses with you. I'll wait here for the Commander." He turned back to Father Alphonso. "I will await the Commander here, if I may?"

"Vespers is in ten minutes," the priest answered.

Geoffrey handed his reins over to Ian. "Do you have enough money for the night?"

"Me?"

Geoffrey sighed and dug deep into his purse. It was almost empty. The money the Templar treasurer had put at his disposal for his return journey had almost been used up, and he hadn't a clue where he was to get more. His brother had begrudged him the very food on the table and hay for his horses .... "You may have to look for a new employer soon," he suggested to Ian, giving him a coin.

"I'll think about it," Ian answered cheerfully, tossing the coin into the air, catching it, and grinning before adding, "Or you could look for a new employer yourself? I expect you can command a high price with your Templar training and that sword." He nodded in the direction of the sword at Geoffrey's hip, then turned his horse around and led both Geoffrey's gray and the captured bay mare out of the Templar ward.

Geoffrey heard Mass, standing in the narthex of the dingy Byzantine church with the lay brothers. The low barrel-arched church, with three parallel apses to the east, had been built in the sixth century. The windows were narrow slits in the yard-thick walls, covered with alabaster. Torches at the door and the candles on the altar provided only unsteady light.

Even so, it was clear to Geoffrey that there was not a single knight in the chapel. Whatever the new Commander was doing in Gastria, he had taken every knight he had with him. The men collected in the church itself were sergeants and priests, while the lay brothers crowded the narthex. These men were gardeners, cooks, and craftsmen such as the baker, the blacksmith, the farrier, and the brewer.

The lay brothers were so astonished to have Geoffrey standing with them that they were audibly restless, trying to get a look at his spurs, and then straining for a glimpse of his sword. More than one of the brothers crossed himself fervently at the sight of the relic in the hilt.

As soon as Mass was over these men crowded around Geoffrey, asking for word of individual knights and sergeants. Geoffrey tried to answer their questions, able to provide relatively detailed accounts of the men who had died at Damietta or on the advance up the Nile, but in too many cases he had only a single-word answer: Mansourah. After they had been talking for some time, one of the lay brothers, a youth who worked in the kitchens, asked about Geoffrey's sword.

"It was the Master's sword, and he gave it to me so it would not fall into Saracen hands," Geoff explained, unbuckling it from his hips and holding it up so the others could see it better.

"Is that a relic in it?" the youth asked.

"A finger bone of John the Baptist," Geoffrey explained, holding the sword in the direction of the kitchen servant so he could see it better.

The youth gasped and took an awed step backward. The sergeant smith took the sword from Geoffrey, but he did not dare to hold the hilt. Rather, he grasped the leather belt, then leaned forward and reverently touched his lips to the crystal enclosing the sacred relic. He passed it to the man beside him, and one after another, they kissed the hilt in wonder.

They were interrupted by the call to dinner, and the brothers scurried to wash their hands in a deep stone basin just beyond the narthex of the church, in the cramped inner courtyard formed by the old Byzantine church, the modern keep looming up to the west, and a single-story tract built along the south wall of the fortified enclosure. The Templar brothers formed two lines to ascend the exterior stairs leading to the first floor of the keep, where the refectory was located in a long, vaulted room with two windows along the exterior and a fireplace on the interior wall.

Brother Bartholomew hung back at the bottom of the stairs to be the last man in line, beside Geoffrey. "The horse you were riding: I did not recognize him," he remarked.

"No, Megalo was one of Master de Sonnac's horses, brought from the Kingdom of Jerusalem but, I believe, bred in the Holy Roman Empire," Geoffrey conceded. "The Master let me ride him because despite being so strong and willing, Megalo had a sweeter temper than any of the other horses; he was the only horse I could really handle," Geoffrey admitted to his old riding instructor, who knew his shortcomings well.

But Brother Bartholomew wasn't interested in Geoffrey's continued inadequacies as a rider; he wanted to know what had happened to his horses — because Brother Bartholomew not only taught horsemanship, he bred, backed, and trained the Templar horses at Limassol as well. Not enough for their needs, to be sure, but Brother Bartholomew prided himself on producing a handful of first-class mounts each year, the kind of horses the Commanders liked to keep for themselves.

Geoffrey hesitated and then said the most comforting thing he could: "The Arabs love horses more than women. They will look after those of our horses that survived."

"And how many was that?" Sergeant Bartholomew pressed him.

Geoffrey stopped in the doorway to the refectory. "Nine."

Sergeant Bartholomew stared at him. That was less than one in ten. "And were any of the survivors mine?" he asked in a voice that was raw with pain.

Geoffrey shook his head slowly.

The look on Sergeant Bartholomew's face made Geoffrey ask again what right men had to misuse God's creatures. After all, men joined the Order voluntarily, and they consciously committed themselves to obedience, to hardship, to danger and the risk of death, but what choice did horses have? Geoffrey was certain that God had made horses trusting and loyal, and so it was almost sacrilegious to abuse the trust God had put in the beasts for their own destruction. Wasn't it?

Sergeant Bartholomew turned his back on Geoffrey and trudged up the stairs to enter the refectory with sagging shoulders. Geoffrey would have liked to sit down next to him, as he often had when he lived here, but Father Alphonso loudly called him up to the high table. "*Sir Geoffrey*," he called, making it sound almost mocking. "Do join me here at the high table."

Geoffrey drew a deep breath and moved up the hall to take the place pointed out to him. Already a young clerk, evidently a new priestly recruit whom Geoffrey did not recognize, was climbing the stairs cut into the thickness of the walls to take his place in the pulpit that hung over the room between the two windows and opposite the fireplace. He started to read from the Gospels while the brothers ate in silence.

The Commander and the knights still had not returned by Compline, and after joining the brothers at Mass again and sharing the nightly wine with them, Geoffrey was taken to a cell in the knights' dormitory, which was on the ground floor of the keep. It was accessed by descending a narrow stairway from the narthex, carved out of the thickness of the walls. Geoffrey had never slept in a knight's cell when he was a squire; squires were housed over the stables in the outer ward, not in the keep with the monks.

The cells were narrow and windowless. Each was furnished with a low, narrow bed along one wall, a wooden kneeling stool under a wooden crucifix on the other, a niche containing a candle (that the Rule required burn all night) and a chest on the narrow end of the cell, and hooks just inside the doorway to hang one's clothes, a saddlebag, and the like. There was no door in the doorway, however, because no Templar was allowed privacy, and his superiors had the right to see what he was doing at any time.

As Geoffrey removed his clothes, hanging his chain mail and surcoat on the hooks provided and laying his folded shirt and breeches on the top of the chest, he found himself wondering which of his brothers had slept here — before being killed in Egypt. He knelt before the crucifix and prayed for the souls of the dead, then stretched out on the straw mattress and, eventually, fell asleep.

The bells for Matins woke him, and Geoffrey started to rise to join the brothers for Mass. Then he heard men moving in the cells on either side of him, and he realized the knights of the Commandery had returned during the night. He did not want to meet these men for the first time in nothing but his nightshirt, and so he lay down again.

When the bells rang for Prime, however, Geoffrey rose and dressed himself. It took longer for him to get himself into his armor without the help of a squire than for the Templar knights to don their monk's robes, so Geoffrey found himself trailing behind them, almost late for Mass. Again he stood at the back of the church, while the dozen knights in their white robes filled the first two rows near the altar. After Mass was over, while Geoffrey remained in the narthex, letting the lay brothers and sergeants file out, a tall, dark-haired knight approached him. Their eyes locked.

"So." The man halted directly in front of Geoffrey. "You must be the mysterious Sir Geoffrey de Preuthune. *Former* Templar squire. Come to my office!" The knight, whom Geoffrey presumed was the new Commander, turned and started up the stairs that led upwards from the end of the narthex.

Geoffrey cast a look at the other knights, but they were all strangers, and the looks they gave him ranged from curious to contemptuous. He followed the Commander out of the narthex and up the set of exterior stairs to the refectory. Here the Commander dived into an enclosed spiral staircase that led up past the second-floor armory and treasury to the top floor of the keep. Geoffrey found himself in a rectangular room with a barrel-vaulted ceiling that appeared to occupy half the top floor of the keep. A door, now closed, apparently gave access to the rest of the keep. A large fireplace with a mantel adorned with the splayed cross of the Temple dominated the long interior dividing wall. Three double-light windows flanked by window seats more than a yard deep pierced each of the remaining walls. Light from the bright Cypriot sun was streaming in the east window along with sounds from the market in the square outside. Geoffrey was startled; he had almost forgotten there was a world outside, a world full of colors, scents, and sounds.

"So," Sir Arnaud started again, standing behind the heavy oak table that dominated the room. "Father Alphonso tells me you were a squire here once and claim to have letters from the late Master de Sonnac."

"I have letters from Master de Sonnac, including one for the Preceptor of England, who I was told would soon be passing through Limassol," Geoffrey confirmed.

"You missed him," Sir Arnaud retorted.

Geoffrey started. "When?"

"Yesterday."

"I was here all day yesterday," Geoffrey protested.

"And Commander Bérard's ship put into Gastria, rather than Limassol."

Geoffrey said nothing. It was hard to know if he had been given misinformation in Acre intentionally — or if the English Preceptor's plans had simply changed.

"If you have a letter from a former Grand Master addressed to an Officer of the Temple, then you should hand it over immediately — along with William de Sonnac's sword." The latter was said in an accusatory tone of voice.

"Master de Sonnac belted this sword around my hips," Geoffrey answered steadily. "Why should I give it to you?"

"Precisely because it was Master de Sonnac's sword and it contains a priceless relic. As a man who spent six years living with us, you must know that Templars are not allowed *personal* property. Even the Grand Master *owns* nothing. The weapons and armor a Templar wears belong to the Temple. Master de Sonnac had no right to give you that sword. It belongs to the Temple!"

"You are right that the sword did not belong to Master de Sonnac. The sword was *loaned* to him, and hence Master de Sonnac was neither obliged — nor able — to give it to the Temple."

"Who then is the *real* owner?" Sir Arnaud's tone suggested he didn't believe a word Geoffrey had said.

"I don't know," Geoffrey answered honestly, "but his name is recorded in the archives of the Temple kept in the vaults of Castle Pilgrim." Sonnac had told Geoffrey this the very first time he had held the sword in his own hands as Sonnac's squire. Geoffrey had been awed by his sudden elevation from squire to an ordinary (and familiar) Templar knight to squire of the Grand Master, and then stunned a second time within the hour to find himself holding the bones of Saint John the Baptist in his hands.

Sonnac had smiled at him. "Don't be afraid of it, Geoffrey," he'd said softly. "Just as Saint John reached out his hand to baptize Our Savior, so his hand still brings blessings to those who hold it in good faith. It is said, but I cannot prove it, that no man has ever died while holding the hand of the Baptist in his."

The memory of these words sent a shiver down Geoffrey's spine despite the heat in the office in Limassol. Despite all the odds against him, Master de Sonnac had not died the day he wielded this sword — but the very next time he fought *after* he had given it to Geoffrey, he had been mortally wounded.

"You expect me to believe that fairy tale?" Commander Arnaud snapped back. "Hand it over!"

Geoffrey was hearing a different voice in his head, that of William de Sonnac himself. "Don't surrender this sword to anyone who demands it, Geoff. The Baptist's Hand is a gift, and it must not be captured, stolen, or extorted. Guard it with more than life and blood. Guard it with love."

Geoffrey met Commander Arnaud's eyes. He was acutely aware that he was three flights of stairs above the exit and that he didn't stand a chance of getting out alive if he tried to flee or fight. Outwardly, he remained calm. "If the

Marshal and Seneschal of the Order *and* the Commander of the Kingdom of Jerusalem did not see fit to take this sword from me, sir, why should you?"

"My superiors have a great deal on their minds in the midst of this crisis. The fact that you were wearing that sacred sword without being entitled to it undoubtedly escaped their notice."

On this point Geoffrey was unsure. The Marshal and Seneschal had indeed been preoccupied with the implications of the French King's defeat, but Geoffrey thought that the Commander of the Kingdom of Jerusalem had cast a pointed glance in the direction of the sword after reading Master de Sonnac's letter to him. It had been the Commander, too, who had escorted Geoffrey down to the harbor to board a galley for Cyprus two days later. He had embraced Geoffrey and kissed him on both cheeks. "Go with God, my son, and in the knowledge that even if you have doubts, you are in good hands — sacred hands." That might have been a reference to the relic in the hilt of the sword, but then again it might just have been a turn of phrase. Likewise, when the Commander added, "When the time is right, Saint John will show you the way," that too might have been a reference to the sword. On the other hand, maybe it was a reference only to the main Hospitaller Church, Saint John of Acre, which at that moment started ringing its bells for Nones.

"*You* may idolize the late Master de Sonnac," Commander Arnaud was continuing, "but there are good reasons to believe that William de Sonnac was not what he pretended to be."

"You mean he was not the Grand Master?" Geoffrey asked, intentionally provocatively.

"Of course he was the Grand Master!" Arnaud retorted, irritated. "But his election was —

manipulated. The information about his past was not available to the Chapter that elected him."

"What information?" Geoffrey asked.

"I don't have to explain myself to you! You aren't even a Templar squire anymore, much less a member of the Order! All you need to know is that William de Sonnac, *late* Master of the Temple, was a man tainted by the evil Albigensian heresy. It is absolutely certain that he was related to some of those vile creatures who preferred to burn alive at Montségur rather than accept the mercy of Holy Mother Church!"

Geoffrey felt himself burning, too — with indignation. The accusation of heresy was absurd! William de Sonnac had been hot-tempered and impatient with fools. He had not been a saint by any means, but Sonnac had been a man of humbling piety and inspiring faith. It had been their shared love of Christ that had made Sonnac and King Louis such close friends.

"Each man will be judged for his own deeds — not the sins of his relatives," Geoffrey answered the Commander, while trying to move imperceptibly closer to the door.

"And you will be judged a thief, if you try to walk out of here with that sword!" the Commander countered.

With a ringing rasp, Geoffrey drew the sword, the relic firmly in the palm of his right hand. Commander Arnaud drew back sharply. He had expected Geoffrey to be intimidated, and was stunned to find himself facing a naked longsword held in battle-hardened hands. Commander Arnaud was, after all, completely unarmed and not even wearing armor.

"King Louis is my witness, sir," Geoffrey told the startled Templar Commander. "This sword was given into my keeping in the presence of half the nobles of France."

"Most of whom won't return from Egypt alive!" Commander Arnaud scoffed.

"King Louis will return," Geoffrey insisted stubbornly, although there was no certainty of this. King Louis, by all accounts, had been so sick he had been given up for dead by half his army. Certainly he had been too weak to stand when he was taken captive. There was no way of knowing if he would survive captivity.

But there was no certainty that he would die, either. Commander Arnaud did not want trouble with the King of France, or with the King's close friend, Maréchal de Vichiers. Vichiers stood a very good chance of being elected the next Grand Master of the Temple — and he was completely subservient to the French King.

Commander Arnaud's eyes moved away from the naked blade, glinting in the sunlight, to the spurs at Geoffrey's heels. What a ridiculous situation, he thought. Here was a youth, hardly old enough to grow a beard, the son of some obscure English knight left behind by the Lionheart on the Island of Cyprus, and he was holding one of Christendom's most precious relics hostage in his hand while wearing the spurs of the King of France!

"Get out of my sight!" Commander Arnaud ordered with an angry gesture of his hand. "Get out! And don't you ever dare to set foot on Templar property again, or we will take that stolen sword from you by force!"

Geoffrey nodded once to indicate he had understood. Then he sheathed the sword and ducked out the door to pound down the spiral stairs two at a time, his hands stretched out to the wall and the central stone column to keep from falling. He did not trust Commander Arnaud, and he expected any second to hear the man shouting orders to his knights and sergeants to seize the "thief."

Instead, just when he reached the first floor and was about to duck into the refectory to cross to the exterior stairs, he heard Commander Arnaud calling his own name. "Geoffrey de Preuthune!" he called. "You do not fool me! You are not what you pretend to be! You too are tinged with heresy!"

The words made Geoffrey's blood run cold. How could this stranger know he had denied Christ?

But he did not stop. He stormed across the refectory and burst out into the sunlight of the landing. Outside, life was normal. The sun was hot, the market loud. Geoffrey pounded down the stairs to the ward and made straight for the gate.

Today another sergeant was on duty, but he nodded to Geoffrey respectfully. "Will you be coming back, sir?" he asked in a friendly tone as Geoffrey passed.

Geoffrey paused, glancing past the sentry toward the entrance to the keep, half expecting Commander Arnaud to appear in the doorway. He did not, but his words echoed in Geoffrey's head, mixed with his own voice. The words rang in his skull accusingly: "Christ died on a cross in Jerusalem, but he was never God's son ...."

"No," he told the sentry. "No, I will not be coming back anytime soon."

Chapter 6

Of Shipwrecks

Eleanor descended the spiral stairs to the solar, feeling pretty for the first time in half a decade — a feeling promptly buoyed by Lord Tancred's gallant compliments and courtly bow when he caught sight of her in his wife's made-over dress. Eleanor blushed with pleasure, and Rosalyn admonished her husband, "That's quite enough, Tancred. You're too old for courting."

"I may be too old, but Eleanor is clearly in need of a little more male attention! And if she's out of practice, then we need to help her get fit for flirting again before the bachelor knights return from captivity, starved for the sight of a fair lady."

Yes, Eleanor thought, I am very much out of practice, since the last time anyone courted me was eight years ago. That had been when her brother Henri introduced her to her betrothed. Sir Jean had been thirty-four, tall and thin, a little solemn but very courtly. Eleanor trusted Henri by then. If he said Sir Jean was a good man and she would be happy with him, then she was prepared to believe it. Certainly Sir Jean had treated her like a "lady" — although she was only twelve at the time. He had bowed to her in greeting, offered her his arm to escort her from room to room, poured her wine, and cut her meat at table. It had made her feel so grown up! And she had loved it when he played the lute and sang love songs to her, too. After less than a fortnight, however, it was time for him to go. He kissed her chastely and gave her a ring when he left.

Three weeks later he was dead at the battle of Taillebourg.

Eleanor had cried her heart out, and her mother had stroked her hair and sung lullabies to her as if she were a child. But there had been little time to grieve, not with Roger an outlaw with a price on his head ....

"Here!" Lady Rosalyn's cheerful voice snapped her out of her memories. "This is the scarf I've been looking for! It matches that dress, and it's perfect for you!" She held up a green silk scarf embroidered with gold sunbursts. "It will bring out the green in your eyes and the gold highlights in your hair." Rosalyn was enjoying this transformation of Eleanor from a brown mouse into a beautiful lady almost more than Eleanor herself.

Eleanor had never thought of her eyes as green or her hair as gold, but she took the scarf in her hands reverently, stroking it without thinking. After her father's death her mother had never worn bright colors, disdaining all luxury in the end. She had not actually forbidden Eleanor to dress according to her station, but funds were increasingly short. Roger needed horses and weapons and men-at-arms, and Henri was loaning money to Comte Raymond, who was always in desperate straits for one reason or another. No one seemed to think it was important to outfit "little Nel" in any kind of finery.

"Come!" Lady Rosalyn offered. "I'll tie it around your head."

Eleanor submitted willingly, ignoring the page who had come up to report to Lord Paphos about something. Tancred grunted and then excused himself to go out.

He followed the page out the door, across the drawbridge to the wooden stairs, and down to the outer ward to find Sir Geoffrey with his squire and packhorse in tow. Sir Geoffrey was dismounting.

"Back already, Geoff? I mean Sir Geoffrey."

"Geoff's fine," Geoffrey answered. "I'm here to — to ask if you have need of my services."

"Your services?" Paphos asked, astonished. "Aren't you going to join the Temple?"

"I can't. Not yet. Meanwhile, I'm out of funds, or almost. I need to find employment, so I'm here to offer you my sword."

"*Your* sword?" Paphos asked with raised eyebrows. "You mean the Grand Master's sword? Or should I say the sword of John the Baptist?" He paused dramatically and reproachfully, then added, "I'm not sure I'm prepared to accept it. I doubt very much that the Grand Master entrusted you with it so that you could put it in the service of a secular Cypriot baron."

Geoffrey just gazed at his former lord, as if he didn't know what to do or say next.

Paphos relented. "Well, we don't have to resolve your entire future today. You're welcome to stay for a while. Thibault," he addressed his squire, "show Sir Geoffrey's squire the horse boxes and make sure Sir Geoffrey's stallion has a large outside box. He's the real hero of Mansourah, and deserves to be treated like it. See that all three horses get straw, hay, and water. Then show the young man — what's your name?" Paphos addressed Geoffrey's squire.

"Ian, My Lord."

"Show Ian where he can bed down with you and Antoine. Come with me, Geoff," Paphos added, leading the way back up the external stairs to the narrow drawbridge that gave access to the first floor of the keep.

At last, after a fortnight at Paphos, Eleanor was to continue her pilgrimage. The idea was to travel by way of the fishing village where she had first been nursed after the wreck, then to continue on to the Shrine of St. George in Pegeia, her original destination. There was a convent at this particular shrine, which was why the Queen Mother had chosen St. George's as the most suitable destination for Eleanor's pilgrimage. Like the Queen Mother, the Lord and Lady of Paphos were certain that Eleanor would find comfortable accommodation there, and would be able to stay as long as she liked.

Geoffrey and Ian were detailed by the Lord of Paphos to see Eleanor safely to her destination. They loaded provisions for several days on their saddles, but left the packhorse behind, and Lady Rosalyn loaned Eleanor her aging and well-behaved palfrey.

"Have the sense to stay out of the rain this time, will you?" Paphos admonished the younger man as Geoffrey mounted in the outer ward. "Lady Eleanor is not going to turn to stone if you have to seek shelter in someplace less than a castle."

Geoffrey just nodded. He knew the route between Paphos and Pegeia well, and there were several places along the way where they could seek temporary refuge from the elements.

Eleanor was led across the drawbridge from the first-floor solar by Lady Rosalyn, who held her firmly around the waist, so she was not frightened despite the twenty-foot drop down to the salty moat. She was wearing her partly ruined riding dress because she did not want to risk damaging one of the lovely gowns Lady Rosalyn had given her, but her hat was held in place by pretty bright-red scarves, and her expression was one of excited anticipation.

Lord Tancred led his wife's fat palfrey to stand next to a bale of hay, then climbed onto the bale so he could help Eleanor up beside him. From here she could put her toe in the stirrup without having to reach for it. After two weeks of rest she felt not a twinge of pain as she settled into the saddle, and as on the morning she'd first set out on her adventure, she felt full of energy and curiosity for the outside world.

"What's her name?" Eleanor asked her hostess as she patted the mare under her. She felt much safer than on Geoffrey's "packhorse."

"That's Polly," Lady Rosalyn told her, coming over to give the faithful mare a pat on the shoulder. She added, "You'll need a crop with her, I'm afraid."

Her husband at once ordered one of the grooms to bring a riding stick, and when this was turned over to Eleanor, he nodded to Geoffrey and ordered the gate opened.

Geoffrey led the little party out of the castle, but then paused to let Eleanor fall in beside him. Ian followed a length behind, while Anna on her donkey brought up the rear. To ride north, they passed through the city of Paphos, but by now the Lord and Lady of Paphos had already shown Eleanor the sights, so there was no need to linger.

When they passed out of the city by the north gate, however, Eleanor found herself enchanted by the splendor of the Mediterranean on a calm sunny day. This morning there was hardly a breath of air, and the sea seemed as tame as a duck pond. It was hard to believe this was the same stretch of shoreline that had greeted her with raging waves and screaming winds a year ago. Hard as she tried, Eleanor could see nothing that looked even vaguely familiar. She stopped looking and turned her attention to her companion.

"Would you mind telling me a little more about yourself, sir?" Eleanor asked in what she hoped was not too forward a tone. She was curious about this knight who had come to her rescue so unexpectedly two weeks ago, and she had been sorry to discover he had already left Paphos by the time she awoke the day after her arrival. She had not wanted to show too much interest in him, however, because she did not want Lady Rosalyn and Lord Tancred to think she was immodest. Besides, she did not entirely trust her own emotions. She had been so cut off from the world these past six years that she did not know what was normal anymore. The simple kindness of Lady Rosalyn and the courtesy of Lord Tancred had utterly disoriented her that first night. Maybe the sense of safety she had felt in Sir Geoffrey's arms was also nothing more than a naive over-reaction.

"What would you like to know, My Lady?" Geoffrey asked, acutely aware that for all his exceptional education, he had not been taught how to converse with a lady — at least not since he had left Paphos' household a half-dozen years ago.

Eleanor, however, had her first question ready. "The day we met, you said your father was a vassal of King Richard of England. That interested me, you see, because my father was, too. He was Guy Sire de Najac, and he owed Richard fealty as Duc d'Aquitaine. He was a banneret under him with more than a score of knights." She was clearly proud of this.

Geoffrey was pleased that Eleanor's father had been King Richard's vassal, but he did not want Eleanor to think he was pretending to be something he was not. "My father was a landless knight, My Lady, not a vassal. A landless English knight."

"And that was the reason he stayed here in Cyprus after King Richard sailed home?"

Geoffrey thought about that. "In part, perhaps, in the sense that he had nothing to return to and so did not resist the King's suggestion, but the real reason was that he knew the island somewhat. You see, when the storm dispersed King Richard's fleet, driving the King's ship to Rhodes, my father's ship, like the ship carrying the King's betrothed, Berengaria of Navarre, and his sister, the Queen of Sicily, was driven ashore here — very close to where your own wreck occurred." Geoffrey pointed vaguely to the coastline ahead of them.

Eleanor was astonished and even more excited by this coincidence. Joanna Plantagenet, Queen of Sicily and King Richard's sister, was a heroine in her family. Her example of fortitude, and the fact that she too had endured imprisonment and betrayal, had helped Eleanor endure the last six years.

"My father and the other knights who managed to survive the wreck of their ship were first given comfort and aid by the local residents, but then officers of the tyrant Isaac Comnenus took them prisoner. They were locked in a tower and given no food until they signed huge promissory notes. My father said he indebted himself for more gold than even a great baron could have paid — and still they were not set free, but rather told they would be sold to the Arab slavers. As if to give them a foretaste of their fate, they were set to work restoring some of the ramparts at the Castle of Buffavento along with other forced laborers. The combination of brutally hard labor from dawn to dusk and almost nothing to eat was murderous. My father said men died of starvation and exhaustion before his eyes — and others lost their footing on the nearby sheer cliff and fell to their deaths." No sooner had he said this than Geoffrey stopped himself and glanced sideways at Eleanor, unsure if this was an appropriate topic of conversation for a young lady. He really had no idea. But Eleanor did not look offended, so he resumed.

"My father and three other crusaders decided they had to make an escape attempt before they were too weak to do so or were killed in an accident. Together they attacked one of the guards. One of my father's companions was killed almost at once, but the remaining three managed to wrest the guard's sword away from him, kill him, and then open their fetters. As they fled, a second one of them was shot in the back by the archers of Isaac Comnenus, but my father and the fourth man escaped. They found refuge with a shepherd, who helped them regain their strength with sheep's milk before pointing them toward the shore, indicating that other crusader ships were at Limassol.

"When they arrived at the port, they discovered that the great galley carrying the King's sister and bride was at anchor in the harbor, too badly damaged in the storm to continue the journey. Fortunately, however, the ladies had not yet gone ashore. My father swam out to the ships —"

"My father was aboard that ship!" Eleanor said excitedly. "He was one of the knights guarding Joanna Plantagenet!" That struck Geoffrey as an amazing coincidence, which in turn could only be the hand of God. He crossed himself automatically. "Did your father then take part in the assault on Limassol?" Eleanor asked eagerly.

"Yes. When the King arrived a few days later, he was furious about what had happened to the shipwrecked crusaders — and about the ill-disguised threats Isaac Comnenus had made to his bride and sister. He stormed Limassol, without even waiting for the horses to be offloaded."

"Yes!" Eleanor agreed excitedly. "That's just what my father told me, too. He said King Richard's companions urged him to wait, but he said, 'The horses be damned!' and ordered his galley into the harbor, smashing its way through a chain of boats full of archers that the Byzantine tyrant had ordered across the harbor mouth. His galley went alongside a quay, and King Richard was one of the first men to spring ashore. His knights had to rush over the side to keep him from being completely exposed. But my father claims the Cypriots put up hardly any resistance. He said King Richard had control of the city within hours."

"So it was," Geoffrey agreed with a smile, pleased that the accounts they had heard from their respective fathers did not differ. "In the weeks that followed, Richard made use of the fact that my father had already traveled across the island during his escape, and particularly that he knew the fortifications of Buffavento intimately — if unwillingly."

Eleanor laughed at his little joke, which encouraged Geoffrey to smile at her before resuming. "When Richard continued his voyage, leaving only a handful of men behind to protect his interests, he asked my father to stay with his chosen lieutenants, Richard of Camville and Robert of Thornham."

Eleanor nodded. That made sense to her.

Geoffrey added, "What you may not know, since your father continued with King Richard to Acre, is that the Cypriots, although they hated Isaac Comnenus, were nevertheless loyal subjects of the Byzantine Emperor. They had no desire to become part of a Latin kingdom. They rebelled against the Templars, to whom Richard had sold the Island of Cyprus shortly after his arrival in Christian Palestine. Because of the revolt, the Templars decided the Island was too much trouble to control, so they returned it to King Richard. Meanwhile my father and King Richard's other knights were all but trapped in the port of Kyrenia.

"Fortunately for them, King Richard sold the Island a second time — this time to Guy de Lusignan, who had been King of Jerusalem by right of his wife but had lost his kingdom at her death. Guy de Lusignan raised an army composed of lords and knights who had recently lost their lands to the armies of Salah-ad-Din. When Lusignan launched his invasion with these men, my father joined them. Guy de Lusignan, like King Richard before him, found my father's knowledge of the island valuable, so he granted my father a fief after he won control of Cyprus. It's on the other side of those mountains." Geoffrey gestured vaguely toward the Troodos Mountains.

Eleanor looked toward the massive pine-clad range, whose snow-capped peaks thrust upward to the brilliant blue sky, and then back at Geoffrey. Eleanor had seen enough of Cyprus to know it was a rich island. Cyprus received enough rain to sustain forests, orchards, and valuable crops like sugar, cotton, and wine. Furthermore, it was known as the breadbasket of Christian Palestine. Eleanor suspected that a knight who helped a king win this rich kingdom would be well rewarded. Geoffrey's horses — and his spurs — matched such wealth. His unbleached linen surcoat did not.

"Why don't you wear your coat of arms, sir?" It was one of the questions Eleanor had been burning to ask almost since the moment they met, and only after she had blurted it out did she realize how rude she sounded. Six years cut off from civilization had made her an inept conversationalist, she thought bitterly.

"I am a younger son, My Lady ... and I was intended for the Church."

"The Church?"

"The Templars."

"Oh!" The disappointment in her voice was audible, and it made Geoffrey turn and look at her, but Eleanor looked away ashamed. Why should she care that he was destined for the Church? It was not as if she were free to marry whom she pleased. The Comte de Poitiers would choose her husband, assuming he was freed from Saracen captivity. And if he was not, she would die an old maid. One way or the other, the income from her lands would go to pay the Comte de Poitiers' ransom, leaving her impoverished.

"I have not taken the vows," Sir Geoffrey said into her thoughts, "and that is the reason my brother is very angry with me. He thinks I have disgraced the family." Geoffrey added mentally, "... a second time."

"And why haven't you taken your vows?" Eleanor asked, only to again bite her tongue. How long would it take before she learned again how to behave in company?

Geoffrey shook his head and would not meet her eye. "It is difficult to explain, My Lady. It has to do with what happened on this last crusade. Will you not tell me of your father instead?" he replied, changing the subject.

Eleanor was not averse to talking of her father; her memories of him were untainted by the horror that came afterwards. "My father was over sixty when I was born. I was a late, unexpected child: the last, the youngest, and the most spoiled — or so my brothers claimed." She almost laughed as she said this, and the sight of her smiling made Geoffrey smile as well.

Then Geoffrey started to ask, "But if you have brothers …" He stopped himself.

"If I have brothers, how did I become an heiress and a ward of the Comte de Poitiers?"

He nodded.

"They were killed," Eleanor answered bluntly, and the smile was gone.

Geoffrey regretted his stupid question. Of course they were dead. That should have been obvious. He fell silent, ashamed of his lack of social graces. It was little use being able to translate Scripture into three languages, he reflected, when he couldn't even carry on a casual conversation with a young lady.

Eleanor, realizing she had killed a conversation she wanted to pursue, pulled herself together and started talking again about her father. "My father used to tell me stories about the Lionheart, and about the Lady Joanna, Richard's sister. As I said, my father had been one of the knights tasked with guarding her, and I think he fell a little in love with her, too. She was only twenty-six when she joined her brother on crusade, and by all accounts she was very beautiful."

Eleanor had loved her father's stories of the 'fair Joanna,' Eleanor of Aquitaine's daughter. "In any case," she continued, "when King Richard arranged a marriage between Joanna and the Comte de Toulouse, he gave our lands as part of her dowry. My father always saw himself as *her* vassal, not a vassal of the untrustworthy Raymond VI de Toulouse."

Geoffrey nodded to indicate he was listening, and Eleanor, a little desperate to keep the conversation alive, pressed ahead. "Raymond VI maintained a harem just like a sultan, and he had a violent temper, which led him into conflict with his vassals as well as the Church. He was excommunicated twice, you know?"

Geoffrey hesitated to admit his ignorance, so he nodded again.

"Anyway, while he was putting down one rebellion, another flared up at the other end of his lands, and Joanna, although pregnant with her third child at the time, set out to put it down." Eleanor continued her story, conscious that she wasn't telling it as well as her father had. "Joanna laid siege to a castle held by the rebels, but traitors managed to set the besiegers' camp on fire. My father only just managed to get the Lady Joanna out as her tent went up in flames. She was badly burned, but insisted on riding north, certain that her brother King Richard, who was then in Poitou, would come to her aid and destroy her enemies. She was in such a terrible state, however, that my father had to carry her in his arms as they rode through the night. In Niort, word reached them that King Richard was dead. The Lionheart had been killed only a few days before at Châlus."

Eleanor fell silent, hearing in her head her father's voice as he closed with these words; he always said them with great sadness. She knew that many men nowadays were detractors of the legendary Lionheart. They said he had been vain and overly proud, that he was quick to insult others and even quicker to take offense himself. He had made many enemies, and had committed acts of violence that shocked even his comrades-in-arms. But her father was not one of King Richard's critics. He had always said simply that "All men are sinners, Eleanor. The greater the man, the greater the sins."

Geoffrey could see that Eleanor was lost in her memories, and hesitated to intrude. He looked over his shoulder to see how Ian and Anna were doing. Ian grinned at him, but Anna's donkey had fallen a hundred feet behind. Geoffrey drew up to give the donkey time to catch up, and when Eleanor looked at him questioningly, he gestured toward the orchard on either side of them. "Would you like a pomegranate, Mademoiselle?"

"A pomegranate? I've never had one," Eleanor admitted.

Geoffrey jumped down, handed his reins to Ian, and stepped into the orchard to look for an edible pomegranate among the fruits that had already fallen to the ground. By the time he returned, Anna's donkey had caught up with them.

Geoffrey took his eating knife from his belt and cut the top off the pomegranate. He then sliced into it carefully and broke out a section. He bent back the outer skin and held up the contents to Eleanor. Her face lit up in delight. "The kernels are like rolled rubies!"

Geoffrey laughed, surprised by the analogy and infected by Eleanor's delight. Then he urged, "Try them!"

Eleanor looked a little hesitant, but she dropped her reins and reached down to pick one kernel from the offered fruit. Geoffrey shook his head. "Cup your palms and I'll give you enough to taste."

She did as he ordered, leaning down from the saddle, while he used the tip of his knife to free the kernels from the skin. When he had picked the section clean, he threw away the skin, and Eleanor timidly raised her cupped palm to her lips. "They're delicious!" she exclaimed in amazement a moment later, eliciting laughter from both Geoffrey and Ian.

Geoffrey looped the reins over his left arm and sent Ian to collect some more, while he broke out another section and again filled Eleanor's hand. He did this twice more before, to Eleanor's utter amazement, he turned and spoke to Anna in Greek.

The old woman's face lit up, and she started chattering. Eleanor all but fell off her mare; she had never seen the old woman smile before. The next thing she knew, Anna was nodding vigorously and then blessing Geoffrey. Geoffrey turned and called to Ian, who threw him a second pomegranate. Geoffrey deftly caught it and handed it to Anna, who blessed him again, smiling broadly, before she tucked it away in her saddlebag.

Geoffrey and Ian remounted and they started forward again. Geoffrey renewed their conversation. "Was your father rewarded for his loyalty to the Angevins?"

Eleanor nodded, "Queen Eleanor remembered him in her will with a forest." She paused, unsure if she should also reveal the other gift, but then she couldn't resist. "She also sent a ring that had belonged to her daughter. Joanna must have been wearing it when she died in Fontevrault with her mother beside her. The Queen said that Joanna had wanted my father to have it ...."

Geoffrey nodded, commenting, "You must treasure it greatly."

Eleanor started. Treasure it? She would have loved to treasure it, but it was gone — along with everything else that had ever meant anything to her. Lost or stolen; who knew? "I don't have it anymore," she told Geoffrey bitterly. Geoffrey looked over at her, startled by her sudden change of mood, but she avoided his eyes. Her face was a mask again.

"Lost in the wreck?" he asked innocently.

"I wish it were that simple," Eleanor snapped, not meeting his eyes, her face stiffer than ever.

Geoffrey could sense that there was a story behind those words that Eleanor did not want to share with him. He respected that and looked forward along the road, admonishing himself not to be too curious.

For a second time Eleanor regretted her brusqueness. It was so hard to know what to say, much less find the right tone. She did not dare say too much for fear she would alienate Sir Geoffrey. As a man destined for the Church, he would surely scorn the daughter of an executed heretic. Certainly he would not look on her as kindly as he had up to now. She searched for another topic of conversation, and her eyes fell to his spurs. She had not been mistaken at their first encounter: his spurs had blue enamel fleurs-de-lis embedded in the gold. How did a Cypriot knight, the son of a man who had served the Angevins, come by spurs with the lilies of France?

"Sir? Forgive me," she ventured timidly.

Geoffrey was relieved that she had forgiven him for his earlier impertinence. "Yes, Mademoiselle?"

"Would you tell me about your spurs? When we met, I thought you must be a knight of the

King of France because of the fleurs-de-lis on them ...."

Geoffrey glanced down at his heels. "I was with King Louis on crusade, Mademoiselle, but I went as a squire. It was only after the Battle of Mansourah that I was knighted." He paused, conscious of how much it would seem like bragging if he just told the truth. He tried to put it in context. "The King had just lost his brother and scores of good knights, including almost three hundred Knights Templar. I was told that when he learned that the Grand Master of the Temple had been carried out of Mansourah alive, albeit unconscious from a head wound, he wanted to reward the knight who had saved such a good man. But the knight was not a knight at all, only a squire. So he resolved to make that squire a knight, and put a pair of his own spurs on the squire's heels."

"Oh!" Eleanor looked at Geoffrey with so much open admiration that he was flustered. She looked again at the spurs, thinking that her first reaction had been right: they were the King of France's own! But Geoffrey could not be blamed for the crimes of the man who had owned his spurs before him. He had nothing to do with those crimes. "You are to be congratulated, sir," she said sincerely.

Geoffrey laughed from embarrassment. "The Lord of Paphos says my horse did more than I did. He carried two fully armored men out of Mansourah, at one point jumping over a barricade." As he spoke Geoffrey patted his massive gray stallion on the neck affectionately. The stallion snorted contentedly in response. "His fetlocks were badly strained and he was covered in cuts. It is a miracle he was not seriously injured. Too many horses are killed and injured, although they are completely innocent," Geoffrey noted, focusing again on his stallion. "Horses are so loyal. They do all we ask of them, and we reward them by exposing them to thirst, starvation, battle, and fire ...."

"The victims of all wars are the helpless, Monsieur. Not just the four-legged variety, but women and children as well," Eleanor reminded him.

They stopped by a stream for a midday meal of bread and cheese and pomegranates, and then continued on to Coral Bay. As they approached by the road on the bluffs above the bay, Eleanor felt tension rising in her innards. It tied her stomach in knots even before they crested a slight rise and saw spread out below them a beautiful sand beach cupped between two rocky headlands, and there — clear as day — the wreckage of a ship lying just under the surface.

The day was still practically windless, sunny, and so warm Eleanor was sweating under her gown and scarves. The bay was clothed in shades of blue and turquoise woven in an irregular pattern by the rocks underneath. The water was so pure and clear, it was easy to see schools of fishes darting among the rocks and a big turtle paddling slowly along the shore. It would have been a peaceful, enchanting scene if it hadn't been for the wreck.

From up here it was easy to see that the ship's back was broken, and the wreck actually lay in two pieces, separated by two or three yards. The bows lay on their starboard side, the deck facing the bluffs where Eleanor sat. The stern was still on an even keel and seemed remarkably intact from up here.

"Do you wish to go closer, Mademoiselle?" Geoffrey asked politely.

Eleanor glanced at him uncertainly.

"If you like, I could swim out and see if there is anything left in the wreck."

"Lady Rosalyn says the locals scavenged everything of value from the wreck long ago," Eleanor countered defensively.

"They will have looked for things of value to them. You lost things of value only to you."

How do you know that? Eleanor asked herself, gazing at him in wonder, but Geoffrey had already turned away. He swung down from his stallion and called to Ian to come give him a hand. He led his stallion down into the olive grove on the far side of the road and hobbled him there. Anna trotted over on her donkey, evidently to ask him what was going on, and he explained in Greek. She nodded agreement, got down from her donkey, and spread out a blanket in the shade, with the evident intention of taking an afternoon nap.

Geoffrey was back at Eleanor's bridle. "If you wait here, Ian and I will see what we can find."

Eleanor nodded and dismounted. She joined Anna in the shade while Geoffrey hobbled her palfrey. Then he and Ian disappeared as they descended the steep bank toward the bay.

Within minutes Anna was snoring loudly, but Eleanor could not rest for thinking about the wreck. She couldn't just sit here waiting. She stood and returned to the road to look down at the bay and the wreck.

Below her, Ian and Geoffrey had stripped out of their clothes, leaving their things piled between some boulders. As she watched, they started to wade out into the water. The water was evidently cold, because Ian was making little yelping protests with each step. Eleanor's eyes were riveted on Geoffrey's back. A swath of hideous scars covered his left shoulder and shoulder blade almost to his waist. Those were burn scars, she registered in horror, and looked at the palm of her left hand, where the blisters were healing but the old wound stood out more than ever — or so it seemed to her.

With a shout Ian plunged into the water and started swimming with a great deal of splashing, and Geoffrey followed him silently. They swam on the surface until they were above the wreck. Then they started diving.

After waiting a few minutes, Eleanor couldn't stand the suspense anymore. She started cautiously winding her way down toward the shore, following a goat track. She had to watch her footing to find her way between the rocks, and her skirts caught again and again on thorns and brambles that grew between the boulders. She was sweating heavily by the time she reached the beach itself, and was grateful that a gentle breeze had sprung up out of nowhere.

From this level, when the breeze ruffled the surface of the water, it was not possible to see the wreck at all. The bay was just a basin of sparkling sunlight and brilliant aquamarine water. The breeze caught the ends of her veils and they fluttered, while her surcoat billowed out, letting in the coolness to her sweating body underneath. Eleanor closed her eyes and lifted her face to the sun. It felt good. Then she held out her arms to feel the wind wrap its arms around her completely. Her skirts flapped and her veils flew, and she felt almost like she was flying — like she was free.

After standing like this for a moment, Eleanor sat down on the closest rock, unbuckled her shoes, and removed them. She reached up under her skirts and rolled down one stocking after the other so she could place her bare feet on the sand. It was a heavenly sensation.

Mentally she tried to picture the night of the shipwreck again, to reconcile that nightmare with the serene beauty of the scene around her. She called to mind the lightning and Father Xavier's hate-filled face leering over her, shouting that she was to blame for it all. "You shameless heretic! You cannot hide your heart from God! Look at His anger!" He had gestured to the lightning and the waves and the raging shoreline. "Listen to the voice of the Lord! Cleanse your heart of heresy or you will die like this ship — broken by Divine justice!"

Eleanor put her hands over her ears and closed her eyes tight. Then, after a moment, she raised her head slowly and looked at the sparkling aquamarine water and the turtle leisurely paddling with his head above it. He blinked at her wisely and stretched his claws contentedly. Father Xavier is dead, he seemed to say, but *you* are still alive.

Eleanor drew a deep breath of the clean air and called out to the cloudless heavens: "Look at me, Father Xavier! Look at me! I am alive and free, and I rejoice that you are dead!"

The sun did not darken. No sudden thunder rumbled from behind the mountains. The waves did not leap up and drench her in reproach for such sentiments. A bird frolicked against the sky, and it struck Eleanor that the heavens were far too beautiful and peaceful to house Father Xavier. He was not there, nor did he linger here among the rocks. She confirmed this with a searching sweep of the cove, just to be sure. No, he wasn't standing threateningly among the rocks and the brambles. He was not scowling and pointing an accusing finger at her.

He was dead. She would not meet him again in this life.

And the next? her irrepressible brain inquired.

"According to Father Xavier," she answered the voice in her head, "he will be in heaven and I will be in hell, so we will never meet again!" She tossed her head defiantly.

But what if Father Xavier was wrong and your mother was right? the intelligence at the back of her head persisted.

"I don't want to think about that!" Eleanor answered, shaking her head sharply, and was startled by a shout from the water. She looked over guiltily, because she had completely forgotten about Geoffrey and Ian.

Ian appeared to have found something and was calling to Geoffrey. A moment later they dived together below the surface. Eleanor pushed herself to her feet and held her hand over her eyes to try to see better. Her heart was beating in agitation. What could they possibly have found after so much time?

When Ian and Geoffrey resurfaced, they had something heavy between them. "Jesus, Mary and Joseph!" Eleanor gasped; it was a strongbox just like the one that Father Xavier had kept.

The two men were struggling to swim with one arm while holding the heavy strongbox between them with the other. Eleanor registered that their clothes were on the rocks not far from her. She blushed at the thought that they must come ashore naked — and she was blocking their way to their clothes. Without bothering with her stockings, she shoved her feet back into her shoes and turned to work her way back up the bank to the road.

If it *was* Father Xavier's strongbox, she was thinking, she would actually, for the first time, be able to read the Inquisition summary of her case. She knew that the Bishop of Albi had interceded in the proceedings at the behest of the Comte de Poitiers. Eleanor had no illusions about Poitiers' motives: the property of convicted heretics fell to the Church, and Poitiers preferred to retain control of her property so he could plunder it himself.

When she reached the blanket in the shade of the orchard, she found Anna still on her back, snoring. The horses were grazing contentedly. It was as if she had never departed. She sat down, brushed the sand off her feet, and pulled on her stockings just in time.

Geoffrey and Ian crested the bank and came toward her with the box between them. "We found something, Mademoiselle!" Ian called out eagerly. He was grinning with triumph.

Eleanor bent and shook Anna awake before getting to her feet. Ian and Geoffrey dropped the strongbox on the ground beside the blanket, Ian grinning and Geoffrey looking vaguely uncomfortable. "Is it yours, Mademoiselle?" he asked hesitantly.

Something about the way he asked the question made Eleanor think he knew better. The seal! The strongbox was closed with a wax seal, and on that seal was the mark of the Dominican Order. As a cleric — or anyway, a man intended for the Church — Geoffrey apparently recognized it. "It's not mine," Eleanor admitted; "it belonged to my confessor, Father Xavier. He was traveling with me on the ship, and had all my valuables with him." Eleanor did not dare meet Geoffrey's eyes as she said this because, although everything she said was true, she was sure he would see through her. She feared he would guess that Father Xavier had control of her valuables not out of protective concern, but to punish her.

"Was he killed in the wreck?" Ian asked cheerfully, earning a frown from his employer.

"Yes," Eleanor answered, trying to keep her tone neutral. "Yes, I'm told I was the only surviving passenger, although four or five of the sailors managed to swim to shore safely."

"I'm sorry, ma'am," Ian apologized contritely, crossing himself and praying automatically for the dead.

Geoffrey, however, had his eyes fixed so steadily on Eleanor that she did not dare look at him. Instead, she crossed herself and closed her eyes as if praying. She was surprised to hear Geoffrey declare rather matter-of-factly, "If he's dead, he can have no objection to us opening his box."

Geoffrey's sword rasped in the sheath, and a moment later he had slipped the blade between the lid and the box. He stood astride the box, took hold of the hilt of his sword with both hands, and yanked upwards. On the third try, the locks broke and the lid flipped open.

Eleanor twitched involuntarily at the renewed evidence that force could overcome any obstacle. Nothing in this world is safe from a man with a sword, she thought with an involuntary shudder, before gazing into the box.

The others were staring, too — obviously disappointed. There were no jewels, no gold, not even coins of silver, only documents. Geoffrey reached in and gingerly removed the first parchment, neatly folded and sealed — and falling apart. The ink on the document was smeared to mere blue-black smudges, and water dripped from the limp document as he held it out to Eleanor. She held out her hands palm up and he placed the document in them. It was wet and heavy. Only the seal was legible: the seal of the Dominicans.

"Are the documents important?" Ian asked.

Eleanor stared at the ruined records of her past and took a deep breath. "Not anymore," she concluded.

Chapter 7

Demons

The exploration of the wreck had taken up too much of the afternoon, and Sir Geoffrey insisted on continuing straight to Agios Georgios. He promised to escort Eleanor to the fishing village on the return trip. Even so, the bells were ringing Vespers as they turned off the main coastal road to wind their way the last half-mile down to the monastery, which sat halfway down the steep shoreline toward the sea. A barren, flat-topped island sat not far off the coast, and now that the wind had picked up, waves were crashing dramatically against it. To the left of the road the coast fell away in sheer cliffs to the narrow, rocky shore below, but to the right on a level bank the silhouette of the large basilica loomed out of a walled enclosure against the fading daylight.

The domes highlighted against the orange sky were clearly Byzantine, and the other pilgrims seemed mostly Greek, which Eleanor found reassuring. After passing through the outer gate, however, rather than turning to the right and the large, somewhat noisy complex of buildings to which the other pilgrims streamed, Geoffrey turned to the left. He led past a complex of rundown stone buildings, which smelled of horse, to a second walled complex. Cypress trees flanked the arched entrance to this inner wall, and the door was firmly closed, but Geoffrey reached down and rang a bell beside the door.

In that moment Eleanor recognized the mark of the Dominicans over the peak in the arch. "This is a Dominican house?" she asked, unable to suppress the alarm in her voice.

Geoffrey had just jumped down from his stallion, and he emerged at her off stirrup. "Yes, Mademoiselle," he said softly, his eyes watching her closely.

Again Eleanor evaded those uncomfortably perceptive eyes. He will see my terror, she told herself, and she clung to the pommel of the saddle to stop her hands from shaking. In her head Father Xavier was laughing mirthlessly. "Did you really think you could escape Holy Church? Did you think that just by destroying a few pieces of paper, the record would be wiped clean? He sees everything! And *we* are His servants."

"Do you need a hand dismounting, Mademoiselle?" Sir Geoffrey asked solicitously, thinking her paralysis was due to exhaustion or pain, as on the day of their first encounter.

"No, Monsieur. I can manage." She looked away from him as she leaned forward and slowly swung her leg over the cantle.

Already the heavy wooden door had opened and a nun was bustling out to receive the evidently important visitors. Sir Geoffrey did the introductions. "The Lady Eleanor de Najac. She has come to pray for the safe return of her guardian, the Comte de Poitiers, for the King of France, and for the other crusaders. She plans to stay at least a week. I presume you can find suitable accommodations?"

"Najac? I've never heard of it," the nun retorted haughtily with an appraising look at

Eleanor, making her conscious of her simple gown and worn shoes.

"Najac is in France, Sister," Sir Geoffrey told the nun reprovingly, and Eleanor couldn't help being pleased by the way he so firmly put the Dominican sister in her place. He added, "The Lord of Paphos sends his greetings and requests you show Lady Eleanor your best hospitality."

Now the nun inspected Geoffrey. Like Eleanor before, she found the signals somewhat contradictory. His horse and armor were absolutely first rate, but his surcoat was plain and frayed, his saddle unadorned, and his saddlebags thin. She cast a glance at Ian and Anna, but quickly dismissed them. "The Mother Superior is already housing a party of Venetian ladies, but we have a spare cell, if that would suit you, My Lady? After all, since you are here to pray, that would be the most suitable accommodation. You will have complete privacy there." Then, without awaiting Eleanor's answer, the nun turned back to Geoffrey and added, "You, your man, and the Greek woman can bed down in the hostel." She pointed back the way they'd come, toward the buildings beyond the church from which light and noise spilled, adding, "The stables are right behind you in the Roman baths." Then she turned to enter the convent, gesturing vigorously to Eleanor and ordering, "Come with me!"

Eleanor clung to Lady Rosalyn's mare, paralyzed with fear. Her tongue stuck to the roof of her mouth, and her stomach contracted. She wanted to say "no," but Sir Geoffrey was already tossing Polly's reins over her head, preparing to lead her away. Ian had the stallions and Anna was easing herself off the donkey, chattering to Geoffrey in Greek. Geoffrey was distracted by her questions and didn't even notice Eleanor's paralysis.

"Are you coming?" the nun asked sharply. "We don't have all night. We'll be late for Vespers."

Eleanor's feet responded to some inner discipline. She had learned long ago not to fight openly. Appear to cooperate, her brain was urging. Go, before they become suspicious, that part of her brain said. There's nothing to be afraid of, another part said; you're being hysterical. God is cruel! a third voice protested. Where are you now, Mother? Eleanor asked the darkness that closed around her.

But, of course, her mother could not enter a Dominican convent, not even as a ghost.

The sisters kept a strict rule. After Vespers, absolute silence was observed. Eleanor heard Mass with the nuns in their own generous chapel which, like the main basilica, was built in the Byzantine style and, so Eleanor presumed, hundreds of years old. She then took her meal with the nuns in silence in a much smaller, dingy, vaulted chamber that lay parallel to the chapel. Eleanor counted only fourteen sisters, and there was no sign of the Venetian ladies the nun had referred to. But then, they were probably dining with the abbess, she decided, when she discovered that dinner consisted of stale bread, dried fish, and a bowl of onion soup. Only a single glass of sour wine was allowed per person.

After the meal the nuns attended Compline, and it was only after this that Eleanor was led to a narrow cell that opened onto a gallery running around a cramped inner courtyard.

The lay sister who had led her here put the candle she was carrying in the window sill, nodded good night, and backed out, closing the door behind her as she withdrew.

The light of the candle wavered and the shadows leapt and quivered. The wooden crucifix over the prie-dieu seemed to sway forward. Eleanor felt a shudder of terror run down her spine, and she broke out into a cold sweat. Spinning around, she grabbed at the door and wrenched it open. It was not locked. The chill air of the spring night poured into the room. Eleanor stood, filling her lungs and staring at the brilliant stars hanging close overhead, until her galloping heart calmed itself. Slowly the cold got the better of her and, reluctantly, she closed the door again and turned to face the cell.

The room presented her with whitewashed walls, a narrow loop window shuttered against the night, a straw pallet on the floor to the right of the window, and a prie-dieu to the left of the window. A coarse woolen blanket was folded on the foot of the straw pallet. An earthenware pitcher of water, a bowl, and a chamber pot were lined up against the wall beside the door. Her bundle of possessions sat in the corner.

Eleanor swallowed down the resurgent panic, unconsciously winding her left hand in her surcoat. Only as she became aware that she was trembling from head to foot did she start pacing back and forth between the window and the door.

You are on Cyprus, she told herself. The door is not locked. You are free to go, to return to the gallant Lord Tancred and kind Lady Rosalyn. Sir Geoffrey is just beyond the convent wall in the hostel, ready to escort you back to Paphos. Tonight nothing will happen to you. No one here will come for you in your sleep. No one here has any questions about you. Father Xavier is dead.

But in these surroundings, this thought did not bring her the same comfort it had brought in the sparkling sun this afternoon.

Looking around the room in fright, Eleanor confronted Father Xavier everywhere she looked. He held the crucifix in his hands. He held the candle ....

Eleanor lunged at the candle and blew it out, retreating slowly from it to stand with her back to the door, the palms of her hands pressing against the wooden planking.

Father Xavier laughed. "Do you think you can blow out the fires of hell? A candle is harmless compared to the fires at the foot of the stake ...." She could smell his foul breath as he leaned over her and spoke.

She was sweating again, but her hands were icy and her feet freezing. They had tied her mother to a stake and burned her alive, but Eleanor had not withstood the pain of a single candle on the palm of her hand.

Her mother's belief in the teachings of the Cathars had been so great that she had *preferred* the flames to abjuring her faith. But Eleanor didn't believe in anything: not her mother's religion, which called earth hell and all flesh the work of the devil, nor a Holy Church that had created the Inquisition and called for a crusade against Christians.

"My mother was a Christian," Eleanor insisted, speaking to the crucifix. "She followed in Your footsteps, giving all that was hers to the poor, tending the sick and aged, spreading the Faith as she understood it. You were her model and she lived according to Your example. She even died for her beliefs as You did. Would you have burned her?"

Christ hung in agony upon the wooden cross, His head sunken upon His breast, the crown of thorns tearing the flesh of His forehead, and His life's blood draining from the spear wound in His side. But it was the nails in the palms of His hands that pierced Eleanor's heart. With her right thumb she kept massaging the burn scar on her left hand and thinking that it had taken hours for Him to die. She stared until the tears hesitantly dripped down her face.

Calmed, she lay down upon the pallet, still fully clothed, and wrapped herself in the blanket. She had spent two years in the hands of the Inquisition, and three years as an unwilling "guest" of the Dominican nuns, but she had never felt so close to Christ as on this night.

For two years they had kept her locked in a cell, taking her out only to interrogate her at irregular and unpredictable intervals. Sometimes she was alone for months, receiving her food through a slot in the door. Sometimes she was interrogated night after night for hours on end. They had only employed "sharper methods" once: they had held her hand over a burning candle to impress upon her what she could expect in hell if she did not truly repent of her presumed heresy. Eleanor had repented and bitterly cursed her mother's soul.

Eleanor had hated her mother and Christ in equal measure, blaming them both for her condition. Her hatred had fueled her will to live. She had been consumed by a single passion: the passion to survive. And to survive she had to outwit Father Xavier. They had given her the New Testament to read, and she had not just memorized it, she had dissected it — chapter and verse, phrase for phrase. She had turned it into a weapon against the Inquisitors.

That had infuriated Father Xavier. "You presume to quote Scripture to me?" he scoffed. "You, a woman stained with the sin of Eve, carrying the guilt for the Fall from Grace in your womb? You dare to take the word of the Lord in your filthy mouth? Your mouth needs washing!" He had grabbed her at the back of the neck and tried to force soap into her mouth. She bared her teeth and struggled, but the lime soap bruised and bloodied her lips, and the blood and saliva carried the foamed soap into her mouth until she gagged on it.

Father Xavier had never been convinced of her innocence. She knew that. He had simply been forced to capitulate to the greater power of the Bishop of Albi and the Comte de Poitiers. Because Poitiers did not want Eleanor declared heretic, the Inquisition was pressured into releasing Eleanor to the Bishop of Albi. Father Xavier was ordered by his superiors to let the case rest.

If the two years with the Inquisition had been hell on earth, then the three years with the Dominicans had been purgatory. The sisters knew she was the daughter of a burned heretic. They knew the Inquisition suspected her of heresy. The Mother Superior had orders to watch for any indication of a "relapse." Eleanor suspected she wrote regular reports to Father Xavier, who was the convent's confessor in any case. Father Xavier had access to her any time he wished, even after she was officially under the Bishop's care.

And it was while she was with the nuns that she had been forced to watch the execution of a handful of weavers found guilty of heresy. The nuns had crowded onto the grandstand like ladies at a grand tournament. Some of them had squabbled over the right to have a place in the front row. Eleanor would have been happy to stand at the back, but the Mother Superior asked loudly, "Where's our Eleanor?" and then put her at the front, causing resentful looks and nudges from the others. Eleanor had closed her eyes, but she couldn't cover her ears or close her nose. And with her eyes closed, she kept seeing her mother tied to the stake. Halfway through the burning, when the stench became overpowering, she had started vomiting violently, all over the ordinary people on the square below her. The Mother Superior was outraged, but the Bishop saw what was happening and took pity on her. He had one of his clerks take her off the grandstand and escort her to his palace by the river. He'd ordered his servants to prepare a bath and give her a change of clothes. He sent for her later, and together they had strolled through his magnificent gardens, her hand looped through his elbow. He had spoken to her like a grandfather, stern but loving. She hated him because he had ordered the burning of the weavers, but she played the helpless, grateful child with all the cunning at her disposal. Within a month she was aboard a ship bound for the Holy Land to join the household of the Comtesse de Poitiers — with Father Xavier as her escort and confessor.

Eleanor was starting to drift off to sleep. Had God's wrath really shattered her ship? If so, God's wrath with whom? If he was angry with her, why was she still alive? Why had He sent fishermen to lift her from a doomed wreck and deliver her to safety? Why hadn't He delivered Father Xavier? Or had He? Was Father Xavier in heaven?

And if her survival had been the Grace of God, did that mean He considered her more worthy of His mercy than her mother? How could she, a selfish, foolish girl, be more worthy of His Grace than her mother, who had done so much good for the sick and the poor? And what about the others? What about her brothers, her fiancé, and all the other slaughtered men, women, and children of the Languedoc?

Eleanor squirmed miserably on the pallet to avoid those images as well. On the steps of the church the beggars gathered: the man whose eyes had been gouged out by Montfort's soldiers, the whore who had been a sheltered maiden until she was gang-raped by Montfort's men, the girl whose lovely face had been destroyed by the Inquisition's hideous brand, and the mad widow, who wandered about with a blank stare and a voice like a crow, screeching out the judgment of the Papal Legate as the crusaders sacked Beziers: "Kill them all! God will recognize His own!"

Eleanor tossed and turned. Her brothers were arguing in her head. "The Young Count knows what he's doing!" Henri insisted. "We're too weak to confront the King of France openly. Do you want to call a new crusade down on our heads?"

"Can you deny that Trencavel is the true lord of Carcassonne? Can you ignore what the Inquisition is doing?"

Eleanor saw again the night Roger had left, never to return. There had been a dozen other knights with him that night. It had been pouring rain, the torches sputtered, and the horses kept slipping on the wet cobbles. Eleanor had slipped out of her chamber to find out what was going on, and she hid herself in the shadows and out of the rain dripping from the gutter over her head.

Her mother came down from her chamber in such haste that her hair was uncovered and free about her shoulders, streaks of gray evident even in the dark. "Roger, no!" she heard her mother plead. "Don't do it!"

"They are murderers! The vilest of murderers — because they don't get their own hands dirty, but make others soil their hands with innocent blood!" her brother answered vehemently.

"I know, but an eye for an eye will bring us all nothing but blindness! Please! For the sake of your own soul, don't do this!"

"For the sake of my soul, Mother, *for the sake of my soul*, I *must*! I do this not for me, Mother, surely you know that? I can defend myself well enough. All of us can!" He gestured to the armed and armored men waiting uneasily on skittish horses all around him. "We do it for the defenseless, the weak and humble and gentle. For you, Mother, and for little Nel."

At the mention of her own name, Eleanor had caught her breath, and tried to shrink farther into the shadows.

The men around her brother were getting impatient. Someone murmured something about the time. The word Avignonet was mentioned.

"Roger!" their mother cried out. "Is this what we've come to? Assassins in the night?"

"I am not ashamed," Roger retorted, with so much pride it rang off the stones of the castle and echoed across the courtyard. Then he'd drawn his longsword so vigorously that Eleanor had gasped and cowered in the shadows. He'd clutched it in his hand with the blade long and sharp and glittering in the torchlight. He held it out to his mother. "Bless it, Maman! Bless it in the name of all our slaughtered countrymen! Bless it in the name of the innocents tortured and the children orphaned. Bless it, for it does God's work come Wednesday."

"You know I can't do that, Roger," his mother answered steadfastly. "If it is God's work you do, then you do not need my blessing."

Roger had sheathed his sword and spurred his horse out of the inner ward, with the others clattering at his heels. They had splattered Eleanor with rainwater — and she had found herself shivering in the darkness after they had left, terrified even though she still didn't know what they intended. It was weeks before she learned that her brother and his companions had killed two Inquisition judges and nine of their servants in Avignonet on May 28, Anno Domini 1242.

Brother Xavier was bending over her bed. He leaned so low that she could smell his foul breath on her face, hot and garlic-laden. "The blood of those martyrs is on *your* hands, Eleanor," he told her in a low, threatening voice. "It is the blood of martyrs that soils your sheets at night — a symbol of your guilt!"

Eleanor tried to get away from his horrible breath. How could she be held responsible for her brother's crimes? she protested.

But the blood was real, pouring out of her body from between her legs, thick and black, clotted and stinking. It had terrified her. And the pains in her abdomen were real, too. The pain kept her from her sleep. She did not understand what was happening to her. No one had told her it was normal for women to bleed once a month.

"Do you want to die in this state of sin?" Father Xavier asked. "Confess your heresy, and His Mother may take mercy on you. But if you persist in this farce, this pretense of innocence, you will surely bleed to death."

But she hadn't bled to death. After three days the bleeding stopped, though they did not let her wash or change her sheets for another four days. The filth seemed to cling to her now, too. How she hated the unwashed bodies of the nuns, who called bathing "vanity" and perfume "devil's water." Even the stench of the fishwives had been better, because at least it was not mixed with self-righteousness.

Eleanor sat up and stared at the window. Was it getting light at last? Had she survived the night yet?

No, the bells were ringing for Matins, and the light outside was from the candles of the nuns as they moved along the gallery to go down to the chapel for Mass.

Eleanor lay back on her pallet and closed her eyes, telling herself to think of something positive. Think of this morning, she told herself. Think of the taste of pomegranate. And Sir Geoffrey's smile.

"Whore!" Father Xavier screamed at her. "Craving the sins of the flesh!"

"How can I crave what I have never even known?" Eleanor sobbed back.

"Liar! You heretics all engage in orgies! Admit it! You knew your brothers carnally, didn't you? You fornicated with them and all their men! One after another, again and again, just like any whore!"

"No!" Eleanor screamed, waking herself from the nightmare. Her scream was only a whimper in the night, but her heart was pounding against her breast and the sweat ran between her breasts and her legs, making her feel filthy again. Would the night never end?

Chapter 8

The Springs of Aphrodite

Geoffrey woke when the bells rang for Prime. He slipped from under the blanket, careful not to wake Ian. He pulled his aketon over his shirt and donned his hose and boots, but left his hauberk and surcoat where they hung over the pallet. He took his sword and spurs with him only because they were too valuable to risk leaving behind. Thus dressed, he slipped out of the dormitory into the central courtyard of the complex. He paused at the stone fountain in the center to splash water on his face and wash his hands. Then he passed through the door leading from the courtyard to the atrium in the forecourt of the basilica.

The pillars here were ancient, probably Roman, Geoffrey noted, remembering what he had learned, but they had been reused, brought here by the Byzantines. The Byzantines had also created the decorative geometric patterns in tile on the atrium floor. From the atrium he passed through the narthex and on through the south door into the basilica itself.

Only a handful of other pilgrims had risen so early. The vast church was almost empty except for the priest and acolytes reading the Mass at the altar. Geoffrey dipped his fore and middle fingers in the bowl of holy water by the door, crossed himself, and then tiptoed up the south aisle, so that neither the heels of his boots nor the scraping of his spurs on the mosaics disturbed the priest. About two-thirds of the way to the altar, he stopped and crossed himself again. Then he went down on one knee, bowed his head, and folded his hands in prayer. Sunlight poured through the windows in the east-facing apse to fall on him.

"Please, dear Lord, show me Thy will. Show me what it is You want of me. Help me to *understand* Thy will. Help me to understand why You tolerate the presence of Muslims in Your holy cities. Enlighten me with understanding of why You allow so many good Christians to die in Your name in vain. Bless me with the Grace of understanding why You condemned good King Louis to humiliation, defeat, and capture. Grant me understanding of why you allowed good Christian knights and men to become prisoners and slaves. Please, help me to understand Your will, so I can return the sword of Your servant Saint John the Baptist to the Temple of Solomon, and so that I may take my vows to serve You as a knight of your Holy Order the rest of my days." Geoffrey crossed himself as the bell rang at the elevation of the Host, and with his lips he followed the service, but in his heart he was still praying for enlightenment.

As he emerged from the basilica after Mass and retraced his steps, he was aware of the hostel starting to come to life. The smell of frying fish wafted in from the kitchens, and there was now a crowd around the central fountain. In the dormitory Ian was already fully dressed and looked relieved to see Geoffrey, although he knew his lord well enough by now to guess where he had been. Ian helped Geoffrey into his hauberk, tying the leather thongs at his wrists without the chain-mail mittens, and handed him his surcoat. Then, taking their saddlebags over their shoulders, the two men headed for the stables.

Megalo was waiting impatiently, and he snorted and kicked his stall door at the sight of Geoffrey. The former bath complex made a poor stable, as the roof was in poor repair and evidently let in the rain in many places. The stalls were improvised wooden structures, but the flooring, once magnificent mosaics, was now pitted with holes and treacherously uneven.

"What's the matter?" Geoffrey asked his stallion with an unconscious smile, as he reached over the stall door to clap him on the shoulder. "Isn't the hay good enough for you?"

"You can't blame him, sir," Ian commented, with a nod in the direction of a heap of nearly rotting hay, pitched into what had once been a decorative niche for a statue long since stolen.

Geoffrey lowered his saddlebag and opened the grain sack he had inside. He scooped out a handful of oats and fed Megalo from his hand four times. He then carefully reclosed the sack and the saddlebag, clipped the lead onto Megalo's halter, and led him out to water him at one of the ancient pools, filled now with rainwater because it stood open to the sky after the roof had collapsed sometime in the last several hundred years. When Megalo had drunk his fill, Geoffrey tied him to one of the rings in the wall, picked out his hooves, and brushed him down. Meanwhile, Ian fed, watered, and groomed his own gelding.

When Geoffrey went to fetch his saddle from the "tack room," however, Ian protested. "Don't you want to have breakfast first?"

"Fried mackerel?" Geoff asked back.

"Smells good to me," Ian insisted.

"Where did you grow up? On a fishing smack?"

"Practically," Ian answered, still grinning. "Newcastle on Tyne."

Geoffrey seemed on the brink of giving in, but then he shook his head. "I hate fighting with the rest of the pilgrims over the food. We'll find a tavern on the coast on the way back."

So they fetched their saddles and tacked up the horses. As they started leading them around the baths along the wall of the convent, Eleanor's voice wafted through the early morning stillness, calling, "Sir! Sir Geoffrey! Please don't go!"

The two men turned around, startled and bewildered. They couldn't see Eleanor anywhere. Then she called again, and they spotted her waving from a narrow window in the far end of the wall. She was one floor up, her hair was loose, and she looked quite frantic.

"My Lady?" Geoffrey called back. He hurried forward, with Megalo trailing him, to stand below the window so they didn't have to shout.

"Sir, please! I don't want to stay here. Not another night." From this distance Geoffrey could see that Eleanor had dark circles under her eyes and that her hair was not just loose, but tangled. She looked as if she hadn't slept at all.

"I am at your disposal, Mademoiselle," Geoffrey assured her with a bow of his head.

"We can leave today?" Eleanor asked anxiously. "You'll wait for me?"

"Of course, Mademoiselle."

"Thank you, sir! I'll go find Anna."

Eleanor was gone from the window, and Geoffrey turned and told Ian to saddle up Lady Rosalyn's mare and the donkey.

"Why? What's happened?" Ian wanted to know.

"Ian, do as you're told and stop asking questions."

"But something must have happened," Ian insisted.

"So what happened between you and the Bishop of Durham?"

"I'm getting the horses! I'm getting the horses!" Ian answered, raising his arms in surrender and backing away.

Fifteen minutes later they were all mounted, and Geoffrey led the party out of the main gate and back up the road leading down to the highway. At the main road, however, he had to stop and ask Eleanor where she wanted to go.

"The fishing village," Eleanor insisted. "I want to give my thanks to the fishermen who saved my life."

"Could we find a tavern for breakfast first?" Ian asked, with a charming smile in Eleanor's direction.

Geoffrey frowned at him, but Eleanor readily agreed. "Of course — breakfast and a bath. I feel so filthy."

Geoffrey and Ian looked at one another, a little perplexed, and Eleanor was about to feel ashamed, when Ian suggested, "Why not take her to Aphrodite's springs, sir? There are several good taverns nearby, and there's no better place to bathe on the whole island."

"It's in the other direction from the fishing village," Geoffrey protested.

"But not that far," Ian reasoned. He turned to Eleanor and asked her directly, "Wouldn't you like to see the springs that the natives say were sacred to Aphrodite? They bubble up into a cave, not far from the surface, and there is this deep pool of sweet water under the dome of the rocks. It's like being in a natural cathedral! There are several chambers, actually, one exclusively reserved for women, so you could bathe in complete modesty." Ian spoke with genuine enthusiasm; he had seen these springs for the first time only a few weeks earlier, when traveling with Geoffrey to his brother's estates.

"I'd love to see them," Eleanor admitted with a glance at Geoffrey. As a man intended for the Church, he was bound to disapprove of this, but Eleanor felt a childish, defiant delight at doing something scorned by the Church. What had the Church ever done for her but torture her and kill her mother and brothers?

To her surprise, Geoffrey shrugged and turned his horse to the left, pricking him with his spurs so that the big gray leapt forward and broke into a canter. Eleanor had to use her crop several times to get her mare to keep up, and Anna's donkey didn't have a chance. But already Geoffrey had reined Megalo back to a slower pace.

He glanced over at Eleanor, and she felt his eyes taking in her crushed dress and veils. She was certain he could tell she had not slept and that she had been plagued by nightmares. She was ashamed and felt dirtier than ever.

Geoffrey cautiously remarked, "The Dominicans are a very young Order, Mademoiselle, young and zealous."

Something about the way he said it didn't sound approving. Eleanor glanced over at him, surprised.

Geoffrey avoided her eyes, keeping his gaze fixed on the road ahead. "I was, I think I told you, squire to William de Sonnac, the Grand Master of the Knights Templar."

Eleanor nodded cautiously.

"The Grand Master was from the Languedoc, Mademoiselle."

Eleanor started. Of course he was! Why hadn't she registered that sooner? Sonnac was a fief in the Aude, not far from Termes. The Sires de Sonnac were vassals of the Viscomte de Beziers and Carcassonne. They had been loyal to Raymond-Roger de Trencavel — and had been disinherited along with him, losing their lands to Simon de Montfort! One of Roger's closest companions had been a certain Pierre de Sonnac. Eleanor was not sure, but she thought he might have been one of those who was with Roger at Avignonet .... She held her breath.

"The Grand Master confided in me that the Dominicans were, he said, obsessed with eradicating the so-called Albigensian heresy; he accused them of hubris, Mademoiselle."

Geoffrey was seeing again the inside of the Grand Master's tent. Night had fallen over the desert with its typical abruptness, and by the light of a smoking torch Geoffrey was trying to clean the Master's chain mail. He had a brush with fine wire teeth to scratch the blood and rust off the thousands of links, and he held the heavy mail across his knees as he worked diligently, brushing the chain mail square inch by square inch. Now and again he daubed at it with a cloth dipped in olive oil to wipe away the sand and rust particles freed by the brush.

It had been the day Master de Sonnac had lost his temper and had charged a troop of harassing Mamlukes against the King's orders. When they made camp that night, Sonnac had been summoned to the King, and Geoffrey had been worrying about him. He had been so sunk in thought that he had not realized the Grand Master was standing over him, watching him work, until he spoke.

"Fanaticism is a dangerous thing," the Master remarked softly over his head.

Geoffrey started and looked around sharply. He was astonished to find that not only had the Grand Master returned, but he was directing these words to none other than himself.

Sonnac was dressed in his long white habit, bearing the red, splayed cross of the Temple on his chest. He wore only sandals on his feet and his head was bare, revealing his tonsure. He looked older and weaker in this monastic garb than when he wore the armor Geoffrey was so diligently cleaning. When in armor the coif covered his tonsure, and the aventail covered his beard.

At the sight of him Geoffrey had started to get to his feet, but Sonnac put his hand on his shoulder and signaled for him to remain sitting. Geoffrey resumed his work in silence. To his astonishment, the Master walked over to his traveling wooden cabinet, opened the doors, and removed two silver chalices, usually reserved for important guests. The Master personally poured wine into both of them and brought them back with him. He stopped in front of Geoffrey and offered him one of the chalices.

Geoffrey was so astonished, he just gaped.

Sonnac seated himself on a three-legged stool opposite Geoffrey and ordered, "Drink with me, young man."

Hesitantly Geoffrey put aside the brush and took the offered chalice, ashamed of his dirty fingernails as his fingers closed around the gleaming silver. He didn't know what to make of this.

"Do you know what the most dangerous thing on earth is, young man?" the senior officer of the Knights Templar asked his squire.

Geoffrey hesitated. Was this some kind of test? Was he perhaps being interrogated to see if he was ready to take his vows at last? He had felt a moment of rising panic — that sense of everything being at stake, and the near certainty that he did not know the right answer. He tried anyway. "Temptation, sir?"

Sonnac smiled mildly but shook his head.

"Greed?" Geoffrey tried again, more desperate than ever, as he felt his future slipping out of his hands. How could a man be so well educated and still not ever have the right answers?

"No," Sonnac shook his head again. "The most dangerous thing on earth is a man who thinks he speaks directly with God." Then the Master had raised his chalice as if in a toast, meeting Geoffrey's eye before he sipped the sweet red wine.

Geoffrey took a cautious sip from his own chalice because he felt he had been invited to do so, but he still didn't understand what this conversation was about.

"I once met another man who spoke directly with God," Sonnac remarked, getting up from the stool to settle himself in his armed chair. Geoffrey just waited. "Arnaud Amaury," Sonnac intoned, his eyes fixed on something in his memory.

The name meant nothing to Geoffrey.

"I suspect you've never heard of him," continued the Master, reading Geoffrey's reaction correctly. "He was the papal legate in spiritual charge of the crusade against the Albigensians; later he was Bishop of Narbonne."

"And he spoke directly with God?" Geoffrey asked, awed.

"He *thought* he did," Master de Sonnac corrected, sipping his wine. "What he *did* was to order knights and men-at-arms to kill the entire population of Beziers: twenty thousand men, women, and children."

"Beziers?" Geoffrey asked, totally confused. "Isn't that in France?"

"In the Viscounty of Beziers and Carcassonne," Sonnac corrected gently. "The crusaders, seasoned soldiers and hardened mercenaries, the veritable scum of the earth, had come to plunder and kill heretics, but the great French nobles and knights leading the crusade naturally wanted to spare the lives of the 'good Christians.' The noblemen asked the papal legate how to distinguish between heretics (who, of course, looked just like ordinary people) and Catholics. Arnaud Amaury, a senior cleric of the Cistercians, ordered the crusaders to: 'Kill them all. God will know His own.' And so they did. Every man, woman, and child, even those seeking protection in the churches with their priests. Even the priests themselves! Twenty thousand people ..."

Geoffrey was stunned — and shocked that he'd never heard of this. After a few moments of silence, he ventured to ask, "When was that, My Lord?"

"The Year of our Lord 1209 — and I was exactly eighteen years old."

"Were you there, My Lord?" Geoffrey asked, even more astonished.

"Had I been there, I would not be with you here now. There were no survivors: they set fire to the town, utterly razing it, with the people trapped inside. A thousand people burned alive in the Church of St. Mary Magdalene alone."

Geoffrey mentally noted that the Master could have been on the side of the crusaders and survived, but Sonnac's answer made it clear that the Templar Master sided completely with the victims. Geoffrey asked instead, "Then when did you meet Arnaud Amaury?"

"That was much later," the Grand Master answered dismissively.

"How then did you learn of what happened at Beziers?" Geoffrey asked hesitantly, a little afraid he might be going too far, but also too fascinated by this insight into the man he served to just let the topic drop.

"The word of Beziers spread like wildfire. The very birds seemed to scream of it. Certainly, riders made it to Carcassonne on foundering horses before the fires were even out. The warning was clear: we would be next."

"Then you were in Carcassonne?"

"I was in Carcassonne, representing my father, who was a vassal of Raymond-Roger de Trencavel, the Viscomte de Beziers, Carcassonne, and Albi. Raymond-Roger had called for his vassals to rally to him in Carcassonne after his offer to submit to the Church and cleanse his lands of heresy was rejected by Arnaud Amaury."

"I don't understand," Geoffrey admitted softly. "Why wasn't he given a chance?"

Sonnac looked into his chalice, apparently studying his reflection in the surface of the silver. Geoffrey wondered what he saw: a venerable old knight with a white beard and wrinkles carved by the sun of Palestine, or a youth of eighteen about to face his first battle? Then he remembered his duties as squire and jumped to his feet to pour the Master more wine. Sonnac looked up and met his eyes. "Why, indeed? Was it merely because the Cistercian fanatic doubted Raymond-Roger's sincerity? After all, he had been raised by a notorious heretic, Bertrand de Saissac, he was distantly related to various women who professed the heresy, and he had up to then provocatively tolerated the heretic preachers who wandered at will in his territories. Or was it simply that, having collected a vast crusading army and after offering so many northern nobles and their knights indulgences, forgiveness of debts, and booty, Arnaud Amaury was afraid to send them home again empty-handed? I don't know.

"What I *do* know is that both Raymond VI de Toulouse and King Pedro de Castile abandoned Raymond-Roger to his fate. The 'terms' he was offered were his life, with eleven other men of his choosing, in exchange for opening Carcassonne to the 'mercy' of the crusaders — that is, to the mercy of the very men who had just slaughtered the entire population of Beziers. Raymond-Roger, who was only twenty-four at the time, spiritedly replied that he'd rather be 'flayed alive' than cravenly abandon his people. So the siege started ...."

Geoffrey waited. It was obvious from Sonnac's expression that the siege had not gone well for the defenders. Sonnac took a sip of wine. "In the end he made the reverse deal: he surrendered up his own person in exchange for a free passage for all the people in the town. The crusaders agreed to allow everyone in the city, whether burgher, mercenary, or vassal, to leave the city by the postern gate, but no one was allowed to take anything with them but the clothes on their back. Even that was restricted to a single shirt and breeches for men and a shift for the women. I lost my armor, my arms, and my horse, and walked barefoot for the first time in my life, but I at least had a home to return to. Most of the citizens of Carcassonne had nowhere to go. They had lost everything — their homes, their savings, their livelihoods ...."

"And Raymond-Roger?" Geoffrey asked, identifying with the noble and chivalrous young viscount who had sacrificed himself for his people.

"He was taken to his own castle and chained in his own dungeon by the man Arnaud Amaury named his successor as Viscount: Simon de Montfort. He died in that dungeon, never having seen the light of day again, three months later — whether from a broken heart, dysentery, or poison, I do not know."

Geoffrey was shocked, and Sonnac read it in his face. He nodded soberly. "A chilling story," he agreed, "and an example of what happens when men who think they speak directly with God lead armies ...."

The obvious reference to King Louis made Geoffrey catch his breath. He did not want to associate King Louis with the brutal, self-righteous murderer Arnaud Amaury, nor did he want to think King Louis' crusade would end in unjust slaughter or the humiliation of honorable men.

Sonnac shook him from his thoughts, reflecting in a now conversational tone, "Curiously, St. Dominic, the founder of the Dominican Order, was far more circumspect." Sonnac sipped his wine and then continued. "He was a man of unshakable faith, but equally great humility. He rightly recognized that the main cause of the heresy was the profligate and hypocritical lifestyle of the Catholic clergy. While the Catholic bishops lived like princes surrounded by luxury, the preachers of the heresy went around barefoot in simple homespun gowns, eating no flesh whatsoever, and living entirely from charity. St. Dominic argued that it was the messengers, not the message, that had alienated the people from the True Faith. His entire mission was to win back the misguided by reason and example. He himself lived no better than the Cathar preachers, the so-called "Good Men" and "Good Women.""

"Left to his own," Sonnac speculated in his tent on the banks of the Nile almost forty years later, "St. Dominic and his original, devout followers might have won back the lost souls led astray by a theology that was superficially logical, but in fact insidiously destructive. Unfortunately for my homeland, Pope Innocent III and King Philip, called Augustus, of France were not patient men. They wanted results sooner rather than later, and crusading armies were more suited to rapid conquest than to debate and sermons.

"So the armies came, and for twenty years they ravaged my homeland, besieging every castle held by men loyal to the Trencavels and every city that wished to retain its independence. Men wearing the Cross sacked and slaughtered, pillaged, raped, and burned, and still the heresy flourished — perhaps more than ever before, because now people saw in the Church not just a corrupt and hypocritical institution, but a tyrannical and cruel one as well."

"But why did the Pope tolerate it? Why didn't he stop them? Surely he could have withdrawn the indulgences — even excommunicated these men who had overstepped their mandate?" Geoffrey protested in distress. He wanted to think of crusaders as men of exceptional virtue and devotion.

"But they hadn't overstepped their mandate," Sonnac corrected him cruelly, shattering his illusions. "Pope Innocent accepted Arnaud Armaury's logic that it was better to kill a thousand innocent men and women than to let even one heretic go free. On the one hand, God would recognize his own, and on the other hand even the Catholics of the region were guilty of harboring, or at least tolerating, the heresy of their neighbors. That is the reason that after the military resistance of the local nobility had been broken and the peace of the graveyard had settled on the Languedoc, the Inquisition was sent to root out the heresy that still burned in the hearts of my countrymen." Sonnac paused and considered his squire.

"You know about the Inquisition?"

Geoffrey shook his head.

Sonnac drew a deep breath. "You are lucky. Come, help yourself to some more wine." He indicated the carafe behind him on the open flap of the cabinet.

Geoffrey first refilled the Master's chalice and then poured cautiously for himself as well.

"You see," the Grand Master explained to the young man who served him, "after the good Dominic Guzman died in 1221, the Dominicans were corrupted — not in the usual way of becoming soft, self-indulgent, and luxury-loving, but with something far more dangerous: with fanatical zeal. They saw the extermination of the Albigensian heresy as the justification for their existence — which was not entirely false — and they became obsessed with its eradication.

"Don't misunderstand me!" Sonnac warned. "That goal is in itself a noble one — provided they had pursued it as their founder had intended, by winning each soul through reason and example. But the Dominicans chose a different path: one of intimidation and terror. By rewarding those who reported on their neighbors, they undermined the most fundamental of Christian principles: Love Thy Neighbor as Thyself. To place their own mission above the teachings of Christ is, to say the least, hubris."

The tent on the banks of the Nile faded back into his memory, and Geoffrey turned to look again at Eleanor de Najac. While swimming around the wreck the day before, he had heard her call out to some "Father Xavier," saying she was glad that he was dead. He had seen, too, how frightened she had been by the contents of the strongbox. Geoffrey could not imagine that Eleanor was a heretic, but he could imagine that she had been intimidated and terrorized by over-zealous priests.

"Then you know about the Albigensian crusade, Monsieur?" Eleanor asked, holding her breath. No one else on Cyprus did, not even Lady Rosalyn.

"I know very little; only what Master de Sonnac told me."

Eleanor considered this answer carefully. Both the Military Orders had been conspicuously absent from the Albigensian crusade; neither the Templars nor the Hospitallers had taken part in it. Her father and her brothers had said that was the reason these knights were still welcome at Najac. Geoffrey himself had reminded her that Sonnac himself came from a family tied to the Trencavels and disinherited for their loyalty. If all Geoffrey knew, he had learned from Sonnac, then he would not be too harsh in his judgment of her.

Geoffrey reined in his stallion so he could speak more softly, and he spoke for Eleanor alone. "Master de Sonnac confided in me that before he joined the Templars, he fought on the side of the local lords against the invaders."

Eleanor let out her breath with a sense of relief; Geoffrey understood.

"His family was disinherited, he said, and he twice escaped from sieges with nothing but the clothes on his back. After the second time, he told me, he had a price on his head. He soon despaired of ever regaining his inheritance, and so he sought refuge in the Temple. And your family, Mademoiselle? Did they fight against the crusaders, too?"

Eleanor was relieved that he asked the question, now that she knew he would not hate her for her answer. "Yes. My brothers were loyal to Raymond VII de Toulouse, and my brother Roger befriended the rightful heir of the last true Viscomte de Beziers and Carcassonne, Raymond-Roger the Younger."

"Ah!" Geoffrey recognized the name at once. "I didn't know he had a son."

"He was an infant at his father's death, and was much the same age as my brother Roger. They were very close."

"Isn't that the turnoff to Aphrodite's springs, sir?" Ian called out, pointing to the left.

Geoffrey had been so engrossed in his conversation that he had missed the turnoff. He turned his horse around and led the way on a trail that could only be navigated single file. The countryside around them had become notably more rugged, but it was beautiful nonetheless. Between the white limestone outcroppings, gorse and thorn bushes sprouted and wildflowers bloomed.

After following the path for almost a half-hour, they crested a rise, and abruptly a gorge fell away to their right. Continuing along the crest of the gorge, they descended gradually toward the sea, which could now be seen as an expanse of vivid blue in the distance. Before they reached the coast, however, they came upon a complex of white stone buildings. One of these was marked as a church by a cross and a bell. Tables in front of a second suggested it was a tavern, and Ian announced enthusiastically, "Breakfast at last!"

Eleanor laughed, but she was very hungry, too.

They drew up in front of the tavern, and at once a man came out to greet them, smiling and bowing. He welcomed them in broken French, but

Geoffrey switched to Greek, and after that his smile widened and service was very fast. Boys came and took their horses, cushions were found for the benches lining the tables, and within moments a carafe of fresh water, a board with warm bread, and bowls of olives and oranges were set in front of them. Eleanor asked Anna about a place to "refresh herself," and Anna jumped up and happily led her into the tavern. Meanwhile, Geoffrey ordered a full meal for the four of them.

After breakfasting heartily, Geoffrey explained to the proprietor that Eleanor wanted to visit the baths, and their host called for his daughter. She smiled shyly at Eleanor, giggled in the direction of Geoffrey and Ian, and then gestured for Eleanor to follow. Eleanor looked at Anna, who nodded vigorously. Together they were led around the back of the tavern and down a steep, rocky path lined with trees. This led into the gorge itself, and Eleanor found it difficult going with her injured leg, but their guide was patient and chattered happily with Anna. Eleanor wished she knew what they were talking about, because they laughed frequently.

Abruptly the trail ended, blocked by a stone structure. The building seemed to be in a ruinous state, but the girl gestured for Eleanor to follow her inside. Inside, leaves and debris had collected in the corners, but there were also benches and some old blankets. The girl promptly took one of these blankets and hung it up over the doorway. Then she gestured for Eleanor to undress, pointing to a door in the far side of the building.

Eleanor crossed to the far door and looked out. She was astonished to discover that beyond the door was a cave formed by the white limestone. Brilliantly clear water was filling it almost to the doorway of the hut she was in.

Sunlight broke through a fault in the ceiling to light up the cave. Eleanor caught her breath in wonder at the simple beauty of it all.

The Greek girl was beside her, gesturing again for her to take off her clothes, and then pointing to a little side pool where a pottery jug and some mugs stood. Eleanor gathered from her gestures that the water served at the table came from here. She nodded, smiled, and turned to Anna for help undressing.

The serving woman deftly removed Eleanor's veils, untied the lacings of her surcoat, and undid the buttons down the back of her gown and on her sleeves. Eleanor stepped out of both. The girl folded the garments over her arms and then put them on one of the other blankets, while Anna helped Eleanor out of her shoes and stockings. Eleanor looked anxiously over her shoulder once more to be sure no one had followed them before pulling her shift off over her head and stepping out of her drawers. Fully naked, she stepped toward the invitingly crystal-clear waters. There were stairs carved into the stones under her feet, leading deeper into the pool. She found herself wondering just how old these steps were. Had the tavern owner carved them so he could charge visitors for visiting the springs, or did they perhaps date back to ancient Greece? Were these the steps on which ancient women had trodden when they came to honor the goddess Aphrodite? Or were they older still?

The water was cold, and Eleanor paused to let her feet adjust to it. Then she stepped down the next step, and again waited. When she reached the last step she was up to her waist in water. From here she could see tiny bubbles floating up from the depths, and if she looked up, she could see a patch of blue sky. When she moved her arms, she sent little waves to the edge of the cave, and the sound of the water lapping against the walls echoed around her. What a place for lovers! Involuntarily she pictured Geoffrey and Ian as they slipped into the waters of Coral Bay.

She stepped off the last step and fell into the spring with a splash to wash away her sinful thoughts. She plunged down until her toe touched the sandy bottom and then fought her way back up to the surface, shaking the water and her wet hair out of her eyes. All the sweat of the day's ride — and more important, the terror of the night before — was washed away. She felt herself buoyed up by the waters and heard the echoes of her splash overhead, and was overcome by inexplicable delight. She wanted to laugh. She kicked to keep on the surface and turned herself around with her arms. Who would have thought a cave could be so beautiful?

Anna and the girl were chattering and laughing. They had sat themselves down on a ledge, and Anna was removing her stockings so she could wash her feet. The girl worked her way over to the secondary basin to fill up a jug of water and fetch a mug. She offered the water to Anna, who threw her head back and laughed so hard one could see her rotting teeth.

Eleanor couldn't really swim, but she paddled until she was directly under the sunbeam pouring into the cave and trod water there for a few minutes, breathing in the scent of rosemary and bramble from overhead. Then she paddled back to the steps and pulled herself onto the first one, stood, and slowly emerged from the water, to find the girl offering her a mug of water with a smile.

Anna said something that sounded like a warning, but Eleanor didn't understand. This water was obviously very clean. She drank the water gratefully, while the girl laughed and Anna clicked her tongue.

"Kala!" Eleanor told the girl as she handed the mug back to her. She had learned that much Greek from Geoffrey already. "Kala!"

The girl giggled and Anna laughed again, nodding now.

The girl, fortunately, had brought towels. Together she and Anna dried Eleanor's body and wrapped one towel around her hair. Anna helped Eleanor back into her clothes. Carrying her veils and still wearing the towel on her head covering her hair, Eleanor started back up the trail to the tavern.

Eleanor felt completely refreshed and restored. Father Xavier was dead. The records of her trial were destroyed. She was the heiress of Najac, a free noblewoman — and Cyprus, far from being a treacherous and forbidding land, was an enchanting island full of good people. Today she would thank the fishermen for saving her life, and then she would return to Paphos Castle and stay there until her guardian remembered about her — which might be months or even years. What did she care?

They emerged from the trees of the gorge and were back in the sunshine. From the tavern came the sound of male voices and laughter. Sir Geoffrey was a good man, she thought. Hadn't even her mother's ghost said so? If only he had been the elder son and heir to a barony here ...

They came around the corner of the tavern, and Ian caught sight of them first. "My Lady! You look enchanting."

Geoffrey twisted around to look at her, too, and something in the way his eyes lit up suggested that Ian was right: the short swim must have transformed her appearance in some way. At least she *felt* more beautiful than before.

"Did you drink the water, too?" Ian was asking eagerly, although Geoffrey said something sharply that Eleanor didn't quite catch.

"Yes, of course," Eleanor answered. "Isn't it what they serve at the table?"

"Didn't anyone warn you?" Ian asked, his eyes growing big.

"Ian! That's enough!" Geoffrey ordered.

"Warn me about what?"

"The effects of the water," Ian ignored his knight. "It is a love potion, and makes whoever drinks it fall irrevocably in love."

"Ian, that's nothing but superstitious nonsense!" Geoffrey admonished, scowling.

Eleanor wasn't so sure ....

Chapter 9

The Fisherman

It was well past noon by the time they retraced their steps to the main road, passed the turnoff to Agios Georgios, and found the track leading down to the fishing village they were seeking. Again they had to ride single file for a distance, but at last a huddle of white plaster huts, clinging to the shore and surrounded by drying nets, came into view. Smoke oozed from the chimneys of most of the houses, and chickens scratched and strutted in the unpaved street. Beyond was a cove notably smaller than the one in which Eleanor's ship lay, and the shoreline was rockier. A very short beach was squeezed between some ominous boulders, and here a single — evidently unseaworthy — fishing boat lay drawn up above the tideline.

As they approached the village a couple of children, who had been digging for something on the edge of town, ran screaming to the second house in the village. Their excited voices could be heard even after they disappeared inside. A moment later a woman emerged in the doorway, wiping her hands on her apron. She squinted toward the approaching riders from a leathery face, and Geoffrey cast a worried look at Eleanor. He found it hard to believe that a highborn French noblewoman really wanted to return here and thank these simple people.

Eleanor looked very tense. The bloom the bath had put on her cheeks had faded, and the long, dusty ride had wearied her. Geoffrey drew up and addressed himself to Anna in Greek, telling her to ride ahead into the village and explain to the fisherwoman who they were and what they wanted.

Anna nodded, kicked her donkey vigorously, and trotted past the fine horses of the others.

"Does it look at all familiar, Mademoiselle?" Geoffrey asked Eleanor.

Eleanor shook her head.

Anna stopped in front of the fisherwoman and a lively conversation started. The fisherwoman eventually nodded vigorously, then looked over at Eleanor, nodded again, gestured further into the village, and then sent one of her children scampering up the street. Anna returned and reported to Geoffrey that they were indeed in the right village, and pointed out the house of Eleanor's erstwhile rescuers.

As they passed, women came out of all the houses and stood on their doorsteps, staring. When the riders reached the house the first woman had pointed out, the woman standing warily in this doorway slowly stepped down into the street, and Eleanor let out a little cry of recognition. She stopped her horse and swung herself out of the saddle as quickly as she dared. Geoffrey could only watch in amazement as Eleanor hobbled forward to throw her arms around the astonished fishwife.

"I've come to thank you," Eleanor told the fishwife in French, but then she looked over her shoulder to Geoffrey. "Please, sir! Tell her I'm here to thank her."

Geoffrey duly translated, and the woman looked up at him uncertainly. "It was only our Christian duty, My Lord. You are her husband?"

"Sir Geoffrey," Eleanor interrupted before he could answer, "please explain that I wanted to come earlier, but I wasn't well. And tell her I want to thank her husband and the other men as well. And tell her I wish I could reward her, but I don't have any money to call my own."

It was Eleanor's obvious gratitude, not anything Geoffrey could say, that started to thaw the suspicion of the fishwife. In the face of Eleanor's warmth she smiled a little, indicating with her hand that Eleanor was welcome to come inside. "I can offer you bread, goats' milk, olive paste, and fresh oranges," she suggested hesitantly.

"She's offering you refreshments, Mademoiselle," Geoffrey translated. "Do you wish to step inside?"

"Of course!" Eleanor assured him. Still somewhat skeptical, Geoffrey dismounted, and together with Ian he hobbled the horses before following Eleanor and Anna inside.

Within minutes all the women of the village had crowded into the humble dwelling, and the children sat on their mothers' laps or climbed onto the tables and cupboards to get a better look at the strangers. Everyone seemed to be talking at once, and Anna was chattering away. The women seemed to have forgotten Geoffrey and Ian altogether, as they insisted with gestures that needed no translation for Eleanor to show the scars of her injured leg.

Embarrassed, Geoffrey ducked back outside, dragging Ian with him. "You're too damn fast, sir. I wouldn't have minded a glimpse of Lady Eleanor's legs."

Geoffrey just frowned at him, while exclamations of sympathy poured after them from inside the hut. Anna could be heard telling the audience that Eleanor had been with the Hospitallers for months, but that she was now with the Dowager Queen. Anna, Geoffrey noted disapprovingly, was proud of her position and not above bragging.

"What next?" Ian asked.

"That depends on Lady Eleanor," Geoffrey replied.

Anna, he could hear, was explaining in a loud, amused voice to the audience inside the hut, "No, no, Lord Geoffrey isn't Eleanor's husband. He's just escorting her."

The fisherwomen evidently did not understand this concept. They clearly thought it was improper (and dangerous) for a young woman to travel with a strange man, but Anna insisted, "Sir Geoffrey is a knight of the King of France!"

"But where is her husband?" the women wanted to know, and Anna explained that Eleanor was still a maiden.

"But why? She's old enough to have children! She should have married long ago."

"Her guardian is a prisoner in Egypt," Anna explained.

Oh, yes, they had all heard about the great misfortune that had befallen the crusaders more than a month ago. The women started invoking various saints and cursing the Arabs. Fear of Arab slavers and raiders had dominated their lives for generations, Geoffrey reminded himself, and they could identify with the crusaders trapped in Egypt — and with the women left behind.

"We must pray to the Lord for their safe return!" someone said.

"Someone should fetch Father Demetrius."

"We should celebrate Eleni's return," someone else suggested, and Geoffrey gathered that the women had understood "Eleni" when Eleanor tried to tell them her name. The women started discussing who would bring what, and Geoffrey glanced at Ian. "Maybe I should warn Eleanor they're about to put together a feast."

"Sounds like a good idea to me," Ian agreed. "It's been hours since breakfast."

"Ian! You don't know what these feasts are like! We'll be here the rest of the day. Besides, they can't afford it. Eleanor," he said as he stuck his head back in the hut. "They want to make a feast for you. You must stop it. Tell them you have to leave soon."

"But why?" Eleanor asked, meeting his gaze. She had taken off her hat and veils, and she sat in the middle of the fishing women like a rose among seaweed. Her eyes shone, just as they had when she returned from the Springs of Aphrodite. She really is beautiful, Geoffrey noted in surprise, while Eleanor insisted, "I'm not in a hurry. Lord Paphos isn't expecting us for another week. Why not stay and celebrate ...?" She hesitated. She felt like celebrating, but what? The destruction of her Inquisition records? The death of Father Xavier? Or was it something more daring still? Like the young man in the doorway? "Let's celebrate survival," she suggested to him audaciously.

"They can't afford a feast, Eleanor. These are poor people."

Eleanor caught her breath and bit her lip. Why hadn't she thought of that? "But — it doesn't have to be a fancy feast," she rationalized.

"It won't be in any case, but they're talking about killing a kid. You mustn't let them do that."

"Of course not, but — I have *some* money. The Dowager Queen gave me ten livres." Her expression brightened. "If I compensate them for the kid, surely we could stay? Please, sir, I'd like to stay a little longer — at least until the men return."

Geoffrey found it impossible to say no to her. Besides, she was right that neither of them had to hurry anywhere. There was no rush. And if she was willing to spend some of the money she had, what right had he to interfere? Still, it seemed odd to him that a lady of her rank and wealth would want to stay here with common fishermen ....

Turning to the fisherwomen, who had fallen silent during the exchange between the Latin visitors, he announced, "My lady is deeply grateful for your hospitality, but she cannot accept unless you allow her to make a contribution."

"No, no, no!" the women protested predictably, but Geoffrey ignored them. "I will speak to Father Demetrius," he told the women and withdrew.

"So what happens now?" Ian asked, not understanding the exchange.

"I go talk to the village priest, and we arrange for a donation to the Church that will enable the priest to give a kid or lamb from the Church's tithe, along with some wine — if he's a reasonable man."

"I *do* hope so," Ian agreed with a grin.

By the time the fishing smacks returned to their cove, the kid was already roasting over an open fire. Tables had been set up and the women and girls were busy preparing the rest of the feast. The boys ran down in a noisy horde to meet the little fleet, shouting excitedly about the visitors. The catch had been landed at Paphos, where there was a fish market, and so the men came ashore carrying various purchases rather than fish.

Geoffrey, watching from the edge of the village, noticed that many of the men cast skeptical looks in his direction. He could appreciate their mistrust. Latin knights rarely interacted with the likes of these men — unless it was to make arrests or collect taxes. The Frankish elite considered themselves superior to the local inhabitants of the island.

Geoffrey had been raised no differently. The natives, who clung to their Orthodox faith, were servants and peasants for the most part. The Greek noblemen who had once controlled the island had gone into exile, and only a few of the Greek merchants had decided to remain under the new regime. They formed a largely isolated and insular sub-community, much like that of the Jews, in the major cities such as Paphos, Limassol, Nicosia, Famagusta, and Kyrenia. But the common people, the people who had nowhere else to go and no means to start anew somewhere else, had remained. The Templar efforts to convert them to the Church of Rome had led to a rebellion, so the Lusignan kings had wisely decided to leave them their religion as long as they paid their taxes.

Geoffrey's father's and brother's tenants were all Greek peasants, and the servants in his father's house, including his wet nurse, had been Greek. He had learned the language from them and spoke it fluently as a child, but when he went to Paphos as a page, he had quickly learned that one did not speak Greek in "polite" society. Furthermore, the other pages and squires always spoke of the Greeks as "stupid" or "dirty." Making fun of the Greeks was part of daily life among the youths of the Frankish elite.

It was only when he left Paphos' household to study with the Benedictines that Geoffrey refreshed his knowledge of Greek, this time with ancient texts. Many of the earliest Christian documents were, after all, in Greek, and Geoffrey had been tasked with transcribing and later translating many of them. Among scholars, respect for the ancient Greeks was high as well, and Geoffrey had come to distinguish between "Greek culture" and "native peasants."

Eleanor's fate, however, reminded Geoffrey that his father, too, had been rescued by Greek fishermen such as these, and after escaping from slave labor he had been nursed back to health by a Greek shepherd. Eleanor's willingness to sit among these women, conversing by gesture and expression and sheer goodwill, shamed him. If a highborn French heiress could show so much gratitude to these simple people, shouldn't he?

The men were approaching in a small group, led by a white-haired man with a long, drooping mustache. He had weathered, dark skin and eyes set deep in his skull. He looked warily at Geoffrey, bowing his head to him as he stopped. The other men clustered around, waiting for him to speak. He spoke in halting French, "Sir? Can we help you with something?"

"You have nothing to fear," Geoffrey answered in Greek, startling the men. "A year ago you rescued the Lady Eleanor de Najac from a shipwreck. She has returned to thank you, and she has paid for the kid and the wine." Geoffrey gestured in the direction of the tables, where Eleanor sat calmly while the women bustled around her.

Now the men started talking excitedly among themselves. They all remembered the wreck. It had been one of the worst storms in living memory. There had been more than one wreck, but they especially remembered the French ship that had almost made Coral Bay. Some of the crew had swum ashore, but there had been a priest and a girl on the stern of the wreck. They couldn't go in to leeward of the wreck, one of the men explained, because of the underwater rock ledges, and so had to approach from windward. They came as close as they could, but there was a gap of several feet, and both the priest and the girl had been afraid to jump into the raging sea. Andreas, they said, pointing to one of the men, had jumped in and swum to the wreck with a towline around his waist. He had tied this around the girl, around Eleni, then dropped back into the water, leading her by the rope around her waist. Just as they tried to bring her on board, however, a giant wave had flung the fishing boat crashing against the wreck. Geoffrey sensed the narrator's fear that the fishermen might be held responsible for Eleanor's injuries rather than rewarded for her rescue. Geoffrey supposed the Hospitallers had given them reason to think they were lucky not to be held accountable.

Eleanor had caught sight of the men, and she was hobbling towards them. Geoffrey could sense that she was nervous; her eyes were searching the faces of the men, looking for someone familiar. After a moment they fell on the man identified by the others as Andreas, the man who had swum to the wreck.

"Andreas?" Eleanor asked hesitantly.

The man broke into a wide grin, and the others laughed and nodded and clapped him on the back. Eleanor held out her hands, palms upwards. "I've come to thank you for saving my life," she said, gazing at him earnestly, and her words needed no translation.

The man was so moved that, hardened fisherman that he was, he blushed as he nodded and mumbled something.

"And your son?" Eleanor asked, looking around at the others. "You had a boy with you, didn't you?"

"Petrus!" the man called over his shoulder. "Petrus!" The older men parted a little, and a young man came forward shyly. Geoffrey guessed he was no more than fifteen, possibly younger, but a big youth, who stood with his head down and didn't meet people's eyes. "You sat with me all the way back to the harbor," Eleanor spoke to him. "You covered me in blankets and talked to me," Eleanor remembered. "I was so frightened and shivering, but you kept telling me everything would be all right. Even though I didn't understand a word you said, I knew what you were saying."

The youth looked timidly at Geoffrey for a translation, and Geoffrey summarized, "Lady Eleanor thanks you for comforting her after her rescue."

He smiled and bobbed his head, embarrassed, but his father flung an arm over his shoulders and cuffed him proudly. "He's a good boy, most of the time," he told Geoffrey; "just not very bright." The man tapped his head with a finger in a gesture that implied the boy was a simpleton.

"Come!" The patriarch gestured to the women and to the tables loaded now with grilled octopus, artichokes, olives, goat's cheese, almonds, bread, and stuffed grape leaves. As they went together toward the tables, the patriarch asked Geoffrey, "And who are you?"

"I am Sir Geoffrey de Preuthune, but you will know me better as the younger brother of Sir Richard de Thurn of Meladeia."

"Ah, yes," the patriarch nodded knowingly, looking at him with apparent recognition.

They had reached the tables and settled themselves in a group. Soon wine in pottery jugs was passed around. One of the men went to check on the kid and start carving, while the priest stood and blessed the meal. Then everyone sat down, the women at one end, the men at the other, and Eleanor and Geoffrey in the middle with Ian opposite them.

With a start, Geoffrey registered that the sun was setting into a bank of clouds. The western sky was the color of molten copper tinged with bronze, and overhead the sky was a vivid blue. The evening star, Venus, was rising in the east. "My Lady," Geoffrey turned to Eleanor in alarm, "we will have to spend the night here."

"I know. That's not a problem, is it?" Eleanor asked back.

"No, not if *you* don't mind, My Lady," Geoffrey answered uncertainly.

"Why should I mind? I was here for weeks after the wreck." She met his eyes as she said this, and there was so much certainty in her voice that it was hard to believe this was the same woman who had been almost hysterical this morning in her desperation to leave the Dominican convent. He turned to his squire. "Ian, have you fed the horses?"

"Yes, sir. They're fine."

Geoffrey twisted to try to get a glimpse of the yard beyond the village church, where they had turned the horses loose with the goats. There was plenty of fresh grass this time of year, and the horses had endured worse elsewhere; he thought of Egypt.

Then he looked back toward the setting sun. It was time for Vespers, he registered, and he hadn't heard Mass since Prime. He crossed himself and recited the Lord's Prayer. "Thy will be done," he repeated mentally over and over, but he didn't understand God's will ....

The fisherman beside him held up the carafe, asking if he wanted more wine. Geoffrey nodded absently. "Have you been married long?" the fisherman asked conversationally.

"No, no," Geoffrey protested. "I'm not married."

The man paused in the midst of pouring the wine, shocked. "You are not Eleni's husband?"

"I am in the service of her guardian," Geoffrey explained, exaggerating his status to protect her reputation. "He hired me to protect her on this journey," he insisted.

"But her husband?" the fisherman asked skeptically. "He lets her ride around with a strange man?"

"She is not married," Geoffrey explained.

The man looked over at Eleanor; like the women earlier, he was clearly unsatisfied. The girls in the village usually married as soon as they were old enough to bear children, and Eleanor looked old to him.

Geoffrey changed the subject. "There was a priest on board the French ship. What happened to him?"

The fisherman looked back at Geoffrey, this time with alarm. "He disappeared," he answered too quickly.

"What do you mean, 'disappeared'?" Geoffrey insisted.

"After we rescued Eleni, we planned to go back for him, but he was gone. We thought he had been washed away, and looked for him in the water. We called out, but with the wind and the hammering of the waves, who could hear anything? Eleni was in terrible pain and soaked through. We had to get her back to safety."

"And did the body wash up somewhere?"

"No, it was found inside the wreck. The man must have returned below deck for some reason. At the time, part of the stern was still above water."

"He was found in a cabin?"

"Yes," the fisherman nodded vigorously, pouring himself some more wine.

Geoffrey had the feeling the man wasn't telling the whole story. He pressed for more information. "And later, you scavenged the wreck, surely? Did you find anything of value aboard?"

"No, no!" The man shook his head more vigorously than ever. "There was nothing valuable on the ship. It had a cargo of hides, leather. Ruined." He shook his head and made a disgusted face.

"Lady Eleanor lost all her clothes, her jewels," Geoffrey pointed out calmly.

The man shrugged and made a helpless gesture. "I'm sorry. We never found jewels. Ah, the jug's empty! I'll go get more wine and some meat for us." He made a hasty retreat, and Geoffrey's eye fell on the youth, Petrus, who was staring at him from the far side of the table. He smiled. "Petrus," he asked, "did you swim out to the wreck and look for treasure?"

The youth nodded vigorously.

"Did you find anything?"

The youth's eyes lit up and he nodded his head vigorously again.

"What did you find?" Geoffrey asked.

"Show you!" the boy offered, signaling for Geoffrey to follow him. Geoffrey looked about. The women were chattering among themselves, with Anna managing halting translations for Eleanor. The men were reminiscing about their heroic deeds on the night of the wreck, laughing and teasing one another, and Ian had gotten up to help the priest carve the kid.

Geoffrey climbed over the bench and followed the youth to a shed by the beach where old nets, unused anchors, and other pieces of damaged or superfluous equipment lay about. The youth gestured for Geoffrey to wait while he climbed up a ladder into the loft. He disappeared in the dark under the eaves, and Geoffrey could hear him rummaging around. Eventually he returned, carrying something carefully in the crook of his arm. At the base of the ladder, he proudly displayed the object of his pride: a fragment of a broken glass goblet. The youth held it up against the fading light outside the door. "Beautiful," he whispered, and looked up, anxiously awaiting Geoffrey's judgment.

"Yes," Geoffrey agreed. "Yes, it is beautiful."

"Father says worthless," the youth stammered. "Broken!" He spat the word out and looked disheartened and broken himself.

Geoffrey heard the echo of ridicule and laughter as the boy presented his prize, only to be told it was worthless. "But even broken, it *is* beautiful," Geoffrey assured the youth. "Beauty isn't always about perfection." He thought unwillingly of Eleanor; there were surely women more *perfect*, but few who were so valuable.

He had another thought. "Petrus, would you like a whole glass? A goblet like that, but complete and usable?"

The youth stared at him warily.

"Lady Eleanor lost all her personal things in the wreck. If one or the other thing were to turn up, she would be very grateful. If you find something and bring it to me at Paphos Castle, I will give you a glass goblet."

The boy looked at him, frowning. It was hard to know if he was doubtful or simply having a hard time understanding. Then abruptly he nodded, and darted back up the stairs to hide his treasure again. Geoffrey went outside to get away from the smell of fish and breathe in the clean sea air.

The sun was gone now. The whole sky had turned a luminous blue. More and more stars were visible. From behind him came the deep, throaty laughter of the men still retelling their heroic deeds and the high-pitched chatter of women gossiping about marriages and births. Ahead, the gentle waves slapped and hissed on the sand of the little beach. The fishing smacks rose and fell as if they were breathing in and out.

What am I doing here? Geoffrey asked himself with a searing flash of guilt. The images from Mansourah clamored in the back of his brain. The screaming of the wounded horses, the shouts of the triumphant enemy, the gasping of Master de Sonnac in his arms ... They were all dead, all of his comrades. And the King of France was a prisoner .... How could he be standing here on a peaceful beach listening to the laughter of simple fishermen, as if there had never been a crusade? Much less a catastrophic defeat?

The most dangerous thing on earth is a man who thinks he talks to God, Master de Sonnac said inside his head.

Geoffrey reached for the hilt of his sword, wrapping his hand around the crystal vial holding St. John's bones, and tried to feel the presence of the saint. But how could he expect the saint to favor him with Grace and Presence when he was still so bitter about what had happened in Egypt? When he did not *want* to accept God's will? Because that was the real problem: he didn't *want* to believe that God could *want* what had happened ....

Someone seemed to be approaching him from the beach. Had another boat put in later than the others? Geoffrey made a quick count. Yes, there were now seven boats moored side by side.

The man coming towards him was dressed, like the other fishermen, in a loose linen shirt, bound with twine at the waist, over baggy trousers rolled up above the knee. He walked barefoot toward Geoffrey with uncanny self-assurance, as if he met armored knights at the village shed every evening. "God be with you, my friend," he greeted Geoffrey in a deep, melodic voice.

"And also with you," Geoffrey replied automatically.

The man smiled gently. "Will you not join me for the feast?" he asked.

"Of course," Geoffrey answered, confused. How could the latecomer know about the feast? Then again, the smell of roasting kid reached all the way to here, as did the laughter and the voices. Geoffrey looked around for Petrus, and the fisherman answered his gesture by pointing to the shadow of Petrus already scampering up the incline to the village. "The boy has gone ahead."

Geoffrey nodded absently and fell in beside the fisherman.

When they reached the tables, the fisherman gestured to an empty space at the very end of the table and asked, "Will you break bread with me?"

"Of course," Geoffrey answered without thinking.

"Wait for me here. I'll be right back."

Geoffrey did as he was bidden, while the fisherman withdrew into the darkness beyond the range of the lamps on the table. Geoffrey turned his attention toward the light, to Eleanor.

She looked content but very tired. The sleepless night, the long ride, and the constant chatter in a foreign language had combined to exhaust her. Her eyelids kept falling over her eyes, and she had to shake herself awake. "Anna!" Geoffrey interrupted the serving woman, who was in a lively conversation with the other women. "See to your mistress! She is exhausted!"

Anna looked over at Eleanor, realized Geoffrey was right, and immediately jumped up, ordering the fishwives in a bossy tone. The women took no offense, seeing at once what Geoffrey had seen. Like a hive of fussing bees, they hustled Eleanor in the direction of one of the cottages.

The fisherman returned to Geoffrey. "You are Sir Geoffrey de Preuthune?" he asked.

"Yes," Geoffrey conceded.

"Ah! Then I beg you to bless me, sir."

"Bless you? I'm a knight, not a monk. I did not take my vows," Geoffrey admitted, nervously aware of his guilt.

The man smiled. "But you carry St. John the Baptist's hand with you. I would be honored to be blessed by the hand that has held the saint's in his."

Geoffrey was embarrassed, conscious of his unworthiness. "I assure you, good fisherman, I am not fit to bless you. The sword was only loaned to me until it can be returned to its rightful owner. I am a sinner."

"As are we all," the man answered knowingly. "Here," he gestured; he had brought a loaf of bread with him and a jug of wine. He tore the end off the loaf and handed it to Geoffrey. "Eat this in remembrance of Him that gave His flesh for the sake of all sinners."

Geoffrey was so startled by this mockery of the Mass that he knocked over his cup. The red wine splashed onto the table and splattered his white surcoat with bright-red drops. "His blood that was shed for thee," the fisherman intoned.

"This is not the Mass!" Geoffrey reproached the fisherman sharply.

"Isn't it?" he answered calmly. "Didn't Christ break bread on the banks of Galilee with the fishermen Simon Peter, Andrew, James, and John? Didn't he drink wine and laugh with them as the stars grew bright in the night sky?" He gestured to the glittering heavens overhead. "Do not seek God only in the houses men have built for Him, sir; seek Him rather in the cathedral He built Himself." The fisherman opened his arms wide in a gesture that took in the world around them.

Geoffrey looked up at the heavens and then back toward the peaceful sea. He let his gaze sweep past the village to the orchards beyond. He heard one of the horses snort, listened to the wind rustling the trees, and heard the gentle thump and hiss of the incoming waves on the shore. He drew a deep breath. Maybe the man was right, he thought. Maybe there were more ways to God than the narrow path he had set himself. Maybe he did not have to take Holy Orders in order to serve Him ...

Chapter 10

The Sword of John the Baptist

Eleanor had not slept so soundly since her first night at Paphos. As then, she woke up in the morning feeling refreshed and full of faith in life. The nightmares of the night before were just that — silly nightmares. She resolved never to spend another night in a convent. She would rather sleep in a fishing village any day!

She stretched and drew a deep breath, then sat up and slipped her feet into her shoes without bothering about stockings. Anna was still snoring on the pallet at her feet. She had rejoined the feast after putting Eleanor to bed, so her night had been comparatively short. Eleanor, wearing only her shift, sought out the privy.

When she returned, she took her gown and surcoat off the hooks. She pulled on the gown and buttoned her sleeves, but left the back undone, as she could not do those buttons without help. Instead she pulled the surcoat over her head, covering her open back, and tied up the laces at her sides. She found her comb in her saddlebag and sat on the bed as she combed out her long hair until the last of the snarls were gone. Then she braided it in two strands, bound the ends with ribbons Lady Rosalyn had given her, and entered the main room of the house without bothering about hat and veils.

The fishermen had long since taken to the sea again, and the women and children were tending the gardens and flocks. Oranges and bread were left waiting on the table for Eleanor, however, so she took an orange and went outside to peel it on the front step in the fresh air. Only now did she start to wonder where Sir Geoffrey and Ian might be.

She looked around and realized that only her mare and Anna's donkey were still in the goat paddock. The men's horses were gone. Eleanor felt a rush of irrational alarm. Although she was not afraid of anything specific, she didn't like the feeling of being without Sir Geoffrey's protection. Besides, she liked his company. She had looked forward to spending the day with him. Was there anything wrong with that? Sir Jean was dead and she had not been promised to anyone else. What could be wrong with enjoying the company of a young man? Didn't other maidens dance, hunt, and hawk with young men of their class? She was sure of it. Her nursemaid had told stories of when her mother was "young and lovely." Her mother had wanted Henri to remarry, too, and had insisted that he travel to several weddings and christenings and to the Christmas court of the Comte de Toulouse, so he could cast his eye at the eligible maidens.

Eleanor had wanted to go with him, but she was too young and the route was considered too hazardous; Henri and Roger had gone alone. Henri brought her a book of hours as a Christmas gift, and Roger had given her a pretty crystal pendant, but what she loved most was the way Roger described the court to her. He made the great hall come to life. He described the dresses of the ladies and the fashions of the knights. He showed her the dance steps, and then sang for her the songs he had sung at court "to the pleasure of all the ladies — if not their jealous chevaliers!" Roger claimed that all the girls gathered around when he sang, and joked about falling in love first with one and then another, until his mother scolded him.

Clearly, Eleanor argued in her mind in self-defense, the young maidens had been allowed to enjoy his company, and no one thought the less of them for it. There was no harm in being a little in love with Sir Geoffrey, surely? He was a knight intended for the Church, so he would not take advantage of her, and she would marry whomever her guardian chose for her like a dutiful ward — when the time came.

But today was today, and Eleanor wanted to spend it with Sir Geoffrey. She looked again for him, but the horses were definitely gone. Tossing aside her orange peels, she returned inside the cottage and helped herself to a second orange.

The Lord and Lady of Paphos had assured her that she was welcome to stay with them as long as she liked. They had, of course, written to the Dowager Queen immediately after her arrival to explain where she was, thinking the Queen might be alarmed by the return of the archer with the lame horse. The Queen (just as Eleanor expected) had shown no interest whatsoever, beyond saying it was "not her affair."

In short, as long as the Comte de Poitiers was captive in Egypt, she could remain with the Lord and Lady of Paphos. There were many things worth seeing on the island of Cyprus, or so Lord and Lady Paphos assured her, indicating they would be happy to show them to her. Eleanor was beginning to hope the Comte de Poitiers — not to mention his hated brother — would be imprisoned for a very long time.

The last news that had reached Paphos from Damietta was that the Sultan of Egypt wanted a million gold bezants for the French King's release. The sum was unimaginable to Eleanor. She thought she remembered her brothers saying the income of Najac was something over two thousand livres a year, but she wasn't sure whether a gold bezant had the same value as a livre tournois. Whatever the exact relationship, it did not seem likely that even the King of France could put his hand on a million pieces of gold quickly.

Eleanor was reminded that the Lord and Lady of Paphos had received no ransom demand for their son, which distressed them — until they learned that King Louis had promised to pay the ransom of all his men. The King allegedly said the return of Damietta was his ransom and the million bezants would be paid for the men he'd led into captivity. Eleanor found that hard to believe. Hadn't King Louis mercilessly hounded her homeland? But the news had comforted Lady Rosalyn greatly.

The sight of horses coming down the track distracted Eleanor from her thoughts. She jumped up and strained her eyes against the morning sun. After a moment, however, she was certain that the lead horse was Sir Geoffrey's big gray stallion. The horse was snorting and fussing at the bit, evidently excited, and Sir Geoffrey rode him at an unreasonably fast pace for the terrain. Ian followed several strides behind, his horse wet with sweat as if they had ridden a long distance already. As soon as Geoffrey's horse had navigated the slope, he sprinted forward to come to a halt in front of Eleanor.

"My Lady!" Sir Geoffrey exclaimed in an agitated voice as he swung down. "The Mamlukes have murdered the Sultan of Egypt! If the rumors are to be believed, they cut him to pieces in front of King Louis!"

"But why? I don't understand!" Eleanor exclaimed honestly, alarmed only because Geoffrey seemed so.

Geoffrey's expression was dark and earnest. "We don't have reliable accounts, or not yet," Geoffrey admitted, "but if what they say is true, the Mamlukes felt the new Sultan had not rewarded them well enough. They felt he had favored unworthy men and insulted them. They have now installed one of their own in his place — a former slave, with not a drop of Salah ad-Din's blood in his veins!" Geoffrey was clearly appalled by this thought, although Eleanor found it hard to grasp its significance. Geoffrey, meanwhile, continued in agitation, "They say the Mamlukes cut out the Sultan's heart and thrust it in King Louis' face, then threatened to kill him and all his knights and nobles. The prisoners were locked in the holds of the galleys, and everyone thought they would be killed at dawn. By the next morning, however, the Mamlukes appeared to have changed their minds, or at least their new Sultan had. He sent for King Louis and demanded a renegotiation of the terms of his release."

That's good, Eleanor thought to herself. Then it will take even longer for King Louis to be set free, and I will be free longer than ever.

Geoffrey, however, was continuing in obvious distress, "Meanwhile, the lesser knights and common soldiers have been sent back to Cairo."

Eleanor sympathized with the rest of King Louis' army and their relatives, particularly with the Lord and Lady of Paphos. "What about Matthew, the Lord Paphos' son?" she asked anxiously. "Do you think he is important enough to be with the King?"

Geoffrey grimly shook his head. "Matthew is a younger son, and he was ill. They —" he stopped himself, and turned away.

Eleanor found herself staring at his back as he stroked the neck of his stallion — with an intensity that bespoke volumes. Eleanor knew better than to be insulted. Geoffrey might not be as gallant as Sir Tancred or Sir Jean, but he had natural courtesy. Even as she waited, he remembered himself and turned back to her. "Forgive me, My Lady; I did not mean to be rude."

"I know," she assured him, adding tentatively in hope of an explanation, "Something upset you."

He shook his head, either to indicate that he didn't intend to answer or to clear his thoughts. "I'm sorry, Mademoiselle, but I think we should return to Paphos at once." As he spoke he glanced toward Ian, who had just caught up with him and had pulled to a halt in front of Eleanor.

Eleanor nodded. "As you think best, sir. I'll wake Anna." She turned and went inside.

Sir Geoffrey's agitation conveyed itself to his high-strung stallion, and the big horse strode out energetically, leaving the lazy Polly behind. Eleanor urged the mare with her heels and the crop, but the effort was only partially successful. She was soon sweating in the hot Cypriot sun. It seemed particularly intense today. In any case, there was only a light breeze, and the sun was merciless. Within an hour Eleanor's fair skin started to burn, and it was this later fact that provoked Anna. Emboldened from her prominent role at the fishing village, Anna called out to Geoffrey in Greek: "My lady is burning up! It's not proper for a lady to ride at this time of day in summer," she scolded.

Geoffrey was instantly contrite. He drew up, confirmed with a glance at Eleanor's bright-red face that Anna was right, and gestured toward a grove of cypress trees off the road that backed up against the mountains. "We'll pause there," he told Eleanor. "There's a fountain and shade where you can cool off," he promised.

He led the way down off the road, around the edge of a field, and then through an olive orchard, to bring them to the cypress grove. As they approached, first a rounded stone basin came into view, and then a ruined building behind it.

The shade of the cypress trees was instantly refreshing. The fountain was made of marble, and long weeds swayed in the softly flowing pool, but apparently cracks underground allowed water to seep out: the ground was soggy and overgrown all around the base. Megalo sank to his fetlocks in the mud as he eagerly stretched out his neck to drink. Geoffrey jumped down, but directed Eleanor to ride deeper into the grove. "I'll bring you water," he promised.

Eleanor followed his instructions, looking curiously at the ruined building, whose purpose she could not decipher. The construction was solid and almost perfectly square, but the roof, which appeared to have been domed, had caved in. The flagstones in front were evidently marble. There were remnants of a large porch or terrace, and a column of some sort lay on its side in pieces, half overgrown with weeds. Most inviting was a covered porch along the front. Eleanor dismounted gratefully, tethered her mare in easy reach of long grass, and started toward the bench. Anna stopped her with a call of alarm. "Stop, My Lady! Keep away! That's the work of the Antichrist!" She held her fingers crossed in front of her face to ward off evil.

Ian looked from Anna to the ruined building, frowning at first, but then his face cleared as he realized what she was talking about. "She's right, Sir Geoffrey! It is a mosque!"

"It *was* a mosque," Geoffrey replied calmly as he loosened Megalo's girth. "It was built during Arab rule in the ninth century, and has been abandoned for three hundred years. It collapsed in an earthquake sometime in the last century." As he spoke, the others were reminded that he knew the island and its history intimately. "There's no harm in resting here," he assured his companions, repeating this to Anna in Greek.

Although Ian shrugged and was prepared to accept his word, the women remained paralyzed — Anna outraged, and Eleanor simply stunned. She had never been near a mosque before. She didn't know what she had expected, but she was more surprised by how beautiful it must have been, with its fountain and porches, than offended by what purpose it had served. In her homeland Gothic churches, not mosques, represented oppression.

But Anna was not having anything to do with this "Godless" place. She shook her head and complained to Geoffrey, "This is no place for good Christians!"

Geoffrey had had enough of Anna's complaining and was in no mood to cater to her superstitious fears. "What do you want? A cross and a relic?"

Before Anna could even answer, Geoffrey drew his sword and held it up by the blade so the hilt formed the shape of the Cross. Anna's eyes widened in awe when she saw the bones in the crystal. After a moment she dropped to her knees and started crossing herself.

Eleanor caught her breath and looked more closely at the hilt as well. Then she looked at Geoffrey, puzzled. "What is it?"

"One of John the Baptist's fingers," he answered simply, as he sheathed it again and told Anna to get up. The Greek woman pulled herself to her feet, but her eyes were fixed warily on the young man with the awesome relic in his sword. She crossed herself again and kept murmuring prayers. Eleanor looked from the Greek woman to the knight, perplexed more by the fact that Geoffrey had not made a great show of this weapon earlier than by the possession itself; she guessed it had come from Templars, most likely from the Grand Master Geoffrey had served.

Ian took Megalo off Geoffrey's hands, tethering him with his own mount deeper in the grove, and Geoffrey extracted a tin cup from his saddlebag. He dipped it into the fountain.

Eleanor watched him, chagrined that she had failed to notice the sword earlier. She'd been too fixated on his spurs, perhaps, and his lack of heraldic arms, but that hardly seemed a good excuse to overlook something as exceptional as this.

Geoffrey brought her the cup of water. "There really is no cause for discomfort," he assured her, misinterpreting her apparent paralysis as fear of the mosque. He gestured toward the benches. "Sit down and rest in the shade. We'll have a snack as well."

Eleanor crossed the broken terrace to the benches and sank down. The marble was cool under her, and it felt good to sit here in the shade. She drank the water slowly, savoring its freshness. Then she set the empty cup beside her and unwound her scarves so the breeze could reach her throat and cheeks, drying the sweat of the ride.

Geoffrey returned with cheese and bread, which he also set on the bench beside her. "I'll just wash my hands," Eleanor announced, getting up to return to the fountain. Here, as she started to unbutton her sleeves, Anna dutifully came to assist her. Together they undid her sleeves to the elbows and rolled them up so she could plunge her hands deep into the water and rub off the sweat and dirt of the road. Then Eleanor cupped water in her hands and wet her face with it, drying off the excess drops with the ends of her veils. Overhead the wind rustled the tips of the cypress trees, and birds were calling.

Eleanor returned to sit where she had before and looked at Sir Geoffrey with open, curious eyes. "Will you tell me about your sword?" she asked.

Geoffrey could have answered as he usually did, that it was the late Master de Sonnac's sword given to him to prevent it from falling into Saracen hands, but that was only half the truth. Remembering that Eleanor's father had been a vassal of the Comte de Toulouse, he found himself saying, "Master de Sonnac told me that the relic in it was brought from the Holy Land after the First Crusade by Raymond de Toulouse."

Eleanor's interest in the sword increased instantly. Raymond IV had been one of the first nobles to heed Pope Urban II's call to rescue Christendom from the armies of Islam then threatening Constantinople. An experienced fighter who had already helped stem the tide of Islamic invasion in Spain, he had led a large force of knights and men-at-arms from the Provence. He had played a key role in the capture of both Antioch and Jerusalem. Eleanor's gaze went to Geoffrey's hip, and he again removed the sword and held it out to her, hilt first, so she could get a better look at the relic. "The relic, you say," she noted; "and the sword?"

"Is younger. Master de Sonnac said the relic had not been integrated into a sword until the Second Crusade, when Raymond IV's son took the Cross. Master de Sonnac himself inserted the enamel disc with the Templar cross in the pommel when he became Preceptor of the Temple in England." Geoffrey held the sword hilt toward Eleanor so she could see the enamel emblem, roughly two inches in diameter, set in the pommel of the hilt.

"But Raymond IV's son was poisoned in the Holy Land," Eleanor noted, more interested in the sword's connections to the house of Toulouse than in the Temple.

"Yes, but apparently he knew he was in danger, and for some reason he thought the sword itself might be turned against him. To prevent that, he did not entrust the sword to one of his own entourage, for he feared they would die with him — or use it against him. Rather, he gave it to a young knight, Sir Guillaume, in the train of the French Queen."

"Eleanor of Aquitaine!" Eleanor exclaimed, delighted.

"Yes," Geoffrey agreed with a fleeting smile in her direction, before he turned his attention again to the sword. A ray of sunlight had penetrated the surrounding cypress trees to light up a spot on the bench between Eleanor and Geoffrey. Grasping the sword by the blade, Geoffrey moved the hilt into the sunlight. The crystal flashed, and Geoffrey's little audience caught their breath in wonder; Ian and Anna were hanging on his words.

"But the Comte de Toulouse did not *give* it to Sir Guillaume," Geoffrey emphasized. "He *loaned* it to him, saying he must preserve the sword from men who would misuse it for unholy purposes. And *then* he was poisoned."

It occurred to Eleanor that if the sword belonged to the Comte de Toulouse, and so his heirs, then it was the rightful property of her guardian, the new Comte de Toulouse. But she disliked the thought of this precious sword falling into the hands of a Capet, even if he was Comte de Toulouse by right of his wife.

Geoffrey continued his tale. "Sir Guillaume felt it was his duty to take the sword to the Count's heir. So he returned to the West. Raymond V, however, was soon at war with the Duc d'Aquitaine, and Sir Guillaume was tormented by the thought that the sword entrusted to him might be used against his liege. He concluded he had made a mistake to deliver it to Raymond V and somehow retrieved the sword. He then turned the sword over to his son- in-law, Sir Bertrand, a man of great courage and honor who had taken the Cross. They agreed that the sword was not intended for use in the unending wars between Plantagenet and Capet, but rather to free the Holy Land."

Eleanor and Ian could understand that and nodded agreement.

"And so," Geoffrey continued, "Sir Bertrand took the sword with him when he followed Richard, Duc d'Aquitaine and King of England, on the Third Crusade. Here, it is said, he performed great deeds of arms, always in the thickest fighting, but — just as with the others who had used the sword in good faith — he always emerged from the fighting unharmed. King Richard, seeing this, offered to buy the sword from him, but Sir Bertrand answered that he could not sell it, since it was not his. King Richard, predictably, retorted that if he would not sell it he would lose it, and seized the sword from him then and there."

"Now that sounds like the Lionhearted!" Ian snorted, although it was hard to tell if he was approving or the reverse.

Geoffrey ignored his squire and continued, "But that same night King Richard came down with a fever. In his delirium he had a vision of John the Baptist, who ordered him to restore the sword to Sir Bertrand. The next morning, to the wonder of those who knew him, King Richard went barefoot and repentant to Sir Bertrand and returned the sword."

"I would have liked to see that!" Ian commented skeptically. He had seated himself cross-legged at Geoffrey's feet and was contentedly chewing some stale bread.

Geoffrey cast him a wry smile. "No doubt King Richard gets humbler each time the tale is told, but just as undoubtedly he returned the sword." Ian accepted this, and Geoffrey continued. "When Sir Bertrand returned home to the Aquitaine, he hung the sword in his castle chapel, awaiting the next man who would take up the Cross. He was convinced that the Hand of the Baptist was destined to lead Christians back to River Jordan.

"Instead a crusade came to him, the crusade against the Albigensians." Geoffrey took the sword out of the sunlight and laid it in the shade. "It was not a holy war, for all that the Pope had blessed it," Geoffrey declared, warming Eleanor with these definitive words. Eleanor shook her head in agreement and waited eagerly for him to continue the story.

"One cold and wet November night, Sir Bertrand was riding hard to get home to the comfort of his own fire and his wife's company after a long journey, when his horse suddenly shied. Sir Bertrand was thrown and his horse ran away. Although he was not seriously injured, he was winded, and he sat by the road to wait while his men went after his horse.

"Sitting there alone in the rain and the dark, Sir Bertrand smelled something vile, and realized the smell came from something moving slowly in the undergrowth. This, he realized, was what had caused his stallion to shy. On looking closer, he discovered a young man sick with dysentery.

"When his men returned, he ordered them to wrap the beggar in a blanket and lay him over the back of one of the packhorses. At Sir Bertrand's castle, the sick man's filthy rags were stripped off and he was washed and fed, but there seemed little hope that he would survive the night. The priest heard his confession and gave him the last rites. Sir Bertrand retired to bed, having done his Christian duty.

"But he could not sleep." Geoffrey's audience was hanging on his words, but he hardly noticed. He was hearing the voice of William de Sonnac in his head. "He could not forget the young man lying on a bed of straw in his stables. Mumbling an apology to his wife, he rose and went to his chapel. He took down the sword that had hung there peacefully for over twenty years." Geoffrey reached out and touched it reverently.

"By now the rest of the household was sound asleep. Only the horses stirred when Sir Bertrand entered the stables. They snorted gently, and a cat meowed. Sir Bertrand half expected to find the beggar already dead, but he was not. So Sir Bertrand knelt and held out the hilt of the sword to the man. 'This is the hand of John the Baptist,' he told him. 'Take it in yours that you may be restored to health.'

"The young man, who was so weak he could not lift his head, reached out his hand ..." Geoffrey imitated the gesture for his fascinated audience. By now even Anna was caught up in the drama, although she could only understand half of what was said. "... and grasped the hilt." Geoffrey gripped the hilt in a desperate grasp.

"The dying man closed his eyes, took a deep breath, and the fever broke. In the morning he was able to retain food, and within two days he could sit up and speak.

"Only then did Sir Bertrand learn that he had given refuge to an outlaw, one of the faydits, or disinherited, with a price on his head."

Eleanor gasped audibly, thinking of her brother Roger. Ian, on the other hand, knew nothing about the Albigensian crusade and asked, puzzled, "You mean he wasn't just a beggar, but a criminal?"

"No!" Eleanor burst out indignantly, then blushed and looked down.

Geoffrey answered his squire, "Hardly. The faydits were all noblemen, mostly the sons of the dispossessed hereditary lords of the Languedoc, who had lost their lands for remaining loyal to the Trencavels or for allegedly harboring heretics. They were not criminals or heretics, but noblemen and knights."

Eleanor nodded agreement and thanked him mentally.

"This particular young nobleman," Geoffrey resumed, "had been very close to the heresy. He had come within a hair's breadth of taking their heretical sacrament, the consolamentum. But then, as he lay in such agony and hopelessness, he had been given Christian charity by a Catholic nobleman, Sir Bertrand — and more than that, he had felt the power of Christ through the bones of St. John the Baptist.

When he recovered his speech, he vowed that he would dedicate his life to Christ."

Geoffrey's audience nodded approval, most vigorously Anna.

"Sir Bertrand nursed him back to health, and when the young man was fit again to ride and fight, he contacted the Templar Commander at Cahors. The Commander and two other knights came to Sir Bertrand's castle, and there they tested the young faydit. They were soon convinced of his sincerity and agreed to accept him into the Order. Just before he departed, Sir Bertrand gave him this sword."

Geoffrey paused, and his audience waited expectantly.

"Sir Bertrand knew that Templars are allowed no personal possessions, so he made the Templar Commander take down a deposition that was witnessed, signed, and sealed by all five knights and the chaplain. That deposition was for the archives of the Order in Acre and is there to this day, or so I have been told. In this deposition, Sir Bertrand stated that he loaned his sword to Sir William de Sonnac for use in the service of Christ. He said that no one, not even the Grand Master nor the Pope himself, had the right to take the sword from him out of greed to possess it or in order to punish Sir William for any failing or crime — unless Sir William had turned against God and the True Faith. If, Sir Bertrand made them swear, William de Sonnac abandoned the Church, then the sword was to be taken from him, but so long as Sir William was a true servant of Christ, he had the right to bequeath the sword to whomever he chose."

Geoffrey fell silent. For a moment the others waited expectantly. When Geoffrey said no more, Ian proudly told the ladies, "Master de Sonnac personally belted this sword around Sir

Geoffrey's hips at Mansourah, right after King Louis knighted him."

Geoffrey nodded slowly in confirmation, but his expression was far from triumphant. Instead he looked deeply troubled, and Eleanor suspected his distress was related to whatever had prevented him from taking his Templar vows. Out loud, he said: "The sword carries great responsibility with it. It cannot be used like another sword, in idle sport or self-interest."

"I'll bet the Hospitallers would give you a pretty penny for it," Ian suggested. "Their Order is dedicated to St. John. If you sold it to them, we —"

"Ian! I can't *sell* this sword!" Geoffrey was appalled, and Ian beat a fast retreat, protesting, "I was just kidding, sir! It was a joke!"

Eleanor looked from one to the other, not at all sure the squire had been joking. Geoffrey wasn't either, apparently, because he was still frowning fiercely. He ordered Ian sharply, "See to the horses; we need to get back on the road."

Anna at once came over and rearranged Eleanor's veils so that the silk hung completely over her face, held in place by her hat. Air came in from underneath the veil and the silk was so light that it blew and fluttered, but the sunlight could not burn her skin.

Shortly afterwards they resumed their journey.

Geoffrey pressed the pace throughout the afternoon and, as if he regretted being so communicative earlier, he hardly spoke a word to any of them. They reached Paphos in the late afternoon, with Eleanor's mare and Anna's donkey both lagging unhappily.

As they were passed through the outer gate, the gatekeeper shouted out excitedly, "We've had word from the Comte de Poitiers!"

Eleanor hardly had time to absorb this shock before Lord Paphos' squire was at her stirrup, offering to take her up to the solar. "The King of France is free, Mademoiselle!" he told her exuberantly, unable to keep the good news to himself.

Eleanor felt as if she had been kicked in the stomach. How could that be? So suddenly? Already? Just this morning they had been told the Mamlukes wanted to renegotiate the ransom!

Paphos' squire was chattering excitedly, repeating much of what Geoffrey had already said about the Mamlukes killing the Sultan and putting one of their own in his place. As they climbed the external stairs, Eleanor only caught fragments of his sentences: "cut out his heart," "a million bezants," "two hundred thousand livres in advance ..."

"Ah! You *are* back! I wasn't sure my message would reach you!" Lord Paphos greeted her with his usual deep bow and hand-kiss.

"What has happened, My Lord?" Eleanor answered anxiously.

"Oh, it's quite a story!" Paphos assured her. "Sit down and let me send for refreshments. Where's that boy got to?" He looked around for a page. Soon Eleanor was comfortable in the window seat with watered wine and fresh-cut watermelon, while Sir Tancred and Lady Rosalyn animatedly related the news. "The Mamlukes," they explained, "agreed to release King Louis, his brothers, and all the important nobles in exchange for the surrender of Damietta and a payment of just two hundred thousand livres tournois!"

"The others will not be released, however, until the remainder of the ransom is paid," stressed Lady Rosalyn, clearly thinking of her son.

"Yes, but who would have thought the King would be released so soon?" her husband reminded her, evidently encouraged by this turn of events.

"And he had two hundred thousand livres to pay just like that?" Eleanor asked, still hoping that somehow it wasn't true.

"Well, not really, he was short — what was it? — forty thousand livres, or something like that, but the Templars were persuaded to advance the sum."

"How could they do that?" Geoffrey asked. "Most of the money in Templar hands is on deposit from others."

Paphos laughed, "Exactly, Geoff! And so they at first refused to help, saying the money entrusted to them was held on condition that they swear never to turn it over to anyone but the rightful owner. However, the Seneschal of Champagne, Jean de Joinville, threatened to use force, raising an axe to break into the chests in the hold of the Templars' galley. At that point the Marshal of the Order, Reginald de Vichiers, who loves King Louis dearly, intervened — saying, since it was clear Joinville was determined to use force, that the Temple would lend the sum needed and take recompense from the King's funds deposited at the Temple in Acre."

"By then," Lady Rosalyn picked up the narrative from her husband, "the King, his brother of Anjou, and all his highest nobles were aboard galleys and free to sail, but the Comte de Poitiers was still in captivity. The Mamlukes held him back until they had counted and weighed every single piece of silver!"

"Some of the other noblemen did not wait for the release of the Comte de Poitiers," Paphos noted with an expression of mild disapproval. "They put to sea at once. Some, I was told, set course straight away for France, although the King told everyone he would go to Acre, to join his Queen and continue his crusade."

"The Queen is in Acre?" Eleanor asked, confused. "I thought she was in Damietta."

"No, she left for Acre as soon as it was agreed that Damietta would be surrendered as part of the ransom. She and all her ladies are in Acre now," Rosalyn informed her, adding with a forced smile, "which is why we are going to have to part with you, my dear."

Eleanor could hear the regret in Lady Rosalyn's voice, and she wanted to protest. She didn't want to go to Acre, to be with strangers. She wanted to stay here among her new friends. All she managed to say was, "Is that certain, then?"

"I'm afraid so," Lord Paphos confirmed. "After the ordeal in Damietta, the Comtesse de Poitiers feels she has need of your support."

How could she feel that? Eleanor protested mentally. She has never met me! She hasn't given me a single thought up to now! What difference can it make to her if I am here or there? But Eleanor knew better than to say her thoughts out loud. If the Comtesse de Poitiers had sent for her, she had no choice but to go. And maybe, just maybe, she would find in the Comte de Toulouse's daughter a friend ....

Chapter 11

Arrival in Acre

Kingdom of Jerusalem
June, Anno Domini 1250

The crossing had been uneventful. In fact, the wind had been so light that the galley had been rowed much of the time. Still, Eleanor was relieved when the coast of the Kingdom of Jerusalem came into view on the horizon and she was certain there would be no repeat of her disastrous first sea voyage. Only after her fear of a new wreck faded did she start to worry about what lay beyond the voyage's end.

Soon she found her stomach knotting itself as the galley nosed its way into Acre harbor. Acre was like no place she had seen before. In retrospect, Cyprus seemed benign and familiar. At least the Cypriot harbors did not stink like this! And they had been comparatively orderly and quiet, Eleanor thought nostalgically.

Anna, who had been given no more choice than Eleanor about embarking on this journey, crossed herself and started praying at the sight of the oriental city spilling like refuse along the coastline. There seemed to be as many minarets as church spires crammed within the city walls, Eleanor noted with hardly less horror than Anna. And these weren't abandoned ruins as on Cyprus, but taunting symbols of the alien culture that was trying to overwhelm the Christian kingdom clinging to the shore of the Mediterranean.

Acre was built on a small promontory that jutted out from the coast, and the harbor was formed by a breakwater extending south from the farthest tip. The harbor was entered from the south, and the entrance was guarded by two fortified towers with a chain stretched between them to restrict access when needed.

The captain of the Hospitaller galley paused to point out the tall tower of the Hospitaller church of St. John and the massive castle, on the shore north of the harbor, that flew the black-and-white banner of the Knights Templar. He also pointed out the Court of the Chain, a massive multi-story building at which customs were collected and disputes settled, and the almost equally large Palace of the Doge, but Eleanor could not take it all in, and the captain was soon distracted by his duties.

The galley maneuvered expertly alongside a quay at which a large Egyptian vessel was already made fast. Eleanor was unsettled to realize that the men aboard the vessel wore turbans and long beards, while on the quay men in the baggy trousers or long kaftans of the Arabs swarmed about like flies. A moment later she saw a black man, and found herself holding her breath in terror. Fortunately one of his fellows said something that made him break into a grin, and Eleanor's fear melted as he laughed heartily. Still, she was reluctant to venture among such men, and she lingered on deck until the captain pointedly urged her to go ashore. Two lay brothers had met the ship, he assured her, and they would escort her to the main Hospitaller pilgrim hospice. There she could relax while her luggage was offloaded and word was sent to the Comtesse de Poitiers.

Eleanor had no choice but to thank the captain for his hospitality and the safe passage. Then she very cautiously started down the gangway on unsteady legs. At the far end she was met by a Hospitaller lay brother who, noting her unsteadiness, offered his arm with a cheerful "Careful, My Lady, you wouldn't want to fall in this filth." He indicated the puddles of dirty water and the mixture of mud, feces, and refuse that had collected all over the quay. Turning to his companion, he ordered the other man to find a litter for hire.

Five minutes later Eleanor and Anna found themselves sitting crushed together inside a rundown litter with a crude lattice-wood screen. Two half-naked, barefoot men with skin the color of burnt chestnuts carried it between them. Eleanor felt neither safe nor comfortable in the vehicle, and the latticework interfered with her ability to see her surroundings. She had the impression of dark, narrow alleys that twisted and turned and sometimes even tunneled under buildings and crowds of men. There did not appear to be a woman in the whole city, she thought, until she realized that the black sacks that cowered in the shadows and faded into the alleys were probably women — although she could not be entirely sure, since not a square inch of skin, much less a face, was visible.

At last the litter stopped and they were awkwardly settled on the pavement. A Hospitaller monk opened the door, and with a deep breath of relief, Eleanor climbed out of the litter to gaze up in wonder at the towering white façade of a great church. She crossed herself in genuine gratitude, and the Hospitaller monk smiled faintly — as if he'd seen the reaction often.

Eleanor was led through the lower nave of the church, which was full of people talking and conducting business, even though Mass was being read behind the screen. She was led to the cloisters, but rather than being met by silent nuns or contemplative monks, she was greeted by a bustle of activity. Clerks with pen-cases hanging from their belts were rushing to and fro, while three squires in bright silk hose and short tunics were laughing loudly in one of the arches. The Hospitaller monk led her past the squires, who stopped laughing to give her long, appraising looks as she passed.

Eleanor was acutely aware of her practical traveling gown, her unadorned leather shoes, her plain white veils, and most of all, her lurching gait. She did not expect to win the admiration of young dandies like these, but she was not prepared for the volley of laughter that burst out behind her back, either. It made her blush in shame. Anna caught her arm and squeezed it in a gesture of wordless sympathy. For a moment Eleanor clung to the older woman, but she knew that Anna would be of little help in the world they were entering. They were among the wolves — unless the Comtesse de Toulouse turned out to be a friend. She was, after all, a compatriot, Eleanor told herself, clinging to this hope with desperation.

The Comte and Comtesse de Poitiers were housed in the Palace of the Doge of Venice, the official guest residence of the Venetian merchants of Acre. The palace was built in the Venetian style, with checkered marble floors and high-ceilinged rooms that opened into one another. It being June, the fireplaces were empty, and the batteries of windows were left open only as long as they faced away from the sun. As the sun crept around the building, the shutters were closed to keep the interior rooms dark and cool.

Eleanor was shown to a chamber shuttered against the sun, but oppressively hot nevertheless. It was almost completely filled by a raised bed with carved drawers under it. Told she would have her audience with the Countess "shortly," Anna hastened to help Eleanor out of her traveling clothes and into the prettiest of the made-over dresses Lady Rosalyn had given her. The gown itself was light green, and the surcoat was saffron yellow with broad horizontal bands of blue and green embroidery. Both were high-waisted, a flattering style for Eleanor, who had well-developed breasts. Anna fluttered about muttering in Greek as she brushed the outfit vigorously to reduce the creases, and then gestured for Eleanor to sit down so she could redo her hair. Eleanor had the feeling Anna was growing into the role of lady's maid. In the Dowager Queen's household she had been deemed too lowborn for such a role, and had only cleaned up after the ladies and helped the laundresses.

The page returned and summoned Eleanor before Anna was finished with her hair. Complaining in Greek, Anna took Lady Rosalyn's pretty green scarf with the sunbursts and draped it over Eleanor's head and hat. "*Kala!*" she proclaimed, stepping back and looking at Eleanor approvingly. "Very pretty!"

Encouraged, Eleanor stood and followed the page over the polished marble floors of several shuttered chambers to a large vaulted room with an enormous, but now empty, fireplace. The two double-light windows evidently faced the street, since considerable noise filtered through the wooden slats of the shutters, and the sound of hooves and wheels on cobbles mixed with the yelping of dogs and the babble of voices.

The Countess was seated before the empty fireplace with an embroidery screen in front of her and a long-haired little dog in her lap. She was surrounded by no fewer than five other women already. A man was playing a lute in one of the window seats, but no one appeared to be paying any attention to him, and all the women appeared to be chattering at once.

Eleanor's arrival silenced them. They stared at her as she approached to curtsy before the Countess. Eleanor thought she heard someone gasp as she limped forward, but then someone whispered, "What a *quaint* gown! I think my mother used to wear things like that!" Another giggled, "We haven't worn high-waisted gowns since the reign of Philip Augustus!"

Eleanor tried to ignore the court ladies and focus on the Countess herself, her sole hope that life here wouldn't be hell. The Comtesse de Poitiers was only a little older than Eleanor. The first thing Eleanor noticed, perhaps because her own skin had developed freckles in the Cypriot sun, was that the Countess' skin was a beautiful, flawless white, which she emphasized by wearing a very dark blue gown. She also had dark, almost black, hair, which she parted very precisely down the middle of her head, and then pulled back across the tops of her ears to be encased in a barbette at the back of her neck. The barbette was studded with turquoise beads that stood out sharply against her hair. A heavy collar of turquoise and coral encased her neck, and the hand she held out to Eleanor was laden with rings. Her expression was not welcoming, Eleanor noted, remembering Lady Rosalyn's smile.

"So, you've made it at last," the Comtesse de Toulouse greeted Eleanor, in French rather than the langue d'oc. Eleanor's hopes of a warm welcome died as the words lost themselves in the vast room.

"Yes, Madame," Eleanor answered automatically, straightening and facing the Countess with external calm. The Lord and Lady of Paphos had rattled her with their warmth and kindness; hostility, on the other hand, was something Eleanor had learned to endure long ago. "I came as soon as passage could be arranged. I received your summons less than ten days ago."

"Yes, well, be that as it may, you managed to avoid all the *unpleasantness*, didn't you?" the Countess asked with raised eyebrows and a reproachful expression.

"I'm not sure what you mean, Madame," Eleanor answered steadily. "I was shipwrecked, and my leg was broken in five places."

"Yes, so we heard," the Countess dismissed this as an insignificant irritation, "but you've been living in *safety* on Cyprus while we were *trapped* in that *horrid* Egyptian city, terrified day and night that we might fall into Saracen hands!" Eleanor could think of no suitable reply, since this was undoubtedly true, but hardly her fault. The Countess apparently had similar thoughts because she concluded, "Well, you're here now. I daresay you'll make yourself useful. Can you read?"

"Of course, Madame."

"Oh, excellent. Then maybe you could read to us from the romance my husband gave me. He will undoubtedly ask me what I think of it, and no one else has been willing to even look at it!" She cast this remark to the rest of her ladies, who now protested their innocence in various forms. Two pointed out that they couldn't read Latin, and a third had the boldness to assert that the

Countess herself had told them to "let it lie." Eleanor took careful note of this, because it suggested the Comtesse de Toulouse was the kind of woman who never took responsibility for her own failings — a dangerous woman to serve.

"It's lying there on the window seat," the Countess told Eleanor, ignoring her other ladies. Then she turned and called to the lute player, "Stop making that noise. I want to hear the romance my lord gave me!"

Eleanor dutifully seated herself on the window seat, outside the circle of women, and picked up the book, *Perlesvaus*. It was a very expensive book, with beautiful calligraphy and bright paintings every few pages. The first letter of each paragraph was elaborately drawn in red and green ink. "Do you want me to start at the beginning, Madame?"

"Where else would you start?" the Countess asked back, harvesting twittering laughter from her ladies.

"I thought you might have read a *little* already, Madame," Eleanor replied, refusing to be flustered. Eleanor was disappointed that her dreams of friendship had not come true, but she was not intimidated by this evidently spoiled woman. This Comtesse de Toulouse was no worthy granddaughter of the fair Joanna Plantagenet!

The key to retaining her inner calm, she reminded herself, was not caring what the stupid woman thought of her. She did not care what *any* of them thought of her, she added, letting her eyes sweep over the entire pack of women. They were all young and pretty in their way, and all had undoubtedly led sheltered lives in their fathers' castles, Eleanor thought bitterly. No doubt they had danced and gone to tournaments while she was locked in a cell and interrogated day and night by the Inquisition!

She started reading fluently and confidently, conscious that her command of Latin surprised some of the ladies, who exchanged whispered comments, but she did not get far before the Countess cut her off. "That's enough for now." Eleanor concluded that the Countess had a short attention span.

"Beatrice!" the Countess addressed one of the other ladies, "fetch my nail file. I have a snag on my nail that is ruining the silk of my gown."

"Everyone's nails are in terrible condition," one of the other ladies chimed in, while Beatrice stood and glided out of the room in search of a nail file. "It's because we get too little cheese! If we don't go home soon, our bones will become so brittle we'll soon all be too weak to bear or nurse children!" a third replied.

"When will the King see reason?" the first lady asked plaintively. "It is already a fortnight since he received his mother's letter! She told him he could lose his whole kingdom if he did not return soon! In his shoes, I would have sailed at once!"

"Indeed!" the Countess agreed firmly. "That's just what my lord husband wanted to do — *and* what he told his brother!"

"All the nobles agreed that he should go!" another woman complained.

"All except that sniveling parasite Jean de Joinville!"

"Why did he want to stay?"

"Oh, he made a speech about it being dishonorable for a lord to return as long as the men who had taken service with him remained in captivity."

"What a lot of nonsense!" the Countess scoffed. "What can we do for the prisoners? There are thousands of them! The Sultan will never turn them over to us. Besides, by now most of them will have abjured the True Faith and accepted Islam! Common men have no backbone, and always do what is in their own self-interest. We should not waste another day here for the likes of them!"

"Ah, now I understand why I've heard people calling Joinville a 'colt' — the term for peasants in these parts! Apparently Joinville cares more for peasants than for the fate of France!"

"But it isn't just peasants that are still in captivity. There are many knights, too!" one of the ladies dared to point out. Eleanor looked over sharply, thinking of Paphos' son Matthew. From what she had heard from the Hospitallers, of the twenty-eight hundred knights who had sailed with the King of France from Cyprus, only the one hundred most senior noblemen had been released with the King. Although as many as a thousand knights had died in the course of the crusade or from illness, the Hospitallers estimated that that some fifteen hundred knights were still in captivity, not counting the common prisoners.

"Yes, but how will staying here do them any good? It makes no sense to me at all!" the Countess insisted, frowning reprovingly at the one lady who had dared to voice a different opinion.

The conversation was interrupted by a commotion at the door. The page was pushed aside, and with pounding footsteps and deep voices men surged into the Countess' chamber. They were led by a tall young man with long blond hair, dressed in a blue-and-gold satin-brocade tunic that came barely to his knees. The wide sleeves of the tunic stopped at the elbows, revealing a silk under-shirt in the same bright blue as his hose. His hat was blue and yellow, with a thick velvet band on the brow decorated by a large topaz brooch. This finery, as well as the gaggle of men attending him, suggested it was the

Comte de Poitiers. This guess was confirmed when the ladies around the Countess got to their feet and sank down before him with bowed heads.

Eleanor dutifully followed their example, but her senses were alert for every word and gesture that might provide her with more information about this man who now controlled her destiny. The Count himself was roughly thirty years of age. He was tall and handsome, as his brother was reputed to be, athletic in stature, and darkly tanned by two years in the Near Eastern sun.

The Count raised his Countess up by the hand and announced forcefully: "My Lady, we have come to relieve you of your boredom!"

"And why should you imagine I am bored, My Lord?" the Countess answered, looking her husband straight in the eye and raising her eyebrows in a challenging fashion. Eleanor sensed intense, almost brittle, tension between the Count and his Countess. If she remembered correctly, Jeanne de Toulouse had been betrothed at the age of nine and had gone to live at the French court when she was twelve or thirteen. The marriage, however, might not have been consummated until several years later. The Queen Mother was reported to be so jealous of Louis' Queen that she tried to keep her younger sons away from their wives — a fact that had encouraged them all to come with Louis on this crusade.

"Because women are *always* bored when they have no male company," the Count answered with a laugh, dropping himself onto the arm of the Countess' chair and swinging a leg. "Besides, you will like the news I bring," he announced, as the men of his entourage spread out to find seats for themselves on vacant chairs or in the windows.

"Then by all means, tell us poor, bored women the news," the Countess replied, leaning back and fixing her eyes on her husband.

The Count's eyes, however, had lit upon Eleanor, and he looked startled. "What have we here? Your ladies are multiplying! How is that?"

"That is the Lady Eleanor of Najac, the maiden you —"

"The heiress! Of course!" the Count cut his Countess off, adding as he jumped up and wound his way around the other women to stand directly over Eleanor, "God, I have need of her!"

Eleanor sank again into a deep curtsy, but Poitiers reached out and raised her up. "Let me get a better look at you," he ordered, and took her chin in his hand and turned it this way and that as if she were a piece of pottery or jewelry he was examining for faults. "Not bad!" he concluded, then turned and called over his shoulder to his entourage. "This is the heiress I was telling you about! The lordship of Najac is marvelously rich and, as you can see for yourselves, the maiden is — well—" he looked disdainfully at her dress, "a bit out of fashion, but I'm sure you'll agree that it's how she looks *without* clothes that matters most!"

The remark was meant to be provocative — to make Eleanor blush, which she did, and the Countess protest, which she did, and the men laugh, which they did. The Count, pleased with himself, turned his back on Eleanor and returned to his spluttering Countess to stand over her chair, his hands on each arm locking her into her place. His eyes only inches away from hers, he said in a low, but audible and ominous, voice, "After all, that's the way I like *you* best, My Lady — for all that you put me in debt to keep you dressed in the very height of fashion!" He drew back just enough to tug at one of her turquoise buttons with a raised eyebrow. "New gown, isn't it?" he asked.

The Comtesse de Poitiers was bright red, but it was hard for Eleanor, who knew her so little, to tell if she was outraged or embarrassed. She answered very slowly, unspoken and undefined tension in her words as she continued to stare her husband in the eye. "It is indeed a new gown, My Lord. I hope it pleases you?"

"Well enough — if I could afford it." He broke off his confrontation with his wife to spin about and fling open his arms in an expansive gesture of generosity to announce, "And, of course, I *can* afford it — as soon as I've sold off the Lady Eleanor de Najac to the highest bidder! Or should we dice for her instead?"

Everyone, including the Countess, burst out laughing — except Eleanor. She sat frozen in the window seat, the book on her knees, and felt ice-cold hatred for her guardian. He was every bit the barbarian she had imagined him to be.

Her eyes shifted to the other men in the room, any one of whom might soon be a suitor for her hand. More than one of them was staring at her appraisingly. The gown she had been so delighted to receive from Lady Rosalyn a month ago and had put on proudly only an hour ago, now shamed her. She could feel these courtiers in their bright silk hose and short tunics scorning it. Worse: she could feel them stripping it off her with their eyes. She was relieved when the Countess, impatient not to be the center of attention, drew their eyes back to her by demanding, "So, what is this news you bring?"

"Ah! The news!" Alphonse de Poitiers replied with a smile and another grand gesture. "The news is that we will all be going home soon! My brother the King, in his great wisdom, has resolved — against the advice of his entire council

and every important nobleman of the realm —
that he is going to remain here in Acre, but he has
told Charles and me that we may return to
France!"

At this news the Countess jumped up and
flung her arms around her husband to give him a
passionate kiss, while the other ladies clapped and
took each other in their arms in relief and joy.
Eleanor sat rigidly in the window seat, dreading
another sea voyage, dreading living with these
people, and wishing she were back in the
comfortable little solar of Paphos Castle.

Chapter 12

The Prophet in the Cave

Kingdom of Cyprus
June, Anno Domini 1250

"There's a boy asking after you, Sir Geoffrey," the page announced excitedly. Geoffrey was standing in the castle armory, knee deep in broken crossbows, bent lances, shattered shields, and broken swords, trying to conduct an inventory for the Lord of Paphos. His status remained ambiguous. Paphos still refused to retain him, but he fed him, his squire, and his horses, so Geoffrey doggedly tried to make himself useful.

"A boy?" Geoffrey asked the page, wiping the sweat off his forehead with the back of his arm.

The page made a face. "A Greek boy who stinks of fish," the page elaborated.

"Ah!" Geoffrey guessed it was the youth from the fishing village whom he'd asked to bring things from Eleanor's wreck. Stepping over the pile of crossbows, Geoffrey bounded up the stone steps and crossed the ward to the gate. At the sight of Geoffrey the young fisherman smiled with relief, then grew serious and nodded shyly.

"Good afternoon, Peter," Geoffrey greeted him in Greek, and the smile returned. "Have you found something in the wreck?" Geoffrey asked.

The boy shook his head vigorously, which disappointed Geoffrey until he added, "Found something."

"You found something, but not in the wreck?"

The youth nodded.

"Will you show it to me?" Geoffrey asked.

The boy looked over both shoulders, but no one was lurking about. He pulled a little sack he was wearing around his neck out of the front of his tunic, unknotted the string, and pulled open the sack. He reached inside with his dirty fingers and removed a stone. He handed the stone to Geoffrey and waited.

Disappointed, Geoffrey rolled the stone back and forth between his thumb and forefinger. It was a piece of crystal. Possibly it had once been set in a piece of jewelry or had adorned a sword or other precious object, even a reliquary. Alternatively it had perhaps been part of a larger crystal object, long since broken. In any case, it was no longer recognizable as anything particular. The boy was waiting for a reaction. Geoffrey was sorry to disappoint him, but this was hardly anything he could send to Lady Eleanor.

"It's pretty," he told the boy, "but it's just a stone." He handed the stone back.

The boy looked down at it, dejected. Then in a burst of temper he threw it away, as far as he could. Geoffrey noted professionally that the boy had a very strong arm. The boy started to put the little sack back inside his shirt, and Geoffrey noticed that it wasn't empty. "What else have you got there?" he asked, stopping the boy.

The boy frowned and looked at him suspiciously. Then he wordlessly reopened the sack and dumped the contents into the palm of his hand. There was a clump of gold that appeared to have once been a ring, and another flat stone. "Gold! I sell gold!" the boy told Geoffrey aggressively.

"Of course," Geoffrey agreed absently, because his eyes were fixed on the flat stone. It had been oval, but a piece was broken off. He strongly suspected it had been inserted in the gold ring. "May I see that stone?" he asked the boy.

"Broken," the boy told him sadly.

"Yes, but I'd still like to see it."

The boy put the gold ring back in the sack before he held out his hand to Geoffrey. Geoffrey removed the oval stone, which he guessed was onyx, and felt the surface with his thumb. It was definitely carved. He turned it over and used his right thumb to press the etched side into the soft flesh on the back of his left hand, and counted to ten. When he removed the stone and saw the image briefly imprinted on his skin, his heart missed a beat. There were three lions — or leopards — passant: the symbol of the Plantagenets. There was something else as well, in the upper portion above the lions, but Geoffrey could not make it out because of the damage to the stone.

Geoffrey looked again at the boy. "For this, I will give you the goblet I promised."

The boy's face brightened. "Truly?" he asked.

"Truly," Geoffrey answered.

"It's a rose!" Lady Rosalyn exclaimed as she removed the stone from the sealing wax. "No question about it!" She held the wax out to her husband and Sir Geoffrey to see for themselves. The two men bent over the stone, their heads almost colliding in their attempt to see the little image on the red wax.

"What does it mean?" Paphos asked Geoffrey.

"I can't be sure," Geoffrey replied, frowning, "but the Lady Eleanor told me her father had once been given a ring by Joanna Plantagenet, the former Queen of Sicily and Comtesse de Toulouse. Apparently, her father had been her sworn man." Geoffrey left it at that, but Paphos raised his eyebrows, and Lady Rosalyn exclaimed, "How romantic!"

"Hmm," Paphos commented with a reproving look at his wife; then he turned to Geoffrey. "So you want to send it to the Lady Eleanor?"

"I think we should," Geoffrey agreed.

"Why don't you take it to her personally?" Paphos suggested.

"She's in Acre," Geoffrey protested.

"Exactly — where the remnants of King Louis' army are."

Geoffrey frowned. They had been through this before. Paphos felt strongly that if he was not going to take vows as a Templar, he should offer his service to the Kingdom of Jerusalem, in the form of crusading vows. But Geoffrey could not forgive God for letting the last crusade fail, and he was not prepared to dedicate himself to a new crusade.

"Geoff," said Lady Rosalyn. "Do you remember when you were little that the people here revered an old hermit, Neophytos?"

Both men were irritated by the interruption and looked over at Lady Rosalyn in annoyance, but they were too polite to say anything.

"Now people claim he is performing miracles. More and more pilgrims travel to his tomb every year, and his last disciple, a man approaching eighty himself, has gained a reputation as a wise man and kind of a prophet as well. I think you should go talk to him."

"The man's Orthodox, Ros!" Paphos exclaimed, exasperated.

"I'm perfectly aware of that, Tancred, and I know Geoff is a devout Catholic, but if the Lord in His Divine insight has granted wisdom to an Orthodox monk, then it would be sheer bigotry for us not to listen to him. Geoff speaks Greek, after all, and is quite capable of understanding the man — and making his own decisions," she added pointedly.

For a moment Geoffrey and Paphos stared at Lady Rosalyn dumbfounded, then Paphos turned and looked at Geoffrey. Geoffrey shrugged to disguise the fact that he was taken by the idea. "There's no harm in going to the hermitage and seeing what he has to say — assuming he'll see me. He doesn't talk to everyone, I've heard."

St. Neophytos had retreated from the world in a narrow gorge of the Troodos Mountains just north of Paphos. He had gone to live in a natural cave that opened up in the sheer face of the cliff. His little retreat consisted of three rooms, reached by a ladder from the floor of the canyon. Daily he had climbed down to cleanse himself and collect food at the foot of the cliff, but he retreated to his cave to pray. Over the years he had felt the need to decorate his cave with images of the saints, and he had painted the interior surface of the cave meticulously and with great skill, until every inch of the walls and ceilings was covered with holy images. The first chamber was thus transformed into the nave of a church, where his disciples and pilgrims could come to hear him read Mass in the small second chamber, which contained an altar. In the third chamber, the hermit had carved himself a flat stone bed on which he could sleep, or sit when he read or took his meals at the stone table he carved beside it. He carved niches in the wall for his few belongings, and for lamps. He had also instructed his disciples, upon his death, to lay out his corpse on his stone bed with the Bible beside him, and then close up the chamber as his tomb.

His disciples had crassly disregarded his wishes. By the time he died the little community had a church, a dormitory, a refectory for the monks, and a hostel for the increasing number of pilgrims. Neophytos' followers decided to inter their master's body with great pomp in the church so the pilgrims could pray at his grave, while the disciples used the beautifully decorated caves for their own worship.

In recent years the last of Neophytos' disciples, Brother Hilarion, had taken to living in the third cave, just as his master had done. He too read Mass in the little chapel, and sometimes pilgrims were allowed to attend his services — and sometimes they weren't. Pilgrims seeking out Brother Hilarion first had to report to the Orthodox monks who lived in the growing monastery in the gorge and maintained the church with the saint's grave.

Geoffrey set off from Paphos very early the next morning. He did not take Ian along, because he did not consider the squire particularly devout, and he suspected the young man would have little respect for a Greek monk. He was happy to be alone with his stallion.

Megalo was eager, and Geoffrey took advantage of the early morning to ride as far as possible before the heat became oppressive. Despite the early hour, Geoffrey passed two other parties of pilgrims after leaving the main road; because they were on foot, Megalo easily overtook them. By the end of the journey the trail was so steep and rugged, however, that Megalo could go no faster than a man on foot. By now the sun was hot, and Geoffrey was glad that the sides of the gorge were steep enough to cast the trail in shadow. Even so, both he and Megalo were drenched in sweat by the time they reached the monastery.

Here Geoffrey jumped down and led Megalo to a large drinking trough. The stallion stretched out his neck and drank deeply with large, noisy gulps. Geoffrey stood watching the pleasure his horse derived from the fresh water, and was surprised to be addressed from behind in Latin. "Can we be of service to you, My Lord?"

Geoffrey turned around to find himself facing an Orthodox monk. He answered in Greek, "My name is Geoffrey Thurn, and I have come to consult Brother Hilarion."

The monk looked at him skeptically, but he graciously pointed to the stables, the hostel, and a large chestnut tree with tables under it. "We will be serving bread and milk to the pilgrims shortly," he told Geoffrey.

"And Brother Hilarion?" Geoffrey persisted.

"I will see if he will receive you," the monk answered, pointing again to the stables.

Geoffrey took Megalo to the small, ill-appointed stable. It was made of wood and had only crude standing stalls, more suitable for donkeys or mules than horses. The big stallion took one look inside and balked, evidently insulted. Geoffrey sympathized. He looked around and opted for hobbling Megalo after removing his tack. After all, he did not intend to spend the whole day here.

Returning to the chestnut tree with the tables under it, he found that unglazed pottery jugs with fresh milk were already on the table; evidently no wine was to be offered. Bread was heaped on large platters, however, still warm, and the other pilgrims snatched it up with evident hunger. Geoffrey hated fighting over food, and knowing he could fast all day if he had to, he focused his attention on the other pilgrims. There was one man with a festering wound on his leg, a child with a cleft lip, a blind woman, and a deaf old man — everything but a leper, Geoffrey thought in dismay.

But then he realized he was the leper, the spiritual leper.

"Sir Geoffrey de Preuthune!" The sound of his own name startled him from his thoughts. He had already started to get up before he registered that he had been called by his knighted title, although he had only identified himself by the name of his birth.

The man who had called for him was evidently the abbot. He was older than the first monk and he exuded authority, despite the fact that he dressed no differently and the cross he wore was wooden. "Father," Geoffrey addressed him politely.

"Brother Hilarion is anxious to see you," the abbot replied, looking Geoffrey up and down critically. "He says he has been waiting for you."

Geoffrey had no answer to such an astonishing announcement. The abbot ordered, "Come with me, but you must leave your sword here. No weapons are allowed in the sanctuary."

Geoffrey dutifully unbuckled his sword and held it out hilt first, awaiting the reaction.

The abbot started, caught his breath, and stared at the hilt. Then he looked at Geoffrey in confusion. "Is that a relic?"

"Yes," Geoffrey admitted, but left it at that, since saying any more would have seemed like bragging; he was conscious that he had already committed the sin of pride in this exchange.

The abbot was clearly uncomfortable with the sword thrust at him. He was torn between a professional contempt for weapons and a professional respect for relics. The Orthodox Church had no equivalent of the Militant Orders, no knights sworn to defend the Church. Knights in the Byzantine tradition were secular only. At length he grabbed the sword by the scabbard below the hilt and handed it off to another monk, with orders to take it to the sacristy for safekeeping. Then he led Geoffrey to the ladder leaning against the rock face of the gorge and pointed to the entrance overhead. He told Geoffrey he was to go into the little chapel, kneel at the screens, and wait to be called.

Geoffrey climbed agilely up the ladder and ducked through the low entrance into the rock chapel. The air here was pleasantly cool and smelled of wax. Smoke from many candles had darkened the paintings on the ceiling, almost obscuring them, but the images on the walls were vivid and, although painted in the Byzantine tradition, remarkably lifelike and individualized. Some saints had long white beards and many wrinkles on their faces to indicate they had lived to a great age. Others had the brown hair and tanned faces of youth.

Geoffrey knelt on a wooden bench in front of a screen that separated this chapel from the altar. He folded his hands and recited the Lord's Prayer until, from behind the screen, he heard someone moving about. He held his breath. A disembodied voice asked, "Geoffrey? Is that you?"

"Yes, Father."

"You may enter."

Geoffrey opened the wooden door in the screen and entered the next chamber. Here an altar had been set up to the right, and a Eucharist candle hung over it from silver chains. To his left the ceiling of the cave hung down almost to chest height and the paintings were very near at hand. He had no time to examine them, however, because from the room beyond, the voice was calling. "Come! Come!" Geoffrey crossed himself and bowed to the altar, then continued through the far door. The last chamber was also completely painted with vivid images, and it was a moment before he noticed the old man sitting hunched over in the wall niche on the left of the entrance.

"So!" the man said, stamping a cane between his legs. "Here you are at last. What has taken you so long?"

"I waited for you to call for me, Father," Geoffrey answered humbly.

"I mean, why didn't you come as soon as you returned to Cyprus? You have been wandering around for months now, wasting time with your bigoted brother and doing nothing for the Lord of Paphos. Do you think God gave you so many gifts and lifted you out of the jaws of death and captivity in Egypt so you could do nothing?"

"No, father," Geoffrey admitted, going on his knees before the old man. "I — I know that I have been blessed, but — but I swore to the Grand Master of the Knights Templar that I would not take my final vows until I accepted God's will."

"What do I care about your vows to the Knights Templar?" Brother Hilarion answered irritably. "The Knights Templar may think they do God's work, but I am not so sure. You — you must find you own way."

"Yes, Father," Geoffrey agreed meekly, paused, and then admitted, "But I don't know what that is."

"You were given a great gift, Geoffrey."

"Yes, Father, I know."

"I'm not sure you do!" the old man answered back irritably. "You are a very young man with a good mind and a strong will, and you were given a second chance to live when most of your brothers were killed."

"Yes, Father; that is exactly what torments me. I know that many of my brothers were more deserving —"

"How dare you presume to know who deserves to live or die?" Brother Hilarion cut him off sharply. "Do you think you know better than God Himself?"

"No, no, of course," Geoffrey assured the hermit, mortified by such a thought and flushing with embarrassment. "I don't mean that I know better than God, but I — I know that many of my brothers were — were good men, devout and pious men, men who loved God above all else!"

"Well, then, maybe He called them to him because he loved them best!" Brother Hilarion retorted. "The fact that you were elected for life does not make you *better* than those who died; it only makes you *different*. God chose to give you *life*, but you should not presume it was a *reward*! Perhaps He had a mission for you. Perhaps He thought you needed more time to learn about

Him, or absolve yourself of sin. *We* do not know why He saved you, but we can be sure it was for a reason."

"But —" Geoffrey started and then fell silent, tormented by his lack of understanding. Ever since he was very small he had been told he was intelligent, exceptionally intelligent, but he felt like an idiot.

"But what?" Brother Hilarion demanded.

"But I do not *understand*. Or rather," Geoffrey corrected himself, knowing that only brutal honesty would help him here, "I do not *want* to believe that God could have *wanted* the defeat of his own soldiers, the death of so many good men."

"Hmph!" Brother Hilarion responded as if annoyed, but then he reached out a gnarled old hand and tapped Geoffrey on the shoulder in a gesture of sympathy. "When God is ready to grant us understanding, He will. But only in His own time. Believe an old man: you cannot force Him to grant you that Grace — not even with blackmail, like claiming you don't believe in the divinity of Christ." He chuckled at this, leaving Geoffrey baffled about how an Orthodox hermit on Cyprus could know what he said to the Grand Master of the Knights Templar in a tent outside of Mansourah in Egypt.

Brother Hilarion was speaking again in his gravelly, low voice. "You need to stop ruminating and expecting God to answer your prayers today. He *will* answer them — when He wants to, and the way He wants to. And don't forget that sometimes the answer is 'no.' Answering our prayers is not the same thing as granting our requests! You're old enough to know that!"

Geoffrey winced inwardly, knowing that this elementary lesson was one he had indeed learned as a boy — but had been ignoring ever since Mansourah.

"It is time you stopped sulking and started acting. You have too much energy and too much passion for the life of a monk. A monk is called by God to the Church — not sent there by parents trying to preserve an inheritance — much less jealous brothers."

"But the sword — The Grand Master —"

"I know, I know," Brother Hilarion silenced Geoffrey, "the sword with the finger of St. John the Baptist in the hilt. The Grand Master entrusted it to you, but did he tell you how you had to use it?"

"For good and the True Faith," Geoffrey answered earnestly.

"Is that really what he said?" the hermit persisted.

Geoffrey tried to remember, but Sonnac's exact words now seemed to escape him.

"I think the good William de Sonnac wanted you to put the sword to good use, Geoffrey, but I doubt he was foolish enough to specify what that might be. William de Sonnac was too wise to try to second-guess the Lord. It seems to me, however, that a good start would be to put a saint's hand in a saint's service."

Geoffrey could not make heads or tails of this advice. He tried to think what it could mean, but at last he shook his head in helplessness and admitted, "I do not understand, Father."

"Look at the painting on the wall behind you, young man."

Geoffrey turned around and studied the wall mural.

"What is it?" Brother Hilarion asked.

Geoffrey ventured cautiously, "The Anastasis?"

"Yes: Christ leads Adam out of hell, and Adam leads Eve. Don't forget that! Adam leads Eve! Christ's forgiveness is for Eve as well as Adam. Now, tell me, doesn't Christ remind you of someone you know?"

Frowning, Geoffrey looked more closely at the figure of Christ and caught his breath. "King Louis of France!"

"Saint Louis," Brother Hilarion corrected.

Geoffrey looked back at the old hermit, uncomprehending. "But —"

"He may not be sainted yet, but he will be. Offer your sword to Saint Louis, young man. He will not misuse it — or your trust in him."

Chapter 13

The King of France

Acre, Kingdom of Jerusalem
July, Anno Domini 1250

"A joke?" the King asked his brother, flabbergasted. "A joke? You verbally stripped a young noblewoman naked in front of all your knights, and you call it a joke? Alphonse, in my *entire* life, I have never been so ashamed of a Prince of France!" King Louis was in his private chamber at the palace of the Patriarch of Jerusalem in Acre. There was no one with the brothers except the Queen, who was embroidering in the window seat behind her husband.

Alphonse de Poitiers balled his fists together to keep his temper under control. He was not afraid to argue with his brother on matters of policy, but he had long since learned it was pointless to argue with him when he was feeling pious or self-righteous.

"And if *that* weren't enough, you said you would auction her off to the highest bidder!" King Louis continued in a tone of outrage. "A French heiress!"

"Well, what else are heiresses good for?" Alphonse snapped back, too exasperated to put up with this patronizing lecture any longer. "We use them to reward —"

"To *reward*, Alphonse, to *reward* courage and loyalty and service to the Crown. We don't sell them like Arab slave girls! I cannot believe you did this — and in front of so many witnesses. If I had not heard the tale from half a dozen outraged men, I would not have believed it possible. I would have called it slander against the Crown. But you don't even deny it!"

Alphonse rolled his eyes mentally; how could he deny something said in front of so many witnesses? Although he would indeed have liked to know which of his knights, who had laughed no less than he had at the time, had come running to Louis pretending outrage. Then again, by now no amount of court intrigue ought to surprise him; there were always men looking for an opportunity to make a rival look bad. "I can only repeat, Brother, that it was a joke. I was simply trying to counter the oppressive boredom and gnawing sense of uncertainty about our future that undermines morale with a little lighthearted teasing."

"Lighthearted teasing," Louis repeated, his expression making it clear just how little he was amused.

"For Christ's sake, Louis, is this something —"

"Do not take the Lord's name in vain!" Louis cut him off, frowning for the first time. "Your behavior has been inexcusable! Absolutely inexcusable! I will not tolerate it! If you have no better appreciation of your duties as the guardian of a gentle maiden — a crippled orphan at that — then you cannot be entrusted with those duties. Effective immediately, the lordship of Najac will be held directly from the Crown."

Alphonse felt the blood rising to his head. He clenched his fists again and clamped his teeth shut. Too late, he recognized that this had nothing to do with outrage at all: all his brother wanted was the income from Najac to help refill the royal coffers depleted by his ransom and this stupid crusade. Louis had probably been looking for an opportunity to snatch the rich Najac heiress away from him from the start. Still, Alphonse knew he had blundered with his stupid joke about auctioning her off, and he knew there was no reasoning with Louis when he had worked himself up into a fit of righteous indignation — regardless what his ulterior motives were.

Alphonse comforted himself with the thought that Louis might be talked into restoring the heiress of Najac to him later. For all his other weaknesses, Louis genuinely loved his family. At some future date, after a good laugh over a particularly good wine, if reminded in the right way of his highhandedness today, he would probably relent. But there was no point arguing with him today, Alphonse rationalized, because Louis was still very disappointed with him for deciding to return to France.

With a glance at the Queen, Alphonse decided that this whole charade might, in fact, have less to do with the heiress of Najac and more to do with punishing him for opting to go home, rather than stay on in Acre. Louis had told his brothers they could return to France, but he had expected them to "set a good example" by refusing to "abandon" him here. Louis had complained that "Robert" wouldn't have left him alone like this — referring to their brother, Robert Comte d'Artois, who had died in the assault on Mansourah.

Well, Alphonse thought, Robert had certainly proved he was too stupid to see defeat, even when it swallowed him whole!

"With your permission, Your Grace," Alphonse bowed to indicate he wished to withdraw.

"Oh, Alphonse! Don't be petulant!" Louis reproached him. "You brought this on yourself!"

"Undoubtedly," Alphonse replied distantly, knowing this was how to hurt his brother most.

Already Louis' indignation had blown over, and he appeared to be regretting his harsh decision. Alphonse observed the softening of his expression, saw him tilt his head slightly and then lift his lips in a tentative smile as he asked, "We will dine together tonight?"

"As you wish, my liege." Alphonse mercilessly retained his formal tone to increase his brother's sense of remorse.

"I do wish it, Alphonse. I will miss you so much once you are gone," Louis admitted, already anticipating his sorrow, but Alphonse left him to his regrets and withdrew.

Packing the Comtesse de Poitiers' things for a long sea journey was the task of her ladies, and since Eleanor had so few things of her own, she found herself with the bulk of the packing. She did not mind particularly, because it was a straightforward task and gave her the opportunity to discover what was in fashion. The Countess had the most beautiful things Eleanor had ever seen — and so many silks. Eleanor had not been in the East long enough to become accustomed to entire shifts made of silk, and she found herself stroking them as she folded them carefully.

It must be wonderful, she thought absently, to wear silk against your naked body. Even three layers of silk (shift, gown, and surcoat) would feel almost like nothing at all, and it would be possible to keep cool even in the oppressive heat of Palestine. She admired, too, the beautiful weave of the heavier fabrics, with intricate designs worked directly into the cloth; in subtle tones they re-created coats of arms and floral patterns. Eleanor would have liked to wear such clothes ....

The door crashed open, making her jump and look up. "There you are!" the Countess exclaimed, as if Eleanor were not exactly where she was supposed to be, doing what she had been told to do. "You can stop all that and go fetch your own things! You aren't coming with us." It was said maliciously, although Eleanor could not understand what she had done to arouse animosity.

"Where am I to go, Madame?" Eleanor asked, setting the Countess' things aside and slowly getting to her feet.

"Nowhere!" the Countess retorted. "You're staying right here in this stinking cesspit!"

"But why, Madame?" Eleanor asked, with an irrational sense of alarm. She did not like the Comte and Comtesse de Poitiers, but they were still her best protection against the disordered and alien world outside, against the Inquisition and against the King of France. "What has happened?"

"Nothing has happened!" the Countess snapped back. "It *pleases* my brother-in-law the King" — the Countess' tone of voice was so acid that Eleanor began to understand that the Countess' anger was not directed at her at all, but at the King — "to take control of you — and your lands, of course — himself."

Eleanor was so startled that she took a step backward. "What?" she gasped out.

"Have I expressed myself unclearly? Dear *brother* Louis wants to dispose of you himself! No doubt he has already chosen which of his impoverished noblemen would profit most from Najac! If he hadn't beggared them all with this insane adventure, maybe he wouldn't need the likes of you just to keep men loyal, but it is as it is. He left most of his army in Egypt, dead or captured, and the sane survivors are going home. No one in his right mind is willing to stay on with him here, so no doubt he hopes to buy someone with your hand."

No doubt, Eleanor thought, numbed. No doubt.

"What are you standing about for?" the Countess demanded irritably. "You're not my affair anymore. Take your things and your black Greek widow with you, and go join my sweet sister-in-law's sorry household. I wish you luck!"

Eleanor made it to her chamber in a daze. There she sank down on the bed and tried to collect her thoughts. She was being turned over to King Louis — directly. There was no one between her and her worst enemy!

Oh, why had she been so contemptuous of the Comte de Poitiers? Yes, he was arrogant and self-indulgent, but hadn't he snatched her from the hands of the Inquisition? Hadn't he rescued her from the Dominican convent? He had liberated her! And who was to say the man he would have given her to would have been any worse than the man the King would give her to?

The Countess was quite right. Everyone knew that hardly one of the King's barons had agreed to remain in Acre. They all pleaded business at home. They had been away from their estates too long already. The situation in France was deteriorating. The Plantagenets were casting greedy eyes across the Channel. The absence of so many lords and knights had emboldened robbers, and the roads were increasingly unsafe. Sons needed to be knighted and daughters wed. Wives needed to be comforted and mothers buried. There were a thousand excuses for going home. Only the poor and the mercenary would stay on in Outremer, only men who had little to lose by staying and fighting in a lost cause. Such men would undoubtedly find Najac a mouth-watering prize — no matter what the heiress looked like.

Oh, my God! Oh, my God! Eleanor found herself praying hopelessly, and immediately cut herself off. Praying had never done her any good. If there was a God, he had long since turned his back on her whole family. He had let them kill Roger and burn her mother at the stake and throw Henri in a windowless dungeon to die, although he had not once raised a sword against the Capets.

No, praying had never helped.

She had to think.

But her mind was blank, overwhelmed. The magnitude of this disaster was beyond her ability to grasp. She was at the mercy of her worst enemy, and there was nothing whatever she could do about it. Nothing.

She could run away, her mind whispered.

Where? she answered herself furiously. She was penniless in a strange city full of Saracens. She would only deliver herself to the slave traders!

Maybe she could seek sanctuary with the Hospitallers? She had always felt safe with the Knights of St. John; they were good men, dedicated to protecting pilgrims and healing the sick. And they wouldn't dream of defying the King of France, at least not *this* King of France, who was known as the most pious king in Christendom!

Oh, my God! She put her hands to her face trying to calm herself. Her heart was pounding in her chest and her breathing was shallow. This was worse than the day the French seized Najac. Then she had been too young and naive to understand what was happening to her. Besides, it had all happened so fast. They were just suddenly there, inside the ward. Henri had not closed the gates or tried to defend Najac. He had said it was pointless. They had taken him away at once. They had barely had time for a single hug, a whispered, "God be with you, Nel," and then they tied his hands behind his back and led him away. Eleanor had tried to run after him, to watch him as long as possible, but a priest barred her way. "You are the girl? The sister of the assassin Roger de Najac? The daughter of a putrid heretic? Come with me!" He had her in an iron grip and marched her to a horse; he ordered her to mount. She had not been able to imagine what would come next ....

"What is it, madam?" It was the rough but kindly voice of Anna.

Eleanor took her hands down from her face and looked at the Greek widow. "We are not going to France, after all," she told her woodenly. "We're to stay here with the King."

Anna crossed herself in relief and sent a prayer of thanks to Heaven; she had never wanted to go so far from her homeland. She could sense how upset Eleanor was, however, so she put an arm around Eleanor's shoulders and leaned her head on Eleanor's, murmuring, "Don't worry, Madame, don't worry. God knows what is best. Have faith."

Eleanor wanted to scream at the stupid woman for such an infantile remark. What sort of God let the cruel and corrupt triumph, while the good burned alive or rotted in prisons? Faith was for fools! But Eleanor also knew that Anna meant well, and was too simple to question platitudes such as these. Besides, Anna was the only friend she had left in the world ....

The King was not alone, but Eleanor was far too tense to take note of anyone else. She was only vaguely aware that there were far too many priests and monks and far too few knights. She could sense the presence of the Inquisition, whispering insidious things about her into the King's ears, while the shortage of fighting men underlined the King's hopeless situation. His brothers had sailed for home the day before, and they had been some of the last of the crusaders to depart. Surrounding King Louis now were not French but local barons, men who could not sail away because their land — what was left of it — was here, and officers of the Knights Templar and Hospitaller.

Eleanor kept her eyes fixed on the King. He was tall and blond with a strong resemblance to the Comte de Poitiers, except that the King was much thinner and frailer. Poitiers looked like the kind of man who earned his living with the sword; the King looked like a monk. He was dressed quite simply for a king, too, with none of Poitiers' bright-colored clothes and glittering jewels. He was not wearing a crown or any form of collar. His belt, while tastefully made of brass and enamel disks, would not have been inappropriate on a merchant's waist. He wore no armor, but instead a long blue robe dusted with the lilies of France, over a silk shirt of a lighter blue. He wasn't even wearing boots and spurs, Eleanor registered, with a pang of remembrance and a futile wish to be back on Cyprus with Sir Geoffrey at her side.

Perhaps it was this moment of inattention, or just the fact that she was so tense, but her foot caught on the edge of a carpet and she pitched forward headlong. As she tried to recover, the carpet slid on the polished marble floor, and she crashed down on her hip so hard the thump was audible throughout the room. She gasped in pain and then felt what seemed like a dozen hands reaching out, voices asking if she was all right. Had she hurt herself? She tried to get up, assuring everyone that she was fine, but no one paid her words any attention. Strong hands had hold of her and were guiding her to a seat, ordering her to sit down. "I'm so sorry," she stammered; "I'm so sorry."

The hands were warm and dry and reassuring. "Just sit and catch your breath, my dear," a voice said gently.

A chalice with wine was pressed into her trembling hands. "Sip this. It will calm your nerves."

Eleanor accepted the wine out of embarrassment, and grateful for anything that deferred her ultimate confrontation with the King. It had been bad enough meeting the Comte de Poitiers in an old-fashioned gown, but to have stumbled and fallen before the King was even worse. She was certain the King was watching this ridiculous drama with impatience.

And then she realized that the hand offering the cup of wine bore a signet ring with the lilies of France on it. She froze. The sleeves of the gown beyond the wrist were blue. Her eyes crept up toward the elbows to the broader sleeves of the gown: dark blue with powdered lilies. She looked up and straight into kindly blue eyes. "Your

Grace!" Eleanor gasped, and tried to get up again so she could curtsy.

"Just relax," the King ordered her. "You may have injured yourself more than you know."

"But —"

"Hush," he insisted, his eyes smiling at her. When she went still, he pressed the wine on her again, remarking, "As our ward, child, you are as a daughter to us, and we intend to do our best to make up for the hardships you have already endured. We hope you are not too disappointed not to be going home with my beloved brother of Poitiers?"

"Home, Your Grace?" Eleanor was still too disoriented to fully grasp how she had come to sit next to her worst enemy. The mention of home, however, roused the dead, and she realized with horror that she was drinking from the King's blood-soaked hand. It was as if the blood of her brothers had colored the wine he held. She drew back, fighting the temptation to let herself get seduced by his superficial kindness. "How can I ever go home," she asked, seeing Roger's face, "when everyone I loved is dead? Killed, not by the Saracen, but by —" on the brink of saying "you" she stopped herself and substituted "France."

King Louis caught his breath, and Eleanor winced, expecting him to slap her for so much impudence. When the blow did not come, she held her breath, waiting for the inevitable anger that would bring the full weight of royal fury down upon her head. Now it was Henri who spoke in a tone of desperate sadness, "Oh, Nel! How could you do that! Why insult a King to his face?"

Still King Louis did not answer. He considered her intently, while Eleanor looked down at her hands, clutching her skirts in her lap. Then he took a sip of his own wine before remarking, "I was still a boy when my father died;

I became very dependent upon the advice of my mother. My mother saved my kingdom for me — from Flanders, from the Plantagenets, from the rebellious barons Hugh de Lusignan and Pierre de Dreux. Who was I to doubt her when she said I must crush the rebellion of the Comte de Toulouse? I do not mean to place blame on someone else, but I would like you to consider the fact that a king, too, must learn his trade. Your brother Roger murdered unarmed men of God, but your brother Henri, had he not died in prison, would have been pardoned."

"I loved my mother too, Your Grace," Eleanor countered softly but intensely, "and you burned her at the stake."

The silence in the chamber was so intense Eleanor could hear the voices of the gardeners in the courtyard. She could feel the stares of all the other men in the room, and sense their outrage.

Louis nodded slowly, and his eyes searched her face. She did not dare meet those eyes. She looked down at her hands; she had unconsciously wrapped her left hand in her skirts to cover the ugly burn scar on the palm.

"Will you try to forgive me?" the King asked softly, and Eleanor snapped her head up in astonishment. Their eyes met, and she felt her heart start to quaver. He meant it. He was asking for her forgiveness.

"Forgive us our trespasses as we forgive those who trespass against us ...." It was her mother's voice in her head now. Her mother, who taught that forgiving the sins of others was the basis of *all* Grace. Did Christ clothe himself in gold and jewels and ask his disciples to bow down to him? Did he ask for praise and flattery? Her mother asked rhetorically inside her head. No! All he asks is that we forgive the sins of others, if we expect Him to forgive our own.

"Yes, Your Grace," Eleanor heard herself saying in a weak but clear voice that carried across the room. "Yes. I will try to forgive you."

Suddenly, she and the King of France were smiling at each other.

"You are telling me," Louis confronted the Constable of France, Gilles le Brun, "that there is not one knight in all of Acre who is willing to take service with me?"

"Your Grace, we have approached every knight still here in Acre, but those who remain are here *not* out of the desire to serve, but rather because they do not have the funds to return home. They put such a high price on their own services that we cannot afford them in our present financial straits."

The King gazed at Gilles le Brun, unwilling to believe what he said, and then turned to Geoffroy de Sargines, the one knight who had defended him from the Saracens when the rest of his army surrendered. On his face was an expression that begged Sargines to tell him this was not true.

Sargines drew a deep breath and shook his head with regret. "The Constable speaks the truth, Your Grace."

"And the Seneschal of Champagne?" King Louis asked, remembering that this was the young man who had advised against returning to France, saying it was a shame to return when so many of the men they had brought with them were still in captivity.

The Constable and Sargines looked across the vaulted chamber toward Jean de Joinville, who was in a window seat playing chess with Reginald de Vichiers, the Marshal of the Templars.

"Seneschal?" King Louis called out. "If you would be so kind ..."

At once Joinville left his game to kneel before the King. "Your Grace?"

The King gestured for him to rise and sit beside him, then opened: "Seneschal, you know how much I love you, but I am told you are difficult to deal with and demand too much pay." There was a mixture of jocularity and reproach in his voice.

"Your Grace, you know that when I was taken captive I lost everything I owned. I fell naked into the hands of the Saracen and was given only a single robe, cut from one of my own, to cover my nakedness throughout our captivity. If you had not agreed to pay me four hundred livres, I would not have the money to buy a meal or rent a roof over my head. What I request is pay not for myself alone, but to hire three bannerets at four hundred livres apiece, and to provide for them and re-equip myself with armor and horses."

"And what payment did you request for all this?"

"Two thousand livres until Easter next year."

The King calculated in his head. That was three thousand livres annually for thirty knights and horses. He nodded and announced to his Constable, "I see nothing excessive in this," and then turned back to Joinville and assured him, "I retain you in my service."

Joinville went down on his knees again, offering his folded hands in a gesture of homage. King Louis clasped them in his own, then raised him up and kissed him on both cheeks. They smiled at one another.

Then the King turned back to the Constable with a look of open triumph. "There, you see, it is not so difficult! What other men have you approached?"

Before the Constable could answer, a herald entered and bowed deeply. "Your Grace, there is a knight requesting an audience with you."

"Excellent! Admit him. Who is he, and do we know him?"

"That is the problem, Your Grace. I have never heard of him before, and his arms are unfamiliar to me." This was saying a great deal, since the heralds in the service of the French King were the best of their profession; they usually knew more about every knight that anyone else wanted to know.

"Be careful, Your Grace!" Vichiers jumped up. "He might be an assassin."

For a moment the threat seemed to hang in the air of the room, as every man thought of the danger. The so-called "Old Man of the Mountain" was the head of a Muslim sect who forced all the local lords to pay him tribute — or die. His fanatical supporters believed that dying in his service would give them instant access to Paradise, and so they had no fear of retribution. More than one had entered, like this, right into the heart of their victim's palace, and killed their target even when he was surrounded by his own men. King Louis had paid no tribute to the "Old Man."

King Louis broke the tension by inquiring, "And who does the man say he is?"

"A certain Sir Geoffrey de Preuthune, Your Grace —"

"Ah! Preuthune!" King Louis' face cleared. "You see, my lords? No sooner do you tell me that no one wishes to take service with me than not one, but *two*, knights appear. The good Seneschal of Champagne, and now young Preuthune! Let him in! Let him in!"

Somewhat bewildered, the herald withdrew, while the King turned to his companions to explain. "This is the young Templar squire who saved the life of our beloved William de Sonnac at Mansourah. William asked me to knight him, as he had decided not to join the Temple," Louis noted to Vichiers.

"Yes, I remember him," Vichiers conceded, moving closer to the King. "He passed through Damietta on his way to Acre with dispatches from Master de Sonnac." As Vichiers spoke he frowned slightly, remembering rumors that this squire had also denied the divinity of Christ. He decided this was not the moment to raise that issue with the King, however, since the King was obviously pleased by the thought of another recruit. Nevertheless, he unobtrusively positioned himself where he could spring between the King and this knight if necessary.

A moment later Geoffrey was at the entrance to the chamber. The herald announced him properly, and Geoffrey advanced up the room to go down onto both knees before King Louis.

"Sir Geoffrey de Preuthune," the King greeted him warmly. "What a pleasure to see you again — and looking so well!" Louis was not simply flattering him. Geoffrey looked much healthier than the last time they had met. Not to mention that his armor, rather than being torn and covered in dried blood, gleamed. Furthermore, he wore not a filthy black tunic of coarse wool, but a surcoat of marigold silk trimmed in black and bearing three Catherine wheels.

"Your Grace, you will remember that Master de Sonnac gave me this sword." As he spoke, Geoffrey unbuckled his sword belt and drew it off his hips. He held the sword, still sheathed in its scabbard, on the palms of his outstretched hands.

"Of course I remember!" King Louis assured him. "Master de Sonnac could not let such a sacred relic fall into the hands of the Saracen."

"It was God's will that I should prevent that, Your Grace, but now I offer you the sword."

King Louis glanced at the Templar Marshal and then slid down on his own knees opposite Geoffrey. He leaned forward and kissed the hilt, and then sat back on his heels to look Geoffrey in the eye. Geoffrey dropped his gaze.

"How much do you want for your services?" the King asked, with an amused glance at his Constable and Geoffroy de Sargines.

"Nothing, Your Grace. I — I am giving you the sword, the Hand of John the Baptist." Geoffrey held it out again, but the King did not take it.

"We need knights, Sir Geoffrey, knights that can use a sword such as this."

Geoffrey looked down and shook his head. "I came to give you this sword, and the relic it contains, Your Grace. Please accept it." Geoffrey expected Louis to seize the sword eagerly, as once Richard the Lionhearted was said to have snatched it from its rightful holder.

King Louis was not even looking at the sword, but at the young man holding it out to him. He cocked his head and asked in a low voice, "Why do you despise my service, Sir Geoffrey?"

Geoffrey quickly looked up. "Your Grace! Service to so Christian a King is the greatest honor a secular knight can know! No honest man would despise it! But I — I cannot — I ..." He broke off and looked down again.

"You cannot what?"

"Your Grace ... I lost all my brothers on the last crusade," Geoffrey pleaded for understanding.

King Louis nodded slowly, and then asked in a voice so low that only Geoffrey could hear, "Do you still doubt the divinity of Our Lord Jesus Christ?"

So Master de Sonnac had told the King everything, Geoffrey registered, as he drew a deep breath and met the King's eyes. "God is my witness, Your Grace, I believe in Our Lord Jesus Christ. I believe he was our Savior. My outburst at Mansourah was a foolish cry of childish agony. But — but if I accept that it was God's will that we failed — as we so miserably failed — then how can I take up the sword again? In a new crusade? Why should He favor the next crusade any more than the last? To take the Cross again, Your Grace, would be —" Geoffrey hesitated a fraction of a second, unsure if he should say out loud what he had started to believe since visiting Brother Hilarion. But the King of France was still on his knees and only a couple of feet away. He seemed to demand honesty. Geoffrey took a deep breath and spoke his thought: "— blasphemous."

King Louis frowned, puzzled. "Blasphemous?"

"To take up this sword in a new crusade would be like saying I refuse to accept His judgment, Your Grace. It would be like saying I know better than He does what is right."

"That's preposterous!" one of the King's advisers spoke out. Geoffrey did not recognize the voice and did not dare take his eyes off the King's to try to see who had spoken, but he suspected Vichiers. King Louis, however, signaled for silence without breaking eye contact with Geoffrey. Finally he asked, "And if I were to promise you, Sir Geoffrey, that in my service you need not fight in a new crusade, would you then consider taking my offer?"

"What would you expect of me, Your Grace?"

"Loyalty, integrity, piety, and courage. All things that I know you have in abundance."

"You know, too, that I am weak, Your Grace, and foolish —"

"I know that you showed great love for your brothers. I would rather have a knight who loved his brothers too much than one who loved them too little. You see, even my own brothers have abandoned the men who came out here with them. But as the Seneschal of Champagne said" — here he glanced toward Jean de Joinville — "we discard our honor when we discard our followers. We, we few who remain, must find a way to convince the Sultan to honor his promises to release them. I am not the fool my advisers take me to be," Louis continued, glancing toward the Constable. "I do not believe I can force the Sultan to release his prisoners with a new crusade. But nor can I crawl away on my belly with my tail between my legs. I must put fear into the heart of the Sultan of Egypt by showing him he is not as powerful as he thinks, and that the King of France is a man he does not want for an enemy."

The other men in the room moved somewhat uneasily, apparently surprised by the King's announcement, but by no means displeased, or so Geoffrey sensed.

"Are you prepared, Sir Geoffrey, to serve me under these conditions?" King Louis pressed him.

"With all my heart and all my soul, Your Grace, if you think such a man as I can be of any use."

"I am certain of it, Sir Geoffrey, with the support of St. John the Baptist." With these words, King Louis gently pushed Geoffrey's hands away from him, indicating he would not take the offered sword.

For a second, Geoffrey still hesitated. It had never occurred to him that King Louis might not take the Baptist's sword, and he had looked forward to freeing himself of the burden it put upon him. Brother Hilarion had told him to offer his sword to the King, and he had done that. Brother Hilarion had said the King would know how to put it to best use — and the King apparently wanted Geoffrey to keep it. Geoffrey shook himself mentally, reminding himself he must stop trying to understand everything that happened to him. He bowed his head and took the sword back, laid it across his knees, and then offered his folded hands to the King, just as Jean de Joinville had done before him.

King Louis covered Geoffrey's hands with his own and announced, "I hereby take you into my service, Sir Geoffrey de Preuthune, at a rate of one hundred livres per annum."

Chapter 14

The Lily of France

Acre, Kingdom of Jerusalem
August, Anno Domini 1250

It did not take Eleanor long to discover why the Comtesse de Toulouse detested her sister-in-law, Marguerite of France. They could hardly have been more dissimilar. Not only was the Queen now middle-aged and the mother of a half-dozen children, she was also profoundly different in temperament. The Countess was haughty and high-strung, the Queen calm and modest. The Countess had a short temper and a short attention span; the Queen was patient. The Countess loved fashion and light entertainment; the Queen, like her husband, was very pious and heard Mass before breakfast and usually, if not detained by business, after lunch as well. The Queen also took her duties seriously, daily distributing alms to the poor and frequently visiting the sick.

"Would you like to join me today, Eleanor?" she asked her lady in waiting, coming to stand behind Eleanor. Eleanor was brushing out one of the Queen's dresses, which had been splattered with mud on her excursion of the day before.

She looked up, startled. The Queen was smiling at her gently as she added, "I understand you have seen very little of Acre since your arrival."

"I have seen nothing of it at all, Your Grace," Eleanor confessed.

"Then it is high time you did," Marguerite insisted, looping her hand through Eleanor's elbow and pulling her away from her work.

"We've had far too little time to talk since you joined my household," she continued as she led Eleanor out of her apartments. "These state audiences and dinners can be interminable," she remarked, her voice echoing on the stone ceiling of the narrow, spiral stairs, "and since my brothers-in-law left Acre, my lord husband requires my presence more than before."

In the courtyard, squires and knights of the Queen's household waited.

"You don't mind if we walk, do you?" Marguerite asked. "It's not that far and the streets are too narrow for a horse-litter."

"Not at all, Your Grace," Eleanor stammered, unused to being asked her wishes by anyone, much less a Queen.

Marguerite, however, was sincere in asking. "It won't be too much for your leg?" she asked solicitously.

"No, Your Grace. I would appreciate the exercise, of which I have had too little of late."

They set off with the Queen's herald striding ahead announcing her and her knights clearing a way through the crowds that otherwise jammed the narrow streets and often made progress almost impossible.

Marguerite smiled and waved to those people who backed up against the buildings or hung looked down from the windows, but mostly she pointed out the sights of the city to Eleanor:

the Cathedral of the Holy Cross, the huge infirmary of the Knights of St. John with its soaring two-story arches, and the massive headquarters of the Knights of St. John, built around several courtyards and taking up the space of several city blocks. Here they turned left and headed toward the harbor, passing the palace of the Doge, where Eleanor had lived briefly with the Comte de Poitiers' household, and then continued behind the imposing but sober façade of the customs house and Court of the Chain before entering the Pisan quarter. The Queen showed a remarkable familiarity with the city, although she had been here only a few months herself.

Between the outside distractions, she started speaking to Eleanor in the langue d'oc. "You don't know how delighted I am to have you with me. I've become quite rusty in my native tongue, since I have so little opportunity to speak it; most of my ladies, of course, returned to France with their husbands."

Marguerite had only Eleanor and two other ladies in her household at the moment, the latter being the wives of local barons. "The time in Damietta was very hard on some of my ladies," Marguerite reflected.

"But not so hard as for you, Your Grace," Eleanor countered, remembering how much she had admired the Queen for remaining in Damietta after her husband's capture; it would have been so easy to panic. "At least, to my knowledge, no one else gave birth to a child while in Damietta."

The Queen waved the objection aside. "That was what helped me to stay focused. I had no time to imagine what *might* happen to us — I had to ensure that my child was born healthy, and that my husband returned safely. Those thoughts took up all my attention. And certainly, none of us suffered as you did — shipwrecked and injured and completely among strangers. I admire you very much, you know, because you have not complained once."

Eleanor was embarrassed. "What should I have complained about, Madame? The Cypriot fishermen saved my life at the risk of their own. The Hospitallers gave me the best care possible. I was allowed to recover in the household of the Dowager Queen of Cyprus —"

"Not the pleasantest person, or so I've been told," Marguerite quipped with a twinkle in her eye, and suddenly they were laughing together.

"I'm sure she was no worse than the Dowager Queen of France," Eleanor managed to say, giggling so hard she forgot herself.

Marguerite doubled up with laughter, gasping out, "And I would rather be locked in a dungeon with the Pope than with my mother-in-law!" Eventually Marguerite stopped giggling and admitted, "I shouldn't have said that, should I? You don't think ill of me for being so disrespectful of a Queen of France, do you?"

"Madame, if I understood your lord husband the King correctly, it was Queen Blanche who advocated the subjugation of Toulouse and insisted on the assault on Montségur." Eleanor meant to assure the Queen that she was the last person to take offense at criticism of the Dowager Queen, but her words made the Queen lose all her lightheartedness.

"I'm so sorry about what happened to your mother and brothers, Eleanor," Marguerite responded soberly. "Louis told me everything. He says that your elder brother should never have been arrested, much less allowed to die in prison. We will try to make it up to you, I promise — but now we are at our destination."

They were standing in front of a large two-story stone building with a tower rising over one corner. Eleanor looked around curiously and realized, by the smell of salt water on the breeze, that they were quite close to the sea. Down one of the streets she could see the towering crenelated walls of the Templar Commandery with the Beauséant fluttering brazenly from the towers.

But Eleanor's attention was refocused by the Queen, who took her arm to lead her to the closed door of the building where they had stopped. The façade was high and plain. It was windowless on the ground floor and had only a few small windows on the floor above. A large wooden cross hung above the door, and Eleanor instantly suspected a convent. Remembering her last experience, she would have liked to remain outside, but then she would have had to explain herself. Besides, there was no time: the door opened and, as expected, a nun stood in the opening, bowing her head to the Queen of France.

Marguerite kissed the nun on both cheeks and then turned and introduced Eleanor, adding, "This is Mother Michelle, the prioress of St. Anne's." Mother Michelle smiled and nodded to Eleanor, then invited her visitors inside. The escort was left in the street.

The interior of this convent seemed very dark after the bright light outside, and Eleanor had to watch her footing so as not to stumble on the uneven cobbles. They were led down a dark corridor, and then suddenly a courtyard opened up. It was surrounded by a double gallery of stone arches. There was a large fountain in the center of the courtyard, and around it some two dozen children ran about, shouting and playing. Apparently the nunnery ran a school of some sort.

The nun clapped her hands and called out, "Children! Children! Silence! We have visitors!"

"Oh, let them play," the Queen countered. "We can talk first."

"As you wish, Madame," the nun agreed with a smile, and gestured for her guests to take the corner stairway up to the next floor.

The stairway was shallow and made of sandstone, with an elegant carved stone banister of very fine craftsmanship. Mother Michelle, noticing Eleanor's look, explained, "This was a caravansary, Madame, undoubtedly one of the better ones. The King of Jerusalem turned it over to us fifty-eight years ago."

She led them to a corner room with a large stone fireplace, a carved mantel, and round-headed windows looking out in two directions over the streets below. There was a heavy oak table with two high-backed armed chairs that Mother Michelle offered to her guests, taking a smaller chair for herself. As she seated herself, she asked if they wanted refreshments.

"Water would be welcome," the Queen agreed.

Mother Michelle rang a little bell, and a moment later an adolescent girl in a neat blue habit, white apron, and headscarf entered with a curtsy. "Yes, Madame?"

Eleanor caught her breath as the girl righted herself from her curtsy; the girl was very evidently Arab, with black brows, black eyes, and skin as dark as any of the sailors in the port. But the Queen did not seem in the least surprised. She smiled at the girl while Mother Michelle explained, "Melusinde, our guests would very much like some cool water and some fresh fruit. Would you be so kind as to bring them to us?" Eleanor was astonished by the polite tone the prioress used when addressing a serving girl. The girl dipped her knee again, and withdrew.

"Is that the girl you wrote me about?" Queen Marguerite asked as soon as the door closed.

"Yes," the prioress confessed. "Yes, it is. I wanted you to see her for yourself."

"She seems most modest."

"I have no reason to think she is otherwise, Madame. She has been with us ten years now, and she has never caused trouble. She is very quick-witted, and for the last two years she has been helping with the younger girls."

"How old is she?"

"We think she is fourteen, but, of course, we never really know."

"She was abandoned?"

"She was found crying on the doorstep of St. Andrew's. She could tell us her Christian name and say the Lord's Prayer. She stammered something about 'being bad,' an uncle, and a ship. It could mean anything. An uncle might be a blood relative or simply her mother's latest protector. She had clearly been made to feel that she was to blame for being abandoned, but we all know that no child's actions can justify abandonment." She stopped, with a sharp look at Eleanor. "Perhaps I should explain. This is an orphanage. We take in any and all children in need, regardless of their faith, their race, or the circumstances of their birth. Many of our children were born to prostitutes, but not a few were sired by pilgrims and sailors on virtuous local girls. The latter were usually lured into liaisons by promises of marriage, or even marriage ceremonies. They had no way of knowing that their 'husbands' were already married — until the time came for the men to return home."

Eleanor looked suitably shocked.

"A port like Acre, which sees so many people come and go — above all, so many lonely pilgrims in desperate need of female affection — is full of such stories, My Lady — but I urge you not to judge *any* party too harshly. We rarely know all the facts, nor can we see into another's soul. I try never to judge the parents of our charges."

"But to abandon a little girl of four or five!" the Queen protested.

"Yes, someone decided they could no longer support her, but maybe that was true, Your Grace. Maybe her mother had to choose between abandoning little Melusinde or prostitution. Maybe her father knew that if he did not turn her over to the Church, she would be sold into slavery while he was away at sea. The fact that she was brought to the Church of St. Laurence suggests that her parents cared what happened to her; they simply could not care for her themselves anymore."

Eleanor and the Queen were both silenced. Eleanor found herself wishing she had been brought here and not to the Dominican nuns in Albi. She sensed that Mother Michelle would not have judged her mother so harshly, much less have blamed her for her mother's sins.

After a pause, Mother Michelle continued, "Our problem, My Lady, is simply that little girls grow up. They cannot all become nuns and stay with us. Over the years, hundreds of children have passed through our hands, and we have a staff of just forty-two. We cannot support more than that — and have no space for more, Your Grace," she forestalled Marguerite, who was obviously on the brink of offering financial assistance.

Marguerite took a deep breath, but her brow was furrowed. "What happens to the others, then?" she asked.

"Well, of course, some go to other convents, but without dowries, it is not easy to find acceptance with the other orders." Her tone was studiously neutral — yet biting all the same. "Most of the girls do not really want a life of prayer for the rest of their lives, anyway," she continued, softening her unspoken criticism of the convents that required dowries. "For the more worldly girls, we keep our ears open for possible husbands — or rather, the Knights of St. John and the Knights Templar keep their ears open, since they travel throughout the Holy Land and often hear of a good man who has lost his wife, or a squire ready to settle down. We also run a needlework factory, which I would very much like to show you on your next visit, Your Grace. Almost twenty women earn their keep there with their needlework. They make very pretty things, as I'm sure you will convince yourself, and live communally with two very loyal watchmen, former crusaders. Other girls we try to place in service with good households ...."

The Queen nodded. "And why do you think Melusinde would be suited to service rather than marriage or needlework?"

"She is too bright and too pretty for the needlework, Madame," the prioress answered with a smile, and then put her finger to her lips as she heard the girl approaching.

Melusinde backed into the room, carrying a heavy tray laden with silver goblets, a silver pitcher, and a platter laden with oranges and pomegranates. She set the tray down on the table, took the goblets from the tray, and placed them before each of the adults. She placed the platter in the middle of the table and handed each woman a sharp knife. Finally she poured water into each goblet, and then set the pitcher beside the platter. "Will there be anything else, Madame?"

"Not at the moment, Melusinde — unless you wish something, Madame?" the prioress looked to the Queen.

Marguerite straightened in her seat. "Melusinde, Mother Michelle tells us you have been here several years."

The girl nodded. "Yes, Madame."

"Do you like it here?"

The girl glanced at the prioress, who nodded encouragingly.

"Yes, Madame."

"Have you given any thought to your future?"

"Yes, Madame."

"What do you think?" the Queen prompted.

"That it is very frightening, Madame."

How true! Eleanor thought, catching the girl's look in her direction.

The Queen, however, was astonished. "What is so frightening, child?"

"I know I cannot stay here, but I am afraid of what is out there." She nodded in the direction of the window.

"Are you not curious?" the Queen asked.

"Yes and no, Madame," the girl replied, weighing her answer. "I think if I were not alone in the world, if I could go with others, it would not be so bad."

"That is very wise," the Queen agreed, and Mother Michelle told the girl that she could now go. The girl dipped her knee and withdrew.

The Queen looked at Eleanor. "What do you think, Eleanor?"

"That the future is very frightening, Madame," Eleanor echoed.

The others thought it was a joke and laughed.

When they finished laughing, the Queen noted, "The problem is that she looks very exotic.

Here it is hardly noticeable, but one day my lord husband will return to France, and then ..."

"Melusinde will not fit in, you mean?" Mother Michelle asked.

"Women can be very cruel," the Queen observed.

"I know," the prioress agreed, looking her straight in the eye.

"Is there no local noblewoman who could find her a place?" the Queen asked next.

"If that is your decision, Madame, I will make further inquiries. Please, help yourself to the fruit." The prioress leaned forward and pushed the tray in the direction of the Queen with a forced smile. She was clearly very disappointed that the Queen had not agreed to take Melusinde.

"May I ask a question?" Eleanor ventured timidly.

"Yes?" The prioress looked over at her, surprised; waiting women rarely took part in discussions.

"I mean, you said she knew the Lord's Prayer, but My Lady is right. She looks very — very Arab."

"There are many Syrian and Maronite Christians here, Lady Eleanor, or she might have been the product of a mixed liaison. Something evidently happened that frightened her mother into abandoning her. In my experience, the most common reason a woman abandons a child is threats from a male — a husband, father, brother, or lover — to harm the child. As I said earlier, abandonment to the Church is not necessarily the worst thing that can happen to a child in today's world."

"Your Grace," Eleanor turned to the Queen, "if you would not think it impertinent, I would be happy to engage Melusinde. My woman, Anna, is very reluctant to accompany me to

France when the time comes, but if Melusinde is willing ..."

The prioress perked up at once and looked hopefully to the Queen, who broke out into a broad smile. "What a brilliant idea, Eleanor! Of course you should have a girl to look after you. How do you want to go about this?" The Queen turned back to the prioress.

"I would like to talk to Melusinde in private, after you have gone. I will let you know in one or two days, if she is agreeable, and then we can arrange for her to join you."

"Very good!" the Queen agreed. They then discussed other things, and went back down to the courtyard to meet the other children. After about an hour and a half they were back outside.

Their bored escort gladly emerged from the shadows, helped them into the litter, and they set off on the return trip. "I want to thank you, Eleanor, for taking on Melusinde," the Queen declared, taking Eleanor by the hand. "It was wonderful of you."

"But foolish, too. I have no means to pay her."

"Oh." The Queen looked at her, astonished. "Didn't Louis say anything about an allowance when you spoke? No, of course not. He's too wrapped up in hiring knights," she admitted with a little sigh. "Well, I will just have to remind him."

As they entered the courtyard of the Patriarch's palace, their escort started shouting in evident annoyance. Eleanor leaned forward to see what was causing the commotion and noticed a very large, dark dapple-gray stallion. The horse reminded her so strongly of Megalo that an irrational pang of longing stabbed her heart. Hadn't she just had a lovely day with the Queen of France? Who could ask for kinder treatment? But the memory of those short days on Cyprus came back to her, and she realized she was still a little in love with Sir Geoffrey.

She had hardly finished this thought when the sight of Sir Geoffrey made her freeze where she was. He was just a few feet away, wearing a marigold surcoat with three Catherine wheels. His chain mail gleamed. The hilt of his sword glittered. Oh, my God, Eleanor thought: he's the handsomest man I've ever set eyes on.

"My Lady." He stepped past the squires and knights of the Queen's household, and bowed before her.

"Where did you come from, sir?" She asked, unconscious of her own smile.

"I have offered my services to the King of France, and the King," Geoffrey turned and bowed to Queen Marguerite, "did me the honor of accepting my oath."

"Then you will be staying in Acre?" Eleanor could not keep the happiness out of her voice.

"At the King's pleasure, Mademoiselle."

Eleanor was elated, but she didn't know what to say — certainly not in front of the Queen. Fortunately, Sir Geoffrey was handing her something. "One of the fishermen found this near the wreck, Mademoiselle. Unfortunately it had broken out of the ring in which it was set, which was badly crushed. I had to let the fisherman keep the gold, but I thought you might want the stone nevertheless."

Eleanor looked down at the stone he held in his palm, and her heart started thundering. "It's from my father's ring!"

Sir Geoffrey smiled.

"Oh, sir!" Eleanor held out her hands, the palms cupped, and Geoffrey put the stone in them.

Eleanor drew her hands closer and gazed down at the stone in amazement.

"I'm afraid it's been chipped," Geoffrey noted.

"That doesn't matter!" Eleanor exclaimed. "It is my father's ring — the one Lady Joanna gave him." Eleanor could not tame, much less express, her emotions. She had not seen or held her father's ring since the day of her arrest. She had assumed, but had not been sure, that it had fallen into Father Xavier's hands. It was amazing that he had carried it with him on the ship, and even more astonishing that it — so tiny and fragile — might have been found. But it was her father's ring, as if he too were reaching out from beyond the grave to encourage her. When she looked up again, tears were streaming down her face. "How can I ever thank you, sir? This is the most precious thing to me in the whole world!"

Geoffrey was pleased, but also embarrassed by the intensity of her emotions. He did not know how to react, and shrugged helplessly.

The Queen of France came to his rescue. "Monsieur," she said, taking him by the elbow, "I can see you have done my dear friend Eleanor a great service. We will not forget it. We look forward to seeing you again, but if you will excuse us, I think Eleanor needs to get out of the sun."

Geoffrey dutifully bowed low to the Queen and took a step back. Marguerite took Eleanor by the elbow as the latter continued to stare, dazed, at the stone in her palms. She guided her into the stairwell.

"I'm sorry, Madame," Eleanor stammered, clutching her precious stone in her right hand and her skirts in her left so she could mount the spiral stairs. "You must think me a perfect fool."

"Why should I think that?" Marguerite countered, leading them into the cool of the high-ceilinged room.

"This — this —" Eleanor held the stone out to her. "I know it looks like rubbish to you, but — but it belonged to my father. It was very precious to him, but I thought it was lost — in the wreck. I never thought I would ever see it again. I lost everything in the wreck. Everything."

Marguerite led her to an armed chair and gently pushed her down into it. "You see," Marguerite of France told Eleanor, "the Lord taketh away, but He giveth, too." She paused, watching Eleanor study the stone, but then she couldn't resist remarking, "And Sir Geoffrey is a very comely and courteous knight. Do you know him, it seems?"

"Sir Geoffrey came to my assistance once before," Eleanor admitted, looking up from the stone. "When I learned what had happened to the King and my guardian, I went on a pilgrimage, but the horse the Dowager Queen loaned to me went lame, and a terrible thunderstorm broke. I don't know what would have happened if Sir Geoffrey hadn't chanced along the road and brought me safely to the castle at Paphos."

"I see," the Queen nodded, adding, "A very good-looking knight, and a bachelor, I believe."

"He was a Templar squire," Eleanor admitted. "I thought he would return to the Temple."

"It seems not," the Queen answered, taking pleasure in stowing this piece of information away for later, and changing the subject. "May I see the stone?"

Eleanor willingly handed it over.

"Hmm. It looks suspiciously like Plantagenet leopards to me," she declared, as if disapproving.

Eleanor caught her breath, but Marguerite laughed. "Come! My sister is married to Henry Plantagenet, the current King of England! You can't think I would begrudge anyone a tie to the Plantagenets? The Lionheart was Duc d'Aquitaine, and Najac was one of his fiefs, if I was informed correctly, before it passed to Toulouse."

The Queen of France, Eleanor noted, was very well informed indeed.

"But I think we need to reset it," Marguerite continued practically. "Is that a rose?" she asked, examining the stone more closely.

"Yes," Eleanor admitted, and the Queen gave her another appraising look. "There is, I think, a very interesting story behind this ring ...."

Eleanor smiled. "I would be delighted to tell you, Madame."

Chapter 15

A Secret Embassy

Kingdom of Jerusalem
February, Anno Domini 1251

The Franciscan friar waited patiently while the King finished praying. Yves le Breton had been in the Holy Land for a quarter-century now, and his joints increasingly ached, so he preferred to pray sitting down. He also prayed standing up, walking, lying in bed, and when taking a meal or a piss, for that matter. He prayed whenever he needed to communicate with God, and that was very frequently. Prayer in the sense of kneeling in a church and reciting Latin was, on the other hand, rare; he didn't have time for it.

As Brother Yves watched the King of France pray, however, he noticed that Louis didn't seem to be praying either perfunctorily or pathetically. That was quite rare — especially for kings. Yves had seen the Holy Roman Emperor attend Mass, for example, and the Emperor had made quite a show of it — but he had never seen him actually pray. Apparently what he had been told about this French King was true: Louis was different ....

The King crossed himself and got up from his knees. He turned to smile at Brother Yves, and then sat down beside him on the wooden pew. They were alone in the small, private chapel of the Patriarch of Jerusalem. "Brother, I am told you speak Arabic fluently," the King opened.

"I have studied the language for many years, Your Grace; I speak it — adequately."

Louis nodded, smiling faintly. "Your profession makes you modest."

Yves did not correct the King; people who did not realize what a refined and complicated language Arabic was often overestimated his skills. Instead he asked, "Are my language skills of interest to you, Your Grace?"

"They are," Louis admitted frankly. "I wish to send you on a very delicate mission, one which will require you to speak Arabic very well."

Brother Yves frowned. "I assure you, Your Grace, there are many men in Acre, and even more in the Kingdom of Jerusalem, who speak Arabic better than I."

"Perhaps," the King admitted, evidently amused, "but I want a scholar, a Christian scholar — who is also a scholar of Islam."

"Aha," Brother Yves nodded, pursing his lips, wondering who had told the King about his studies of the Koran.

"And I want a man of great courage," the King added, noting with amusement, "Scholarship and courage do not often occupy the same body."

Brother Yves laughed, taken off guard by the King's candor. But then he grew serious and asked, "What makes Your Grace believe that I am such a rare cross-breed?"

"Ah!" the King retorted with a smug smile. "My sources tell me that you have demonstrated astonishing courage on more than one occasion."

"If your sources were referring to the way I called the Holy Roman Emperor an ass to his face, then they were mistaking pigheadedness for courage, Your Grace."

"But I am told that only the intervention of the Saracen saved your life."

"That could well be — and your source could only be the Templar Commander of the City of Acre, whom I will take to task for gossiping about me." He tried to look angry, but couldn't keep up the facade and laughed instead, remembering a youth and a friendship. Then, focusing on the present, he asked the French King, "So, how can I be of service to you, Your Grace? Presuming, of course, that I have the kind of courage you require."

"You will have heard that the so-called 'Old Man of the Mountain' sent an emissary to me demanding tribute."

Brother Yves nodded. "I also heard that you sent him to the Grand Masters of the Hospital and Temple, who told him off properly. You acted wisely, Your Grace."

Louis bowed his head in thanks for the compliment. "I did not repeat the Emperor's error of caving in to such preposterous and godless blackmail, but I wonder if there isn't more that might be gained ..."

"Your Grace?"

"You know our situation. The Sultan of Egypt is refusing to respect our bargain — one pressed on me when I was a helpless prisoner in his hands and one I did not even haggle over. He had all the advantages. I agreed to a huge ransom, I turned over Damietta intact, yet he still refuses to release our remaining prisoners."

"I know," Brother Yves agreed with a deep sigh of sadness and resignation. He did not think the Sultan of Egypt could be compelled to return the prisoners, because he believed most of them were already dead — from disease, wounds, maltreatment, and sheer despair ....

"I was a prisoner, Brother. I know what it is like — No, don't look at me like that. I don't mean I was kept in the same conditions as our poor soldiers, but I saw with my own eyes how the sick and weak, although they had surrendered and were more helpless than any of us, had their heads whacked mercilessly from their shoulders. Brother Yves, believe me, I know that every day in which we haggle over who owes what to whom, lives are lost."

Brother Yves was moved by the sincere anguish in the King's voice, and he concluded that King Louis sincerely cared about the men still in Egypt; unlike his brothers and his barons, he cared not only for the rich and mighty, but about the ordinary men as well.

The King continued. "I have sent envoys to the Sultan of Damascus and to the Mongols in search of allies who might make the Sultan of Egypt fear my animosity, since I know he has no reason to fear my *own* strength, such as it is," Louis admitted. Then he added with a stern voice and a frown, "But he is a usurper! The descendants of Saladin despise him, and everyone fears the Mongols."

"And rightly so, Your Grace," Brother Yves agreed, still unable to see what the King was trying to say. When King Louis did not continue on his own, Brother Yves asked respectfully, "What is it you want of me, Your Grace?"

"I want you to go to the Old Man of the Mountain."

Brother Yves started so violently that the King saw it.

"Yes," the King turned to look him intently in the eye. "You see, there is no one the Sultan of Egypt fears more than the Old Man of the

Mountain. He knows the Old Man can snuff out his life with a snap of his fingers." He snapped his own fingers to underline his point.

Brother Yves nodded, but said nothing.

"Brother," King Louis lowered his voice a fraction. "What if the Old Man could be convinced to threaten the Sultan of Egypt? To send him the message that he must release the Christian prisoners — or face certain death?"

"That would be a miracle, Your Grace," Brother Yves replied dryly.

King Louis laughed, although Brother Yves thought this laugh was forced. "I do not intend to leave everything to Him. I will arm you with rich gifts."

"Bribes."

"Gifts."

"The Old Man, or so I have been told, is very devout, Your Grace. He prays to a different God — or should I say, he prays to God in a different way? I doubt he can be bought with any amount of gifts."

Louis weighed his head from side to side. "He demands 'tribute' from all the secular lords of Syria and Palestine in exchange for the promise *not* to murder them. That sounds like a man very interested in income to me," Louis argued reasonably.

"Yes," Brother Yves agreed cautiously.

"What, then, is so different about accepting from me a small token of my appreciation in exchange for telling the Sultan to release the Christian prisoners? It is a simple three-way deal: the Sultan pays me what he owes, and I pay the Old Man for making him do so."

Brother Yves was more intrigued by the idea than he wanted to admit. The Old Man, a Shiite, was said to hate the Sunni Sultan of Egypt. He might indeed have no objection to threatening him — might even welcome an excuse to eliminate him altogether. If the French King were willing to pay for him to do what he wanted to do anyway ... "It might work," Brother Yves admitted out loud to the King.

The Franciscan looked so uncertain, however, that the King felt compelled to assure him, "I will provide you with an escort, of course."

"No, no!" Brother Yves protested. "We could never get through to the Old Man in force."

"I know that. I meant a single knight."

"No knight in Christendom can save me from the young men who answer to the Old Man of the Mountain, Your Grace, and men of the sword overestimate the value of force. Such a man would only interfere with a delicate mission of this sort."

"This one won't," Louis replied smugly.

"What do you mean?"

"He's not your ordinary knight."

"Meaning?"

"Well, he was schooled by the Benedictines, trained by the Templars, and speaks Greek as well as Latin and French."

"Hmm." Brother Yves could not deny that he was intrigued. Greek was a language he did not speak — but which many natives still did, particularly the Orthodox clergy that lived like hermits in the same mountains as the "Old Man."

"And he will protect you with a sacred relic," Louis added.

Brother Yves raised his eyebrows.

"He carries a sword with a finger of John the Baptist in the hilt."

"Ah! I've heard of it!" Brother Yves looked at Louis, more astonished than ever. The Holy Land was cluttered with "relics." After all, every piece of sand was potentially the "soil Christ trod upon," and charlatans sold enough "pieces of the True Cross" to build a fleet of galleys. But some relics were genuine, and Brother Yves had heard that the remains of John the Baptist, his severed skull lying cradled in his pelvic bones, had been discovered shortly after the First Crusade. The small finger of his left hand had been removed and put in a reliquary by the Comte de Toulouse, so he could take it back to Europe with him. One of the Count's successors had placed it in a sword hilt, and that sword had been used to great effect on the Third Crusade. Richard I of England had allegedly possessed it briefly, but then it had disappeared. Some presumed it had been seized by the Duke of Austria when Richard was held prisoner. Others claimed it had been turned over to the Knights Templar.

"It was Master William de Sonnac's sword," King Louis explained, "but he personally belted it on the hips of young Sir Geoffrey de Preuthune and charged him with using the sword in the service of God."

"And this Sir Geoffrey is not a Templar?" In Brother Yves' experience, the Templars were hoarders — of relics, wealth, land, influence, power.

"He was William de Sonnac's squire — and he saved William's life at Mansourah — but the young man refused to take Templar vows."

"Very interesting," Brother Yves admitted, more intrigued than ever. "Why?"

"Why don't you ask him that yourself?" Louis countered.

"Have you told him about this mission?" Brother Yves wanted to know.

"Not yet. I wasn't sure you would be willing to undertake it," the King admitted.

"Nor have I agreed, Your Grace. I would like two days to think about it. I will give you my answer on Sunday after morning Mass."

"Alms! Alms for the poor!" The brown-robed figure loomed up out of the alley so abruptly that Megalo, hardened veteran that he was, shied sharply to the left. Instantly, Ian's horse decided that if Megalo was afraid, it was time to clear out. He tried to spin around in the narrow street, lost his footing on the cobbles, and went down on his knees, flinging Ian to the ground.

By this point Ian was cursing like a sailor in a brawl, and when the hooded figure came closer, still holding his hand out for alms, he turned on him. "You idiot! Haven't you ever been around horses before?"

"I just wanted to give you a hand," the friar answered, still holding out his hand.

"Get out of my sight!" Ian shouted, humiliated to have been dumped to the ground and furious to feel undefined filth soaking into his sleeve, where he'd landed in some sort of puddle. The streets of Acre were filled with rubbish and animal dung, and he was wearing a new shirt that was now probably ruined. "You stinking whoreson —"

"That's enough, Ian!" Geoffrey admonished sharply, looming over him on Megalo.

"Look, Champion's knee is bleeding!" Ian shouted back, noting that his horse had hurt himself in the fall.

"That is hardly the friar's fault," Geoffrey answered, but he dismounted and bent to examine the damage to his squire's horse. It was quickly clear that Ian's horse had torn open one of his knees and was bleeding profusely. Geoffrey looked around for something with which to stanch the bleeding. The friar was beside him, offering his sleeve, which he had ripped out of his robe. Geoffrey looked astonished at the begging friar with, now, one naked arm. Most Franciscans had only one robe, and this act of generosity was most unusual — particularly for a horse.

"It is the least I can do," the friar insisted, still holding out the sleeve.

Since the damage was already done, Geoffrey took the sleeve and bound it around Champion's knee, then pressed hard on the padded wound with the palms of his hands. The horse snorted and fretted, at first trying to evade his hands, but then went still as the pain apparently ebbed.

The friar and Ian just watched in silent admiration until Geoffrey ordered, "Ian, give me your belt."

The squire dutifully removed the narrow belt he was wearing and handed it to Geoffrey, who used it to deftly bind the improvised bandage more securely. "That should hold until we can get him back to the stables," he announced as he straightened. "If you come with us, brother," he added to the friar, "I'll give you compensation for your ruined robe."

"Thank you, sir," the friar replied. "That won't be necessary, but I would appreciate your donations for the poor."

"The poor be damned!" Ian snapped back, still shaken by the fall and his horse's injury. "We're poor, too!" He was thinking that he didn't have the money to replace his ruined shirt, much less buy a new horse if Champion were seriously injured and turned up lame.

"Ian! If you hadn't gambled your wages away, you wouldn't be poor!" Geoffrey admonished, adding, "Forgive him, Brother; he is still very young."

The friar laughed, because in his old eyes Geoffrey looked at least as young as his squire. He patted Geoffrey on the arm and assured him, "I've got a tough old hide, and I don't take offense at few heartfelt curses from a boy like your squire."

The stables were only around the second corner, and they reached them quickly. Here Geoffrey removed the improvised bandage and ordered the livery grooms to bring buckets of water and sponges, while Ian was sent to fetch bandages from the Hospitallers further up the road. Only after Champion was properly tended, and both he and Megalo had been watered, untacked, and provided with hay nets, did Geoffrey invite the friar and Ian to a meal at the tavern across the street.

Geoffrey and Ian were renting rooms above a cobbler's shop in the house in front of the stables, but had to take their meals elsewhere. Although entitled to eat with the King's household, Geoffrey rarely did. He found the constant gossip, speculation, and scheming of the courtiers trying, while the protocol of the royal household struck him as tedious.

He led the friar across the street to a tavern, ducking to pass through the low door, and then turned right into a dark, poorly lit room that smelled of roasted meat and stale wine. They were early for dinner, and most of the tables were empty. The sight of a friar with one ripped-off sleeve in the presence of two armed men raised an eyebrow from the proprietor, but no more. He was a man of mixed blood and had seen stranger things in his life as a tavern-keeper in Acre. He went back to the kitchen, and reappeared with a wet rag to wipe down the wooden table. Without looking at his customers, he asked, "What can I bring you, sirs?"

"What's the specialty of the day?" Geoffrey asked.

"Kidney and carrot stew."

"Wasn't that the specialty yesterday and the day before?" Ian asked.

"It hasn't been selling so well," the proprietor admitted with a shrug.

"There might be a reason for that," Ian speculated, while Geoffrey asked, "Don't you have anything else?"

"Hare soaked in red wine and garnished with cloves and onions," the proprietor answered readily.

"That sounds good!" Ian exclaimed.

"How much?" Geoffrey curbed his enthusiasm.

"No matter," the friar interceded. "I will pay."

Ian and Geoffrey gaped at the strange friar. Franciscans never paid for anything.

The friar smiled. "I am only doing my Christian duty to help the poor," he added with a wink at Ian.

"Really, Brother, that is not necessary," Geoffrey protested. "Ian earns a decent wage."

"I don't know about decent ...." Ian muttered under his breath.

"Please. I insist, Sir Geoffrey."

Geoffrey stared at the friar more intently. Since the friar knew his name, he presumed they must have met somewhere, but he couldn't place him. Then again, many people came and went in the King's hall; it was impossible to remember them all. "You have me at a disadvantage, Brother. I do not remember your name."

"No reason why you should. I am Brother Yves — often called Yves le Breton because of my roots and Breton accent, which even a quarter-century in Outremer has failed to erase. As your squire suggested, I am to blame for today's accident. The least I can do is pay for a meal. Bring us three portions of your hare dish and a carafe of red wine," he ordered the proprietor, who bowed and withdrew.

They seated themselves around the table, and Brother Yves continued, "Sir Geoffrey, I have a confession to make."

Geoffrey raised his eyebrows. "Shouldn't it be the other way around?"

Yves laughed and admitted, "Indeed, normally, but all the more reason why I must make my confession now: I was lurking in wait for you today, and I intentionally surprised you as I did."

"Why?"

"Have you ever heard of the Old Man of the Mountain?"

"Of course. He claims to head a Muslim sect, but in reality he is little better than a highway robber, who forces kings and sultans to pay him tribute just to stop him from murdering them."

"That's one way of looking at it," Brother Yves conceded, amused. "But if I had been one of his followers, sent to kill you, you would both be dead men." He looked from the knight to the squire and back again. Ian looked duly shocked, but Geoffrey was unimpressed.

"Why would the Old Man want to kill an obscure knight like me?" he asked.

Yves laughed. "Good point — but King Louis has refused to pay tribute, and we must assume the Old Man might feel compelled to set an example against such behavior by killing the King of France."

"Had I been escorting the King, I would have been on my guard," Geoffrey countered.

Yves bowed his head. "Let us hope so."

"The King sent you to test my vigilance?" Geoffrey pressed him.

"No, no! It wasn't King Louis' idea. It was my own .... You see, the King has asked me to take gifts — not tribute, but gifts — to the Old Man. The Old Man does not receive large hosts, and so I plan to keep my party to a minimum: besides the three native boys to lead and look after the packhorses, I will take only one knight. I thought you might be suitable."

"Why me? I am Cypriot. I am not familiar with the roads. Indeed, I have never traveled north of Tyre. You would be better served with a knight from Tripoli."

"We will have guides and a Hospitaller escort as far as the Hospitaller fortress of Kamel. For the last portion of the journey, I am told, we need make no particular provision, because the Old Man will himself send guides to take us to whichever stronghold he then occupies."

"Blindfolded with our hands tied behind our backs!" Geoffrey concluded sharply.

"Do you fear that, Sir Geoffrey?"

"I'd be mad not to!"

Brother Yves laughed, and then admitted, "You are refreshingly straightforward, sir." The project that had seemed so crazy yesterday had already become his own mission, and he was fast becoming convinced that Sir Geoffrey was the man he wanted to accompany him.

"Brother Yves." Geoffrey stirred uneasily and frowned. "My father was over seventy years of age, and an unarmed pilgrim on his way to

Jerusalem, when he was set upon by Muslim robbers. I was a boy of fourteen, and I'd been raised for a future in the Church. My feeble attempts to defend my father resulted in me being batted aside like a fly. I owe my survival to the fact that I was so weak and light that the robber's thrust sent me flying farther than intended. I landed on the edge of the road and rolled down the steep, rocky slope to land unconscious at the bottom. The robbers left me for dead. When I regained consciousness and crawled back up to the road, I found all our pack animals had been stolen, the women and children had been taken captive, and five men had been left dead or dying, including my father. I was in rugged, arid country with no water. I had no idea where the nearest village or town might be, and I was too weak to carry my father. All I managed to do was drag him into a sliver of shade cast by a large rock ledge and stay beside him, reciting every prayer I knew, until he died. By then my mouth was swollen with thirst and I was having trouble breathing. I stayed beside the body to fight off the vultures that were already feasting on the other bodies. Have you ever fought with vultures?"

Brother Yves shook his head slowly.

Geoffrey nodded. "I never want to do it again. In retrospect, however, it was probably the vultures that saved my life. A patrol of Templars spotted them and came to investigate. They buried what remained of the other pilgrims, but at my insistence agreed to bury my father's body in Jaffa, where they were headed. After that experience, I was determined never to be helpless again. I swore I would learn how to fight, how to survive. Being blindfolded with my hands tied and surrounded by Assassins would make me feel as helpless as I did when I was fourteen."

Brother Yves was relieved that the arrival of their dinner made an immediate reply unnecessary. While the proprietor poured the dark red wine for them, Brother Yves had time to think. He liked Geoffrey intuitively, and he had long since learned to trust his instincts. He liked the very fact that Geoffrey did not leap at the chance to serve the King of France on a mission of this sort; he could think of half a dozen hotheads in the King's entourage who would have. He also liked the fact that Geoffrey did not underestimate their adversaries. But he had not been prepared to argue against a man who did not want to feel helpless, since undoubtedly they would be that once they were in the hands of the Assassins.

Geoffrey broke the silence, announcing, "I assure you, there are many more qualified knights who would serve you better. Let us eat together and drink to your success." Geoffrey lifted his glass in a toast.

Brother Yves smiled and raised his glass as well. They set their glasses down, and while Ian eagerly cut into his meat, Geoffrey bowed his head and prayed silently. When Geoffrey finished and looked up, he saw the Franciscan still considering him thoughtfully.

Geoffrey misunderstood his look and excused himself. "Old habits. I spent six years with the Templars."

"So I was told," Brother Yves admitted, "but not why you did not join them." It was a question, and Ian looked up attentively, clearly curious about what Geoffrey would answer.

"The Templars who rescued me after my father's death were fulfilling the Order's original mission: providing protection to pilgrims in the Holy Land. But as a Templar squire, I saw all my brothers from the Commandery at Limassol cut down in an attempt to seize control of Egypt. I understand the military reasoning behind the Egyptian crusade, Brother Yves, but God was not with us. *God — was — not — with — us.*"

"You are wrong, Sir Geoffrey," Brother Yves replied, softly but firmly. "God is *always* with us." He let this sink in before adding, "But he does not always approve of what we do, and His will may differ from our own."

"For that very reason, I will not undertake a new crusade," Geoffrey told the friar.

"Yes, but what about the men still in Egyptian captivity?"

"I mourn for them, Brother Yves, with all my heart. It is a cruel fate — one crueler than they deserve, regardless of what sins they committed in the past." Geoffrey was thinking again of Matthew of Paphos.

Brother Yves nodded. "Then come with me to the Old Man of the Mountain, Sir Geoffrey, for he may have the key to set them free."

Chapter 16

The Old Man of the Mountain

Syria
March, Anno Domini 1251

Even though they had been warned to expect it, the ambush still took them by surprise. The Assassins cut off their advance and their retreat. Rocks rolled down the slopes of the mountain, knocking one of the packhorses off his feet and breaking a leg in the process. While he squealed in pain, the other horses whinnied in fright, and even Brother Yves' mule started braying, but they had nowhere to run. Brother Yves started shouting in Arabic, while Ian cursed in English. Geoffrey saw steel flash in the sunlight and had time to think: This is a stupid, senseless death. How could King Louis imagine the Old Man would hear them out?

A moment later men swarmed around his horse, and Megalo lashed out with his teeth and hooves with the same ferocity that had saved Geoffrey's life at Mansourah. Terrified they would harm him, Geoffrey called out to Brother Yves, "Tell them to get back! Tell them to keep their distance! Tell them I surrender!"

"Then you must dismount!" Brother Yves shouted back, setting an example by sliding off his mule and kneeling beside it.

Geoffrey jumped down and grabbed Megalo's bridle right behind the bit, talking to him to calm him down. Only after the stallion had settled down did he kneel slowly, still holding the reins, but more loosely. Ian did the same, while the native boys had long since prostrated themselves before their attackers.

Within minutes Geoffrey was blindfolded and his hands were tied behind his back. To his surprise, however, his sword was not removed, and he took comfort in that. It suggested they were indeed going to be led to the Old Man, rather than just executed. Besides, the familiar feel of the sword on his hip, and the knowledge that St. John was still with him, gave him courage.

A horse was brought in front of him, and Geoffrey was ordered by one of their "escort" to mount. Geoffrey could tell the horse offered him was not Megalo because the stirrup was much closer to the ground. This was a smaller, more docile horse, and the saddle felt completely different from his own.

The ride that followed seemed interminable. Blindfolded, Geoffrey could not be distracted by the unfolding landscape, nor could he anticipate changes of incline or direction. With his hands tied behind his back he sat less securely in the saddle, while the stirrups were too short for him, soon causing his legs to cramp. Geoffrey kept asking himself what he was doing here in the mountains of Syria. Why had he agreed to undertake a mission that was patently futile? Why risk his life like this? For the prisoners in Egypt?

That sounded noble, but the reality was surely that he had been bored with the life of an apparently superfluous household knight. Or had he simply dreamed of winning King Louis' favor, King Louis' gratitude?

The image of Eleanor de Najac appeared before his blinded eyes. There had been opportunities to meet now and again at court, to exchange a few words — in full view of the Queen, her ladies, and other courtiers. Only once had they managed to sit together, at a banquet during Christmas. Eleanor had shown him the ring, set with her father's stone, that the Queen had given her as a gift. She had seemed happy — happy, too, to sit beside him. Certainly she had shown interest in his own plans. But court rumors said she was promised first to one lord and then to another. Again and again Geoffrey had watched helplessly while men of better birth and higher station paid court to her. It was not reasonable to think he might win the hand of Eleanor of Najac — even assuming Brother Yves was successful in his mission here. After all, any credit for their success would rightly go to Brother Yves.

His mount lurched over some obstacle, and Geoffrey felt as if he were about to be flung from the saddle. He instinctively tried to grab for something to hold on to, but only wrenched his shoulders. The bonds securing his hands cut into his wrists. Someone shouted something and the horses stopped. Geoffrey heard men jumping down, and a moment later they were jostling his knees and hands dragged at his arm, pulling him down. He tried to dismount, but the explosion of shouts was clearly negative. Someone pressed his thigh and hips against the saddle to hold him in place, while someone else pulled his upper body down, and a third man fumbled at the back of his head until the blindfold came free.

Geoffrey immediately knew why. Above and to the right was the most powerful castle he had ever seen. It had at least two walls of outer defense and what looked like a dozen crenelated towers, the tallest of which reached skyward with a lookout platform surrounding it. Furthermore, the steepness of the mountainside on which the castle sat made it virtually impregnable. They were about to cross a gorge by a narrow drawbridge, and the Syrians clearly wanted Geoffrey to see this: to see that he had no hope of escape once he was beyond the bridge.

Megalo, however, had no intention of crossing the narrow bridge. Several men tried to lead him, but the stallion's resistance only became more furious. Geoffrey watched with detached approval as his stallion lived out his own inner emotions; he felt a certain pride that even blindfolded Megalo sensed the moment he approached the bridge and immediately started rearing, backing up, and lashing out.

After this had gone on for almost half an hour, the patience of their escort gave out. The commander of the escort party, through his translator, demanded that Geoffrey lead his own horse across the drawbridge. A man cut his hands free, and he was allowed to jump down from the mare he'd been riding.

Rubbing his bruised wrists, Geoffrey advanced toward his stallion. Megalo was drenched in sweat and trembling with outrage. Because he was blindfolded, he could not know who was approaching him, but fearing some new form of force, he tried to break free of the man holding him as soon as his nervously twitching ears registered that someone was approaching.

Geoffrey called to him softly by name, and at once Megalo froze and turned in the direction of the familiar voice; his ears strained, searching for the sound, but his nostrils were wide with anxiety. Geoffrey stopped beside him. He reached up and stroked Megalo's neck and shoulders, talking to him softly in Greek. Megalo calmed down somewhat, but the moment Geoffrey took the reins and started forward, Megalo leaned back on his haunches and balked just as furiously as before. Geoffrey imagined he felt betrayed, and gave up the attempt instantly. He shook his head and turned to the Syrians to announce, "There's no point. I can't lead him across that bridge any more than you can."

The Syrians chattered among themselves in outrage, sneering at a nobleman who had so little control of his own horse. In alarm, Brother Yves approached Geoffrey and muttered softly and nervously, "Sir, please don't try the patience of our escort. They are beginning to get angry."

"Tell them to leave my horse in the village there," Geoffrey countered. "Tell them I will pay for his feed and care. We should leave our grooms and Ian here as well," he added. "There is no need for anyone except you and me to go beyond this point."

Brother Yves met his eye. He understood that Geoffrey did not believe either of them would return alive. After a moment he nodded, and passed his suggestion about the horse and their servants to the escort.

After some initial resistance, the escort agreed. The three native grooms were untied and told to take Megalo and their own horses to the village. When they started to lead Ian away in the same direction, however, he called out to Geoffrey in panic. "You can't leave me here, sir! I don't deserve this!" he protested.

Geoffrey looked at Ian, baffled, unable to understand why Ian would resist a gesture meant to save his life. But Ian was pleading, "Why are you abandoning me? After all we've been through together! What have I done to deserve this? It's not fair, sir. You can't abandon me now!"

"If they kill me, I want you to look after Megalo," Geoffrey explained, nodding toward his stallion.

Ian looked at Megalo, who was now resisting being led away from the bridge out of pure stubbornness, and then up at the castle on the opposite side of the gorge, and appeared to grasp the danger at last. He gaped up at the castle for a moment and then turned to ask Geoffrey plaintively, "How long should I wait for you, sir?"

"I don't know, but I expect our hosts will give you some indication of when you are no longer welcome."

In punishment or contempt, the escort transferred the load from the wounded packhorse, whose throat they cut, onto the mare Geoffrey had been riding, and made Geoffrey walk up the steep, winding road to the great castle. The road curved and reversed itself several times, and the castle seemed as far away as ever. Geoffrey was not used to walking, and too soon he could feel blisters starting on his feet where the chain mail rubbed against his heels. The Syrians were impatient with him and clicked at him as if he were a lazy horse. Once they seemed on the verge of kicking him or using one of their riding sticks to make him move faster, but Brother Yves said something in Arabic that made them move away and become more respectful.

At last they reached the first gatehouse complex, where Geoffrey could see the flat roof crowded with men, many of them archers. Just as he entered the dark, evil-smelling vaulted chamber under the first gate, a wailing started that made his hair stand on end.

"The call to evening prayer," Brother Yves commented beside him. "Let us pray. Our Father, who art in heaven ..."

They emerged on the far side of the gatehouse and were confronted by yet another gate, but now their guards were driving them forward angrily. "Hurry," Brother Yves urged; "they don't want to be late for prayer."

The mosque occupied one side of the central courtyard, with a small forecourt housing the fountain. The minaret rose up white and slender behind the mosque. With orders to stay where they were, the two Christians were left standing with the mule and packhorses while their escort hurried into the mosque, leaving their shoes outside. Within moments the entire courtyard was abandoned, except for the beasts and the Christians.

Brother Yves looked up beyond the ramparts of the castle enclosing them to the luminous blue sky, and pointed to the evening star: "Venus, beautiful and unobtainable as ever."

Geoffrey turned to look west instead, toward the gorge, Kamel, Tortosa, Cyprus .... The sky was a blood-orange red, with wisps of clouds that caught the light of the setting sun so that they seemed to glow golden in the near darkness. It was a breathtakingly beautiful sky, accompanied by the twitter of birds preparing to sleep — and the murmur of male voices from the mosque.

Geoffrey looked at Brother Yves, and the Franciscan smiled at him. "We are in His hands, my son."

Geoffrey nodded. The sense of acute danger had receded. Obviously the Old Man was going to give them an audience, or they would be dead already. If he was prepared to listen to them, then he was more likely to laugh or simply dismiss them as fools than to kill them. Even if he were very angry, he would more likely threaten the King than the messengers.

Now that Geoffrey no longer believed he was on the edge of his grave, he could afford to be curious. "Tell me about these Assassins, brother. I have heard they are as likely to kill Sultans as Christian lords."

"More likely," Brother Yves corrected him. "They view the more numerous Sunni Muslims as heretics. And vice versa, of course. Sunnis see Shiites as heretics. They have hated one another for nearly six hundred years, and there have been frequent massacres on both sides. They built these mountain fastnesses to defend themselves from the Sultan of Syria more than from the King of Jerusalem."

Geoffrey nodded, thinking of Montségur.

When the evening prayers ended, their hosts streamed out of the mosque, dispersing in various directions. Each man seemed to have a job to do and knew exactly where to go, just like the brothers of a monastery after Vespers, Geoffrey thought. Men came to offload the packhorses, promising that their things and gifts would be brought to their chamber, while other men led the horses to the stables.

Only after the others were gone did Geoffrey and Brother Yves notice an elegant young man who had waited at one side until the others were finished. At last he came forward and bowed before Geoffrey and Brother Yves. This young man was evidently of higher status than their escort. His wide white trousers were tucked into soft leather boots. His close-fitting, long-sleeved tunic was made of elegant sky-blue satin brocade. It ended just below the knee, was slit up the front for riding — and was lined with chain mail. Likewise, his broad silk sash concealed a leather belt that upheld a slender, straight sword hung in an engraved silver scabbard. Most significant, on the sleeves of his upper arms were bands of white silk embroidered in gold Arabic script; Geoffrey knew these were a mark of rank and presumed they were sayings from the Koran.

When the young man straightened from his bow and looked Geoffrey in the eye, Geoffrey was shaken by the sense of looking into a mirror. The Syrian and he were the same age, height, and coloring, and the Syrian wore a full beard, just as he had done when with the Templars. The sense of eerie familiarity was reinforced when he announced in flawless French, "My name is Yusef, and I have the honor of showing you the hospitality of my Master. You must be tired and hungry from your long journey. Please, let me show you to the baths." He gestured with his long fingers toward one of the towers.

Still discomfited by the uncanny similarity between them, Geoffrey followed their guide, and was further astonished to discover that this castle possessed a large and well-appointed bath complex, complete with steam bath, pool, and massage. Brother Yves had been in the Holy Land long enough to be an avid adherent of bathing, and as he stripped out of his dusty, sweat-soaked habit and undergarments, he joked, "The Old Man wouldn't want to receive a couple of filthy Christians still stinking of horse sweat."

Geoffrey was less enthusiastic. Although he had been raised with baths like this, and would normally have welcomed the chance to wash away the sweat and dust of the journey, he felt some reluctance to let go of his sword — not for its value as a weapon, but because of the relic in his hilt.

"You need not worry," Yusef read his thoughts with a smile. "We will return everything to you. Please," he gestured again toward the bath, "relax."

Geoffrey could not refuse, so he capitulated.

After they had bathed, silent barefoot attendants wearing baggy white trousers massaged them with oil, shaved them, and clipped and filed their nails. Finally they were presented with clean white robes, trimmed with beautiful embroidery, and Yusef, with a smile and a bow, handed Geoffrey his sword. Geoffrey belted the sword around his hips over the Arab robe.

But their expectations of meeting the Old Man were not met. Instead, Yusef led them to a tower chamber with beautiful glazed tiles on the walls and a double window looking west. Light still lingered there, Geoffrey noted, but the room was lit by oil lamps that hung from the ceiling or stood on carved wooden side tables. The chamber was lavishly furnished with highly decorated wood and ivory chests on which their saddlebags were laid out, two low beds overflowing with blankets and cushions, and a low table surrounded by more cushions.

"Please," Yusef gestured again, "sit down. You must be very hungry." Geoffrey and Brother Yves lowered themselves onto the cushions, and

Yusef sat down cross-legged opposite them. He clapped his hands, and a half-dozen barefoot boys in baggy trousers and short kaftans entered the chamber. One boy brought a silver bowl with cool water and towels for the diners to wash their hands, another carried two silver pitchers, one with wine and one with water, while a third brought goblets, plates, and cutlery for the table. The remaining three boys carried large trays laden with bowls full of food.

After the boys had withdrawn, Yusef identified the dishes for the guests. There were several varieties of cheese, tiny grilled birds, lamb chops, roast kid, and calf liver. "Everything but pork," Brother Yves summarized. There were spicy sauces to garnish the meat, and side dishes featuring cashews, pistachios, almonds, raisins, dried apricots, and figs. The flatbread was still warm and covered with sesame seeds. Geoffrey concluded it was going to be one of the best meals he had ever had — in part because four hours ago he had not been sure he would ever eat again.

Yusef scrupulously refused to drink wine, taking only water in his goblet, but he shared the food with them, and in the congenial atmosphere Brother Yves asked, "So, young man, where did you learn your French?"

"It is my mother tongue," he answered, provoking a raised eyebrow from the friar. "My mother was a Frank, but she was raped and abandoned by a crusader." Both Christians stiffened at this bald statement. Yusef cocked his head. "Do you doubt what I say?"

"Why should we?" Brother Yves answered. "There are good — and bad — men of every faith. But how did the bastard son of a Christian crusader and a Frankish woman come to serve the Old Man of the Mountain?"

Yusef bowed his head to Brother Yves. "My mother and I were discarded by her family, who wanted no part of a disgraced woman, and so she came into the home of a Muslim merchant."

"As a slave," Brother Yves underlined the point.

Yusef shrugged. "Was she worse off as the slave of a kind man than the whore of a bad one? She converted and joined the harem, while I was raised with the other boys of the household. I attended the Koran school and became a devoted follower of the Prophet."

"Where did you grow up?" Brother Yves asked, helping himself to more bread and tearing it in two.

"In Damascus, for the most part, although twice I was allowed to travel with a caravan to Aleppo and back."

"How and when did you come here?"

"When I was a youth of fourteen or fifteen, on one of those trips, I heard for the first time about the Master. At once I was fascinated. I sensed in my heart that Allah was calling me to go to him, but I was still young and unsure of myself. I started asking everyone I could about the Master, particularly travelers who had been in these mountains. One man told me about a mullah in the mosque near the bazaar in Damascus, and I discovered he was an admirer of the Master. He taught me many, many things. When he thought I was ready, he introduced me to one of the Master's men. After he had tested me many times and in many ways, he agreed to take me with him when he next reported to the Master. That was six years ago, and I have been here ever since."

"What about your family?" Geoffrey asked, surprised.

"Didn't you leave your family when you joined the Templars, Sir Geoffrey?" Yusef asked back, laughing at Geoffrey's surprise. Then he asked almost reproachfully, "Did you think we would bring you here without knowing who you were?"

"We knew you would have heard of our mission," Brother Yves answered for Geoffrey, who was still unsettled, "but not necessarily everything about our past."

"We try to do thorough research," Yusef explained. "The Master likes to be prepared for his visitors. Would you mind answering one question, however?" he added politely.

"Ask," Brother Yves invited.

Yusef turned to Geoffrey. "I am told that you could not get your horse to cross the bridge at the foot of the mountain, but surely that is not true? A knight must have control of his horse at all times."

"What need have I for a horse here?" Geoffrey countered, gesturing to the room around him to indicate the narrow confines of the fortress.

"It was a long, steep climb on foot!" Yusef answered with a grin.

"Christ walked to Calvary."

"You believe you will be crucified here?" Yusef asked, astonished.

"Not anymore," Geoffrey admitted.

Yusef laughed. "I think we will get along, Sir Geoffrey. And you, Sir Friar," he turned politely back to Brother Yves, "we understand you are a scholar of the Koran."

"I have read the Koran many times," Brother Yves admitted, adding modestly, "but I do not claim to comprehend it."

"Understanding is a gift of Allah, Sir Friar, but if you read the Koran and memorize it, and you follow the Laws of the Prophet, you will surely find favor with Him."

Brother Yves bowed his head to Yusef. "And if you read the Bible and follow the Commandments of Our Lord Jesus Christ, you will find favor with Him, too."

Yusef lifted his shoulders in a questioning gesture, "Why should I read the Bible, when everything is written in the Koran? Now, if you are finished with your meal, I will leave you to rest from your strenuous journey — or is there something else I can bring you?" He looked from Brother Yves to Geoffrey and back again.

Both Christians shook their heads to indicate they had no further wishes. Yusef stood, bowed to his guests, and withdrew.

Brother Yves looked at Geoffrey and said to him in Latin, "The walls have ears, Brother, or I would say more. Let us pray."

They knelt, folded their hands, and recited the Lord's Prayer together. When they had finished, Geoffrey removed his sword and laid it on the floor beside the bed. Then they both stretched out on their beds, still in the white robes they had been given.

Whether the wine had been laced with a sleeping potion or the exhaustion came simply from the tension of the day, Geoffrey slept very well that night. Indeed, his sleep was so deep and his dreams of Cyprus so vivid that he woke disoriented. The room was chilly and smelled fresh. The remains of their dinner had been spirited away and their clothing had been stacked inside the door, freshly cleaned and pressed. Geoffrey's chain mail had been brushed and oiled.

Geoffrey sat up sharply and saw Brother Yves sitting in the corner, reading a book. "What time is it?" he asked.

Brother Yves shrugged. "Midmorning, I think. They've called to prayers twice."

Geoffrey looked around the room again. By daylight it was possible to see the vivid colors of the tiles, cushions, and sheets. "What a beautiful prison," he remarked. "All that's missing is a fair maiden to share it with."

"Oh, they're here," Brother Yves told him, with a smile at Geoffrey's look of astonishment.

"The Assassins may share the reputation for religious zeal and military success that our militant orders have, but not their monastic values. After all, Islam puts no value whatsoever on male chastity. You can be sure there is a harem somewhere, and that the Old Man keeps a hundred concubines or more — or so the legend goes."

Geoffrey was left reflecting that he would be happy with only one maiden — provided it was the right one.

Yusef appeared shortly afterwards and bowed to them again. "I trust you slept well?" he inquired.

"Thank you, very well," Brother Yves answered for both of them.

"The Master will see you after noon," Yusef announced next. "I see, Sir Friar, that you have found the copy of the Koran my Master sent you, and are content. But you, Sir Geoffrey, perhaps you would prefer to join me in the exercise court?"

"I would indeed." Geoffrey jumped at the chance to get out of his prison — no matter how lovely it was.

"Then I will send a boy to help you dress, since you did not bring your squire with you."

"That won't be necessary," Brother Yves announced, setting the book aside and getting to his feet. "I will assist Sir Geoffrey. He'll be ready in ten minutes."

Yusef withdrew, leaving Brother Yves to mutter at Geoffrey, "No reason why we should help them learn how to kill us better."

"They had my clothes all night," Geoffrey pointed out.

"We couldn't prevent that, but it's one thing to see a heap of dirty laundry and another to help a knight into his defenses." Geoffrey noted, however, that Brother Yves carefully inspected and sniffed each piece of clothing before helping him into them. He evidently suspected that they might be poisoned, but fortunately found nothing.

Wearing his armor again, but without his helmet, Geoffrey opened the door to their chamber and stepped out. Two armed men stood flanking the door and at once drew their weapons. At a signal from Yusef, they returned them, and Yusef gestured for Geoffrey to follow him down the winding stairs into the central courtyard with the mosque. From here, Yusef led Geoffrey into a dark corridor that led down a steep flight of straight steps until these opened onto a second courtyard. This courtyard was unpaved and the buildings surrounding it were austere. Two young men were crossing swords at one end of the yard, while in a sandpit in the near corner two youths were wrestling. A trio of youths took turns throwing knives at a target beyond the pit.

Geoffrey presumed all these activities were staged for his benefit, and he took his time watching. The knife throwers were particularly impressive, he noted. They were unsettlingly accurate even from a hundred yards. The swordsmen impressed him less. "Why do you use such narrow swords?" Geoffrey asked Yusef.

Yusef turned and called over his shoulder. A moment later a youth came running with a thin silk banner. With a smile to Geoffrey, Yusef drew his sword and held it at the ready as he threw the banner up into the air. As the silk fell on the tip of the sword, it was sliced and ended on the hilt, draped over Yusef's hand. Yusef looked over at Geoffrey with a smile.

Geoffrey answered by slipping his right hand into his chain-mail mitten and grabbing Yusef's sword by the blade. Their eyes met.

Yusef held out his left hand. "Give me one of your mittens."

Geoffrey stepped back and removed his left mitten, handing it to Yusef.

Yusef laid it on a wooden bench. Then he stepped back and jabbed down with his sword. It pierced the chain mail and went an inch or more into the bench.

Geoffrey nodded, unimpressed. He'd seen far too many of his comrades gutted by Saracen swords to doubt that they were lethal, but Yusef had still not answered his question. "The bench was not defending itself," he pointed out.

"You think your sword is superior?" Yusef asked, sounding surprised.

"I do."

"Then you would not hesitate to fight me with it now?"

"No," Geoffrey agreed.

"A friendly contest," Yusef underlined.

"I have no reason to wish you harm, but can you afford to lose that sword?" Geoffrey gestured toward the pretty weapon in its elaborate sheath.

Yusef laughed. "I will not lose it. Can you afford to lose *yours*?" The question suggested he knew just how valuable and unique it was.

"I trust you would return it to me if I did," Geoffrey countered. Yusef laughed and agreed, "Well said!" He called over his shoulder and one of the ubiquitous boys came running with two shields, but Geoffrey shook his head. "No shields. I have never fought with such a small shield, while you are familiar with it. Sword to sword only."

"All right," Yusef agreed with a nod; "as you like." With an order he sent the boys away, but more and more men and youths emerged from the shadows and surrounding buildings, while turbaned mullahs appeared on one of the balconies. Geoffrey registered that if he were humiliated, it would be in front of the entire garrison.

He paused, crossed himself, and then prayed silently, "St. John, for the glory of Christ, guide my hand."

Yusef waited respectfully for him to cross himself again. Then he raised his sword to the ready and took up a defensive stance. Geoffrey drew his own sword with an audible rasping and felt a surge of excitement. He had never been more than mediocre with a lance, and his archery was deplorable, but during his Templar training he had become an outstanding swordsman. He knew, of course, that Yusef would have a completely different style from the Templar trainers, but he had had his share of encounters with Arab swordsmen during the crusade. He stepped slowly to the right and started to circle his sword, unconsciously enjoying the feel of it in his hand and the increased strength that motion gave the weapon. He was moving back almost imperceptibly, drawing Yusef after him, trying his patience.

Yusef lunged with a shout. Geoffrey parried the blow easily with an underhand thrust. Had he had a shield, he would have used it against his opponent to effect, because Yusef's arm was flung upward, exposing his vital organs. Yusef recovered rapidly, however, feinted left, and then came in again from the right. Their blades crossed and held for a moment; Geoffrey could feel how evenly matched they were in strength. Geoffrey stepped back abruptly, and Yusef pulled back as well, with a grin as if to say, "You can't catch me with a cheap trick like that."

Geoffrey just grinned back and let him make a second attempt. Yusef was much lighter on his feet than Geoffrey, and he included a dramatic twirl in one of his attacks, but it did not increase the power of his sword. Geoffrey held or parried every attempted blow. At the end of the second round, for the first time Geoffrey thought he saw respect in Yusef's eyes.

Yusef's third offensive was much more intense. The blows were faster, and he was now breathing hard — as if he were finally making an effort. Advice, cheers, and complaints were called from the sidelines. Geoffrey continued to evade or rebuff each sword thrust.

As the fury of Yusef's attacks increased even further, Geoffrey decided it was time to launch his counterattack. He went over to the offensive, and in just three quick blows he broke Yusef's sword four inches from the hilt. Yusef staggered as he lost his balance, and a wave of amazement went through the audience. Yusef stared at the stub of a weapon in his hand, while some of the boys rushed to pick up the blade, which had landed a dozen feet away.

"It's not strong enough," Geoffrey commented, and put his own sword back in its sheath.

Yusef frowned and tossed his hilt into the sand. Before they could leave the courtyard, however, another, older man blocked their way.

He was also frowning, and by the way Yusef greeted him obsequiously, Geoffrey gathered he was of higher rank or status than Yusef. Yusef nodded repeatedly, then turned to Geoffrey and asked if he would be willing to fight "the emir."

Geoffrey looked at the man, who scowled back at him, and suspected a trap. He strongly surmised that the emir was an expert swordsman and that he would be completely outclassed, but he could not think of a credible excuse. He agreed. The audience cheered.

Geoffrey returned to the starting point and drew his sword again. The emir wasted no time going on the offensive. With a loud shout to Allah, he lunged at the Christian with all the fury of the righteous against the damned.

The very fury of his attack, however, gave Geoffrey the advantage, because the emir was also armed with the slender, elegant sword of the Syrian cavalry. These swords were dangerous weapons that could easily cut through the quilted linen armor of footmen and horses. The points, as Yusef had already demonstrated, could pierce through the finest chain mail. Geoffrey had seen Christian knights cut to pieces by these swords — when surrounded. The key to Saracen success with these weapons, however, was superior numbers. The odds were almost always heavily in favor of the Saracens. Thus while a Christian knight dealt with one or even two attackers, a third, fourth, or fifth found it easy to plunge his weapon into a vital organ.

Here, one to one, Geoffrey discovered that even the Assassin weapons master was no serious threat. When the emir's sword broke he screamed in disbelief, and Geoffrey took advantage of his shock to knock him down and pin him to the ground with his foot, pointing his sword at the emir's throat. Dead silence reigned in the exercise court. Then Geoffrey stepped back, sheathed his sword, and offered his opponent a hand up.

The emir spat at him, rolled over, and got to his feet on his own. He stalked out of the courtyard without looking at anyone. Geoffrey looked at the stunned audience around him. Yusef appeared at his elbow, anxious. "I apologize profusely! He should not have done that," he muttered.

"What? Challenge me or spit?"

"Spit," Yusef whispered. "The Master will be very angry."

"He need not be," Geoffrey assured Yusef with a shrug. "I humiliated him in front of everyone. I understand his fury."

"You are the Master's guest," Yusef insisted, shaking his head. "He should not have insulted you like that. It was a fair fight."

Yusef led Geoffrey to a fountain so they could wash their hands and quench their thirst. As he bent over the fountain to plunge his hands into the cool water, Yusef whispered in French, "You have made more than one friend just now. The man you just defeated trained us all — and he was not an easy man to please."

Geoffrey glanced over his shoulder at the excited chattering of the other young men. Yusef was right. Most of the young men seemed amused rather than angry. However, he noted that the balcony of the mullahs was empty, and some of the young men were frowning fiercely and looked both insulted and threatening.

"Come!" Yusef urged him, with a clap on his shoulder. "Let me show you the view from the ramparts."

Geoffrey readily agreed and again followed through a labyrinth of tunnels, corridors, and stairways to emerge on the roof of one of the towers. It was not the tallest tower — that one still loomed above them some ten yards higher and off to their right. Nevertheless, the view was spectacular. Yusef pointed out the village in which (hopefully) Ian awaited him with Megalo, and several other landmarks.

"You learned to fight like that from the Templars, did you not?" Yusef asked, as they stood side by side gazing out over the Syrian mountain landscape.

"Yes."

"But you do not wear the mantle of the White Knights."

"I am not one of them."

"Because you lost faith in your false religion on this last crusade, is that not so?"

Geoffrey felt as if an earthquake had just jolted the foundation of the tower. What didn't the Assassins already know about him?

"No," he insisted as firmly as possible. "Because I realized that God wanted me to serve Him differently."

Yusef nodded, as if in agreement. He gazed out across the dramatic countryside, not at Geoffrey, and when he spoke it was in a soft and reasonable tone. "Allah has blessed you, Geoffrey. I believe that. He let you live, when all your brothers died, because he could see you were a man of intelligence and understanding. I believe that. Allah has brought you to us."

Geoffrey shook his head. "I am here at the orders of my King and because Brother Yves wishes it."

Yusef rested his elbows on one of the merlons and smiled at Geoffrey over his shoulder. "But Brother Yves is a man who reads the Koran, Sir Geoffrey. What makes you so sure he is not already one of us? That he still serves your false religion?"

Geoffrey thought about that a moment and then shrugged. "It makes no difference to me what Brother Yves believes. My faith in God is between myself and Him."

"Indeed, and Allah has shown you the truth: for you said truly, Sir Geoffrey, that Christ died on a cross in Jerusalem, but he was never God's son, and he was not the Messiah."

Geoffrey felt the hair stand up on the back of his neck. Clearly Yusef had been detailed to talk to him about this, but how had the Old Man found out about it? But then Geoffrey remembered there had been other wounded in the infirmary tent when he confronted the Grand Master, and many of them would later have been taken captive. No doubt one or another of them converted to save his life. The Assassins were known to have a network of spies everywhere; it would not be so surprising that they had taken an interest in this last crusade — and particularly in a Templar who denied the divinity of Christ. Geoffrey concluded there was no point denying it. "I said that in grief and shock, Yusef; I know better now."

"Know better? Can a man who has seen Truth go back to ignorance?" Yusef raised his eyebrows as he asked this.

"King Louis once said that he had never seen a bad Christian become a good Muslim — or vice versa."

Yusef laughed. "Your King is very wise, I have been told, but surely it does not make a man 'bad' if he sees enlightenment?"

"If it does not make a man 'bad,' why do you kill men who convert to Christianity?"

"Because they have betrayed the True Faith for darkness, not the other way around!" For the first time in their acquaintance Yusef seemed angry, his polished veneer of friendliness cracked.

Geoffrey nodded slowly and noted sincerely, "I hope you will not be punished for failing to convert me, Yusef, because I would rather die for Christ than abjure him."

Yusef turned to look him squarely in the eye. "I am sorry about that, Sir Geoffrey," he said solemnly, "for I would have liked to welcome you as a brother." He let this sink in, but when Geoffrey made no response, he added, "But I respect you for your steadfastness. I feel the same way."

Geoffrey nodded, relieved that Yusef did not seem unduly upset by Geoffrey's refusal to convert.

"I hope that I will soon be selected by the Master for a real mission," Yusef told him next.

Geoffrey tensed, realizing he had relaxed too soon. He cast a furtive glance over the ramparts to the rocky floor of the valley, more than a thousand feet below. No one could survive being pushed off this tower, and he wondered if he had just signed his own death warrant. He stopped breathing as he tried to anticipate an attack from Yusef, but the other man was again gazing out over the mountainous landscape, apparently lost in thought. "I can confide in you as I cannot in the others. They look on me as inferior because of my birth. But if the Master selects me — if I can but die in his service, in the service of Allah — then I will go instantly to paradise!" Yusef's voice was uplifted, his cheeks flushed with the mere thought of this.

"A man's whole life," Geoffrey countered cautiously, wondering where Yusef would hide a knife. His sword, at least, was disabled, but the knife was the Assassin's weapon, and he could easily have concealed it in his tunic, his sash. "A man's whole life, not a single act," he continued, in a voice he hoped sounded calm, "determines his entrance to paradise."

"Don't crusaders think that taking the Cross outweighs all other sins and crimes?" Yusef countered, looking over his shoulder again with a teasing smile.

"Many crusaders think that, and I have heard recruiting sergeants and even priests repeat such things, but the false promises of corrupt men do not make them true. No single act, but rather the cumulative balance of all good and evil committed by a man over the span of his entire life, will be weighed at his death and determine if his soul goes to heaven or to hell."

"But the act of dying for Allah outweighs all other acts," Yusef insisted.

"Why would God want us to die for Him?" Geoffrey countered. "He can kill us at any time." He gestured expansively to the world around them — without taking his eyes off Yusef's hands, watching for him to make his move. "We please Him more if we live good lives according to His laws and use our hands to do His work." He brought his hands down to his waist and opened them, palms outward in Yusef's direction, as if offering them to God, but also close to the hilt of his sword.

Yusef considered his words intently, frowning with concentration. "But that is one and the same thing. What the Master orders is Allah's will, and so if I die fulfilling his orders, I have died doing His work, and I will go instantly to paradise."

From the mosque in the courtyard far below came the wail of the call to prayer. Yusef righted himself with a jerk. "It is much later than I thought! We must hurry!" With an apologetic smile he added, "There are so many steps back down!" as he plunged back down the spiral stairway.

Geoffrey followed in his wake, unsettled by the thought that he had unjustly suspected Yusef of seeking his death. In fact, it seemed, he had been confiding in him honestly. Geoffrey, who had often felt like an outsider, was quick to identify with Yusef's position. He was a man of Frankish blood, a bastard by birth, a slave by virtue of his mother's position, and a runaway. He had no home anywhere on earth, unlike Geoffrey, and no future but here in this austere fraternity of fanatics. It was natural that he would want to prove himself. Geoffrey found himself regretting that he had broken Yusef's sword in their friendly match.

It was late in the afternoon before the Old Man sent for the Christian emissaries of the French King.

Accompanied by boys carrying their gifts, Brother Yves and Geoffrey were led by Yusef through the labyrinth of corridors, tunnels, and stairs that characterized this fortress, until they came to a stairway hidden in the thickness of the walls of the highest tower. They climbed, slowly because Brother Yves needed to stop and rest periodically, to the very top room of this tower. Here they found themselves in a chamber encircled by a balcony and with doors that opened in all four directions of the heavens. This room was so luxuriously appointed with carved wooden and ivory furniture, rich carpets, silk cushions, and colorful tapestries that it was a moment before the Christians even noticed the man sitting cross-legged on a pile of cushions at the foot of a bed. Indeed, it might have taken longer to locate him if Yusef had not flung himself face down onto the floor, as if he were praying in a mosque.

Brother Yves at once went down on his knees, and Geoffrey, somewhat reluctantly, went down on one knee beside him.

The Old Man said something and motioned for them to rise. Geoffrey looked at him more closely. He was dressed austerely in simple black robes and a white turban. He had a beard that reached to the middle of his chest. Although the beard was white and his face wrinkled, he did not look as old to Geoffrey as his father had at the time of his death; Geoffrey surmised that the title "Old Man" was more respectful than descriptive.

The Old Man spoke so softly that it was difficult to hear what he said, but Yusef readily translated for him. "My Master asks if it is true you come from the King of the Franks."

"We are here at the behest of King Louis of France," Brother Yves corrected; the "King of the Franks" might be interpreted as the King of Jerusalem.

The Old Man nodded, then glanced toward the boys holding trays laden with gifts. Without looking closely, it was clear that spread out on scarlet velvet were jewels, silver bridles, and cups of gold. He nodded. Then he turned to Geoffrey and spoke at some length.

Brother Yves looked over, amazed, and Yusef translated. "My Master congratulates you on teaching our weapons master a lesson in humility, and begs you forgive his rudeness. He asks you to accept the following gift."

The Old Man snapped his fingers, and a young man emerged out of the shadows to kneel before Geoffrey with his head bowed. On his outstretched hands he held a dagger in a magnificent sheath studded with jewels.

"Don't touch it," Brother Yves hissed in Latin. "The gift of a dagger from the Old Man is the gift of death."

Geoffrey took a deep breath. "Thank you, My Lord. I am honored that you wish to give me a gift, but I am most undeserving. Not I, but my sword, defeated your weapons master. Not my hand, but that of St. John the Baptist, whose hand is in this hilt, guided my sword." He drew his sword from the sheath and offered it hilt first to the Old Man.

Beside him Brother Yves drew a sharp breath, and Geoffrey surmised he'd blundered.

The Old Man ordered Yusef to bring him the sword. Yusef complied, and the Old Man studied the relic curiously. Then he handed it back to Yusef. "I do not understand how intelligent people can believe bones and other inanimate objects have any power," he commented dismissively. Then, pointing his finger to the ceiling, he scoffed, "Allah, praise be to his name, does not work wonders through pieces of wood or the bones of the dead!" Yusef duly translated this commentary, which Brother Yves had understood in the original. Finally, in a normal tone of voice, the Old Man added, "But if you do not want my gift, then so be it." He waved his hand, and the young man offering the dagger withdrew backwards.

Brother Yves breathed out with relief, and Geoffrey concluded this meant the sentence of death had also been withdrawn. The conclusion was reinforced by Brother Yves muttering from the side of his mouth, "The Old Man has ordered the dagger be given to the weapons master; it means he will die before the day is over."

Before Geoffrey could fully absorb the implications of this, the Old Man's attention returned to Brother Yves, announcing, "I am told you have been reading the Koran, Franciscan."

"I have," Brother Yves confirmed, adding, "and I see that you have been reading St. Peter." He indicated a book on the shelf beside the Old Man's bed.

The Old Man broke into a smile. "Yes! You know this book?" He reached for the leather-bound book and took it lovingly into his lap.

"Indeed!" Brother Yves replied enthusiastically. "For God's sake you should read it many times, for it is full of many good words."

"In fact, I have read it many times!" the Old Man answered with obvious satisfaction. "Peter is very dear to me!" he continued, leaning forward confidentially to explain, "You know, at the beginning of the world his soul dwelled in the body of Abel, and after Abel was murdered, his soul entered the body of Noah, and after Noah died, his soul went into the body of Abraham, and only when Abraham died did this great soul go to the body of Peter."

While Yusef translated this, Geoffrey kept looking at Brother Yves, remembering that the Cathars, too, believed in reincarnation. Master de Sonnac had told him that some Cathars claimed Christ Himself had come to Earth in different bodies — though most alleged He had never taken the flesh at all, but remained an angel. Geoffrey was anxious to hear Brother Yves' rebuttal.

Unfortunately, Brother Yves chose to respond directly in Arabic, and Yusef naturally did not feel obliged to translate for Geoffrey's sake. Within moments a lively discussion had developed between the Old Man and Brother Yves. Both men gestured with their hands and spoke with obvious passion; the light in their eyes and the expressions on their faces clearly indicated they were enjoying themselves.

Puzzled, Geoffrey looked at Yusef, and the latter murmured, "They are arguing about theology. My Master is quoting the Bible and Brother Yves the Koran."

Geoffrey nodded and again turned his attention to the two principals. While he welcomed an exchange that on the surface seemed suited to building rapport and trust between the Old Man and Brother Yves, he couldn't forget that the Assassins were famed for luring their victims into a trap by providing a sense of safety. They had been known, for example, to plant a man in the household of an intended target; for years the Assassin might serve his intended victim with loyalty and sometimes even personal sacrifice. Then, at an order from the "Old Man," the Assassin would turn on the very man he had served for years and kill him mercilessly.

But they were the Old Man's guests, Geoffrey reminded himself; surely that offered some protection. He glanced at Yusef for reassurance, and Yusef, thinking he wanted a translation, remarked in a low voice, "They are now discussing the French King's request." Yusef was obviously more tense, and Geoffrey looked again at the Old Man. His attitude, too, had changed subtly, but decisively. His eyes had narrowed and his lips were lost in his beard. The friendly twinkle was gone from his eye.

Brother Yves was making a point, but the Old Man cut him off with a gesture of his hand. The Old Man turned pointedly to Geoffrey, and Geoffrey's mouth went dry. "You are the sworn man of the French King?" he demanded, through Yusef.

"I am," Geoffrey confirmed, sensing a yawning trap. Something terrible was about to happen. He could sense it coming; he just couldn't imagine what it would be.

"Yusef!" the Old Man called, and Yusef dropped on his knees and bent his head to the floor. The rush of words that followed made Brother Yves gasp, and the next thing Geoffrey knew, Yusef had jumped to his feet. With a cry of triumph, he ran out of the chamber onto the balcony and flung himself over the railing of the balcony with a call to Allah. His wail descended with his body, downwards, and downwards, until it was silenced by the unforgiving earth at the foot of the rocky valley.

Deathly silence gripped the tower chamber. The Old Man smiled smugly at Geoffrey, while Brother Yves closed his eyes, his lips moving in silent prayer. Geoffrey was too stunned to pray. He was hearing Yusef's friendly voice and soft laughter, seeing his smile and the resemblance to himself — and sensing his longing for acceptance ....

The Old Man spoke. He pointed at Brother Yves and said something sharply.

Brother Yves drew a deep breath. His throat was working, his voice distorted. "He wants to know, Sir Geoffrey — he wants to know if the King of France can command such loyalty."

Geoffrey looked from Brother Yves to the Old Man of the Mountain, and they both stared at him, waiting with equal intensity for his answer. "Why," Geoffrey asked slowly but distinctly, "would he want to?"

Ian had been in some god-awful places in his short life. The mere thought of the cold, drenching rain of southwest Scotland could still make him shiver at night. The damp there crept into everything, turning the hay moldy and making the bed sheets clammy. Mold soiled the walls of cottage and castle keep alike, and moisture dripped from the ceilings, as if the saints were weeping, when the mist hung low and oppressive — even in high summer. The winters were even worse! The cold came then, on a sharp wind that whistled through the cracks of the shutters, howled in the rafters, and thundered across the moors. Ian had seen snowstorms that buried the cottages of the poor and left the tower houses peering over the empty landscape like wrecked ships. Nor did things improve when the snow melted, as then the landscape was transformed into a morass of mud under low-hanging clouds that trapped the smoke from the cottages, turning the air a murky yellow, stinking of peat bog.

No, Ian's dreams were not of "home" and a father who thought a birch rod could teach a boy anything he needed to learn — much less a Church that punished a man for wanting a full stomach or a lassie to warm his bed. His dreams had always been of someplace warm, sunny, green, and comfortable. He had followed those dreams to Durham, where he'd taken the Cross, and to Southampton, where'd he boarded one of the Earl of Salisbury's ships.

His dreams had taken him to Cyprus, a place as enchanted as any on earth, and for a short interlude he had thought himself in paradise. But then they sailed for Damietta, and Ian had learned there was something worse than the damp and cold of Scotland: the burning sands of Egypt. Where once the damp and cold had seeped, the gritty sand soon found its way: into a man's bed, his food, his hair, the spaces between his fingers, between his teeth, in his crotch.

And then they started dying — a stinking, nauseating death, soaked in their liquid excrement, vomiting on themselves, their skin covered with ulcers and their teeth loose. There was no heroism in the camps of men suffering from dysentery and scurvy at the same time. The King and his nobles, the militant orders, had supplies and discipline and servants to keep the diseases at bay, but not the ordinary men — not men like Ian.

More than once Ian had walked into the desert, thinking he would rather be killed than stay another minute among the dying, but the desert sun had burned so intensely that it was surely a foretaste of hell, and the thirst was worse still. He had always returned, returned to the Nile, and had fallen into her arms like a man returning to an old whore; the Nile was ugly and worn out, yet comforting nevertheless.

When they made the assault on Mansourah, Ian was not alone in welcoming battle, convinced that death at the end of a sword was better than the alternative. But nightfall had brought only the certainty that he still lived in hell.

It was pure chance that he heard that a newly knighted squire was being sent back to Damietta with dispatches. "Newly knighted," Ian asked his informant. "Has he a squire?"

"Why should I care?" was the stupid answer.

Ian spent the next four hours finding out who and where this new knight was and presenting himself. "You need a squire, sir."

"I'm fine," Sir Geoffrey answered.

Ian ignored him. He had clung to Sir Geoffrey like a barnacle to a ship, and that ship —

his talisman, Sir Geoffrey — had brought him out of the jaws of hell. Together they had escaped Mansourah and captivity. They had traveled to Damietta, to Acre, back to enchanted Cyprus and the baths of Aphrodite, to the dream of leisure and luxury, food in abundance, pretty, willing girls .... And now this.

Ian scratched the flea bites and flung off the stinking blankets. They were so rough they scraped his skin, tough as it was. He stood up, naked as the day he was born, and crossed the dirt floor of the cottage to duck out of the low door and stare again at the castle on the far side of the gorge. The moon had set, and the sky was slowly graying with a new dawn. The castle was only a silhouette against that lighter gray, as much his imagination as real.

Ian was certain he had not slept at all. How could he sleep when that horrible scream repeated itself in his brain, again and again and again? In fact, there had been two screams. After the first, Ian had convinced himself that it was surely Brother Yves they had killed, and he had watched anxiously for some sign that Geoffrey was on his way back down the mountain. But within the hour a second scream had followed. After that, he knew there was no hope. They had thrown him to his death! And his body lay down there in the gorge, set upon by vultures and flies.

Ian shuddered, remembering how Geoffrey had talked of fighting the vultures off his father's corpse. In Ian's nightmares, Geoffrey's corpse fought off vultures with human heads while Megalo whinnied furiously.

No, the last part wasn't a dream. Megalo was going mad again. Twice now he'd nearly killed one of the villagers. Ian wasn't sure what had happened the first time, but certainly after they'd thrown Geoffrey off the cliff, the villagers figured the valuable horse was theirs to sell, and they had tried to put a halter on him to lead him away. Megalo wasn't having any of it. Ian smiled to himself. He couldn't handle Megalo, either, but it was rather satisfying to watch the way the stallion made mincemeat of the Arabs.

Megalo's hooves bashed against wood, and voices were raised in alarm. Ian's borrowed horse (because Champion had not recovered from his injury, Geoffrey had borrowed a horse from Jean de Joinville for Ian) let out a high-pitched whinny of sympathy or protest.

Ian ducked back into the cottage to get his braies and a shirt, but by the time he came out, Megalo was charging down the street, trailing two leads and shaking his head in defiance. Ian's stallion followed him, half trotting, half cantering, clearly just tagging along. Ian stepped out in front of his horse and spread his arms. The stallion drew up and looked at him, looked over his shoulder at the Arabs advancing in a group, put his head down, snorted conversationally, then abruptly kicked up his heels and plunged down the street past Ian, following Megalo.

Ian turned and followed the horses, cursing. He needed that damn horse to get back to Kamel! Even if last night, in his shock over what had happened to Geoffrey, he had been lamed into inaction, he was now not prepared to stay here another minute. It was time to look to his safety.

Megalo reached the bridge across the gorge, the bridge he had so stubbornly refused to cross two days ago. Again he drew up sharply, spun about on his haunches, took two strides back toward the village, then changed his mind again and with raised head and tail, pranced back and forth before the start of the bridge. He was magnificent, Ian registered, fit for a king! — Or a Templar Grand Master ....

Megalo came to an abrupt halt and turned toward the bridge, tense and quivering in anticipation of new flight. Someone clicked at him out of the darkness, just as Geoffrey used to do. A voice murmured something about pomegranates. Surely only Geoffrey (and Ian) knew that Megalo had a weakness for pomegranates.

Ian advanced cautiously; his attention was no longer fixed on the stallion, but on the bridge itself. There were men on it. Two men, one stocky and robed, the other half a head taller and wearing armor.

"Sir Geoffrey? Brother Yves?" Ian asked, disbelieving.

"Yes, Ian. I'm afraid you won't be able to keep Megalo after all. The Old Man let us go free."

"He kept the gifts, however," Brother Yves added, "and my mule."

"But — but —" Ian thought about the screams, "they flung two men off the cliff yesterday."

"Worse, Ian, much worse. I'll explain later. Don't you have any pomegranates for Megalo?"

"Where the hell —"

"Watch your tongue in the presence of a man of God," Geoffrey admonished, but Brother Yves laughed. "Let him speak of hell, Sir Geoffrey — for we have surely been there, you and I."

Chapter 17

Dieu St. Amour

Kingdom of Jerusalem
May, Anno Domini 1251

"Three thousand Christian prisoners have been freed, Your Grace," Brother Yves told the King.

"Is that certain?" King Louis asked, afraid to believe the good news.

"Yes, Your Grace," Brother Yves assured him. "I have seen them myself. I did not make a head count," he admitted, "but I saw them boarding the ships. They filled more than twenty-two galleys."

"They boarded on their own feet?" Louis asked next. He had suffered too many disappointments to easily believe good fortune, even when it seemed to smile on him.

"They boarded on their own feet: many, I would venture to say, in better shape than when they were taken prisoner." Brother Yves did not mention the others, the ones who had been killed because they did not improve in health fast enough to make their captors believe they were worth holding for ransom.

The King of France fell to his knees with a thud, as if he'd been knocked from behind, but he held up his hands to the Franciscan friar. "I have you to thank for this, Brother, you and Blessed Christ!"

"We must indeed thank Sweet Jesus and his Mother, who surely felt great pity for the mothers of these men, Your Grace," Brother Yves agreed, going down onto his knees more gingerly than the King of France. He took the King's hands in his own. Louis was clearly overcome with emotion, and tears were streaming down his face.

"I never believed it," the King admitted to the Franciscan what he dared not admit to his vassals or the barons of Outremer. "I never thought that after losing my army in Egypt, I could ever convince the Sultan to send my poor soldiers back to me."

Brother Yves nodded, smiling, and admitted, "I can't say I was very optimistic either, Your Grace."

"Brother, tell me the truth," the King pleaded. "Did I do the right thing, choosing the lives of my men over Jerusalem itself?"

"Your Grace, that is for you to decide. But as a man who has been to Jerusalem, I can assure you it is a city like any other — for all that Our Lord lived and died there twelve hundred and fifty years ago."

Louis bowed his head and closed his eyes. Brother Yves waited patiently.

King Louis had been a king for a quarter-century. It was to his credit that he could still be overcome by emotion, but he recovered rapidly. He nodded and pulled himself to his feet. "When will the prisoners arrive?"

"Very shortly. Templar galleys are fast, but not *that* much faster than others."

Louis nodded. "We will celebrate a special Mass, and prepare to feast our released men. I think, however, that you deserve a special reward, Brother. You have represented me to the

Sultan of Damascus and the Sultan of Egypt both. If any mortal has played a role in this diplomatic victory, it was you, Yves le Breton. What thanks would you have from the King of France?"

Yves met the King's eyes. On the one hand, the King was entirely sincere, but on the other hand he expected a man of God, a Franciscan, to be humble. He did not expect — and was not prepared — to pay an exorbitant reward.

"Your Grace, I was your ambassador not only to the Sultans of Egypt and Damascus, but also to the Old Man of the Mountain. I can assure you that the former missions were pleasurable compared to the latter. Furthermore, we do not know if it was fear of Damascus — or of the Assassins — that convinced Sultan Aybak to release the prisoners. I think it would please God if you would reward the young man who defended your honor in a most emphatic and exceptional manner to the murderer from Syria, when I was myself struck dumb with horror."

"Sir Geoffrey de Preuthune?"

"Yes, Your Grace."

King Louis looked doubtful, and Yves wondered if he had some reason not to want to reward Sir Geoffrey, but he had no opportunity to argue his case any further. The Constable of France was at the door, a herald hovering behind him. The sound of hooves clattering on cobbles wafted up from the courtyard along with self-important shouting, and the bells of St. John's were clanging for joy. King Louis had to return to reigning.

Melusinde had blossomed in the household of the Queen. Her body had grown soft and round, and her exotic beauty turned male heads, from the sculleries and squires to the highest nobles in attendance on the King. She had an eye for color and fashion and nimble fingers trained by the nuns, so she soon transformed Eleanor's wardrobe and her own. Most of all, she had an infectious laugh that could cascade through the chambers of the Queen's household like the ringing of cathedral bells at Christmas.

Now she burst breathlessly into the end chamber, where Eleanor was diligently polishing the silver cover of the Queen's prayer book. "My Lady! My Lady! The King has chosen a husband for you!" Melusinde announced excitedly.

Eleanor looked up, alarmed. "Where did you hear that?"

"Plaisance had it from Arnaud, who overheard the King discussing the details with the Seneschal of Champagne."

That was plausible enough, because Arnaud was one of the King's body-squires, and Plaisance was the laundress he had been "courting" for some time. Eleanor decided she could not dismiss the rumor. "And *who* is to be my husband?" she asked tensely.

"Arnaud didn't quite catch the name. Apparently he was preparing the King's robes in the next room and couldn't hear everything that was said. The King was mostly concerned about just how much your lands were worth and whether they were encumbered in any way." Melusinde paused and considered Eleanor, who had not reacted at all as she expected. "Aren't you happy, Madame?"

"How can I be happy without knowing who it is?" Eleanor countered sharply.

"But to be married, Madame! It will surely be to a great nobleman, and soon you will have a household of your own, with castles, and servants and horses, and you will be a great lady! You will take me with you, won't you, Madame?"

"Until we know who my husband will be, we know nothing about how we might live," Eleanor pointed out soberly. She had the sinking feeling that the elderly baron from Antioch who had shown an interest in her this past spring had obtained the King's consent to a marriage. She supposed he was not a bad man, but he was not particularly attractive, either. He had been widowed twice already. He had two almost-grown sons and a married daughter from his first marriage and a young son and daughter from his second, and he seemed to want her mostly as a way of ensuring the family had a place to go in the West, if the Mongols or the Saracens captured his lordship on the exposed border between Antioch and Syria.

"But it might be the Lord Philippe," Melusinde suggested, referring to the handsome and gallant younger son of the Lord of Scandelion, who had paid considerable attention to Eleanor at the Easter court.

"No," Eleanor corrected; "younger sons don't get heiresses — unless they perform some special service for the King. Lord Philippe has only made a nuisance of himself, and the King is displeased with him because he swears and gambles too frequently."

"Ah! Then there is Sir Charles!" Melusinde concluded. Sir Charles was not as handsome or gallant as Lord Philippe, but he was attractive in a rugged, masculine way. He had a scar on his neck and a reputation for courage.

Eleanor shuddered at the mention of the name. Sir Charles was a Norman knight who had participated in the siege of Montségur. He seemed to think he was "owed" a piece of the Languedoc for his services, and he had staked a claim to Najac very bluntly and loudly. In some warped way, he implied that the fact that he had been part of the army that killed her mother and brother entitled him to her lands.

"I would rather kill myself than marry Sir Charles," Eleanor told Melusinde firmly.

"Is there no one that you would *like* to marry, Madame?" Melusinde asked, deflated and slightly hurt that her exciting news had received such a cold reception.

"Ah, child," Eleanor answered, feeling ancient compared to the optimistic fifteen-year-old. "There is, indeed, one knight I fell in love with almost a year ago."

"Who?" Melusinde asked, perking up instantly.

"Sir Geoffrey de Preuthune."

Melusinde looked blank. She could not even picture the man. After thinking about it, she finally asked, "Isn't he the man who escorted Brother Yves to Cairo?"

"Yes, and to Damascus."

Melusinde did not look convinced. "He never pays you compliments or any kind of courtesy at all!" she protested.

"He came to my aid without any thought of reward — and that is the greatest courtesy of all," Eleanor corrected.

"But he refused to even take part in the last tournament, didn't he? The tournament where Sir Charles and Sir Philippe both asked for tokens from you!" Melusinde pointed out.

"That is because he, like King Louis, considers tournaments frivolous. Nor does he have to prove his courage in such games, for he was on crusade and earned his spurs at the Battle of Mansourah."

"Then you think he might be your husband?" Melusinde asked hopefully.

"No," Eleanor answered, shaking her head sadly. "He, too, is a younger son, and from a far more obscure family than the Lords of Scandelion. He is not the kind of man to whom the King would give an heiress."

Not since that first interview with King Louis had Eleanor been summoned by the King. She had seen him often enough at court and when he came to the Queen's apartments, or when the Queen accompanied her husband on official business attended by her ladies. On various occasions, King Louis had graciously inquired whether she was comfortable and settling in. He had even apologized for forgetting to give her an allowance at their first meeting. He always treated her with respect and kindness when they met, but he had not summoned her to his presence a second time — until now. That told Eleanor that Melusinde's rumor was correct.

Eleanor was told she would find the King in the walled garden that stretched between the palace of the constable of Jerusalem and the Cathedral of the Holy Cross. This was a very pretty oasis of flowering trees and plants, punctuated by a fountain and Roman sculptures. Peacocks strutted slowly along the gravel paths, occasionally meowing like cats, while parakeets fluttered and cheeped among the foliage.

Eleanor loved this garden, and had spent hours daydreaming about how she would copy this or that aspect of it in the garden that opened off the inner ward at Najac. Her mother had turned that plot, where her grandmother had once raised roses, into a medicinal garden. Under her mother's regime it had been planted in neat, utilitarian rows. Eleanor told herself that if she were ever allowed to return to Najac, she would transform that garden back into a pleasure garden like this one.

The King was seated on a marble bench with a bishop and the Grand Master of the Hospitallers standing before him. When he caught sight of Eleanor limping toward him, however, he dismissed the men, who bowed and withdrew. He smiled and held out his hands to Eleanor. She dutifully curtsied before the King, and he lifted her up to deliver a kiss on each cheek. "My Lady of Najac," he greeted her, indicating the marble bench beside him, "you look more lovely than ever. Red is a good color for you," he told her, referring to the red silk scarves, covered with tiny yellow crosses, that Melusinde had made for her, and the red trim on her surcoat. Eleanor thanked him.

"My dear Marguerite tells me you are a great comfort to her, and have eased her homesickness by speaking with her in her beloved langue d'oc," he continued, but he had said this before. Eleanor answered, as always, that she was happy to serve the Queen, and pleased that the Queen found her company agreeable.

"But Marguerite also reminded me that you are no longer a child but a young woman, who has every right to a husband and household of her own," he added this time.

Eleanor bowed her head in acknowledgement of this fact, but avoided comment. She was very tense; her stomach twisted in knots.

"Nor has it escaped my notice that you have inspired the devotion of more than one admirer," the King continued genially.

"If I may speak plainly, Your Grace?" Eleanor paused and waited for the King to nod. "It is the lordship of Najac, not my person, that attracts interest."

"You sell yourself short, my dear!" the King protested.

Eleanor thanked him with a bow of her head, but added, "Even if I were as beautiful as my maid Melusinde, Your Grace, it would be Najac, rather than me, that lured the likes of Sir Charles de Cholet."

"Ah," the King nodded, "I understand. You need have no fear on that score. Marguerite was very emphatic that Sir Charles must not be considered on any account — and, in fact, I never did consider him suitable. However," he paused, "I must confess, I have delayed so long because I could not make up my mind among the other candidates. At length, my eye has fallen on two men — each in his own way admirable and worthy, but very different. One is a man of wealth and maturity who can be trusted to look after your interests with circumspection and fatherly concern. I believe you would want for nothing as his lady, but I doubt you would ever see your homeland again. I am not sure, however, if that is a significant shortfall, given what you said to me at our first meeting about not being able to return home. Indeed, I wonder, do you perhaps *want* to remain here in the Holy Land the rest of your life?"

Eleanor's throat went dry. She was going to be condemned for her own stupidity at that first encounter with Louis. She wanted to scream, but she drew a deep breath and tried to get a grip on her rising panic. "Your Grace, Najac can never be *the same* without my brothers and my mother. I mourn them still. But to abandon Najac altogether would be an insult to their memory — and to my father. Kind as you and Her Grace the Queen have been to me here, I long to return home, Your Grace." She stopped there, holding her breath for a reaction.

King Louis nodded. "I can understand that, my dear, but I must tell you some very bad news."

She waited for the axe to fall on her exposed neck.

"Your lands have not been well administered during your wardship. They have been mortgaged, and are seriously encumbered with debt."

Eleanor almost laughed from relief. She had expected *that*. The lands of minor heirs and heiresses were routinely plundered by their guardians. But she shied short of saying this, or suggesting that a husband would administer her inheritance better — since her inheritance was now in the hands of the King himself.

Louis continued, "In short, you will need a husband who is either already very rich or very frugal, sober, and good at estate management."

"Who did you have in mind, Your Grace?" Eleanor asked, unable to bear the suspense any longer.

"I thought, perhaps, that a man like Sir Geoffrey de Preuthune, who is very well educated, of sober and devout temperament, but diligent and ambitious, might be suited to this task — if you would not be offended to be married to a man of humble origins?" Louis seemed genuinely skeptical.

Eleanor was stunned. Since the day they took her away from Najac, a prisoner of the Inquisition, she had not experienced such a sense of hope. "You are serious, Your Grace?" she asked, not daring even now to believe it was possible.

"Yes, I am serious. The Queen seemed to think you were well disposed toward Sir Geoffrey, but if there has been some mistake, I will not force you."

"No, Your Grace. There is no mistake. I — I have the highest regard for Sir Geoffrey. I simply — never thought — that marriage — might be possible," she found herself stammering. "I have not dared to hope that you would be so generous." As she spoke she realized that any last remnants of resentment against this man had melted away. She forgave him everything he had done to her family in the past, because he was now giving her a future.

Louis beamed, obviously pleased with himself. "Then it is settled!" he declared. "All that remains is telling the lucky bridegroom of his fate!"

No sooner had the King spoken than Eleanor knew she had rejoiced too soon. Sir Geoffrey had pledged himself to the Templars in his heart. He would not marry her.

Geoffrey woke with a start. He did not know where he was at first, aware only that he was stiff and aching. He was lying in the dark on a stone floor, and for an instant he thought he had been thrown in some dungeon. As he tried to sit up, his knee knocked against something that made a scraping noise as it skidded across the floor, and then clunked as it hit something solid. He reached out automatically to see what it was, and his hand closed around the familiar hilt of his sword.

It started to come back to him. He was in the crypt of the Church of St. John. He had come down here to pray and had laid his sword on the stone altar in offering. He didn't understand how the sword was now on the floor beside him.

He looked around in the darkness for someone else. The candle had gone out, but very faint light was seeping down the stairs at the back of the crypt, suggesting that a new day was breaking above ground. The light was not enough to make out colors, but strong enough to enable him to see the four solid columns holding up the vaulted ceiling of the square chamber. The capitals of the pillars were carved with foliage and beasts; in the blind arches on the side of the crypt were frescoes depicting the life of St. John.

Geoffrey turned back to the altar. It stood solid and mute before a mural of the Baptism of Christ. On the bare slab of stone a gold crucifix stood, glinting faintly in the light slowly creeping in from the stairs. There were jewels of some kind in the splayed arms of the cross and a relic in the heart. Nothing suggested that the peace of his vigil had been in any way disturbed. But the sword had clearly been taken from the altar by an unseen hand and placed beside him.

Geoffrey swallowed to wet his throat. He still did not understand what God wanted of him, but he was beginning to accept that he did not have to understand. It was enough to accept the opportunities God offered to him, and to strive to make the most of the Divine Grace shown to him. He had offered King Louis this sword, and King Louis had returned it to him. Now King Louis was giving him a bride — and not just any bride, but the bride he had long coveted in his heart. That was a miracle in itself, Geoffrey thought, because

Geoffrey did not think he deserved such a bride, even while he wanted her more than anything else — save the Grace of God itself.

But if the King (who would be a saint, according to Brother Hilarion) saw fit not only to let him keep the sword but also give him a bride, maybe he was intended only to be the steward of the sword? Maybe it was his calling to take the sacred sword back to the safety of the West — until another generation, a son or grandson or son-in-law, came into the world who would know how to use it for the glory of Christ?

With this thought, Geoffrey surrendered to his fate and got joyfully to his feet. As he buckled the sword around his hips, it seemed strangely lighter than before. It was as if the burden it represented was being shared. Geoffrey bowed to the altar. He crossed himself and said the Lord's Prayer, stressing "*Thy* will be done."

Then he turned and started out of the crypt. With each step the light increased, and he was filled with new energy. It felt like when the Templars, after prayers, got the order to arm and mount for battle. The time for reflection and prayer was past; the time for action had come. The Templar battle cry rang out clear and inspiring in his brain: "Vive Dieu St. Amour!" He smiled. It seemed a fitting start — and thought — for his wedding day.

Historical Note

Sir Geoffrey, Eleanor de Najac, and the sword with the finger bone of St. John the Baptist are all fictional.

In contrast, the background — the crusade against the Albigensians and the Seventh Crusade — are history, and I have endeavored to render them as accurately as humanly possible. Richard the Lionhearted did seize the Island of Cyprus after several of his ships wrecked and the crews were mistreated. The fate of the Viscomtes de Carcassonne and Joanna Plantagenet are also historical fact, as were the murder of Inquisition judges at Avignonet and the burning of heretics at Montségur. The depiction of King Louis IX and his crusade in Egypt is based heavily on Jean de Joinville's *Life of St. Louis* — as many readers familiar with this lovely work will have recognized.

The lordship of Najac did exist, and it came to Alphonse de Poitiers on his marriage to Jeanne de Toulouse, but there was no heiress attached to it. The castle of Najac is a magnificent example of medieval architecture that figures prominently in the third book in my "Templar Tales" series, _The English Templar_.

Yves le Breton was a historical figure. He was sent by Louis IX to bring gifts to the Old Man of the Mountain after the latter had sent gifts to King Louis. Yves le Breton was a "master of the Saracen tongue," according to Joinville, who while visiting the Assassin stronghold found the Old Man with a book on the life of Saint Peter, which he praised. (The Old Man of the Mountain, according to Joinville, made the interesting claim that St. Peter was the reincarnation of Abraham, who was in turn the reincarnation of Noah, who was the reincarnation of Abel.)

However, the story of the Old Man demonstrating his power over his followers by ordering one of them to jump to his death in front of Christian visitors may be more legend than history. Nevertheless, it is illustrative of the fanaticism of this sect, and Geoffrey's answer, attributed to another Christian nobleman, is equally illustrative of Christian attitudes at the time; I could not resist including it. The story of the Saracen sword splitting silk, but the Christian broadsword breaking swords, is likewise an old yarn, but based on fact: Christian swords were heavier and more effective one on one, as depicted here.

St. Neophytos is a famous Cypriot hermit, and the descriptions of Cyprus are based on my own travels there.

Book III of the Templar Tales:

The English Templar

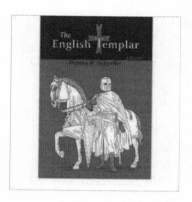

Caught up in the mass arrest of French Templars on the night of Friday October 13, 1307, the English Templar, Sir Percy, is tortured until he confesses to crimes he did not commit. Percy wants only to die, but fate puts him in the hands of two people determined to keep him alive – and resist the injustice of the French King. A novel of faith, fortitude, and love set against the backdrop of one of the most appalling instances of state terrorism in Western European history.

Other novels set in the Age of Chivalry that have already been released, in addition to _The English Templar_, are:

A Widow's Crusade (Tales from the Languedoc)

The melody awakens memories in the heart of a rich widow, Blanche. Long ago, when she was still young and beautiful, she had been in love with a poor knight. He left her to follow Richard the Lionheart on crusade – and never returned.

Blanche sets out on a personal crusade, across the war-torn Languedoc, daring the pirates and slavers of the Mediterranean -- only to find a man, who is nothing like she remembered him, and anything but pleased to see Blanche again.

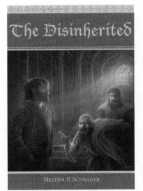

The Disinherited (Tales from the Languedoc)

"The Disinherited" – the faidits – angry young men, born to be lords, raised to play the lance as well as the lute, but now men with nothing left to lose. The Albigensian crusades have taken everything away from them – their lands, their titles, their women and their faith. Invaders from the north have seized their sun-soaked lands – and soaked them with blood instead. While the invaders rule the countryside from their stolen castles, the inquisition rules the towns with terror. The tension is building to a new breaking point, but one faidit has been fighting too long already. He longs for peace -- but has no idea how to find it.

Made in the USA
Las Vegas, NV
26 June 2021

25504210R00189